The Devils Grasp

(handwritten: Don't be Tempted by the Devil's!)

by CHRIS PISANO and BRIAN KOSCIENSKI

SUNBURY PRESS

Mechanicsburg, Pennsylvania   USA

Published by Sunbury Press, Inc.
50 West Main Street
Mechanicsburg, Pennsylvania 17055

www.sunburypress.com

For information about special discounts for bulk purchases, please contact Sunbury Press Orders Dept. at (855) 338-8359 or orders@sunburypress.com.

To request one of our authors for speaking engagements or book signings, please contact Sunbury Press Publicity Dept. at publicity@sunburypress.com.

ISBN: 978-1-62006-566-2 (Trade Paperback)
ISBN: 978-1-62006-567-9 (Mobipocket)
ISBN: 978-1-62006-568-6 (ePub)

Library of Congress Control Number: 2015933713

FIRST SUNBURY PRESS EDITION: February 2015

Product of the United States of America
0 1 1 2 3 5 8 13 21 34 55

Set in Bookman Old Style
Designed by Crystal Devine
Cover by Amber Rendon Cover art by Koa Beam
Edited by Janice Rhayem

Continue the Enlightenment!

Prologue

WYREN WATCHED.

From the precipice of Mount Mythos, Wyren, the mad wizard, peered into the lush valley below and watched.

The sunlight glared down upon a swarming sea of armored men, bristling with purpose like beetles discontent within their carapaces. Plumed helmets, whetted swords, and polished armor glittered. Unit commanders barked out orders, their stentorian commands a clarion rising up amongst the rock outcroppings.

And Wyren watched.

The army below was searching for him. Word of his nefarious deeds had reached the ear of the king, and his Majesty responded by sending this army. Pondering this fact, a smile of self-satisfaction nestled onto Wyren's craggy face, and he ran his fingers through the few scraggly hairs that hung off his chin—an effigy of a beard. No army could oppose him now. No creature of flesh or bone, no matter how numerous, could stop him. His smile widened as he began the madness.

Wyren prepared for battle by stirring the contents of a cask, half his size, with the staff he worked so hard to construct. The wooden staff itself was all too modest; half as thick as his leg, but just as long. Five wooden fingers clenched as a fist formed the crest. The staff warranted little construction time, needing only a sharpened dagger and patience. What cost Wyren decades were the five stones the clenched fist protected—many years of traveling and researching, learning the spells to enrich the stones with the necessary power, sacrificing what little sanity he had.

Looking into the cauldron, Wyren admired the blood, impressed with the amount he drained from the dragon, slain by a ragged band of mercenaries that he had hired. A minor consternation passed through him, thinking about the rumors of this band of sell-swords having a conscious and wondered what they would think if they knew the true purpose of the prize they gave to Wyren.

The army came.

Wyren laughed.

As he watched archers take up positions, he stirred faster. When his thin arms became tired, he lifted the staff out of the cask and used the dripping blood to draw circles upon the ground, small at first. The first round of arrows rained down around him as the archers tested the distance between them and the wily wizard. The projectiles fell short, but not by much, and Wyren knew the next volley posed a viable threat. But as the ground melted and bubbled within the circles, Wyren no longer needed to worry. Again, Wyren laughed.

Within the crimson perimeters, the ground fell away as if devoured by an abyss. Crawling from the small pits scrabbled fist sized insects, demonic in look and purpose. Swarming straight from the holes down the side of the mountain, the creatures made their way to the archers. A wave of mandibles and pincers shredded flesh and bone.

Wyren laughed.

Giddy with power, Wyren used the blood-dripping staff to make more circles, larger and larger, on the ground, on the rare tree, on the rock wall of the mountain. More minions poured forth, larger monsters from larger circles.

Shaggy moths droned from the drawn maw of hell, a cloud forming over a small section of regiment. As the soldiers attacked, the moths burst into a nebulous miasma, devil dust clogging the men's eyes and throats.

As the commanders tried to regain order amongst their trained troops, Wyren drew larger circles upon whatever surface seemed solid enough. Within seconds, Wyren had new troops at his disposal, winged creatures the size of men, but with leathery skin covered in pustules and ridged horns. He commanded them to seek out the order-barking sergeants and carry them off; bat-like wings beat a steady rhythm as they carried the officers high into the air, then dropped them like stones upon their own troops.

Soon the valley floor was strewn with the broken bodies of dead men. Dismembered corpses outnumbered those who had succumbed to a bludgeoning death. Wyren considered the twisted grimaces of the fallen and surmised that asphyxiation was likely a blessed way to die for those few who had found death in that manner. Wyren smiled.

With plenty of blood left in the cauldron, Wyren traced a circle as tall as his arms could stretch and just as wide. Ice petrified his veins as he watched the newest additions to his horrid army stride forth.

Arising from the great circle a monstrous beast emerged, bovine in the leg, though bipedal in its enormous stance, an abyssal lord looming impossibly large and eclipsing the wizard, who shrank into a huddling mass of flesh. Furry legs stretched into a thickly muscled, human torso, then gave way to a mangled face forged from sadistic rage, topped with two ram-like horns, one shorn from a battle waged millennia ago. Its maw split in speech, its voice so deep that pebbles and stones dislodged themselves and rolled down the mountainside. The monster was Ar'drzz'ur, lord of endless toil and general for the armies of hell. He announced his presence, then the blasphemy strode towards the army in the vale below, followed by a legion of equally misshapen demons.

As Wyren scuttled away from the hideousness he wrought, he bumped the cauldron causing a splash of blood to spill over the side. At first, he cursed his clumsiness, but then he watched as a thick stream of crimson flowed down the side of the mountain from the plateau on which he stood. At this, Wyren smiled.

Had the mad wizard known that he was about to be betrayed, he might have rethought his tactic. But as he strategically poured the contents of the cauldron down the side of the mountain in two rivulets, the very mercenaries he had hired changed their hearts, disgusted with themselves for seeing what accepting quick and easy coin had led to.

Being a band of five, the sell-swords were so accustomed to each other's fighting skills and styles that they no longer acted like five individuals, but one organism with five strong and dexterous appendages. With alacrity, they moved between the forest and the mountain base, doing their best to avoid the conflicts. And if some creature found itself in their way, then the mercenaries would send it back to the depths of hell from whence it came.

Finding the mad wizard proved no challenge. He stood at the base of the precipice from where he began the battle, scraping at two oozing, crimson lines with the bottom of his staff. From the cliff where he started the war, over fifty feet above him, to the ground where he stood, two lines of blood, arcing away from each other, streaked down the mountain side. The two lines crossed at the top, but remained uncompleted at the bottom.

Watching the wizard's frenzied scraping, the mercenaries deduced the staff held the power over the demons and must be broken. However, a wall of these very demons stood between them and Wyren.

Wyren howled commands.

Four of the mercenaries formed a square, swords and axes spiked the perimeter while the archer stood firm in the middle. Arrows spewed into the air, a fountain of steel-tipped wood, piercing the marrow beyond the meat of the winged demons. A hurricane of bloody, shredded skin and broken bodies, ranging from massive to minuscule, rained from the sky. The other four warriors pitched throwing knives, daggers, and any makeshift projectile they had at their disposal to ward of the advancing monsters.

Once the archer's quiver emptied, the mercenaries relied upon hand-held weapons as they charged into the melee. Within the flurry of teeth and steel, claws and swords, they witnessed the completion of Wyren's mammoth blood circle.

The ground quaked, throbbed as if hell itself was expanding beyond its limits. Like a stone plunging into a lake, the mountainside rippled, changing hue from slate gray to fecal brown to apocalyptic black. All conflict ceased, eyes upon the gaping hole, even the demons stood awed.

The blackness rippled again and parted, as fingers emerged, each longer than any man in the valley. Bile green and covered with coarse hairs, the rest of the hand, larger than most houses, appeared.

The mercenary leader possessed the instinct to take advantage of the situation and snapped his attention back to the battlefield. Lopping the heads off the few demons in front of him, he rushed forth and drove his shoulder into Wyren's back, knocking the staff from his grasp.

Wyren shrieked.

The mercenary crawled toward the staff fighting off the mad wizard's desperate attacks, biting and scratching worse than the demons. Upon grabbing the staff, the mercenary rolled on his back and folded his leg to his chest, snapping the staff in half against his knee.

Wyren screamed; his shrill voice echoing throughout the valley. The agony reflected both the destruction of his power and the revenge enacted against him as the hand from the mountain reached down and grabbed him. Wyren continued his scream as the hand retreated with the wizard in its grasp into the fading hole on the mountainside.

The five mercenaries turned to examine the battlefield. Any demon left alive had fled. Bodies of monsters and soldiers blanketed the valley, scarred and charred from the fires of war.

Nudging the staff with his foot, one of the mercenaries saw the cause of such mayhem. The staff's crest, once a fist, now an open hand; the Devil's grasp released five accursed gems: the Sun Stone, the Self Stone, the Spirit Stone, the Shadow Stone, and the Satan Stone. He tried to crush them beneath his boot, then split them with his sword, but to no avail. Not uttering a single word, each of the five mercenaries scooped up a gem. With nary a backwards glance, the mercenaries were no longer, now paladins as they walked in five opposite directions, making it their quest to vanquish the stones. ...

ONE

"... AND THAT'S THE story of Wyren and the five stones."

Nevin Narrowpockets stared at the portly bard across the table, wondering if the story he had just heard held even the slightest iota of truth. The bard was an ugly man with round cheeks and a bulbous nose. His desperate smile revealed a piece of bread stuck at the base of his inflamed gums and did nothing to hide that a few of his yellowing teeth had gone absent. Drink froth bubbled from the corners of his mouth, and he had no facial hair to mask it.

Trying not to stare at the bard's lolling right eye or the raised mole at home on his left cheek, Nevin remembered listening to his Elven tribe's elders tell tales of wonder and fancy even more improbable than the bard's tale of an army getting slaughtered by a madman wielding a demon summoning staff over four hundred years ago. However, Nevin wanted a lighthearted tale of whimsy to accompany his drink of ale while visiting this tavern, not what the bard had offered. He turned to his partners for their reactions.

The human who simply went by the name of Silver leaned back in his chair, hands behind his head, and propped his feet on the table. Long and black, his hair flowed over his shoulders like an ebony waterfall. He had a permanent squint, the bar's dim light from the oil lamps made his eyes look like stab wounds. His perfectly white teeth glinted, catching what little light the room offered, as did the medallion resting on his chest, six silver rings encircling each other. The sleeves of his black shirt were snug around his shoulders, but billowed as they fell toward his wrists. His choice of jewelry also showed his affinity for the shimmering metal; a fist full of silver rings on one hand and silver bands hugged his other arm from his forearm to his palm. More silver speckled his body from his cloak clasps to his belt buckle down to even his boot buckles.

Nevin looked at Silver, a wrier smile he had never seen. He knew very well that the human had heard only half the story, at most, while he drank his ale and wondered which woman in the bar would look better naked. And the half Silver did hear, he obviously did not believe.

The elf turned to his other human partner, Diminutia, whose lip corners twitched as he tried to keep from laughing. Diminutia looked quite the opposite of Silver—his eyes were wide and bright blue, while his flaxen hair was short, except for the two shoulder length braids, as thick as his finger, sprouting from just above each temple. He chose his clothing, brown leather, not because the thinness allowed him to retain his agility, but because it made him look good. He, too, only paid attention to half of the tale, using most of his attention to flirt with the buxom serving wench.

Nevin turned back to the bard and said with a smooth derision that only an elf can muster, "That's quite an interesting story. However, I'm afraid my partners and I are not looking for an undertaking quite like what you are offering."

Disappointment forced the bard to slouch. "But, the map ..."

"Yes, we understand that you have a map. But what you are failing to grasp is that we are professional thieves. If you wanted us to *steal* a map, then we would do the job in a heartbeat. We don't *buy* maps and *follow* them."

The bard reached in his rear pocket and pulled out the map in question. Unfolding it, he placed it on the table. "Look. Look at the markings and insignias of those who created it. Look at the ink and the parchment, the notes made by those who tried to follow it."

Picking up the map using only his thumb and index finger, Nevin tossed it in front of Diminutia. The blond man cast his leer from the serving wench to the map just long enough to say, "All I see are blood and burn marks."

"Half. Just give me half my original asking price," the bard pleaded.

"If the stone that this map supposedly leads to is so valuable, why are you so eager to get rid of it?" Silver asked.

"Didn't you listen to the story? This is a very powerful stone! One of the five that the mercenaries hid. Not to mention there are others looking for these stones, and they can be more dangerous than the stones themselves."

"Others?" Diminutia asked. "Who?"

"A band of wizards for starters. I also heard that The Horde is looking for them. Rumor has it that the king himself has been researching the historical accuracy of the same story that I told to you."

"None of those points you mention are inviting us to go on this little adventure," Silver muttered, accompanied by a sneer and an eye roll. "Quite the opposite effect."

"But if you sell the stone to one of the parties you mentioned, then you could ask for more gold than you weigh."

"A king's gold is very tempting indeed," Diminutia said. "But forgive my skepticism. Exactly what is in this for you? I mean, clearly you had some interest and now ..."

"My interest is purely based on the historical. I am a bard with only one tale to tell. I just wish to add yours to my library. I do not have the build for adventure, but I do have the tongue to tell it. Half my original asking price and you spare no details when the deed is done that I might record the tale."

Despite the increasing alcohol content in his blood and the triad of lovely serving women whose attentions he garnered, Diminutia did not miss the way the portly fellow danced and shifted his weight from foot to foot, swaying like a pendulum. Nor did he miss the perspiration matting the rotund man's hair. "Wenches! Another round of ale for the table on this man's tab!" he ordered, using his index finger to identify the bard. Maps on vellum, kings, wizards, hordes, demonic stones, and the cloying scent of another man's terror ... definitely not their line of work, but he would be remiss lest he take full advantage of the situation.

As the servers brought their drinks, Diminutia sought his tankard and drank deeply, the brimming liquid threatening to run down his chin. After using the bard for all he was worth, Diminutia was now eager for the stocky man to leave, but not sure exactly how to achieve that effect.

"What would you do, wench?" Diminutia demanded without even turning to regard the nearest server. Perhaps she would laugh at the notion, cuing the bard to simply stagger away. "Should my friends and I buy this fellow's map and follow it into what surely would be folly?"

"Well, milord," she said, "I must confess that I do find dashing heroes questing with their folded maps ... well ... very manly."

"Manly? Did you say manly?" Intrigued, he looked to her and was met with the blooming rose of her blush. Briefly their eyes locked and Diminutia swore he felt his courage rise within his heart instead of his loins.

"Forgive me, milord, other patrons beckon," she said, hurrying off.

"Manly," he murmured with reverence as though the word were a secret worth remembering.

"Come back to reality, Diminutia," whispered Nevin. Being the elder by more than a decade, he remembered all too well his youth and the meaning of the glint he saw in Diminutia's eye.

"One half the price, elf, and fame awaits your outstretched hand," the bard, picking the moment as his opportunity, offered to Nevin.

"Getting a good price ... now that's manly! Bard, I say one third your original price. Nevin, pay the man and let him be off. Fame is a fickle mistress. Let's not disappoint her," Diminutia said, his mind cluttered with lavish victory parties decorated with many wenches. And gold! Deep troves of king's gold!

Nevin rolled his eyes. "Dim, you cannot be serious about ..."

With perceptible force, the frame of the small tavern shook as the door was shoved inward, hinges groaning in protest at the unaccustomed use of excessive force, cutting all conversation within the tavern short. Even through the thick haze of the room, the twilight backlit the enormous figure of an ogre paused within the doorway, taking in the contents of the tavern, and making the most of his entrance.

Every bit of eight feet tall with the girth of a warhorse, Bale Pinkeye grinned a gap-toothed greeting and stooped under the doorframe as he entered. His thinned, lank, nut-brown hair, a corona atop his knotted, green head, resembled a parched patch of ground, upon which a mule had just feasted. Straightening himself, he brought one gnarled, wart-encrusted hand up to his head, freshly matting the scrub there into an attempted comb-over.

"Must you always be so boorish, Pinkeye?" Nevin asked, sneering.

The ogre laughed, shaking the tavern to its foundation with both his booming voice and the unconfined undulation of his copious folds of fat. "I'm not boorish. I'm very exciting and fun! Everybody in this tavern loves Bale Pinkeye. Wench! Grog!"

Seething stares of discontent from all corners of the room followed the ogre as he stomped to the bar. Whispers and murmurs circulated amongst the patrons, swapping stories of Bale Pinkeye's drunken, and often destructive, stupors. None loved Bale Pinkeye, except for the few close friends that he kept, one being an orc named Zot who trundled into the bar behind Bale. "You idiot!" Zot yelled at his friend. "He said, 'boorish,' not 'boring.'"

Knowing to leave well enough alone, Nevin turned his attention back to the bard. "Look, it is quite obvious that you do not wish to accompany us on this journey. If your intentions of 'purely historical' observation are true, that means we will have to record many aspects of the quest. At the very least, we will have to imbibe less to keep our memories with us, which could be asking quite a bit from the three of us."

In unison, the three thieves pulled an extended drink from their mugs to emphasize the point.

Not being one to leave well enough alone, Silver set his tankard down and nodded toward Zot. "Looks like more trolls are showing up."

Zot ambled from the bar to the thieves' table. "I'm an orc, not a troll!"

An uglier orc did not exist. Half as tall as any man at the table, but easily twice as heavy, Zot seemed to consist of mismatched body parts. Painted with various, uneven hues of green, the creature's left arm was noticeably longer than his right. Cursed with a limp in his gait, either his right knee did not work or it was missing altogether, his stubby legs had the dubious task of carting around a whale's worth of weight.

However, it was his most obvious physical affliction that earned him the name Zot "the Snot." The cavernous nostrils embedded in his mountainous nose were unable to hinder his body's mellifluous secretions.

Silver repeatedly slid his index finger down his nose, as if trying to wipe away an invisible piece of dirt. "Hey, Zot. You have a little something on your nose there. You might just want to ... it's just a little bit of ... do you need a rag for that?"

Mucilage slopped onto the middle of the table, flung from Zot's thumb. With a snort and a sneer, the orc left the thieves to join his ogre friend.

Diminutia reeled back from the offensive bodily fluid on the table. He turned his gaze back to the ample cleavage of the bar wench. To the bard, he said, "One third your original price is our final offer. Take it and leave."

Head hanging low like a child scorned, the bard scooped up the loose coins Nevin tossed in front of him. "Now ... how will I contact you for your tale?"

"We frequent this establishment. Keep coming back until you see us again. You have your coin, now be gone ..."

The bard ceased his fidgeting and, for proper appearance, gave a slight bow. Trudging away wearing a cloak of disappointment, he offered parting words. "Fare thee well, adventurers. Fare thee well."

Nevin turned his mead-glazed eyes to Diminutia. "I believe you have just demonstrated why I do all the negotiating."

"Bahh. This was not negotiation for a regular job. Plus, the bard was annoying me." Though his vision began to blur, Diminutia snatched the map from the table the way a poison victim would grab an antidote. "*This* is for something much more."

"I say we sell it," Silver said.

"I say you let your good friend Pik look at it," came from behind Diminutia.

The three thieves jumped as one, startled by the unwelcome comment. They turned to see Pik Pox looming. Long and lanky, as tall as Bale, with smooth malachite skin, Pik Pox was a hobgoblin. His gaunt body swayed with an eerie calm, like a spider watching a fly encircling its web.

"I'm quite good with maps," Pik smiled, ardent eyes glittering atop Silver's half-drained tankard of mead.

"Someday, Pik, I'll have your eyes strung on a necklace, but for now, hand over my alcohol," growled Silver, angry that he didn't notice his drink being pilfered by the hobgoblin.

"Perhaps, human. Perhaps. I anticipate the effort." As if to emphasize his sarcasm, Pik traded a glance between the double-headed axe that hung from his belt and the dagger that the human wore. Pik's right hand returned Silver's tankard, while his left hand raised a different drink, newly garnered from a neighboring table, to his slick, olive lips.

"Well," Diminutia began, "I'd say both suns are setting on our little reunion. And you know how dangerous it is for three honest and timid gentlemen like ourselves after dark. Be seeing you," he concluded by casting his gaze to the ogre, implying to Pik where he should go. Still leaning up against the bar, which was bowed beneath the combination of his bulk and the weight of the half-dozen, empty tankards loitering around him, Bale waved to Pik. Yellow lips moistened in libation, lower lip stretched over one exposed tusk, Bale stood with a drink in his upraised hand. Pinky extended, he turned his attention to bawling out for another mug full of grog; an alcohol conceived by the ogre scholar Fattous Largemouth, derived by fermenting the bitter roots of the melanoid tree and the funereal leaves of the ravenberry bush, yielding a gelatinous brew of inky hue.

"Let's get out of here before trouble finds us," Diminutia urged his companions. He turned to leave but found his left foot bound to the floor, a green adhesive applied liberally to his honey-leathered boot—the all too familiar work of Zot.

"The inhuman footstool's been at work. Do you think the bar wench could fetch some form of solvent?" he asked of his companions. While the thieves lamented in disgust, Zot, who had crept undetected under their table, flipped the planked and knotted piece of furniture at Nevin, sending the elf sprawling.

Yanking his foot from his very expensive leather boot, Diminutia drew his dagger, ready to slice the cost of the boot from Zot's hide. Nevin stood, wiping a trickle of blood from his lip, ready to send the orc back to whatever fecal pool rejected him. Having never been fond of any green creature, Silver readied himself to tangle with all three miscreants.

"Now gentlemen," Pik said, his words slid from his mouth as smooth as a silkworm's thread. "I believe we have caused enough commotion for one evening. We are certainly more civilized creatures than this."

The thieves looked at each and shared the same thought—how outrageous it was for a hobgoblin to consider himself more civilized than either human or elf. However, a room full of stern and quiet eyes halted their desire to strike. They took great pride in their chosen vocation and worked hard not to be perceived as common hoodlums. "It pains me to say this," Nevin said through clenched teeth, "but we should depart. We have quite a full plate for tomorrow, let's not ruin our appetites tonight."

"Very well," Silver mumbled.

Anger held Diminutia's tongue still; he showed his reluctant acceptance by simply turning away.

Attempting to repair their image, the thieves returned the flipped table and chairs while Zot and Pik, who cared little about their image, joined Bale at the bar.

"They're one up on us, Nevin. They've *never* been one up on us. We *have* to even the score," Diminutia said, using his dagger to cut his boot free from the sticky sludge.

"There is a first time for everything," Nevin replied. "Let's just take the map and ... the map?"

"I don't have it. Silver?"

Silver responded by affixing his eyes upon the three green patrons, enjoying overflowing libations in between uproarious laughter, standing at the bar.

Nevin threw the chair he was holding to the ground and started toward the bar.

"Nevin?" Diminutia asked as he and Silver followed.

"They're now *two* up on us. *That* we cannot allow."

Nevin and Silver strolled up to the bar and stood on either side of Bale. "You know, we want to buy you guys a round of grog. Barkeep! Another round for our friends here." Nevin made no attempt to hide the sarcasm seeping from his lips.

Trying to hide the map, Bale's thick fingers fumbled with it like a child trying to hide a stolen treat after being caught. "Well, uhh ... that's very nice of you. Why?"

"We just wanted to show you that we had no hard feelings about that little misunderstanding a few moments ago."

Being the smartest of his seven brothers and three sisters, Bale flaunted his colloquial mastery. "I ... uh ... ummm ..."

"No need for words, Bale. The look on your face is thanks enough." Nevin finished his sentence with a slight nod to Silver. Faster than a blink of an eye, both men spun, each sweeping their foot across the back of Bale's knees. Stumbling backward, Bale flailed his arms, splashing the grog in each hand throughout the tavern, until he finally fell, reducing two tables to splinters and ruining the evening of five patrons.

Hissing, Pik lunged for Nevin. Before the hobgoblin could reach the elf, Diminutia used his dagger to slash the thin belt that held Pik's baggy pants fast. His pants fell to his ankles causing him to fall as well, missing Nevin. On his way down, reflex dictated he grab for the nearest object, even if it was now the barstool on which Zot sat. Pik unwittingly pulled the legs out from under the barstool, launching the orc across the tavern where he ultimately ended his journey on a nearby table, his rump lodged in a large bowl of broth.

"That's it!" the barkeep screamed, slamming his fist on top of the bar. "All orcs, ogres, and hobgoblins *out* of my tavern!"

Collecting themselves and Pik's ragged pants, the three that the barkeep singled out left the tavern, not caring about the room full of icy glares that accompanied them. Diminutia blew a kiss while waving the map with his other hand.

"They're one up on us again," Zot mumbled as they walked through the night. "They stole back the map we stole from them."

"They're always one up on us," Bale mumbled as well.

"Well, not this time. Ol' Pik has a plan," Pik said.

"What?"

"It's simple. We follow them."

Bale and Zot cheered, Pik quickly joined, laughing and howling as well. They continued raising a ruckus down the street until Bale accidentally stepped right where a horse had recently polluted the road.

TWO

DEARBORN STILLHEART awoke to the morning sun's soft kiss against her cheek. A new day's dawning, existence inchoate. Unthinking, she swiped sleep from her eyes, pale and serene like the morning sky on a cloudless day. Unbound and airy, she slid from beneath the blankets and strode vigorously across the exposed stone floor of her bedroom to regard the faultless form of her womanhood in her mirror, one of the privileges of freedom. Freedom. With all of its elusive and elastic clauses, one wondered at its true definition. Free to do what she could, not what she wanted.

Azure awareness focused on her mirror, glass and steel housed within the coppered frame on the bare wall. Like the mirror, her mind was reflective, but she cast off the miscreant thoughts like anchors from a boat that did not wish to be tethered and slipped into the current of the fleeting moment. *Dismiss the pessimism,* she thought as she brought her gaze to bear on the countenance that the mirror reflected. Gathered beneath the gauzy nightclothes, sinews like springs and muscles of molded perfection piqued her anger as they replicated an image that defied her desired optimism. Unable to turn immediately from her mirror, her glance slid into a stare. Her soul was cast in the silvery glass as with her body—the woman she saw and the woman she hoped to see were two different people.

Combing a few stray tresses of her lengthy hair, as black as midnight, she fixated on her contrapposto form. Substantial hips sprouted from a waist thin enough to be envied by any woman; however, their shape had not been molded by the natural process of child birth and rearing, but through training with the king's army and clinging fast to thunderous steeds while riding into battle. From sternum to pelvis, eight abdominal muscles protruded like angry fists attempting to pound free from fleshy prison walls, and no woman in the capital city of Phenomere, maybe even the entire kingdom of Albathia, had a chest to compare to Dearborn's. That saddened her since her cleavage was minimal, increasing only when she flexed, while the girth of her greatness consisted mostly of her forged back.

Hands still taming hair atop her head, she focused her attention to her arms, thick enough to handle a broadsword with ease; she wondered what man could ever accept her as a wife. Then she flexed; a pronounced web-work of olive veins appeared as her biceps tightened to the hardness of stone. Even her triceps swelled, much the way they did every time a member of the troop challenged her to an arm wrestling match. But even though her arms were strong, they were never strong enough to pull her heavy heart from the deep, dark recesses within.

"Either a career or a man," she whispered. Her hands slid over her sheer nightwear as she hoped that her delicates were not the only distinguishable quality between her body and a man's. But what other choice was available? Being taller and stronger than most men made her no more desirable for marriage than a legless ox for plowing a field. A life away from King Theomann's army would allow her body to shed some mass, but then what means could make her ends meet? Even if she retired and found a man to give her his heart, could he also give her the accouterments to which she had grown so accustomed?

Being a member of the Elite Troop in the king's army did lead to a life of lavish luster. The finest furs adorned her bed. Tapestries of silk flowed across the walls of her room, large enough to house two small families in comfort.

A hot meal was at her constant disposal, as was a warm bath. Even taxation was a burden she had not to bear. She was left wanting for nothing, save an escape from the emptiness inside.

Her only defense against the overbearing emotions that threatened to consume her with hopelessness was to bury them behind a burly façade. This, however, required her to be bathed and dressed, something she could not manage while reflecting in the mirror's vigilant eye. She turned from the sight of her own image, and the loneliness faded, evaporating behind the mental defenses of her own construction.

Time for a bath, she decided, noting that the slant of the sun's rays suggested that others would soon be up and about. She so despised being seen with less than her full regalia to hide the manliness of her form. She donned her silken robe, more concealing than the nightwear, and made for the warm springs, pausing only a moment outside her door to retrieve the pair of buckets affixed to a shoulder bar that were so integral to her daily ritual.

The warm spring fountain stood a few houses from the barracks, scarcely a brief walk if she was brisk of pace. She recently discovered the joy of a long soak when she was breathless from her run to the fountain and back. She made a mental game of it, challenging herself not to spill a drop of the warmed liquid on her return trip.

She set off at a pace that a sleek warhorse would have difficulty keeping for long. She passed Squire Bardeth's cottage, noticing even in her haste that the freshly applied paint was a slightly darker tint than the former one, though still a quite suitable shade of taupe for a cottage amongst the canopy of Catalpa leaves that stretched across its roof. The stalks that were the tree's beans swayed slightly in the light breeze. The gabled roof of the old cottage had a pleasing angle, but she could not help notice that the shingles needed replacement around the chimney. She wondered vaguely if the squire had noticed yet.

Up ahead the familiar form of the widow Palna's homestead greeted Dearborn. Palna was quite a cook and many were the mornings that some fresh baked good beckoned with its sweet scent as she passed by. Today was one of those mornings. A strong scent of apricot drifted across her path as she ran. *One of these days I will stop and savor the taste behind that aroma,* she promised herself.

The remaining houses on her route passed by quickly. She noticed, however, that Perlath, the wheelwright's wife, had replaced her pansies this year with a crop of daffodils, their yellow center beaming out to her like small suns amongst a backdrop of clouds.

The following house had a large retriever the color of burnt taffy. The dog lifted his head at her approach, but did not come out of his shelter as he was wont to do when she passed him. Even animals tire of routines, it seemed, and she wondered briefly when she could trade in hers, but she had reached her destination before her mental reserve could fully elaborate on the subject.

"Morning, Melthas." She knew he was engaged in his tasks and not within earshot, but she always greeted him anyway. The sound of her voice seemed disquieting as if a mere whisper would shatter the perfect silence of this morning. In a large pail she placed a silver coin. Melthas was the peasant responsible for placing heated rocks within the fountain, and he was never lax in his duties, despite the lameness in his right leg. Dearborn always contributed well to his cause. His wife had passed on recently, and his son had grown and gone, leaving the old man with only his labors for companionship. This kinship to the old man she acknowledged with coin.

She stared intently at the fountain, a stone structure with walls about four feet high crafted in the shape of a schooner. It was done to scale, and the mast hid a pump that shot water high into the air above. It was caught in its downward arc on the sails of the foremast and cascaded back into the pool. It was a piece of marvelous craftsmanship and Dearborn had always found peace in its shadow.

"Dearborn! I had no idea you came here this early. No surprise, though, really. I mean, given your dedication to the rigors of training. One simply cannot underestimate the importance of an early start."

Frissons danced down her spine as she savored the sound of his voice. She did not look at her commanding officer as she spoke.

"General, I ..."

"Iderion. Simply, Iderion. How many years have I known you? On the battlefield you may use epithets, but not here. Dispense with the manners, Dearborn. They distance people."

Iderion was a mountain of masculinity and looked every bit the way a general should. None of the forty members in the Elite Troop were taller or wider. No soldier in the rest of the army had his height, and only a handful had the girth, but Iderion wore it the way a king would wear a coat of arms. Even though his waist was forged from many years battling tankards of ale, his chest exploded with muscle, leading into shoulders as broad as a feed wagon and capable of handling a yoke far better than any ox. His arms, thicker than most men's legs, were chiseled from handling pikes and halberds, occasionally considering the mace a finesse weapon.

Like most of the men in the Elite Troop, his hair was thick and long, just as his beard. Iderion stood apart from the others, though, as he kept both impeccably groomed. Dearborn often fantasized about losing her hands in his hair as she would lose her face in his beard.

"As you would have it, Iderion."

"It's a beautiful work, this fountain. I often come here when my mind is overwrought with problems and the answers are evasive. There is solace in the sound of softly falling water. It is nature's laughter, I believe."

"Oh yes! I have often thought as you do. I ... I ... I must be going ... I'm simply a sight ... I ..."

"A sight, you are, but not an eyesore."

Unsure of how to react to his comment, Dearborn shifted her glance to the ground. Attempting to be coy, she shifted her eyes to his; however, he was looking at her left arm, fully flexed supporting the shoulder bar. As ladylike as possible, she set the buckets on the wall of the fountain and replied, "You are far too kind, sir."

"You make it very easy to be kind. In fact, you are the only member of my Elite Troop who bathes more than once a week and refuses to frolic in flatulence."

Dearborn laughed. "Despite my cleanliness, I am still your best warrior."

Dolt! Dearborn scolded herself, never wanting to appear in any way unfeminine in front of Iderion. However, simply standing before the general seemed to counter her comment.

"That you are," Iderion laughed.

"I … have been coming to this fountain since I have been in the Elite Troop and have never seen you here. Any special occasion?" Dearborn asked as she dunked her buckets into the warm water.

"I just came from the armorer. It was just coincidence that I happened to pass through your morning ritual."

Confused as to why he would see an armorer, Dearborn glanced down at the armor he toted along: plate mail for his chest and shoulders, chain mail for waist, while the whole was covered in bear skin.

Iderion never lacked confidence, to the point where a few years prior he proclaimed that he would die from neither weapon nor man. Seeking a true challenge, he sought a battle with nature to learn fear. He had found everything he was looking for in the form of a mountain grizzly and contested it without weapon and free from clothing, save a few strategically placed leather straps to contain and protect certain body parts that defined him as a man. He took from that battle many scars and the bear's hide, which he had fastened strips of to his armor, not as a trophy as some had thought, but as a symbol of respect.

"You're not thinking about switching to new armor, are you?" Dearborn asked.

Iderion laughed. "Not at all. Even though my wife did a fine job attaching the skins to the metal, an expert is needed to readjust and tighten some of the fasten points now and again."

My wife … my wife … my wife … shrieked through Dearborn's mind like an angered banshee. *My wife … my wife …* Thrusting a dagger between her ribs, followed by a twist, would have been more pleasant. *My wife …*

Dearborn's morning had just been ruined. "I must be going," she said as she hoisted the bar and buckets across her shoulders.

"So soon?"

"My ... water ... is getting cold."

Dearborn hurried away as if retreating from Iderion's parting words, "I shall see you at breakfast. And don't forget about our meeting with the king and his sons."

The return trip to her room went quickly, her eyes glazed from unpleasant emotions, unable to concentrate on the surrounding scenery. However, instead of the relaxing soak she desired, she found herself scrubbing, trying to bristle away her lovelorn feelings. Disappointed with her bath and disgusted with herself for her intolerable reaction to the mere mention of Iderion's wife, she resolved to get dressed and simply go about the rest of her day.

Her boots were thick leather and knee high. Running down each shin was a strip of heavy steel, spines sprouting from it, wrapping around her calf like a silver rib cage. From wrist to elbow, she donned the exact same protection. The rest of her armor boasted only slight variations; the same thick hide, except circles of steel in even patterns were fastened firmly, leaving only parts of her thighs and arms exposed. Since the local armory found it difficult to fit a woman, she had crafted the outfit herself, blending the protection of mail with the stealth of leather. Being the daughter of a blacksmith had many benefits. Her cloak, as thin as the air of a stale summer morning and as red as a freshly stoked forge, clasped by a single chain below her neck, flowed as she strode down the hallway. She never liked wearing it, feeling cloaks to be too deceptive, but Iderion requested her to do so whenever she faced a situation requiring formality. And a meeting with the king himself after breakfast certainly seemed a formality.

Her stomach rolled from the thought, ruining the breakfast feast the king's servants prepared as she entered the mess hall. Two inviting tables stood in the center of the room, each long enough to fit an army let alone the motley crew for whom it was intended. With scarcely half the king's Elite Troop present, the din far surpassed that of a full mead hall. The troop force numbered forty, always. Iderion declared that number; any more would be too difficult to control, any less would discount the use of complex battle strategies. In the rare occasion of a member following the path of death, or even the less frequent instance of a member following the path of retirement, a replacement was provided by the regular army. Such was Mahlakore, the newest member, finishing his meal with a few of the other men as Dearborn joined them.

"We were just talking about you, Sergeant!" Grother said, food spraying from his lips as he laughed. "We were just telling Mahlakore here that he wasn't an official member until he tries to best our sergeant."

"I never had to face an opponent so pretty before," Mahlakore said, laughing as well, his eyes never looking below her face to see the outline of her body beneath her thin cloak.

Dearborn squinted, eyes as cold as her sword, her gaze gliding across Mahlakore. He was young. His youth showed in his grooming, with trimmed hair and nails, as well as his health, his waist leaner than his chest. Most new recruits started like that, but quickly turned into Grother— appearance indistinguishable between man and beast.

Under any other circumstance, Dearborn would all but swoon over a compliment, *any* compliment. However, the need to be a sergeant outweighed the desire to be a woman. In one fluid motion, done so many times before, she flipped her cloak open, her broad shoulders burst free like a bull charging through paper, as she sat and planted her elbow on the table with her palm open, waiting for his. Blanching to the shade of a dead man's, Mahlakore's skin kept his jaw from falling clean from the rest of his skull. The mess hall erupted with hoots and hollers, food and drink spraying from every mouth.

As timid as a wedding night virgin, Mahlakore placed his elbow on the table, his hand clasped Dearborn's. Grother signaled the start of the match with an earth-splitting belch.

Like all men, Mahlakore started hard, wasting most of his energy with the first thrust to get only a modest gain. Dearborn always liked to hold fast, forcing her opponent to tire himself, however, today was different: she did not have an enjoyable bath. Veins sprouted in her arm, flirting with rupture from the ire pulsing through them. Slow and steady, the way the oceans reduce shores to sand, she overpowered him, giving one final push to slam and bloody his knuckles against the tabletop. Again the mess hall erupted with cheers and laughter.

Massaging his wrist, Mahlakore looked more dejected than a kicked pup. "What is to become of me?"

"Nothing, boy!" Grother said, slapping the young man's back. "I said 'try' to best our sergeant. *All* of us have lost to her! The only man she has never beaten is ..." A glance to the head of the table replaced his words. There sat Iderion.

Dearborn attempted to stifle a blush, unaware that Iderion had entered. Disgusted with herself for appearing less than feminine twice in one day in front of him, and even more disgusted with herself for caring, she spent the rest of breakfast not once looking up from her plate.

ᴄ𝔥ʀᴇᴇ

THERE WERE PLACES in the world where the land was clean and smooth like unblemished skin; where its voice honeyed and melodious, the air filled with the aria of birdsong and brook speech; where it exhaled steadily and unhurried, its breath a delicious blend of dandelion and marigold. On a stand of countryside just such as this, a contingent of the most finely gifted architects and artisans had erected Phenomere Castle, home to the ruling family of Albathia. Constructed of granite with a pallid marble facing, the castle loomed high above the ground, its highest turret rising spear-like towards the heavens, often transfixing a stray cloud upon its spiny tip. Silver and white banners, the colors of the current monarch, draped from balconies and turrets, flaccid in the stillness, their lengths exposed to view by the surrounding countryside.

There was but one road that led to the castle, and it was well weeded and unmarred, circling off into the temperate day like a band of gold marrying the capital to the country. Beyond the outer bailey, fields of bracken flushed with moss rose, stretched off to either side, extending unbroken beyond the limits of normal vision.

The land to the south was an agrarian paradise, well suited to pasture and vineyards. To the far west grew great stands of trees, and many a man was known to have procured a more than meager existence from their abundance. In the east flowed a mighty river, and on its banks numerous peasants were employed both in spawning and harvesting fish. Northward lay the great stone quarries that had yielded the skeleton of Phenomere Castle and countless other less impressive structures. All manner of professions tied to the virtues of the land were commonplace in this microcosmic paradise. In the country of Albathia, food and drink were plentiful, and, during peacetime, life in Albathia was not a life of wanting.

From atop a parapet on the western wing of the princes' level of the castle stood the youngest of the king's three sons. He gazed in resentment upon all that his family had accomplished and reaped. Eyes of virgin flint lay beneath an unworked brow, furrowed deeper than any valley. This expression was the norm for Prince Daedalus. A trail of sunshine draped from beneath his crown to the middle of his back. Ruddy, well-toned skin stretched tautly across his thin frame, evident beneath the damask cloth he draped about his shoulders. Daedalus ferociously contemplated Father's request for his presence at the military meeting about to take place. As third son to King Theomann, his counsel was rarely sought and even more seldom acknowledged. This could only mean that the matter was serious.

Two scorpions, a brown one and a black one, clattered about in a small brass cage at his feet. He grabbed the tiny and lethargic brown scorpion, leaving its black twin in the cage. Brown for yes, black for no. About its segmented body he secured a thin tube of reed. Satisfied that his message would ride intact, he placed the creature within a basket woven of dried and toughened straw. He then placed the basket within the talons of a falcon as pure white as innocence, making it near impossible to spot against the clouds floating within the blue agate sky that reigned over Albathia. The falcon had come to him some few weeks before bearing news from Praeker Trieste, the leader of The Horde and an ally to Daedalus. When the raptor reached the center of the desert, its tiny passenger would grow agitated from the heat and inject the bird with his venomous essence and plummet to his master's hand. In this manner, no messenger bird could ever be traced. Clever and vicious, this was the nature of Daedalus.

His diabolical thoughts ceased as the din of rapping from his chamber door echoed throughout his room. It was time for the meeting. As if haste were an indignity, Daedalus strolled across the room to the door. With a hand hovering over the latch, he waited. He had little power, and he exerted it whenever he could. Once the person on the other side knocked again, Daedalus opened the door.

"Perciless?" Daedalus expected a servant to fetch him as usual. "What a surprise."

Second in line to succeed the throne, Perciless stood four inches taller than his younger brother, a trait gifted from their mother's side of the family. Having the stature of a decorative tree found in the courtyard, straight and sturdy, his army training teetered the scale from lanky to lean. Of his two brothers, Daedalus hated Perciless the most.

Being the first born prince, Oremethus held the keys to the kingdom. That alone warranted the youngest brother's hate. Perciless, however, accepted nature's cruel joke, accepted that their father decreed him nothing. A year separated each brother, and Daedalus never accepted that *two years* stood between him and a future seat on the throne, unable to fathom how Perciless tolerated *one year.* Even when they played as children, Perciless followed every rule to every game, never wavering from instructions given to him. An acrid taste, brought forth from his stomach, tickled the back of Daedalus's tongue by the mere thought of his brother's blind compliance.

"Let's go," Perciless said. "We don't want to keep father waiting." The words scraped down Daedalus's spine as if a dagger tip scraped raw nerve.

"No, we wouldn't want that," Daedalus said under his breath.

"Father said that we should ..."

The voice of his brother droned on, but Daedalus heard only an incessant murmur. To his ears, it simply trailed off as the hand of memory reached in and reversed the hourglass of years. His vision grew dim as he walked while he was taken back many years to a well-remembered scene from his youth. ...

... The courtyard had been transformed as if by passing sorcery. The daily dust of the marketplace had been replaced with hanging banners, the livestock converted to courtesans with their bright livery and fancy speech, hawkers and gawkers melted into frolicking children, shouts traded for laughter. The midsummer's festival was sponsored by the crown and an event not to be missed. Laborers, craftsmen, and hagglers alike dedicated themselves to their specialties with extra zeal in the months preceding the celebration in preparation for the time off. Such splendor ... such extravagance ... such an incredible waste of time, effort, and resources even to Daedalus's then adolescent mind.

While the adults loitered and chatted idly or strolled down the network of aisles of freshly erected stalls examining foreign-made handcrafts or fresh-from-the-hearth baked goods, the children engaged in all manner of games, some traditional, some extemporaneous. The teenaged Daedalus stood on the stone portico of the market's auction house, the only permanent structure in the outer bailey. It had been designed to serve as the command center for the castellan in times of war to direct the castle defenses but had never been used in that capacity. A simple shame and a squandering of further resources, Daedalus mused. One simply did not build structures one did not intend to use.

From between the columns that supported the edifice's roof, Daedalus stared out at the assemblage of vagrants. Amongst their number, he noted, were his two older brothers. Oremethus and Perciless, swallowed in the midst of the local rabble, engaged in bland banter with the native peasantry about the current status of the kingdom, exchanging handshakes and hugs as though they were smiles. It was one thing to acknowledge the lower class as though they were deserving of royal attention, and entirely another to mingle with the sweat-stained, stinking serfs, let alone come into material contact, as though disease and pestilence were nonexistent.

His eyes swept the field of the inner bailey, until at last they found the field that had been cleared for the games. Disgusted with his brothers and disinterested in everyone else, Daedalus drew up an entourage of guards about himself and moved with haste to the sporting ground.

The rectangular area had been partitioned from the rest of the area by heavy cords bearing banners of alternating blue and silver. Before he ducked beneath the ropes, Daedalus caught the attention of the sergeant of arms, Pendrick, a squat man with a jutting jaw and impossibly large forearms that seemed to be covered with fur, instead of hair.

"Guard," Daedalus hissed, waiting until the sergeant turned to face him before continuing. "Admit none except by noble birth. Let the rest watch from a respectable distance."

Stolid and bowing with as much formality as his brutish figure would allow, Pendrick replied, "As I have been commanded, Your Highness." Pendrick moved off, issuing his commands, administering punishment where adherence was not immediate and precise.

Daedalus turned to regard the center of the field. A large tree, felled but not stripped, lay horizontally across the field, suspended waist high, supported at either end by a large rock carved to hold the bough securely. No one had ever bested the young prince at this event, including his brothers. He circled the great log, examining every nuance and flaw, noting several places where the bark was loose and an unwary opponent might lose his balance. After several minutes of intense scrutiny, he sought out Sergeant Pendrick. "Let them in. And have my quarterstaff brought out."

"As I have been commanded, Your Highness."

Several noble children crowded around, pushing for a good view only to be parted by three guards bearing an elaborately carved box of dark mahogany. As they neared the partition, Pendrick moved out to meet them, taking the case and, with a movement that signified formality, offered the case to Daedalus. The great box opened easily, and the young prince snatched greedily at the quarterstaff held within. A stout piece of oak, it stood eighteen hands high and was thick as a wrist, with both ends butted in a cap of hammered bronze.

Weapon in hand, Daedalus mounted one end of the log, facing the western end where his opponent would be allowed to ascend. Being well before noon, the morning sun would be in his opponent's eyes. Home field should carry some advantage, after all. For the moment, he claimed the spotlight as his own and despised relinquishing it before he could duly appreciate it. A warm breeze teased his ear like the breath of a lover departed and found again. A chill swept through the air leaving his cheek as cold as if resting against a stone wall. ...

"... Daedalus!" Perciless cried, snapping his younger brother's attention from then to now. Daedalus found himself out of balance, his cheek resting against the stone wall of the hallway.

Grasping his brother by his shoulders, Perciless helped him regain his balance. "Daedalus, how fare you?"

"I shall be fine," Daedalus replied, wresting himself free from his brother's grip.

"These fainting spells of yours have us all concerned."

"I do not faint, Perciless! My body sometimes is unable to handle the fire of my passion mingling with the ice of my intellect." He paused to wipe sweat from his brow. "Now if you will excuse me, I need a quick splash before I meet with others."

"But ..."

"I wish to look my best, Perciless. Head along now, I assure you I shall not be tardy."

By the time Daedalus reentered his chamber, he was halfway stripped. *Modesty be damned*, he thought as he left his chamber door wide open and stood completely without clothing, pouring a pitcher of water into a basin. With an obsessive vigor, he swirled the soft fibers of his washing brush over his left shoulder, then his right. And repeated. And again. After all, his brother's hands had touched countless peasants over the decades, making them no less sanitary than that of a peasant itself.

Donning a new tunic, even new robes, Daedalus strode from his chamber into the hallway. His step hastened as he neared the meeting room; all eyes turned to him upon his entrance.

The size of the chamber was incomprehensible to the average peasant. The table, a rectangular slab of slate sliced from Mythos Mountain itself, sat in the center of the room, patiently awaiting any and all meetings. From the vaulted ceiling a chandelier hung. Dozens of small oil wells set within elaborate arrays of hand cut crystal evenly disbursed the light to radiate about the entire room with ease. Statues stood guard around the perimeter of the room like stone sentries, all representing Albathia's greatest citizens. Generals stood by philosophers, as artisans intermingled with warriors, each tenfold larger than the individual it immortalized.

As casual as if no one were there, Daedalus took his seat next to Perciless, whose perplexed gaze went unnoticed. "I assume I have not missed much?"

"Not at all, Son," King Theomann said from the head of the table. "We had just exchanged of few pleasantries and ..."

Daedalus's interest quickly vanished as his sight swept across the others at the table, a veritable who's who of whom he loathed. At table's head was master, the puppeteer, King Theomann. Seated at both perpendiculars were his first and second born whelps, close enough to the puppeteer as to not strangle themselves on their own strings.

Across the table, seated next to Oremethus, was General Iderion Irskine. Daedalus bore no ill will toward the general, the worst thoughts he could muster being the general's undying loyalty. However, his loyalty belonged to the throne, no matter who sat in it.

But there she was, next to Iderion, close to the top of Daedalus's hate list. Trying to fight it, just looking at her propelled Daedalus back to a time she probably did not remember, a time he could never forget ...

... The midsummer festival. There he stood, barely across the threshold of adolescence, at one end of the log with quarter-staff in hand. His first opponent made his way atop the other end of the log. Daedalus cared not to know his name; he simply regarded his opponent by his place in life, the son of the jeweler. Knowing where his opposition fell in nature's hierarchy was the only information needed. As expected, the jeweler's son had a fighting style based on finesse, having spent many long hours with a steady hand setting all sorts of stones in gold and silver stands. However, his strength held his weakness. With perfect precision, Daedalus threw a blow—easily blocked—then retreated a step, threw a blow, retreated, and continued until the jeweler's son grew confident, until he stepped forward when Daedalus did not withdraw. Putting the full weight of his body behind two quick strikes, the young prince smashed all eight exposed knuckles of the jeweler's son, the sparse crowd winced in unison at the noise of cracking bone. Daedalus dealt the finishing blow, leaving a scarring gouge in his opponent's forehead, as callously as swatting away a fly.

Strutting to Daedalus's end of the log came Tallon and Tallia, twins sired by his father's sister. Adolescents at the time as well, they were also two of Daedalus's greatest supporters, a brother and sister who shared the same fate as their cousin—to be unseen in history's eyes due to birth right. And they accepted their fate as well as he did.

"Well done, Cousin," Tallia said, offering a cloth to Daedalus for his shimmering brow. He refused by ignoring her gesture.

"He was but the first match, Tallia. However, I do feel the rest shall end just the same," Daedalus replied.

"We shall stand firm behind you, Cousin," Tallon said. "As we always have."

The second match was with the son of a baker, this particular baker created such pastry that could only be enjoyed by the wealthy and regal, allowing him title of nobility.

Daedalus accurately assessed his opponent's strengths: strong legs from long days of standing, fingers like a vice from years of kneading thick dough, yet a skilled touch from carefully crafting crusts and candied cakes. But Daedalus also calculated correctly his weakness: sore shoulders from ceaselessly slouching over countertops all day long. A few well-placed strikes put the baker's son on the ground. The victory was far less vicious than the prior; Daedalus was fond of the baker's candied cakes.

The third opponent fell even faster, then the fourth, the fifth, and the sixth. One victory blurred into the next. He was unstoppable, defeating all who stepped upon the log, some twice, the longest bout a blink over two minutes. And the people noticed.

A crowd formed, first of nobility, but the peasant curiosity overwhelmed Pendrick's ability to keep order. The penury of the peasant throng assaulted the prince's senses as if a mange stricken canine had befouled a kitchen floor; however, Daedalus coped, as long as they minded their place: in the dirt looking up at *him*. And if a peasant wandered too close to the contest and took a shot from a stray staff strike, then what could he do? They should know better.

All went well for the prince, taking the respect he felt due to him. Tallon and Tallia led the crowd with chants during competition and cheers after victory. Then *she* came.

The daughter of a blacksmith, quarter-staff in hand, took the other end of the log. Blacksmithing was a commoner's job in Daedalus's mind; however, her father fitted the army and shod the horses of the wealthy, earning the king's nod for nobility. Although she had an angel's beautiful face, she had the hard, lean body of a warrior. He knew her age to be around his, yet her size dwarfed his oldest brother.

Why is she doing this? he thought. *To mock me? Belittle me?* Unbeknownst to him, her heart had led her to the end of the log. She desired to get closer to one she had only seen from afar. She had no intention of winning, simply to earn his respect by lasting longer than any of the other competitors.

The battle began, and he charged toward her, staff swinging, hoping to make short work of her. This was no place for a commoner and certainly never a place for a woman, no matter how capable. Determined to make an example out of her in case other undesirables had thoughts of mimicking her nonsense, he unleashed a flurry of thrusts and jabs. To his dismay, she parried them all with ease. Every blocked strike or dodged swing would send explosions through his heart. But when he heard more of the crowd cheer her name, *her name*, over his, ire welled deep within his soul the way unattended broth would boil over a kettle.

More strategy was afoot at that moment than just the match. Unhappy with the happenings, and fearful of the outcome, Tallon and Tallia decided to take matters into their own hands. Making their way closer to the bout, they inspected the crowd, scrutinizing each individual until they found exactly what they sought—Perciless, a dupe they could use to disrupt the match, forcing an early end with no winner.

Slinking closer, Tallon and Tallia positioned themselves behind Perciless, who stood rather close to the action. Too close. Each giving a subtle shove, they knocked the young, gawky prince off balance. They merely wanted him to interrupt the fight, but the prince's own clumsiness dictated that he reach for the closest object—the log, right by the feet of Daedalus. Distracted by the happenings, Daedalus took his eyes off his opponent just as she made a ferocious strike, connecting the end of her staff with the small of his back ...

... Daedalus snapped from his intense recollections with a mild jolt. Only his brother, Perciless, noticed him jump. Even to this day, Daedalus remained unaware of his brother's innocence and returned a murderous scowl, his hatred renewed by the memory of his witless cur of a brother ruining an opportunity for greatness.

Forcing himself to stay focused and not stray back down yesteryear's path, Daedalus could not help but casually rub the small of his back. The shot he took from Dearborn was one he would never forget. It pained him to urinate for a full week after.

"As I was saying," King Theomann droned on. "Oremethus, with the help of General Irskine's Elite Troop, will do whatever is necessary to find these stones of legend. This kingdom has known its share of strife, but it was founded upon the principles of freedom, and we must not allow anything to jeopardize what the scions have passed to us. I know many of you view the tales of these stones as hokum. I myself wonder were the history ends and the fairytale begins. However, the country of Tsinel whispers war. We have been receiving an alarming number of reports from our border farms and villages of larceny and murder committed by those living in Tsinel, yet when we implored our neighbor to investigate, the appointed members of Tsinel's army acted *worse* than the criminals they sought. I wish not to wage war with our neighbor—it would be disastrous to our way of life. If we obtain these stones, even if they do not possess the mystical powers of legend, we may be able to win the war before it begins by proclaiming they do have powers. In addition, I have heard many a rumor of The Horde questing for the stones as well. If The Horde were to find them ... there are those thoughts that a man ought not to have, much less lend voice to."

Daedalus attempted to stay focused on the words of his father, but found that he was unable to pay heed to the incessant droning of patriotism that spouted forth from his father's beard-enshrouded lips. His mind wandered, and as it did, his body seemed to play its own part in his distraction: an itching around his left foot grew more persistent the more he tried to ignore it, lest he be seen as a fidget. But the seconds crawled by slowly much like an insect crawling across his skin.

With as little motion as possible, he stretched a hand down to claw at the offending area. As his fingers scraped across the tight golden skin on the top of his foot, they ran across an object that was certainly foreign to his body. He ran his fingers across the thing, his brain recognizing the shape as oval and hard, a shell. Before he could discover more, the object darted away.

Attempting to appear interested in the conversation, Daedalus gazed at his father as the king spoke. "Perciless, you will assist me in getting the command post ready, seeing to the general readiness of the troops, and the early stages of planning. I do not want the citizens of our kingdom to recognize their king as preparing for war. With you as my liaison, all will seem to be routine inspection and an aging king passing on some of the burdens of stewardship to his maturing son."

Intrigued by the feedback from his fingers, Daedalus risked a glance under the table. All seemed as it should be, but as he stretched his legs, which had been crossed at the ankles, a patch of blackness crept off the leather strap of his right sandal and began to ascend his leg.

Brown if yes, black if no. The statement swam before his eyes as if printed on paper. He had sent the brown messenger back to its master to indicate that their plans should proceed. The black one must have gotten loose and hidden in the cuff of the robe he had changed into when Perciless had sullied the first set! He must not allow anyone to see!

"Daedalus, my son, you will ..."

At this, Daedalus clutched at his forehead with his left hand and made a groaning noise. He slouched in his chair to garner a more advantageous view beneath the table. Offering another moan as distraction, he slapped his sandaled foot against the floor, but missed his scuttling target. Another moan, another twist of his body, and another stomp. This time his action was met with reward, the crushing of the scorpion. Panting from his feigned spell, Daedalus gripped his chair and pulled himself straight, dragging his sandal across the ground, smearing all evidence of the squashed arachnid.

Perciless was the first to his brother's side and helped him to his feet, supporting the majority of his weight as Daedalus overacted the part of someone stricken lame.

From his seat at the head of the table, King Theomann sighed, a mixture of concern and relief. Though disconcerting, this was the perfect opportunity to relieve his son of responsibility and ensure that he would be safe and at hand. "You, Daedalus, will seek physical care ..."

Four

THE TOWN OF Freeman's Way was a humble town, a town where one could lead a fruitful, yet modest, life. The lone road wound its way from the south, as the town was flanked on the east and the west by fertile farm land fit for livestock or crop, crowned on the north by lush forest in which both hunting and gathering were always plentiful. Freeman's Way had one of every shop necessary to get one through the day. There were even a few taverns; enough to keep the populace satisfied after a hard day, but not enough to attract rapscallions, such were the tendencies of most isolated towns. This one even had a few retired adventurers, boasting quite often of their terrific tales and their unbelievable findings. Within this circle of retirees, a few claimed to be experts in antiquities and all forms of art and weapon, no matter how rare or arcane. That was now why the town lay in rubble, besieged mere hours prior. The buildings, more than half, were burnt to point of collapse. A majority of the citizens littered the streets dead or dying, the survivors stumbled around dazed, mystified by the happenings, confused as to why a wrath such as this fell upon their humble town. All except one.

In the center of town stood the remnants of an antique shop. The eastern wall was largely intact, as was a portion of the roof. The rest of the above-ground structure had burnt and crumbled. Undetected by hastily scanning eyes, the floor beneath the rubble had remained completely intact. Made of good hardwood and reinforced from below, the floor covered the secret catacombs beneath the shop where the proprietor conducted some of his more illicit activities. Haddaman Crede hid in these catacombs, while the last vestiges of local civilization struggled on. Ever the coward, when the first screams rent the stillborn air, Haddaman crept below ground and prayed for the violence to pass. His throat tightened at the weeping of women and his voice almost betrayed him at the wailing of infants, but the sound of his own terror pounding in his brain frightened him back into silence.

Once a hush had fallen and the cacophony above had been replaced by the staccato of his heart, he made to creep back into the light of day, but as he reached for the trap door above, a small scorpion squeezed through the narrow crack around the door frame and dropped onto his outstretched hand, scurrying for the cover of his sleeve. Only the lightning-fast reflexes of a coward prevented it from doing so. He flailed his arm; the scorpion sailed to some corner and was lost in the depths of the darkness. He lacked the courage to look for the pest and sat himself upon a dusty table, all the while hoping that scorpions were not as adept at climbing as other, less poisonous insects. Pulling his legs to his chest and hugging them, he hoped for a miraculous rescue.

Climbing the small rise leading to Freeman's Way, three men of dubious background took a pause from their journey to check their bearings. Silver squinted at the dual suns that compassed their journey. Setting in the sky glowered Rosaria, the red morning sun. Just above the horizon was Rellucidar, the blue day sun.

"Almost there. Are you sure that Haddaman can authenticate the map?" Silver asked.

"Of all the people who might verify it, only Haddaman is too spineless to deceive us," Nevin replied. "Let's keep moving. This trip has been quite easy, but I would see its end sooner than later."

In a week's time, their passage had been unmarred, other than an unfortunate incident that had been narrowly avoided when Nevin recognized a leaf that would have given him a bad rash as he sought a suitable reply to nature's call. When his counterparts laughed about his near misfortune he had insulted their lineage, the reason for their immaturity. In the end, it had cost him only a pair of worn gloves that he often used when hiking—he no longer trusted their "purity"—a small portion of ego that he could easily afford to do without, so he wrote the incident off as no great loss.

"It seems we made good time, however ..." Nevin said, his words trailed off as speechlessness struck him. From their vantage point atop the knoll about a mile from the erstwhile town, the group gazed at the smoke spiraling upward in plumes.

"Nevin, maybe we should see if there are survivors and if we can be of use to them," Silver mumbled.

Scratching at the stubble that had consumed his chin during their journey, Nevin regarded Silver with the sightless look of disregard that had always distanced them.

"There's only one person I'm interested in seeing. Let's go see if we can count him among the survivors. I have a very bad feeling our little map may have something to do with this. If so, our moving on is the best help we can offer them."

Within minutes, the trio came to smoldering remnants of the town walls. A charnel odor tainted the air as they neared, overpowering them as they entered. Nevin's delicate senses were offended the most, forcing him to use the corner of his traveling cloak as an ersatz handkerchief, cradling it around his nose and mouth.

Diminutia and Silver walked as if any given step could give way to a trap. They forced their pace faster as Nevin trod down the ash speckled road, nary a glance in either direction; not even to the abandoned waif standing in the charred doorway of a partially collapsed house. As if magnets, her eyes clung to the thieves.

Unable to look away, Diminutia whispered, "Shouldn't we help her?"

"No," Nevin replied.

Usually business minded as well, Silver would normally agree with Nevin in such matters, however, the sight of the orphan would not soon be forgotten. "Nevin, helping her would ..."

Nevin stopped and turned to his counterparts, his callous eyes hiding the layers of pain and anger associated with living through such an ordeal many, many years ago.

"Help her? And how do you propose we do that? Give her the gold we have, or our food, so we have none when we need it? Take her door to door searching for someone to care for her?"

"You elves ..."

"Look, I am sympathetic to her situation. I am just as upset as you two, but we need to find answers to more questions than just what happened here. She will be found soon enough, probably by someone who knows who she is and will be more suited to help her than we are."

"I'm beginning to wish that you did wipe your ass with that leaf."

Nevin disregarded the comment as simple human callowness, as he had done so many times in the past, and continued to make his way to his destination—the antique store of Haddaman Crede. To refer to the store as anything more substantial than debris would have been an exaggeration.

Out of habit, the thieves stepped into the area as if there were still a door. The ash of the burnt roof coated the fist-sized rubble remains of the walls scattered over the floor. The ash swirled like angered spirits around the thieves' ankles, disturbing the wreckage as they continued to search the remains. The store's wares decorated the destruction: hand-crafted gold candlesticks fused to designer shields, entire suits of armor warped or shredded, jade and turquoise ground to green talc.

"Haddaman's dead?" Diminutia whispered.

Despite the horror surrounding him, Nevin could not help but to smirk at his partner's comment. He walked to the far end of the room where a corner would have been, had there still been walls, and kicked away enough debris to reveal part of the wooden floor. Using his dagger, he stabbed the floor, sinking the blade deep into the wood to give his fingers enough leverage to lift away the hatch, exposing the catacombs. "Now, Diminutia, have you forgotten who we are talking about?"

Nevin reached into the small hideaway and yanked the screaming, flailing Haddaman to the surface. Lifting the weasel-framed man posed little effort for the elf. "Haddaman! It's us. Calm down."

"The Horde! The Horde did this."

"The Horde? Why? What did they want?"

Haddaman knew exactly what The Horde wanted. Instead of offering up his knowledge to save half the town, he hid like a coward. "Stones. There's an obscure tale only whispered in the darkest of dungeons. It's quite lengthy, but over four hundred years ago, a mad wizard accursed five gems, giving them a power ..."

"That when placed in a staff, the staff mixed with dragon blood had the power to summon demons," Nevin finished.

Haddaman's face shifted to the color of the bleached ash still sprinkling from the sky. "You have heard that story before?"

Devoid of any emotion, Nevin reached into his satchel and produced the map. "Just a week ago."

Reaching for the map, Haddaman shook, the minor quakes not stopping with his hands and soon consumed his whole body. "You ... you have a map to one!"

"So the map is legitimate?" Diminutia asked.

"Yes, yes," Haddaman answered, looking at the map. "Where did you get this?"

"A bard sold it to us.

"A bard? Who? What was his name?"

Diminutia's face curled, contorting as if an unpleasant odor took his senses by surprise. "He never gave us his name."

"Pity. I would like to meet this fellow."

Silver surveyed the landscape, noting the surviving townsfolk beginning to make their way from various shelters and hiding spots. Two sobbing women trudged past, each holding a hand of the small waif from the town's entrance. "Exactly what happened here, Haddaman?"

"A nightmare. Earlier in the day a messenger had bequeathed the mayor a very peculiar gift—a rare and beautiful cactus from an unknown source. Once the day sun reached the pinnacle of its ascent, the cactus exploded."

"Exploded?"

"Yes. What the mayor did not realize was the cactus was a nursery for thousands upon thousands of baby scorpions. They flowed from the town hall like a pool of malevolent ink, their chattering so loud it drowned out the screams of their immediate victims."

"I thought you said The Horde did this?"

"The scorpions were merely a signal. The Horde burst from the forest just as the scorpions from their nest."

"Well, gentlemen, we came here seeking to authenticate a map and, it would seem, validated the entire myth. Perhaps we should forego the mad pursuit of this stone and simply stay here to lend a hand where one is sorely needed ..."

"But you must pursue this! If The Horde were to retrieve the stones, the consequences would be ..."

"Dire, naturally." Nevin exhaled, and with the stale breath went the acidic remnants of hope. "And there you have it, friends. The choices that lie before us are charity or potential martyrdom. What next?"

"There is much that could be done here," Silver began, looking about him at the devastation as if for advice.

"I will do everything I can to rebuild this place and shelter these people," said Haddaman Crede, his voice suddenly taking on the tone of confidence. "For years I have stashed away gold and always felt too guilty to put it to use. It seems," he said, gesturing about him, "that the purpose I have always lacked sought me out. You have a chance to thwart The Horde ... you must seize the advantage or the atrocities to which you bear witness today will pale before those of the future."

"It seems to me," Diminutia said, "that staying here to help these people might not be such a wise idea after all. It's reasonable to assume that there is a bit of trouble following our boot heels. If we stop now, we'll be responsible for causing more people more grief."

"Sorry, Silver," Nevin said, his voice conveying true regret. "I agree with Dim. I understand your concern, and when this is over, we can come back to see if anything still needs to be done. But to delay here invites the same doom to other towns, I believe."

Silver heaved a sigh heavier than the rubble the townsfolk sifted through. Then Nevin turned to Haddaman and asked, "Do you have any supplies we could borrow? And what of The Horde? Did they find any of the stones? Did you see which direction they went?"

"I, uh, spent most of my time cloaked in obscurity. I wish I could help you more, but I'm afraid I don't know the answer to any of those questions. But take what you need. What's mine is yours!"

When the trio had replenished their supplies only insofar as demand dictated, they made their farewells and trekked to the forest that lay on the other side of the erstwhile town.

Glancing over his shoulder, Nevin wondered, *How close are you, Bale Pinkeye, and do you really know what you're looking for?*

Two days later, the ogre and his group found Freeman's Way. The left side of Zot's head was swollen and bruised with the likeness of Bale's hand. Never blessed with directional sense, the band had wandered in circles for a whole day before a stomach malady had befallen Bale. He barely had time to stoop behind some rocks when the intestinal seizure hit him. By the time the discomfort had passed, his legs could not support him well enough to stand. As luck would have it, a broken plant lay in the dirt at arm's length. He used the leaves to the last, then called for camp to be set up as darkness crept about them.

The next morning, Bale awoke with a terrible itching about the loincloth. Frantically, he searched about for the proper tool. To his companions delight, he ran to the nearest tree and used it as a scratching post, scraping his buttocks across the bark for relief. Hoots and hollers came from Pik Pox and Zot, until, at length, one of Zot's dances carried him too close to the ogre he mocked.

By the time they reached Freeman's Way, Bale's flesh bubbled from top to bottom with the maddening itch. His skin was flushed as though with anger, and he picked at

the thick pustules while surveying the damage of
Freeman's Way.

Trotting along toward the rear of the pack was Phyllis
Iphillus, a satyr. A long-time friend, Phyl, joined in the
adventure as soon as he heard about it.

"Bale!" Phyl called. With every word from the satyr's
mouth, Bale swore he heard the faintest whisper of a lisp,
contrary to all of Phyl's denials. "I've been working on a
new one ... let's see now ...

"There once was a captain named Speld
Who liked to have his privates held
One day while playing with his mistress
He went and got caught by his missus
And now the poor man is called 'Geld'"

Phyl's tittering grated Bale more than his sumac rash.

"Phyl," Bale bawled. "Come here."

As Phyl made his way to the front of the group, the tiny
tinkle of tiny metal against metal forced Bale to stare at the
satyr's ankle. Right above the cloven hoof, a small silver
chain hugged the satyr's ankle. Dangling from the chain
were two miniature morning stars, irresistibly striking each
other anytime Phyl walked.

"I hate your ankle bracelet," Bale mumbled.

"You've been saying that ever since I got it. What is so
wrong with it?"

"It sounds like a bell. A really tiny bell."

"It's not a bell. It's a talisman."

"It sounds like a bell."

"It's a symbol of confidence and virility. All the other
satyrs have one."

"We need to be interpretating and it's hard to be
interpretating with a little bell ringing behind me."

"You mean 'intimidating' and what could be more
intimidating than two morning stars smashing into each
other?"

"It sounds like a bell."

Unbeknownst to Bale and company, one townsperson
heard the whole conversation and approached the motley
crew. "Welcome to Freeman's Way," Haddaman Crede said.
"Might you be here for business or pleasure?"

"No!" Bale barked, thrusting his chest forward while his cronies stood firm behind him, making as many menacing faces and gestures as they could muster. "We're looking for people. But from the looks of things ... What happened?"

"Small disaster, I'm afraid. But we'll get on our feet soon enough. We always do. People, eh? Well, you're in luck. This town has a lot of people. Tall ones, short ones, skinny ones, fat ones ..."

Bale snorted and shook his head as if trying to shake a complex thought from his brain. "No. That's not what I meant ..."

"So, you're not looking for people?"

"Yes, we are!"

"Then you're still in luck."

"No! I mean, yes! I mean ... stop talking!" Bale yelled. As he huffed, his gelatinous belly rolled up on the inhale and squished over his rope belt on the exhale. "We're looking for a statistic group of people."

"You mean 'specific,'" Phyl whispered.

"Very well," Haddaman said. "Who might you be seeking?"

"A group of thieves ..."

"You mean the dastardly trio of Nevin Narrowpockets, Diminutia, and Silver? Those curs?"

"Does that mean he doesn't like them?" Bale asked from the corner of his mouth to Phyl.

"That's correct," Phyl replied.

"Then, yeah!" Bale and his party roared in unison.

"They came through town recently. I assume you want to know where they went?"

"Yeah!" the team roared in unison again.

"Go past the farms on the east, and you'll find a forest. There will be a large clearing and then another forest. The thieves are on the other side of the forest. Now go get them!"

"Yeah!" they screamed again as they hooted and hollered, lumbering down a side street of Freeman's Way toward the farms.

Haddaman Crede laughed, almost feeling guilty for confusing them and then sending them to a vile piece of land aptly named The Fecal Swamps.

FIVE

KING THEOMANN stared out his window, facing east, toward the potential war. If war came, it would rage half a continent away, but the king could see fields of flame and hear earth-trembling explosions mixed with the screams of thousands of young men dying. Any other person could stand at the same vantage point and not be wary of any such threats of war, deceived by the smooth hills rolling among lush patches of forest. Any other person would only hear the muted voices of the city's citizens and bird warbles. Not King Theomann, though. He had to snap his head to shake the image of blood rushing like rivers over the hills and through the forests.

"Am I doing the right thing?" Theomann asked his son.

Perciless approached and placed his hand on his father's shoulder. "Father, your sons and all your people have great faith in you. If there is an opportunity to win a war before it begins, you must take it."

"But to send your brother and the Elite Troop on a potential wild-goose chase? All from the word of a mysterious bard?"

"Sometimes chances must be taken. The Elite Troop exists for a reason—they are the best of the best. If nothing is found within a month, I am sure they will return no worse for wear."

"There is a fine line between taking a risk and flailing in desperation."

"What if Tsinel seeks the gems as well? And we have intelligence that The Horde is looking for them. If we are grasping for phantoms, then they are reaching for the same ones."

Theomann smiled. "Your words are comforting, Son. As much as I would appreciate hearing more of them, you really should be off to see how troop movements are going. Tend to the needs of our generals; see what supplies they need to help fortify the borders. We may not be at war yet, but a presence along our borders should quell any Tsinel sneak attacks."

"Very well, Father. Rest your body and soul, for what you are doing is for the good of all," Perciless offered as his parting words.

My father acted for the good of all, Theomann thought.

Memory flooded through him as light through a transom, and he was taken back many years to his own childhood. Theomann was barely six when his father, Durandenn, was confronted with the first tangible threat to the peace and tranquility upon which the kingdom of Albathia had been forged.

An area of peace and prosperity surrounded on all sides by passive city-states, Albathia was a relatively young monarchy when rumors of conflict drifted from across the ocean of distant Irabel, a land of warmongers steeped in intrigue and political maneuverings. At first, the rumors were as wind over water, gentle and not alarming, but steadily they grew to a clamor that was insistent and dangerous. Albathia, situated as it was, had a standing army, though it was never needed previously, and a local militia that consisted of farmers who required fervent consumption of alcohol before their pitchforks menaced anything other than hay.

As rumor lingered into certainty, many of the surrounding settlements ceded themselves to Albathia in the hopes that such a concerted effort would display a unity of mind and purpose even a violent nation could not lightly dismiss. The event had the opposite effect. Irabel saw this large conglomeration of cultures as a challenge to their sanguinary vision of conquest. Their armies were assembled and dispatched post haste.

Irabel's efficacy depended entirely upon quick success. One good defensive stand, Durandenn hoped, would shatter the illusory cooperation that united the Irabelian army. Once that was accomplished, the confounded Irabelian army would take their frustrations back across the ocean.

His words were viewed as the wisdom of a savior and an army was assembled under his ultimate command, with the various governors and mayors assuming positions of rank. They met the Irabelians at the shore on the morning of their landing. Durandenn held his force together by sheer force of will, but his slipshod army of peasants, farmers, bricklayers, and fishermen was quickly pushed back as far as they could run.

At the close of the first day, they had given up as much ground as could be covered by an army in such a span of time. Durandenn called his officers to him, and they met all night, exhausting strategy and alcohol in a session that lasted until shortly before the morning sun's rise. Just as words of surrender tickled the lips of the officers, an enigmatic visitor appeared as if hand-delivering an answered prayer.

An aged man with a scraggly beard and bare pate to complement his prodigious belly stared at him with eyes of cobalt blue. The stranger professed to be a wizard of some magnitude who expressed concerns of his own for the kingdom of Albathia and claimed that Irabel marched with a rare stone in their arsenal that he deemed too dangerous for them to possess. And that stone was the wizard's only asking price.

The wizard traveled with a dozen equally experienced in the craft. All thirteen were also equal in appearance as well, prosperous waistlines, clothing as unkempt as their beards, as menacing as a band of bristled weasels. But they did Durandenn's bidding, and they did it well—the war ended within three weeks.

The first victory came the following day—the wizards ordered Durandenn's makeshift army to retreat again, leading the forces of Irabel through a narrow valley. Landslides from both sides crushed the entire Irabelian army, taking mere minutes to create a graveyard for hundreds.

Taking offense at such an ignoble defeat, the entire able bodied populous of Irabel had been launched forth upon any ship with the ability to stay afloat. Tens of thousands desired revenge and an undeniable urge to conquer a new continent. The wizards were prepared. Silhouettes of ships appeared against the crystal horizon like insects on a placid pond. By the time they reached the shores, apocalyptic black clouds reigned supreme, unleashing swirling winds and erupting waves; more than a dozen ships became airborne. In the end, all of the ships finished beneath the water.

Even though the events leading to the war's finale seemed more coincidence than magic, Durandenn paid the price with neither complaint nor hesitation. He rewarded the wizards with what they sought—a mysterious black stone, darker than ceaseless night or the emptied grave of a murderer, the void of pitch seemed to whisper poems of fear and death. The wizard refused any other reward and insisted that Durandenn keep the remainder of the Irabelian treasure.

"Father?" the voice of Daedalus snapped his father's ear like the tip of a whip.

Theomann grasped his robes as he stumbled backward as if slipping on the profuse sweat pouring from his brow. A hundred heartbeats seemed to accompany every quivering breath rushing over his parched lips. His head ached as if a battle-axe had split it in two. He even ran his hand through his time bleached white hair to make sure there was no such gash.

"What are you doing?" Daedalus asked.

Panting like a dehydrated dog, Theomann replied, "My mind momentarily escaped me. It ... does that from time to time. Unfortunately, it seems you and I may have that in common."

Daedalus squinted, his thoughts trying to process the meaning of his father's words. *Patronizing old man*, entered his mind, but what exited his mouth was, "I know not what you mean."

Theomann sighed, disappointed with his failed attempt to relate. "We ... also have more in common than just that. You are quite a gifted thinker."

"Not gifted enough to become the future ruler of Albathia, though."

The king sighed again, this time rubbing his temples.

"Daedalus, you know very well the crown must fall upon ..."

"... Oremethus." Daedalus spat the word out faster than he would a rotted piece of fruit.

"Son, I have said many times, my love is spread equally among you and your brothers."

"However, it is Oremethus who receives the best education, Oremethus who receives the best training, Oremethus who leads the Elite Troop on a daring quest to prevent the kingdom from falling off the precipice of war."

"Daedalus ..."

"Sorry, Father, I must leave now."

Feelings of failure washed over his heart as Theomann once again gazed out his window, wondering how his firstborn was faring.

✫ ✫ ✫

Well beyond the watchful eye of Phenomere castle, Oremethus scratched an itch on his palm. From the horse beside him, General Iderion leaned over and said, "That means someone is talking about you."

Oremethus laughed. "Only in good ways, I hope."

Both men laughed as they and their mounts climbed the final hill to the entrance of Freeman's Way. Behind them, Dearborn followed close, leading the rest of the Elite Troop. However, once they reached the pinnacle, everyone came to a halt.

What remained of the town's gates were charred black and withering. Iderion gave a few hand gestures, ordering his troops to continue forward with caution. The troops entered the town silently, save the sound of horse hooves against the dirt road. Pensive, hands ready to draw weapons, the troops made their way past the first block of burned and crumbled shops until they reached the center of town.

The entire populous was there, the women tending to the wounded while the men began repairs to the largest buildings, making sure there would be at least a place for everyone to rest their heads for the night. Even though all were busy or injured or both, Oremethus's presence did not go unnoticed as the assembled took a moment to bow for the crown prince.

Shocked by the desolation, Oremethus barely remembered to gesture for everyone to rise. Dismounting his steed, his words were but a whisper, "What happened here?"

Haddaman Crede approached from the crowd to reply, "The Horde."

"Any indication as to why?" Iderion asked, dismounting as well, signaling the rest of the troops to follow suit.

"They weren't very forthcoming with their intentions, but they did seem to be searching for something."

Oremethus surveyed the surroundings and said, "We will stay and assist with repairs until the morning sun reaches its peak. Send a rider to let my father know of this tragedy."

Being one of the few in the troop who could read and write, Dearborn scrawled a message on parchment while Iderion issued orders to his men. When finished with the communication, she gave it to the second oldest of the Elite Troop, the second message rider of their journey so far, the first being sent with a standard update days ago.

As Dearborn watched the message rider depart, she wondered if she would ever reach that point in her career with the Elite Troop. Before every job, they would meticulously plot their course. The oldest members were given the responsibility of carrying messages back and forth to the king, strictly following the pre-plotted path so the multiple riders could convene along the way, keeping the chain of communication free-flowing. Being assigned messenger duty was a form of reward for many diligent years of service.

Wondering through the near abandoned streets, Dearborn reminisced about her childhood in a village similar to this one. Similar roads led to similar buildings. She found what she was looking for with ease. The blacksmith shop had three men, one working on repairs to the building while the other two hammered and molded what the town needed the most—hinges and nails.

THE DEVIL'S GRASP | 47

Stripping herself of her cloak and armor, she immediately helped the man, more of a boy, wrestling with a post, jamming it under a support beam. Without saying a word, she showed him the futility of his actions. Instead of supporting the top of the beam and trying to kick the bottom into place, which simply dug further into the dirt, she supported the bottom with her foot while pulling the top into place.

"Wow," the young man said, his eyes surveying her massive body, settling on her angelic face. "That was amazing."

"This isn't the first time I've repaired a blacksmith shop before," she replied, choosing to believe his comment was directed toward her accomplishment, rather than her striking height and musculature.

Her own words echoed in her mind, fluttering around like a drunken moth, skimming across latent memories. That day was very easy to remember. It was the day she received her first dress.

Being the child of a blacksmith preordained her with a challenging life—especially for a girl whose mother died during child birth.

As soon as Dearborn was old enough to walk, her father put a hammer in her hand. He was a reclusive man who knew nothing other than his craft and became more so after becoming a widower. His love for his daughter unwavering, he provided well and took every opportunity to give her more than he had when he was her age. The king had a soft spot for the blacksmith, granting him many privileges saved for nobility. When offered, the blacksmith would send Dearborn to every class available for reading and writing. However, he could not provide for her what a mother could.

Even though Dearborn attended schoolings, she spent most of her days helping her father. The lucrative contracts he held with the king provided the best of foods and the fuel needed to put muscle on her tall frame. Forging from dawn until dusk left little opportunity for fat to find a place on her body. Almost as if fate dictated compensation and balance, while her body grew more massive, her face became more beautiful, which caught the attention of a young stable hand named Oshua.

The teenage boy with sapphire eyes and flaxen ringlets haphazardly sprouting from his head showed up twice a week, either to purchase new supplies or for horseshoe repair. A lean body tapering from broad shoulders acted as a harbinger for his future as a strapping man. His acquaintance with Dearborn began with a shy smile to her while she all but hid in the back of the shop. She slowly worked her way up to a pleasant salutation. After inadvertently humiliating her last crush, Daedalus, by being too aggressive, she decided to try being a bit more demure, or at least as demure as her physique would allow.

Within months, quaint conversations accompanied Oshua's visits. Dearborn's father did his part, leaving to find lunch just as Oshua approached. Although Dearborn felt a connection with Oshua, she made it a point to keep a thick animal hide apron over top of her long sleeved baggy shirts. But her infatuation was doomed to be incomplete.

On Dearborn's fifteenth birthday, her father bought her a dress. Her first dress. It was wrapped in the signature paper from the most popular seamstress in town, the one exclusive to nobility. As part of her present, he gave her the remainder of the day off.

Dearborn took her present and ran out of town to the neighboring glen. On the pinnacle of the nearest knoll, she stopped and changed into her new dress. It was two inches too short and too wide in the waist. Her eyes welled up with tears as her heart swelled from her father's love. She knew very well that even at her young age, there were no women in the town even close to her stature. Deduction led her to realize that her father swallowed his pride and used himself as the model for the seamstress to fit the dress—he was a couple inches shorter with a waist made by many ales. She also assumed he slipped the seamstress a few extra coins, insuring she would never speak of that moment again.

Barefoot, she ran, danced, twirled through the tall grass on top of the hill. Laughing, she picked flowers to tuck away in her flowing hair. Daydreams of a wedding, marriage, and a family flooded her thoughts. Until she gazed toward the town.

Thin strands of smoke streamed from the edge of town, the exact spot where the blacksmith shop was located. She ran, wrapping her hair into a makeshift bun along the way. By the time she reached the shop, black billows of smoke engulfed the roof.

She ran inside to find her unconscious father sprawled on the floor near a table with a large gash across his forehead. Flames crawled across every post and every lintel, dancing along the rafters. Charred thatch rained within the shop, smoldering pieces pelting Dearborn. Worried by the wound, she tore off one of her sleeves and wrapped it around his head, stopping only to extinguish stray embers attempting to ignite her dress. Without concern that the structure might collapse, she pulled a wooden chest filled with forty pounds of coins from underneath the table. Normally, she would care little about the money; however, the gold in the chest did not belong to her father, but to others who entrusted him to guard it. It would be quite difficult to divvy it out properly if the coins melted together.

Aided by adrenaline, Dearborn slung her father over her right shoulder. After gaining the balance needed, she crouched down and scooped up the chest with her left arm. Addled by the extra weight, she toddled her way to the nearest door, still ablaze, and kicked it off its hinges.

Relieved by her escape, Dearborn dropped the chest and placed her father on the ground. Onlookers had gathered, many formed a line from the town fountain to the blaze, passing buckets back and forth. However, once she stood from tending to her father, slowly coming to consciousness, all activity ceased.

The townsfolk, even the older ones who were adept at discretion, stared like wide-eyed simpletons gazing upon their own reflection for the first time. Before them stood a sight they had seen before, but never in that way, a girl barely in her teens, the tallest person there with the musculature of a poetic hero. There she stood—sweat-streaked soot hid her angelic face, her dress torn and burnt —feeling like an abomination. The dress only covered one shoulder, the other side so shredded it covered no part of her torso. Had she any bosom, it would have been exposed.

Oshua witnessed Dearborn rescuing her father. He gawked as did every other crowd member. At first, fear paralyzed him as his eyes scanned her body, until he realized her chest was more muscular than his. He ran, never to see her again.

"Dearborn?" Iderion's words snapped her from her unpleasant trip down memory lane. "Why am I not surprised to find you at the blacksmith's shop."

Forcing a smile, Dearborn replied, "Smithing holds many memories for me."

"Well, I hate to pull you away from your first love, but we have a mission to complete. We must be on our way."

Noticing a man standing next to Iderion, Dearborn asked, "Are we getting company for this journey?"

The man outstretched his hand and said, "Yes, Sergeant. Your general confided in me what item you seek. I believe I may be able to help, and I humbly offer you my services for a favorably negotiated price, of course. My name is Haddaman Crede ..."

Six

HALCYON HILLS' appellation was only partially accurate. Not only were the hills closer to mountain range size, but the pelts of lush, green grass and fields of frolicking flowers only grew on one side, the valley side. The other side was as barren and grim as The Scorched Sea, the desert that the Halcyon Hills encircled.

Poets often described The Scorched Sea as a victim of circumstance, despising its lot in the world and making it known to all who entered. A colossal mountain range lined part of the continent's northern shore, hindering any southern bound storms. Any minimal weather front that made it through rarely moved past Halcyon Hills and usually finished its precipitation cycle within the fruitful valley, leaving the desert destitute with no water to nourish the ground and no cloud cover to hinder the blazing rays of both suns.

Open fields of grass lined the valley, sprawling from the Halcyon Hills to the edge of the thick forest. Speckled throughout were flowers of all kinds, adding just the perfect pinch of color. The air was crisp and clear, allowing bird song to flow; even the flapping of butterfly wings seemingly echoed in the valley. Nature had formed the perfect patch of tranquility.

"We're lost!" Diminutia's voice cracked the air like thunder. Startled, small animals raced from the fields to the forest, seeking shelter before taking the chance to examine the noise.

"We're not lost," Silver said, his squinted eyes darting along the perimeter of the forest. "We know exactly where we are."

"Fine! We know where we are, but we don't know where we're going."

"We do know where we're going," Silver replied. "Did either of you see anything suspicious in the forest?"

"If we know where we're going, then why aren't we there yet? And the only thing suspicious around here is that map!"

Nevin stopped walking and sighed, reminding himself that his impetuous partner was a thief, not an adventurer; one who would rather examine the intricacies of a lock, not the landscape. "Dim, this map is quite old, and some parts are very faded. It shows that the stone is located in a small cave in The Scorched Sea. It even shows a short path through the Halcyon Hills leading right to it. The difficulty we're having is trying to find the start of the path. And yes, Silver, I have also noticed some unusual movements in the forest."

Diminutia grunted, running his fingers through his blond hair as if trying to comb away his frustrations. "Sorry. I guess I just need a bit of a break."

"I know of a small town nearby," Silver said. "I wouldn't be opposed to a hot meal and a cold drink."

"Sounds good to me. I must be in dire need of a rest, the ground looks like it's moving."

"Moving?" Nevin snapped his eyes away from the map to look around. Mere yards away, a strip of grass seemed to glide closer. Drawing his knife, he saw another strip of grass move. "Spine snakes!"

Just as the other two thieves brandished their weapons, the spine snakes made their presence known. The aptly named snakes' green scales were long and thin, and when raised offered wonderful camouflage within a field of long grass. Four serpent heads arose from the grass as the snakes surrounded the thieves, boxing them in. Each snake was twice as long as any man was tall and thicker than a thigh. The thieves moved closer together, keeping their backs to one another as the circling serpents slithered closer.

"Okay, Nevin," Diminutia whispered, not even attempting to hide the fear in his voice. "I've never seen one of these before. What do we do?"

"They strike fast, but they aim for their victim's head. When they attack, duck and thrust your blade upward," Nevin whispered back.

"Referring to us as 'victims' wasn't quite the confidence boost I had hoped from you."

Diminutia focused on the snake in front of him, half its body raised from the ground, its morose yellow eyes aligned themselves with the thief's. The snake squinted, then its eyes widened, then squinted again, repeating the process to pull all of Diminutia's focus into them while its head drifted from side to side like a falling leaf. Continuing its lulling dance, the viper waited until the perfect moment, then attacked.

Diminutia had fallen into a slight stupor, unable to react as the spine snake launched itself at his face. Mesmerized, he lacked the reflex to even blink as the open maw of fangs rushed toward him. However, he did jerk back as the snake's head exploded and burnt chunks of reptile meat pelted his body.

All eyes focused on the forest to find a grizzled wizard in tattered layers of cloaks, arm still extended from the fireball he released, rendering the striking serpent to smoldering shreds. The smoke trail slowly sank in the windless air like dismissed cobwebs. Three more wizards appeared from the forest as if oozing free from select trees. One of the other wizards, wearing similar garb as the first, whispered an incantation while extending his fist. As he unfurled his fingers, a cloud of glittering dust mushroomed from his palm. Shimmering particles hovered in place. Pursing his parched lips, the wizard released the slightest exhale. Growing from mote to spear, needles shot from the cloud to pierce a second snake in the blink of an eye. Tens of thousands of impaling filaments struck the snake, killing it long before it hit the ground. Despite being mere animals, the remaining two snakes knew enough to retreat.

"Dim! Are you all right?" Silver asked, running to his meat-covered friend lying in the grass.

Keeping his dagger unsheathed, Nevin turned to the closest wizard. "Who are you?"

"My dear friend, is that any way to thank us for saving your lives?" the wizard replied.

"I assure you, the three of us are very grateful. However, the coincidence of your arrival seems suspicious."

"Typical elf, quizzical and untrusting." The wizard paused to allow Silver and Diminutia, still removing pieces of snake meat from his clothing, to join Nevin. "I am Belhurst. And this is Grymon." Grymon hobbled forward, the crags in his face rivaled those of any mountain range, and his tattered robes did little to hide his wooden leg.

Belhurst introduced the other two wizards, Follen and Moxxen, who followed the pattern of gnarled features and shoddy clothing; however, they each stood apart in their own way. Every labored breath Moxxen took could be seen by all. His shoulders pulled back slightly, and his waist expanded while drawing in a breath; a shrug and a concave waist escorted his exhale.

Follen had a twitch. Nevin saw it right away, always noticing the many imperfections of humans. Follen's right eye fluttered, a quick half blink that twitched faster the more Nevin stared at it. But what annoyed Nevin more was the occasional twitch of Follen's left thumb, tapping nonstop against the staff in his hand.

"Pleased, we're certain. I'm ...," Nevin started.

Belhurst interrupted, "We know who you are, Nevin. We've been following you for some time now."

Nevin gripped his dagger tighter. "And why is that?"

"Because we seek the same thing, one of the sister stones to the Shadow Stone." Belhurst outstretched his arm, resting in the center of his palm was a stone blacker than a starless night, as if he were holding a small hole to oblivion.

The thieves could only stare at the stone as it seemingly stared back at them, through them. No light could escape from the darkness of the stone, including that within their souls, stripping away layers of confidence, leaving only an inexplicable fear. Mouths agape, the thieves slowly realized the precariousness of the situation in which they found themselves, hypnotized until a ground-shaking voice boomed from behind them. "Is that the stone the map leads to?"

All attention turned to Bale Pinkeye, lumbering out from the forest, followed closely by Phyl, Zot, and Pik. Dried mud caked all four from foot to waist, however, Phyl had picked away most of it from his thigh fur.

"So you *did* get a good look at the map. And ..." Diminutia started to reply, but found it difficult to complete his thoughts once the stench of the ogre wafted past his nostrils. "Ugg! Bale! You smell worse than usual!"

Nevin backed away, lifting his shirt over his mouth and nose. "What could precipitate such a foul stench upon you?"

Outstretching his hand and gazing skyward, Bale mumbled, "I don't see any rain."

"The Fecal Swamps," Zot grunted. "We followed you to Freeman's Way, and some idiot antiques dealer gave us wrong directions."

"I don't even see any rain clouds in the sky," Bale continued.

Knowing very well who the "idiot" antiques dealer was, the thieves did their best to stifle their laughs. The wizards did not understand the inside joke, but enjoyed another. "You four traversed through The Fecal Swamps on the word of a stranger? Oh, that is rich!" Belhurst laughed.

Unappreciative of the joke at his own expense, Bale slammed his fist against a tree near Belhurst. "Small animals shouldn't make fun of big animals!"

Contrary to his frail appearance, Follen lunged forward with a youthful nimbleness, gesturing with his right hand. He struck the ground with the staff in his left hand and yelled, "Mollyhogawath. Quandro!"

Streaks of lightning skittered through the grass, nipping the toes of the bumptious Bale and his cronies, reducing them to a memory blanketed by a puff of smoke.

Again, the thieves drew their daggers. "We have never been fond of those trolls," Nevin said, "But they certainly did not deserve death."

Belhurst laughed. "My friends, we are hardly the types
to kill without provocation. That spell merely sent them
back whence they came—in their case, The Fecal Swamps."

The thieves looked at each other and laughed so hard
they had to support each other from falling. "Belhurst,"
Diminutia said, "We're heading to that town over there. It
would be my honor to buy you and your friends an ale."

"We graciously accept. Balfourd's Bounty has a fine
wizard's guild, and we are in dire need of supplies,"
Belhurst replied, gesturing to Moxxen pulling a cart
holding a large cabinet replete with dozens of doors and a
hundred tiny drawers.

The thieves and wizards chortled their way to
Balfourd's Bounty, wasting no time finding a suitable
tavern. Had the Barren Mermaid been a patrician
establishment burgeoning with the upper-class citizens of
Balfourd's Bounty, then its ramshackle roof and decaying
door would have proved an effective disguise to the eyes of
an outsider. For seven exhausted men who earlier that
morning snatched back their mortality from gaping jaws, a
rundown shack with porous walls that failed to contain the
streaming aroma of stews and slurred shanties was a
welcome sight.

With a passing gesture and a fleeting word, Belhurst
caused the wheels on the elaborate cart to lock with an
audible click before entering the establishment. Its current
state of immobility would deter any would-be thieves, while
the doors and the drawers only responded to a wizard's
touch.

Lively eyes found a plain serving wench, to whom Silver
introduced himself with coin. A quick point at the sole
empty table completed the transaction, and within
moments, watery ales and slabs of cheese and bread
appeared as if conjured by the wizards. The barmaid was
swallowed in the shuffle of the bustling throng as quickly
as a coin dropping from a slit pouch. As with any tavern
this crowded came the assault of many different
conversations.

"... A spiny plant ..."

"... Feldryn's an idiot ..."

"... Beer is better ..."

Covetously, the wizards fell upon the food and began several rounds of stuffing their mouths and swigging drinks in a rhythm the ocean would have envied. Nevin watched in disgust, the sight of humans feasting appalled him. Like a drowning man scrabbling for flotilla amongst a churning sea, he turned to Diminutia, but the human was too busy scanning the crowd to notice.

Diminutia found what he was looking for—their waitress. Cheese and bread sated his appetite, but did little to satisfy his desire for flavor. As she passed close to their table, Diminutia, in one fluent motion, spun from his chair, caught her by her arm, and escorted her to a nearby corner.

Even by the miniscule light of the oil lamp, the bar maiden could see Diminutia's eyes were like sky-blue topaz that he had stolen on numerous occasions. His gaze gripped her tighter than his hand. He moved closer, his eyes, his mouth; all the while, his hand caressed her arm, settling on the nape of her neck. Her heart raced as his hot breath tickled her ear.

"Stew," he said.

"Excuse me?" she replied, clearly hoping for a more suggestive statement.

"Stew," he repeated, pulling away. "My companions and I are resting from an arduous job, and we'd like some stew."

"Job? So what do you and your companions do?" She finished her question with an extended lick of her lips.

After a curt glance over his shoulder, Diminutia pulled the bar maiden close, chest to breast, and leaned in again. Her breath shortened to mere gasps as his lips once again grazed her ear. "We're thieves."

"Really?" she asked with a slight giggle. "That must be quite exciting?"

"Very." His fingers began to tangle in her hair.

"Well, dread thief, where might you be laying your head tonight?"

"My companions and I have yet to decide. The night seems fair; maybe we will set up camp in the forest?"

"Nonsense. I know not about your companions, but the tavern owner grants me a room on the second floor. No need for *you* to settle for a stone as a pillow if you have another option."

Watching Diminutia do what he did best, Nevin could only shake his head, confounded by the simple animal desires of humans. Still uncertain of his surroundings, he continued to scan the conversations of the crowd.

"... Strange gift indeed ..."

"... Left the alembic open ... ha, ha, ha, ha ..."

"... Good with bread ..."

Mouth full of bread, Moxxen expressed his gratitude to Nevin. "We would like to express our sincere thanks to your group for this food and drink. Despite our rather hardy appearance," he thumped his sallow chest in emphasis of his sarcasm, "we seldom get to satisfy our appetites."

"... Middle of the night ..."

"... Burned off his eyebrows ... ha, ha, ha, ha ..."

"... Good with meat ..."

Nevin gaped at the wizard, unsure if he had heard him correctly through the din or how to phrase a polite response. "Did you just say something about spanking us to satisfy your appetites?"

"... Front of the mayor's house ..."

"... Ha, ha ... he's hairless now ... ha, ha, ha ..."

"... Women don't like it ..."

"Um-huh." Moxxen smiled past his mastication, picking up as little of their conversation as Nevin.

"... Middle of the night ..."

"... ha, ha, ha, ha, ha, ha ..."

"... Never run out ..."

Silver, all the brief while, watched Belhurst, mindful of the strange wizard companions. During their brief trek from where they met to this tavern, Silver said nary a word, simply watching their new companions with distrust in his eye. He waited for the wizard to place an exceptionally large piece of bread in his mouth before he spoke.

"You wizards are all alike. High and mighty sycophants, you show up when a situation is well in hand, spread some smoke and fire, then drop weighty words down atop the oh-so-lucky-to-be-alive commoners like typical, self-proclaimed saviors, while the needy then satisfy your whims with their lifeblood. It's all sleight of hand and nonsense, if you ask me."

"The life of a wizard," Belhurst said, "is hardly a bountiful existence. Fear and distrust pervade every thankful handshake a wizard receives. Loneliness permeates his being. Young man, have you ever walked through the shadows and stared upon the great eidolon?"

"I have faced death many times without shrinking from the sight, thank you," Silver replied.

"Not death, young man. It is *night* I speak of."

"You speak in riddles, like a poet. Or a fool. It is verbal trickery ..."

"How do you sleep?"

"What? Why do ..."

"A simple question ... no tricks. How do you sleep?"

"Lightly and with one eye open."

"You mock me, but it is no matter. In your mind, you know a different

answer as truth. In the last decade I have slept two complete nights and both of them fitfully. As a shade walking amongst shadows, little upon this world is clear and real to me. All is distorted as by a haze. Paltry concerns of employment, finding a bride, building a home have little value. I can survive ..."

"Save your dissertation for dimwitted peasants and starry-eyed children," Silver interrupted with a wave of his hand. His attention shifted from the wizard's cryptic conversation, and he found himself staring at the older man's mug of ale. It was an earthen-colored drink, but for some reason there was a large, dark splotch rising towards the surface. As Silver stared at it, a small creature, buoyed by the billowing foam, raised from the liquid and perched itself on the mug's rim, ultimately mirroring his stare. Realization struck him at the same instant that Belhurst said, "Children indeed!" and raised the glass to his lips.

"Stop!" Silver shouted reaching out for Belhurst's arm. Belhurst, startled, looked from Silver's pointing finger to his mug.

"Odd! Scorpions aren't indigenous to these parts ..."

"Nevin," Silver called while scanning the interior of the bar.

"Silver, you wouldn't believe the things this guy next to us has been saying," Nevin mentioned to his dark-haired companion, gesturing to a nearby patron.

"Scorpions, Nevin! Scorpions!"

Silver clutched his friend's jerkin, pulling himself to his feet. Wild-eyed, he began pointing and gesticulating in earnest at various points around the bar.

"There ... and over there ... and there."

"How could I be so daft?" Nevin began. "How could I have missed it?"

"Missed what?" asked Silver.

"I overheard patrons talking about the mayor receiving a mysterious cactus. Let's go. Everyone. *Now!*" Nevin said, his rising voice tinged with hysteria.

Quizzical looks aimed at him from all sides missed their target as he was already a blur of movement. Nevin glanced back once on his way to the door, but Silver and Diminutia were already in tow, sucked into the maelstrom of his motion.

He reached the decomposing door and shoved it aside with alacrity. Before the commotion of the streets could be noticed, a man, open-mouthed with a look of disbelief in his eyes, fell into the elf's arms. Without thinking, Nevin pushed the man away and was befouled for his efforts. A great spout of gore issued from the man's mouth as a sword cleft it like an over-ripened melon, covering Nevin's face. Not pausing to wipe himself clean, Nevin locked eyes with the murderous assailant, unable to determine what kind of creature he was dealing with. It resembled a human; however, the skin had a tint of green while its tattered strips of clothing of the same hue and the befouled stench coming from it was more befitting an abomination spawned from mildew. Never being one to allow awe to distract from survival, the elf allowed his trusted dagger to make short work of the creature's throat. Nevin hurried the group on as he stepped over the fallen townsman.

A city under siege, the structures of Balfourd's Bounty smoked like a forest fire. Flames winked at Nevin and his companions as they darted from behind one smoking building after another. Realizing that the wizards had stopped to retrieve their cart, Nevin and his friends waited behind a relatively untouched structure, while Moxxen and Follen pushed the bulky cart with as much haste as the frail wizards were able to muster.

Nameless assailants, hooded with black cowls, tracked down the fleeing residents, severing lifelines with slashing sabers. Nevin noted the movements of one attacker in great detail, noting how he swept a man's feet from under him as he fled, then drew himself up straight, looming titan-like over the fallen wretch, before ending the attempted escape with brutal finality.

As Belhurst drew even with him, Silver dared a brief exchange with him.

"Well, mighty wizard, shouldn't you be helping these poor people?"

"Our duty does not allow us to take that risk."

"Truly? All this talk of 'eidolons' notwithstanding ..."

"Dear boy, the security of what we guard cannot be compromised, or far more blood than was spilled in this town will flood this world."

A huge chunk of earth dislodged beside them as a great torrent of energy blasted through a small gathering of assailants, ending their exchange. From the other side of the square, several of the resident wizards stood atop the parapet of their guild, combining incomprehensible speech and wild gesticulations. Periodically, some dramatic effect would manifest itself as a tangible result of their sorcery. A gout of fire, a lance of energy, a stroke of lightning, each conjured and controlled by wizardly will loosed its primeval fury on the flesh of an attacker, leaving a sundered heap or burned out body.

In response to this display of defense, a wave of insurgents massed against the tower. An arrow from the ground took one of the wizards in the throat, disrupting the verbal element of his spell. As he toppled over from the impetus of the missile, his body blazed with the unleashed energy of his ruined thaumaturgy, catching in a flaming nimbus one of his comrades, who stumbled off the edge of the roof in his blindness.

Ladders were raised against the side of the building, and the onslaught surged up their height. A lightning bolt crackled from an outstretched wizard hand, searing attacker after attacker, hurling bodies to their demise, the ladder exploding into useless pieces. A great deluge of water, created by another wizard, gushed down upon another ladder with similar success.

As the standoff at the wizard guild drew the attention of more of the aggressors, Nevin led his group of thieves and wizards towards the city gates in an area where all of the buildings had been consumed by guttering flames. Such destruction, coupled with the promise of new violence, led the attackers to abandon this gate altogether. Nevin let the others pass him by as they exited, turning one last glance at the second city ruined by The Horde that they had seen in a fortnight. The gravity of world events pressed in on him, threatening to crush the breath from his lungs as reality forced him to understand how pivotal a role he and his friends would be made to serve if they were to continue to enjoy the freedom that had marked their lives.

As he stood there looking at the wizard's tower, a great figure, fully clad in green armor of a bizarre metal, strode towards the town's last defenders. Spells erupted harmlessly around the figure. With a motion of his gauntleted right arm, splinters of some indecipherable projectiles launched towards the top of the parapet. Seconds later, the final few wizards screamed as one, a death knell that propelled Nevin out the ruined gate after his fleeing comrades.

SEVEN

THE LATE AFTERNOON air was cool and crisp; the morning sun long gone, the day sun beginning its descent. Life in the valley began its routine to settle down for slumber: song bird warbles slowed, predators returned to their shelter sated from an earlier meal, prey, fortunate enough to avoid the predators, munched stray patches of grass or an easily accessible berry or nut.

Dearborn caught glimpses of these activities now and again, realizing the Elite Troop would need to do the same. They were near Balfourd's Bounty. However, the afternoon hinted at a pleasant and still evening. She knew Iderion well enough to know that if a glimmer of light existed, so did the opportunity to complete the mission.

Remaining vigilant, Dearborn enjoyed simple pleasures. When the air remained still, she could feel tiny percolations of perspiration form all over her body, especially across her back and neck. But even the slightest breeze caused a quick evaporation that sent warm chills throughout her body. Unfortunately, there was one grating noise that took it all away and sent razor blades scraping down her spine —the voice of Haddaman Crede.

Haddaman rode next to Mahlakore, the youngest and newest member of the Elite Troop. *Typical viper*, Dearborn thought, *isolating the youngest, assuming he's the weakest.*

Guiding her steed closer, Dearborn heard Haddaman's words, full of vigor, "... I knew something was amiss when the mayor received that cactus. Being the man of the world that I am, I knew the intricacies of such a species. I knew that cactus was a breeding ground for that species of scorpion."

"Was there any reason why you kept that knowledge to yourself?" Dearborn asked, hoping Mahlakore did not believe Haddaman's words.

"Ahh, sweet Dearborn. I thought you might be interested in the tale I tell. Being the band of experts, you thought you might gain a clue about the dread enemy who besieged my humble town?"

"My *dear* Haddaman, I assure you I hear enough flatulence from this band of experts with whom I share my travel."

Dearborn saw the sparkle fade from Haddaman's eyes. It was quite obvious to her that his lily-laden words tickled the fancies of tavern maidens; never suspecting a woman could possess an education to actually decode their hidden meanings. She continued, "However, you have yet to fulfill my curiosity—why did you not share your vast knowledge of desert foliage with anyone?"

"Have you ever yelled at a deaf man, Sergeant?"

"I assume you mean that you did mention it to someone, but they did not heed your words?"

A woman capable of logical deduction, how disdainful, Dearborn thought. That very idea was painfully etched across Haddaman's face.

"Very astute. It's no wonder that you're the sergeant."

"Being astute had nothing to do with it. Your message was obvious. It's no wonder that you're retired."

With a feminine flip of her hair, Dearborn led her horse away, knowing Haddaman's flavorful words would no longer taste as sweet to young Mahlakore.

Once her horse paralleled Iderion's, Dearborn leaned toward him and said, "I have my concerns about bringing a civilian along with us on a mission. First we allow Prince Oremethus to scout ahead, and now this."

"First, Prince Oremethus is well trained and so are the soldiers who are accompanying him. Second, are we talking about any civilian, or just this particular civilian?" Iderion replied.

"I truly doubt he has joined us for the good of king and country. And that is even if he knows the workings of The Scorched Sea, as he claimed repeatedly, to lead us along the best path to get the stone. If the stone even exists."

Iderion sighed while a slight smirk crept across his face. "As much as you may wish it so, a man's intentions cannot be revealed by simply pulling away a curtain."

Eyes sparking like a flint strike, Dearborn glared at her superior. "So you're saying a woman's intentions can be revealed in such a manner?"

Iderion let loose a belly laugh that caused his horse's knees to creak. "That's why I love having you as my sergeant!"

"Love ... what?" Dearborn all but stuttered as her skin blanched to the color of snow, her heart fluttered like the moth wings in her stomach.

"Your views and thoughts are so contrary, so fresh! You force me to perform at my best, even when I think I need not."

"I ... I ... was just ... I ..."

"What I *meant* was there is only one way we will find out what his true intentions are. We simply must wait. His true intentions will be known soon enough. He claims to have seen a map to the stone, and I am willing to take him at his word."

Scolding herself for getting flustered like a schoolgirl, she regained control of her senses. "But ... what if his intentions are simply for his own benefit, becoming ultimately disruptive to our mission."

"Dearborn, even the pup Mahlakore knows the *sole* reason our guest is with us is for personal, financial reward."

"*That* motivation I cannot trust."

"Come now, Sergeant. What man ... I mean, person ... would be fool enough to cross forty specially trained soldiers carrying a small armory?"

"I still cannot trust him."

Dearborn's last statement was lost on Iderion; he instead paid great heed to the forest line. As soft as a butterfly's whisper, the mighty general commanded his horse to a firm stop and raised his fist, demanding his troops do the same. He squinted, focusing deep into the forest border; his nostrils flared, drawing in the restless valley air. Every bird flit through the leaves, every rabbit shuffle through the brush echoed like thunder as Iderion concentrated, looking for what set the scenery amiss. There, beyond the first dozen layers of trees, he saw movement, unnatural and awkward. Ominous figures on steeds deemed worthy of further investigation.

As if Iderion possessed his horse's very soul, it moved with the grace of a strand of silk floating on a gossamer breeze. Crossing the forest threshold first, Iderion signaled to his troop to do the same. Slow and steady, every member breached the forest with ease, the crunching of leaves nothing more than nature readjusting itself.

Iderion surmised the mysterious riders were unaware of his troop's presence. Ten riders, single file, all in various sorts of armor with hoods cloaking their faces. His plan was simple: follow the strange caravan until they strayed off the path. But Iderion unfastened every tie to every dagger, every sword, every crossbow anyway.

"What are we doing?" Haddaman's voice shook the tranquil forest with the force of a falling tree. No sooner had the words escaped his lips when an arrow whistled through the air, sinking into the tree nearest Iderion.

"Scatter!" Iderion barked by the time two more arrows struck nearby trees.

Training dictated that when ambushed, even if it was caused by an ignorant civilian, the unit should fall back. Dearborn used the environment for protection and tried to keep a solid view of any and all members of the team for an immediate reconnoiter. She turned her mount in enough time to see a barrage of arrows tear through the neck of Haddaman's horse. With a gurgled whinny, the animal experienced a spasm, its front legs giving way. Haddaman's fate to fall with the beast seemed sealed, and Dearborn would have loved to leave him with that, except her reflexes forced her to grab his arm and pull him onto her steed. However, she made no attempt to hide her feelings on the matter. "Dolt!"

"How was I to know that was going to happen?" he replied.

"Tale after tale I had to endure from that filth-pit mouth of yours about one great adventure after another. Surely, a worldly man such as yourself could have understood the actions of our general!"

"I ... I ... have never seen such a tactic before ..."

"Staying quiet until we ascertain the threat level of strangers? That is quite the strange tactic indeed."

"But ..."

"Haddaman, enough! I have heard more intelligent remarks from the back side of my horse!"

Dearborn seethed, her muscles tensing, as her ride galloped without direction, weaving among the trees. Haddaman, hands on her shoulders, waited for the slightest ease of her stress before he muttered, "But at least I'm versed well enough in military tactics to know you should never lose sight of your battalion members in situations such as this."

She felt his fingers twitch as her muscles transformed from wood to steel. Even though his life was in peril two fold, from the mysterious marauders from whom they fled as well as from his new riding partner, she imagined he felt a mild sense of satisfaction.

Dearborn pulled on the reins. With a muffled whinny and a few grunts, her steed stopped, awaiting the next command. Spinning the horse, Dearborn peered through the trees, squinting as best she could, but to her chagrin, Haddaman's statement was accurate.

Now what? she thought. However, that question was answered by Haddaman, "Sword!"

Faster than the speed of thought, Dearborn brought her blade to her head, blocking similar steel from cleaving her skull.

"Again! Again!" Haddaman screamed into her ear. And again she parried another strike. Horses whinnying, attacker growling, and Haddaman screaming forced her to release a dire bellow as well. Manipulating the reins with one hand, she used her other to slash with her sword. Doing a controlled sidestep and a spin, her steed moved far enough for Dearborn to view her opponent in full. Sitting atop a malnourished and angry looking beast was another beast shaped like a man. Dark shreds flapped in the breeze, but Dearborn was unable to tell if it was tattered clothing or the man-creature's flesh. His skin was clay gray while his eyes were only a shade darker. Inky puss poured from his pores while the stench of death rippled the air around him.

"Aim for the head!" Haddaman yelled as Dearborn ordered her steed closer. Her sword was blocked as she strove to sever her opponent's arm.

"The head! The head!" Haddaman screamed again.

Blocking her prior attack was exactly what Dearborn wanted the creature to do, allowing her to plunge her sword through the center of its chest—to no avail.

"Higher! Strike higher!" Haddaman continued.

Loathing the idea that her detestable riding partner may actually be right, she relinquished her sword, now stuck in the creature's chest, and brandished her short sword, driving it through the bottom of the creature's chin, the tip poking through his skull. After a full twist, she lifted the hilt, causing its face to fall free from the rest of its head.

"Do you not know your anatomy, woman? Or was my instruction too complicated?" Haddaman admonished.

"One more biting comment and I shall have my sword demonstrate how well I know anatomy," Dearborn replied as she retrieved her sword right before the dead creature's steed rode off. "And how did you know stabbing it in the chest would be useless?"

"I didn't. I just know to go for the head. You *always* go for the head when facing an unknown creature. And I thought you were the professional. I can now see why you're only a sergeant and Iderion's a general."

Iderion? Iderion! Dearborn thought. So worried, she retraced her tracks without so much as an ill thought toward Haddaman's insult.

The sounds of fighting came from all directions, but scanning what she could of the horizon, Dearborn was unable to see anyone, friend or foe.

"Haddaman," she said, "do you see anything?"

"Trees," came the curt response. "Now I suggest you find the largest one and we put our backs to it. I'll watch one side and you can watch the other. Then ..."

"Haddaman, I am going back to look for the other members of my team. You can either watch for enemies or stay here and hug the tree of your choosing. Which will it be?"

"And I suppose it goes without saying that you will not be stopping to let me off this horse. Correct?"

"Correct," she said as she urged her mount onward. "Now I suggest you hold your tongue."

Picking her way from tree to tree, the landscape scrolled around her as if she stood still and the land itself were moving. In her mind, Dearborn failed to draw a breath, but her mount breathed deeply and exhaled in long plumes of steam. The smell of freshly turned loam clung in her nostrils. The waiting was intolerable. Her mind raced and whirled, but one thought was constant, *Iderion, where are you?*

Just when she was sure she could bear no more, she made out several figures from the corner of her eye. Ahead were two men, lying on the ground and taking up a defensive standpoint behind several fallen trees, in the joint of the crossed trunks. Closing on their position, Dearborn made out that both men wielded crossbows. The Elite Troop boasted several fine crossbowmen, and much to her relief, she recognized the two men as her own. Barrett was the closer of the two, and from this distance she wasn't quite sure who the other member was, but she could discern the crossfire they were laying out.

And aren't I quite the target, she thought, *mounted on a horse and tall as I please.*

"Haddaman," she whispered. I am going to maneuver behind that tree about forty feet to the left. I need you to watch behind us."

"Yes," he replied.

She would have liked to make comments regarding his sudden terseness, but no time for such foolishness now. *Our lives depend on our stealth*, she reminded herself, and then let her warrior instincts take over. She knew she needed to dismount the horse if she was to make herself a less obvious target, but she was loath to give up the speed it promised. And she still needed to find Iderion.

From behind a tree, she waited and observed the projectile exchange taking place. Her horse was bred for combat and stood still as if sensing what was required of him. Nervously, she patted its neck as she watched Barrett and Glindos, another newer recruit, work their crossbows.

"Make sure you keep a sharp eye on our flank, Haddaman. It would not do to have someone circle around us," she whispered.

"I am quite aware of that tactic. Rest assured my eyes are never still. Since we're not hiding like I suggested, then at what point do you intend to join your comrades there? I'm assuming your hand could help turn the tide."

"I possess no ranged weapons, Haddaman. And I would bear more quills than a porcupine before I ever got close."

"Then you simply plan to stay here and wait? Sounds like we're hiding. Like I suggested," he said, his voice rising a little too loudly for her liking.

"Well, Haddaman, it seems your little display of elocution got us noticed," she hissed as Glindos threw a worried look in their direction. He gave a slight wave and held up a few fingers briefly, indicating the number of attackers with whom he and Barrett dealt. The distance between them and the brevity of the movement caused her to miss the number, though it was clearly five or less. Having made his display of information, Glindos turned his attention back to the task at hand, though Dearborn could see him lean slightly towards Barrett conveying information to the other man.

"Haddaman, we need to move. The enemy probably already noticed our little exchange and this spot won't stay safe for much longer."

"Sergeant, do you mean to say that you are deserting those men?"

She turned full to face him. "Not at all. I am going to drop you off over there and you can follow that line of trees right over to that edge of their barricade. You do know how to load a crossbow, yes?"

"Of course! One does not live through as many adv ..."

At this, she instructed her mount to move in the direction she indicated.

"Good! They seem to have things pretty much under control, but you can load the weapons for them and allow them both to fire. That should be all they need. Oh, and Haddaman, don't forget you have a sword at your hip, if you know how to use it."

"Where will you be?" he asked as he slipped off the horse's rump behind a very stout and majestic looking oak.

"To take stock of the rest of the situation. Someone else needs me. I can just feel it," she said as she let her heels tap her mount's flanks. "I'll be back shortly."

"Delightful," he smiled and then focused his attention on his surroundings. After several long seconds, he pushed himself from the oak tree and, starting from a crouch, began a winding series of dodges and loops, whirling from one tree to the next as if in a dance for his life. He slowed his hectic pace and slid behind a tree not fifteen feet from his final destination. As he rounded the small maple, he bumped into the back of a horrible creature. Haddaman gasped as the beast turned to confront him. It was bipedal and had two long arms, but its skin was a pasty green and covered with hundreds of tiny holes, much like oversized pores. The eyes were solid black and sunken, and they disappeared behind their lids as the creature's entire body began to swell and puff up like a blowfish. Haddaman did a tuck and roll around the tree with what little grace his out of shape body would allow, but with a speed that even he did not quite believe.

The lumbering man-creature bore down on Haddaman. Feeling he had little choice, Haddaman brandished his sword and spun with all the force he could muster. The blade sunk deep within the creature's arm, but did little damage other than to slow its pace. Having performed such a desperate maneuver midstride, Haddaman fell victim to momentum, then gravity.

Staring from a prone position, Haddaman couldn't even escape the waning shadow of the man-creature. Each step it took brought with it a more fetid stench, foreshadowing doom. He guessed the rhythmic gurgling emanating from its wheezing lungs was a putrid form of laughter as it tore Haddaman's sword from its arm, readying it to strike. Feeling foolish for dismissing prayer for a silent curse about the moisture from the ground soaking through his pants, chilling his haunches, he instinctively raised his arm to protect his face. However, had he been any quicker, he might have missed the barrage of arrows tearing into the creature's skull.

Before the creature fell, Glindos pulled Haddaman by the scruff to join him and Barrett behind the tree.

"Are you daft, man?" Glindos scorned. "You should have aimed for the head! You always aim for the head! Don't you know anything?"

Haddaman could do nothing but seethe as he looked over his shoulder to watch Dearborn and her horse fade from his sight....

EIGHT

"TALLON, STOP THAT."

Tallia's voice seemed shrill to her own ear, but only due to the nature of the circumstances, she surmised. She sat upon a rock in quiet repose, while her brother stood a few feet to her left. He had gathered a handful of stones from the dirt and cobbled road at his feet and tossed them one at a time into the woods in what Tallia knew to be a show of indifference.

"I hate waiting, Tallia," he said.

Tallia looked over at her brother, studying his visage. *There it is*, she thought. His left eye twitched spasmodically whenever he was nervous. *There again. At least we share the same distaste on this matter.*

"Tallon," she said, her voice barely a whisper.

With his back still towards her, he turned his head to indicate that he had heard her and she should continue— the nuances of communicating with a twin.

"I'm scared. And it's obvious that you are, too ..."

"I'm not scared," he said. His voice rang out, startling a few birds into flight from their perch in a nearby tree. Pausing from his stone throwing, he turned to face her. "I'm not scared of anything. Or anyone." He suddenly looked away from her and rubbed his twitching eyes. "Damn all this dust. Dries my eyes."

"It isn't the dust, Tallon. It's your nerves."

He opened his mouth as if to retort, but she cut him off. "This isn't a simple case of cloak and dagger anymore. This is for real. If Daedalus finds out we met this man ..."

Tallon picked up the skein of her thought and extrapolated. "But if we don't meet with Praeker, then *he* will think it a betrayal ..." He lifted his head and locked stares with her. "Look, Tallia, maybe this man isn't at all like we've heard. I mean, isn't fear simply conjecture about the unknown anyway? Once we meet him and start to figure him out a little bit, he won't be so alien to us. And nothing that is known is to be feared." His eye fluttered. He turned from her again and muttered, "And it is too the dust."

Tallon went back to tossing pebbles. Those actions he could control. The time passing from seconds to minutes, he could not. Nor, his eye. Another rub, another mumble. "Damnable dust."

"Might I suggest that you employ a helmet?"

Tallon jerked around at the stranger's words, involuntarily backpedaling as his mind struggled to comprehend what his eyes were seeing. Before him stood what he presumed to be the man they were to meet—and a veritable monstrous one at that.

For an instant, swirls of dust wreathed the figure before him. Tallon tried to scrutinize him, but his form seemed to be in constant motion, swaying one way, then undulating the other. No, just his armor seemed to move, a repetitive series of clicks coming from it. He was dressed in a full suit of ornate armor fashioned of foreign, green material. Plates overlapped each other, always shifting to hide potential openings, even at the greave.

Upon his head sat a full helm, offering both protection and anonymity. An opening two fingers thick ran horizontally to keep his vision unencumbered, but the whole was covered by the relief of a scorpion facing downwards, the stinger of its tail looping down over his nose. The body of the creature hid the man's mouth to such an extent that no indication of facial hair could be ascertained. His eyes gleamed like twin emeralds floating in a pool of spoiled milk. "Forgive me if I startled you. For some reason, my presence leaves people ... unsettled."

"N ... no ... not a problem, friend," Tallon said, forcing his words past a jaw that refused to cooperate.

Tallia rose gracefully from her roost, her lean, supple body swaying in the manner of a charmed snake. She had learned at a young age what power a simple pout, the promise of parted lips, or the display of an ample bosom allowed a woman to exert over the simple-minded male species.

"You didn't startle us, sir. Our minds were merely occupied with other things and we failed to take notice of your approach," she said with breathy tones, her stage fright dissipating once she assumed the role of a character that she had acted many times before.

As she approached him, she took full notice of his size. Tallon was of average height for a man, and Tallia had only to stand on her tiptoes to look him full in the eye. This man was a full two heads taller than Tallon. The crown of her head would be swallowed within the hollow of this man's breast, she realized. And of his width ... she estimated that Tallon's chest would need to double or triple to match what this monstrous man offered.

"Ah, where the brother falters, the sister is quick to assist. As inseparable as light and shadow. I wonder, lass, which more correctly describes you. You both reek of mischief and deception. As false as vanity and as reversed as a reflection. Mark me well. I do not trust either of you. But neither do I worry over it. As liaisons of your prince, you need only speak the requisite amount of fear into his ear. He must never forget that his position is one of fealty to me."

"Mercenary rabble," Tallon said in retort.

"Your voice returns, bolstered by a false courage. Let this be the last time you ever address me, boy." With two quick strides the armored man made his way to Tallon and gripped him about the throat with his right hand, casually lifting him clear off the ground with a minimum of motion. "Do I make myself clear?"

"Yef," Tallon said amid as much head nodding as he could muster from his restricted position. Trying to relieve any amount of spinal pain caused by gravity's pull, he grabbed the hulking forearm of his assailant. For a moment fear shifted to pensive bewilderment as he felt the monstrous man's green-plated armor shift and scuttle under his grasp. He relinquished his grip as he saw a number of scorpion tails arise from between the plates. With a dramatic sigh to show his boredom, the armored behemoth dropped Tallon as well as the young man's ego. "Now, to what do I owe the … pleasure?"

Tallia slithered her way closer to answer the question. "Simple. To strike a deal. To offer you something you don't have."

"I am *Praeker Trieste!* I command The Horde! My name alone shrivels the hearts of all men who hear it! What could you possibly have, girl, that I could want?" he asked.

"What is the one thing that separates warlords from generals? Gods from men? You from the vermin you command?"

Tallia could see his eyes squint through the slit of his moss-hued helmet, the way a cat's do before it turns a mouse into dinner. She heard his patience wane through gritted teeth as he growled, "Power."

"What topples kingdoms or turns a flailing attack into a mighty ambush?"

"Information."

"Exactly!"

"I grow weary of your games, girl!"

Fully composed from his embarrassing indiscretion, Tallon stepped in, adding, "Daedalus views you as a puppet."

Praeker clenched his fists, bone and armor cracking, as he turned toward Tallon. "Have you not learned your lesson …?"

Fighting every urge to run or let loose his bladder, Tallon continued, "You recently razed Balford's Bounty, did you not? Did your reconnaissance teams meet resistance from the king's Elite Troop?"

Stopping in his tracks, Praeker growled again. "They killed a dozen of my soldiers. Continue."

"He is playing both sides of the game. Hedging his bet. You see, Daedalus is looking for the stones as well."

"*What!*" the mammoth warlord bellowed. His armor chattered and clicked, springing to life as a hundred score pincers and poison-tipped tails popped up, preparing to strike. "Even that pompous whelp would not be so foolish!"

Unnerved by Praeker Trieste's pernicious suit of living armor, Tallon forced himself to quell his fear. "Our dear cousin views everyone he meets as a puppet. Even us."

"Yes," Tallia said, looking into the forest as if watching a ghostly play upon a phantom theater unfold. She pulled her wrap that lay over her shoulders tightly across her bosom. "We are nothing more than his play things."

"Even you, Praeker. Or is it Lord Trieste?" Tallon continued, trying to judge how far to twist the proverbial dagger. "You are but a toy to Daedalus. Is that the deal you made with him?"

"Far from it," Praeker replied as his armor's angry protrusions tucked themselves away. "But how do I know you two view the world any differently?"

Tallon felt as if his skin moved and shifted the same way Praeker Trieste's armor did; the many creatures that formed it readjusted themselves, once again making a seamless shell over their master. "You know very well what they say about 'the enemy of my enemy,' don't you?"

"Aye. But I have yet to hear what you have to offer?"

"Weapons!" Tallia's voice held the desire to use them. "Far superior to what Daedalus supplies."

"How so?"

"Daedalus gives you pikes with wooden handles. We will get you solid steel. He supplies you bows, we'll supply crossbows. Your troops will have broadswords instead of short swords."

Praeker Trieste squinted, his mind reeling from the girl's words. All prior forms of negotiating he had ever done with anyone consisted of him crushing the windpipe of whomever he was negotiating with while holding them perilously close to fire, spike, venomous scorpion tails, or some combination of the three. However, if her words held truth, he doubted that he could procure the goods by threatening her life, or her brother's. Wondering how to proceed without attempting to rend the siblings limb from limb, he sat upon the very rock she had perched upon moments earlier. The boulder settled further into the ground, groaning from the sheer size of him sitting upon it.

Finally, he fought against his every urge and surrendered to logic. "What do you want from me?"

"What do we want?" Tallia repeated. "The same as you, Lord Trieste. Power."

"I do not see where this is going."

"If you ... *when* you finally get all the stones, this continent will easily succumb to your mighty grip. And then you will move on to others. I do not know entirely what powers the stones will bequeath to you, but I do not believe omnipotence is among them. You will need assistance managing your affairs. My brother and I simply wish to be in your employ."

"I will have armies of thousands by then. Your 'assistance' is certainly not needed."

"From the tales we have been told, your armies are made for fighting, not thinking. Can you honestly think of one soldier, one general or commander, you would entrust with the governorship of this continent while you conquer others?"

Even though the warlord was seated, Tallia still needed to gaze upward to look into his eyes. They possessed the warmth of mildewed tombstones while he pondered her question. "Surely, your cousin would offer you the same position if he were to claim the stones."

"Surely, he will not."

"And you prefer allegiance to a monster than to family?"

"I assure you," Tallia said, clutching her cowl, again drawing it across her chest. "There is more than one kind of monster."

"Come, Sister," Tallon said, holding out his hand. "Let us leave him to his thoughts."

"We'll be in contact soon, Lord Trieste. We know that our cousin will soon be meeting with you in this very spot. Remember our words," Tallia said as she took comfort in her brother's hand. Without so much as a backward glance, the twins followed the dirt path, awakening dusty specters with every step, over the knoll and out of Praeker Trieste's sight.

Praeker Trieste could only savor mere moments, pondering the offer laid before him, before he had to turn his attention to another matter. Daedalus, approached from the other end of the dirt path. There he sat, third born of King Theomann, stick straight and peacock proud, atop a steed that could outrival any of the land. Gifted with such a pristine gait, the creature's hooves released not a single swirl of dust from the road. Praeker Trieste forgot more battles in the past decade than most generals fight in a lifetime, yet, there was no pain greater than in the pit of his stomach and no wound deeper than that done to his pride knowing he had to deal with the likes of Daedalus.

"Good day, my great comrade!" Daedalus shouted once within earshot.

Again detesting the world of diplomacy in which he had found himself, Praeker Trieste fought the urge to rip out Daedalus's gizzard and bite each of his limbs to crack them like chicken bones. He simply stood from the stone and allowed the milquetoast to approach before saying, "What reason have you for not informing me of the Elite Troop's involvement?"

Daedalus remained on his mount. He had done so for every meeting with Praeker Trieste, feeling he needed the horse's height to compensate for his lack of physical prowess when next to the warlord. "I bid thee fine greetings and this is ..."

Desperately grasping at his patience as it slid down a slippery slope, Praeker Trieste gritted his teeth. "I lost soldiers."

"Yes. Well, obviously not very good ones!" Daedalus made no effort to conceal his disdain for someone interrupting him. "I made no mention of it to you, because I had no knowledge of it! My father tells me next to nothing, and my eldest brother, who happens to command the Elite Troop, tells me even less!

"Not to mention, though I'm sure the thought has already occurred to you, should your army strike with impunity and loose nary a man, then it should quickly become pretty obvious that you are receiving help. That tends to tighten even the most willing lips. I suggest, therefore, that this was not a total loss and that things went splend ..."

"That's just it," roared the giant. "If this is to be a joint venture, then I require input as well. I do not doubt the validity of some of your statements. I think you know more than you admit, perhaps. But I, and I alone, shall control the effects of attrition. To my army, a dozen men is but a single tear from a woman suddenly bereft of husband and babe. But these dozen men were mine to march into death, *not* yours!"

His emerald eyes blazed with the passion of his words. Though he couldn't see it, Daedalus imagined spittle running the length of Trieste's chin. Such unbridled rage made a man stronger but more prone to tactical error in the prince's mind. Daedalus quickly made up his mind to stay well out of the behemoth's arms-length during these fits of rage; however, he would not be cowed either.

"Praeker, in the interest of compromise, I will concede the point. If such knowledge is mine to share, then I will make every effort to communicate it to you; however, you will never again hold me responsible for those things I am not privy to, nor will you ever again doubt me. If I say I do not know, then the conversation is terminated. Are we clear?"

At this, the colossus that was Praeker Trieste swelled even larger. His eyes sparkled beneath the sheen of his slivered helmet. Daedalus knew the foundation of their alliance was made more of old wood than of cement, but he had been compelled to deal with this man as he would any other. For the first time, Prince Daedalus, third son of King Theomann, knew fear. He regarded it with the same disdain he reserved for all other emotions, though it was difficult to dismiss the physiological changes that accompanied it. He could ignore the profuse sweating, but his throat was tight and threatened to close off completely under the attack of that pervasive stare.

With nary a word, and a dearth of motion, the warlord moved to the side of the prince's steed, his arms outstretched towards it. The horse, sensing the seething of emotions, tried to skitter nervously away, but Daedalus, refusing to let go of his pride, rigidly held the reins and the beast proved well-trained, holding its ground. Praeker's hands slid smoothly under the belly of the beast, stopping only when they cupped the other side. Without so much as the release of a breath, Praeker Trieste lifted rider and mount skyward not stopping until they were both held aloft an arm's length above his head.

"By the gods," swore Daedalus. Incredulity and fear struggled for control of the battleground of his mind.

"Normally, *Prince*, I would have centered my efforts on you, but that would have left you dead—hardly befitting my diplomatic mood. As you can surmise, I am not a man known for legendary self-restraint, nor will I ever be confused as a great arbiter of compromises. Now I suggest that we recommence this meeting, minus the exchange of pleasantries since we have already progressed well beyond that point. What say you? And remember, your vote does not count."

Daedalus refused to speak, though it wasn't due to the warlord's whim. He refused to give the much larger man the satisfaction of hearing him croak from a throat desiccated by fear. He chose, instead, to let this further fuel his anger. In time, after Praeker had served his purpose, he would see that the warlord received his due recompense for his display of impudence. For the nonce, at least he had learned a thing or two about the man's character and volatility. He could stomach the shame of his seeming servitude as long as these direct meetings were not lengthy.

By the time his mount was settled back firmly on the ground, Daedalus had regained enough composure, accompanied by the requisite amount of saliva, to allow for normal speech so he could once again address the chieftain before him, though he still refused to dismount. "Quite a compelling display. It must garner an unforgettable respect among your troops."

"We have dispensed with the pleasantries, remember?" Praeker growled. "Now, where were we? We were discussing the unauthorized loss of my troops. Since I had to pay a price, dear Prince, so shall you. I need better weapons for my troops. Something fabricated wholly of steel. There will be great resistance from many towns as word of my quest spreads. I require something that will narrow the margin of disadvantage that many of my men will face in the coming months."

"Praeker, the majority of our weapons are as I have previously provided—pole-arms with hafts of stout wood. Have they not served you well that you make this request? Though it may be possible to satisfy such a request, the count on such weapons is closely monitored. It may not be feasible to provide you with them in the amounts that you seek."

"Very well. Consider this my display of faith. I shall modify my tactics to compensate for the inferiority of our weapons until such time as I have cause to doubt you. Pray that never happens, Prince."

At this, the mountainous man moved off, three strides taking him to the edge of the trees that seemed about ten paces off to Daedalus's eye. Before entering the obscurity of their shade, Praeker turned back to address Daedalus once more. "Oh yes. And remember to let me know the whereabouts of this Elite Troop of yours. I will allow them one more small victory at your suggestion. In the meantime, you may wish to send the crown prince your farewells if you were close to him."

He remained in view for but a moment, then was quickly swallowed amongst the trees with which he shared a similarity of stature.

"Well now," whispered Daedalus to himself as he urged his mare towards the area he had designated as a meeting place for his cousin confidants, "I wonder if he is more properly feared as an ally or an adversary? He will need to be dealt with sooner than anticipated, I think. Time to place a few bribes before this game of chance gets too heavily weighted against my favor."

Daedalus rode slowly and took a longer route than he originally had planned. It simply would not do to show up in a rush, nor would he allow himself to be seen by human eyes until he was completely composed. The meeting with Praeker Trieste had left him more than a little unnerved, though his calm demeanor returned as he began to outdistance the incident. Having sweat, from contemptible nerves nonetheless, made him feel positively indecent.

He approached the designated rendezvous point at a controlled cantor. Even over the sound of the hoofbeats, he

could hear his cousins engaged in conversation before he
could see them.

"I'm beginning to worry, Tallon. It may be like him to
keep us waiting, but this is excessive. Given the situation, I
think it best that one of us go to look for him."

"Tallia, I just think it is unwise to separate. What if
something ...?"

"But one of us should wait here in case he shows up in
the meantime, Tallon. How would it look if Daedalus
arrived and neither of us was here?"

"It would look like we simply got tired of waiting for
him, Tallia. We can either be concerned for his safety or we
can be worried about appearances, but we can't do both. It
simply isn't practical."

"Since when," Daedalus called out, "have either of you
ever concerned yourselves with what is practical?"

"Daedalus! Your belated arrival had us concerned. We
were simply discussing whether one or both of us should
go looking for you and ..."

"Your concern is touching, dear Cousin, but as you can
plainly see, it is quite unnecessary. I am well. I simply
found other matters that required my immediate attention.
Those matters have been addressed, and now, here I am,"
Daedalus said. "Shall we talk next of the weather, or
should we concern ourselves with why we are here?"

"Ever the diplomat, eh, Daedalus?"

"Time is a valuable asset, Tallon, a limited resource and
best not squandered. Now, what news do you bring me? Is
everything proceeding according to plan? Or is
improvisation the word of the day?"

"After Tallon and I had spent many hours talking with
many of the king's advisors, it seems a safe bet that your
father has no idea the capitol is a target of The Horde,
Daedalus," Tallia said with a curtsy. "The path to victory is
a wide swath with nary an obstacle."

"Excellent. Most excellent. Whatever your failings, Tallia,
you do know how to begin a conversation. Pray proceed ..."

NINE

"LOOK, NEVIN," Silver said in a hush, slightly louder than a whisper, "all I'm saying is that it seems a little more than coincidental that these wizards appear out of nowhere at a time that was critical to our survival; thus, encouraging us to ask fewer questions out of gratitude."

Standing on a bluff a half-day's walk from Balfourd's Bounty, the three thieves, finding themselves without wizardly presence for the moment, saw their opportunity to discuss their individual concerns regarding their new companions.

"They knew who we are. They knew what we are hunting. They even have one of the blasted stones themselves! Then, there has been nothing but trouble since we met them. Not to mention the fact that they allowed those people to die without lifting a finger," Silver said, all but frothing at the mouth.

"Silver, we are guilty of the same crime."

"What do you mean?"

Nevin's face was more scored than lined: the creases seemed like crevasses. Though deep in the heart of discussion, Silver did not allow his friend's haggard appearance to be lost on him. The elf was normally reticent, but lately he had been flat out uncommunicative. Though Silver and Diminutia had presented Nevin with a form of leadership, he had never willingly accepted any power, and the triumvirate functioned as such. Since

Balfourd's Bounty, however, Nevin had been uncharacteristically dictatorial. Not in a mean-spirited way, Silver thought; it was just so alien to him and Diminutia, who was so laid back that crows would eat crumbs from his chest as he clucked to them. And now Nevin drew a parallel between the thieves and the wizards? Could he not see that the wizards had much more at their disposal to help those people than three ordinary men with a knack for acquiring what was otherwise not for barter?

"Silver?" Nevin asked. "I am used to that look from Bale, but you generally seem to have a greater facility for the language. Does the blank look mean that you agree and we can end this pointless discussion? All this clamoring saps my spirit."

"Um ... yeah, I guess. Hey, listen, Nevin. You don't look so good. Is everything all right?"

"Of course," Nevin mumbled dismissively. "But we have to find that stone. At first I figured this was all just a big joke, a silly distraction and a way to stretch our legs until we found a legitimate heist. It was not so long ago that we acquired this map. But it seems like a lifetime has passed. Can't you feel that, Silver? The world has changed, my friend, and probably not for the better. And those who fail to participate are lost."

"That's exactly my point: we did fail to participate in Balfourd's Bounty. We could have helped those people and ..."

"Silver, there is honor and chivalry in your conscience, and I admire that. Perhaps we could have saved two or three lives. But if we fail to find this stone, many *thousands* will die. It isn't about us matching wits with an ogre and his band of miscreants anymore."

"Nevin, those people were innocent and ..."

"In my experience," piped up Belhurst, appearing announced and uninvited, "innocence is not a label one tosses about arbitrarily. Most people are anonymous and unknown to us, but seldom are they innocent."

"What do you want?" Silver snapped.

Maintaining a patient tone, Belhurst answered, "It was not so long ago that I engaged in this very same argument with my peers, and I took a posture precisely as you have.

Then I was entrusted with the Shadow Stone. In a matter of moments, I had to adopt the same philosophy as Nevin. Since I could not dam the tide of events to come, I had to find a way to divert the floodwaters. It is not long before the deluge, Silver."

"Make no mistake, wizard, I am not like you, nor will I ever be. I am along for this adventure solely because my friends are," Silver said before turning his back to the wizard.

His head still slightly bowed, Nevin addressed the wizard without looking in his direction. "Before we begin anew in the morning, you should divulge the secrets of the stone that you carry. Forewarned is forearmed, after all."

The mage looked around the campsite. Night covered all, save the small portion interrupted by the embers of the dying fire. He gestured to the sleeping forms of their companions as they lay semi-obscured amidst the tall grass or behind boulders. "Perhaps we should sleep first and talk when our minds have more clarity."

"Insomnia is not a condition unique to you, wizard, and there will be no peace for me until I can still my restive mind."

"Very well," said Belhurst, casting glances all about him. "Ah," he exclaimed when he found a stick that was to his liking, and then gestured for the two thieves to join him. The spot he had chosen consisted of a patch of bare ground upon which he could draw mock maps, then cover them up with relative ease.

"We are here," he began, using a pebble to indicate the spot. "Beyond this copse of trees to our left is a large expanse of broken lands before the mountain range. Beyond the mountain range is The Scorched Sea. My best estimation is a journey of two nights, assuming the way is clear and we suffer no setbacks."

"Does that allow for that damnable cart of yours, or are you finally coming to your senses enough to leave it?" Silver asked.

"We can expect to pass through the rest of these lands with relative ease of movement. Though the land itself plays to our disadvantage, it is very conducive to sneak attacks," Belhurst continued, ignoring Silver's question. "I

believe it may behoove us to have you thieves scout
ahead."

Silver grunted and looked around. He disdained the
wizard too much to give him his undivided attention for
any period of time. But it was at this moment that a small
patch of the sky attracted his interest. It was a clear night,
and the stars were visible everywhere. Everywhere except
over Belhurst's left shoulder. With a double blink and a
quick rub of his eyes, Silver saw the stars return. Thinking
nothing more of the anomaly as his mind's reaction to his
ever-increasing anger, Silver let his thoughts fly. "Let us
review your plan. You and your crooked cronies wish to sit
back with your cart of great mystery, and even greater
uselessness, while us three set off to cross through The
Scorched Sea desert with 'relative ease' and clear safe
passage for you? Does that sum it up all tidy? Should we
escort you through Grimwell as well?" Silver shuddered
from the word "Grimwell" as soon as it passed over his lips
and the horrors that the town possessed.

Nevin's muscles tensed as if being cranked tighter by
his partner's very words. He bent his leg, allowing his heel
to dig into the ground, and shifted his weight, readying
himself to tackle Silver should this heated debate come to
blows. When Silver took an ill tone, such as he did with
Belhurst, his dagger never lurked far behind.

Belhurst took things one point at a time. "The cart is
hardly mysterious. And its usefulness will undoubtedly be
demonstrated before this adventure's end. The cart merely
holds special ingredients."

"Ingredients?" Silver emphasized his sarcasm with an
indignant snort. "I thought you were magicians, not chefs."

"*Wizards* and chefs are of similar ilk. However, every
piece of the world, every word made, every motion of our
bodies are all ingredients."

"My flatulence holds more meaning than your words! If
every word and motion and every*thing* is an ingredient,
than why am I not casting a spell now?" Silver mockingly
pulled a handful of grass from the ground and threw the
loose blades in the air. With all the drama of an actor
selling his performance to the balcony seats in a theater,
Silver flailed his arms about and wriggled his fingers. A

mild sense of discomfort washed through him, thinking his antics might have very well cast a spell, because the stars behind Belhurst's left shoulder had gone missing again.

Heaving a sigh that showed Silver was starting to grate his nerves, Belhurst explained his analogy. "Any fool can mix yeast, flour, and sugar into a bowl. But does that make it a pastry? Hardly. It takes training, skill, dedication to learn how to take the measured ingredients and mold them, to take separates and make a whole. And still it does not guarantee that it will be a good pastry, an edible pastry. That is the duty of the chef, the master."

Once again, Belhurst went unheard. Silver instead focused on the patch of black behind the wizard. It was difficult to distinguish black from midnight, but the area almost burned Silver's eyes as he stared at it. Then he blinked, and it was gone. The stars were back.

"I saw the fireball you used to destroy the spine snake, stopping it from ... ahh!" Nevin started, but a prick to the back of his neck interrupted him. Thinking it a mosquito, he reacted with a quick smack, but yielded nothing more than a sting.

"Something wrong?" Belhurst asked, the tone of his voice contained a trepidation unbefitting the situation. "What happened?"

"Mosquito," Nevin replied, examining his hand, wondering how he could have missed.

"Are you certain?"

Before Nevin could answer, Silver yelped as he ducked forward, surprised by tickles under each earlobe. His hand so close to the hilt, he brandished his dagger and sliced at the emptiness behind him. He missed. Growling, he said, "There was something behind me. Something ... touched ... me."

"Me as well," Nevin said.

Panic washed over Belhurst, hoping he did not know the answers to his questions, "What was it? Were you able to see anything?"

"I don't know what it was. I can't see anything," Silver replied.

As did Nevin, "I was stung, but I swatted no insect."

"Oh no," Belhurst mumbled. Unable to pull his gaze from the blackness of night, he stumbled back, his hands franticly searching to arouse his slumbering partners. "Not so soon. They're finding us faster. Our spells aren't keeping them at bay."

"Who, you daft old man?" Nevin asked.

"Nevin. Look. The sky …," Silver whispered. His words started as a shout, but trailed off as uncertainty and fear clogged his throat. He even tried to point, but his limbs had gone numb.

The stars disappeared, giving one final wink as they left, as fast as anyone could have noticed. The surrounding brush and bushes turned to fine ebon mist and thickened, black skeins unraveling to form a blanket of dark horror. The tree canopies turned to shadow and reached to each other, looking like a murder of ravens flapping blindly, merging into each other until all that could be seen was black.

"Manulittim!" broke the silence. There stood Follen, no longer a frail, twitchy, old man, but a diminutive warrior in drab clothing, his right hand on fire. Swinging his arm with the grace and precision of a swordsman, he used his flame ensconced hand to cut through the swarthy air. Undulating as if reeling in pain, the blackness pitched a spastic fit and retreated from the fire, everywhere the flame touched.

Belhurst launched his own attack. A practiced sentence and specific gestures turned the dying embers of the campfire into a raging inferno. The living darkness backed away more, but still surrounded all sides of the small, lit perimeter.

"What manner of madness is this? Please tell me I'm still asleep," Diminutia said, scrambling to his feet as fast as his body would allow. He ran over to his partners as they stood next to the campfire, now spewing impossibly large flames.

"As nightmarish as this may seem, this is real," Nevin replied. "Belhurst! What is happening?"

Ignoring the thief, Belhurst assisted Moxxen and Grymon with the cart, moving it closer to the protective fire. Once in place, Grymon clutched the contents of one of the drawers and whispered to his hand. He unfurled his fingers to expose worms, glowing with the cool, white light of the moon. They floated free from his hand into the air. Each spilt in half, then again, and again, dividing themselves with every heartbeat until they were a dissipating cloud of fine, luminescent sand. The darkness screamed and spiraled, unable to avoid the caustic touch of the glowing and growing nebula. The stars returned, unveiling the forest. The darkness tore itself asunder into many creatures the color of pitch, scurrying for cover, fleeing, or occasionally lashing out in desperate frustration, hoping to do some parting damage. They did.

Confused by the swirling madness, Moxxen lost his footing and stumbled too far from the campfire's protective embrace. An angry tendril of blackness latched onto the wizard's back. Tentacles bound his arms and squeezed his throat, forbidding him from using magical defenses. He opened his mouth, gasping for air, but the squirming blackness forced itself inside. Unable to resist, Moxxen swallowed the creature, ingesting it until it was no longer to be seen.

Belhurst and Grymon bellowed and wailed, remorseful at their loss. Follen extinguished his hand in mournful silence.

"What is going on?" Diminutia yelled. "One minute it's dark, and the next it was blacker than ... black, like the darkness was alive! Now everything's back to normal? And what in the name of all that is holy and unholy is happening to Moxxen?"

Nevin grabbed Diminutia's arm and gave a squeeze, letting his ignorant, human friend know he did not display the proper social grace. "We should let them grieve for their perished comrade, my oafish friend."

"Perished?" Diminutia asked. "But he's still moving."

Moxxen slowly writhed on the ground, black veins like calligraphy on his papery, ashen skin. His hacking gurgles brought unease to the thieves' stomachs.

Follen started to chant and gesture, while Grymon waved his arms and, despite his wooden leg, moved with the elegance of a dancer as he talked to the heavens. Belhurst would have joined them if not for the tip of

Silver's dagger. "Wizard, we want answers and we want them *now*!"

"Very well, you impatient dolt! We were attacked. Attacked by the demons sworn to protect the Shadow Stone, the stone we possess. They are creatures of a darkness none of you could possibly fathom. Fire burns their flesh worse than it would you, and bright lights cause them quite a bit of discomfort. And one such creature is attempting to possess Moxxen."

"Light? It's dawn soon. We simply leave him be and that's the end of that."

"The whole point of a demon possessing a human is for the benefits of the host body. In this case, protection from light."

"Nevin and I were both touched by these ... shadow demons before the ambush. Are we to share a similar fate?"

"No. Demons can only possess the tainted. We wizards have all touched the stone, you thieves have not ..."

Grymon and Follen chanted louder as Belhurst made one final sweeping gesture. The luminescent mist made from glowing worms to ward off the attackers congealed and funneled to a pinpoint right on the tip of Silver's dagger. When finished, the dagger glowed with a brightness a full moon would envy.

"You have bedeviled my dagger!" Silver yelled.

"No," Belhurst said. "Merely turned it into a useable weapon. Now drive it through Moxxen's chest."

"Are you daft? I hardly like you wizards, but I can't *murder* one of you!"

"You had that very tip to my throat seconds ago!"

"Yes, but you were infuriating. You kill him if the deed needs done so badly."

"I can't."

"Ha! Then why do you speak with me in disapproving tones when you can't bring yourself ..."

Belhurst cut him off by snatching the dagger from his hand. No sooner than he did, the glow faded to nothing. "*Your* blade is enchanted now. None here, save *you*, can use it."

Belhurst emphasized his point and expressed his contempt by giving it back, jamming the hilt into Silver's chest.

"So enchant another weapon!" Silver refused to lose this argument.

"The mist that fended off the other demons, and what enchants your blade, is ground moonworm, which we have just depleted."

Before Silver could admonish the wizard's lack of forethought, the sounds of snapping bone brought his attention back to Moxxen. Both of his legs twisted and stretched, flopping like eels on dry land. The possessed wizard rolled, his chest and face touched the ground while his ever-expanding legs continued to whip about.

"Do it, Silver," Nevin yelled, brandishing his own daggers even though he knew they would be of little use against whatever possessed Moxxen.

"Very well," Silver said, his face contorted with anger and disgust.

He approached with the dagger pointing down, ready to drive it through the possessed wizard's back. Moxxen's hands clawed at the dirt as if he tried to push himself up from the ground. The thief raised the dagger, but stopped, shocked to see the wizard's head turn all the way around to look at him. The brutal noises of muscle tearing and bone shattering froze Silver in his tracks. Just as he regained his senses, Silver thrust downward only to be stopped by a pair of gruesome, gnarled hands that formed from the wizard's elbows. One hand struck the dagger from Silver's grip; the other sent the thief flying backwards.

Black bile oozed from Moxxen's mouth as the demon inside commanded the husk to rise. And reshape. Bones were now merely sticks to add a loose frame to a child's kite. Moxxen's prominent ribcage expanded and pressed against the bubbling skin, forming a set of sideways jaws. Moxxen's legs divided and divided again, forming thick tentacles. Intrigued by the use of hands, the demon inside rearranged Moxxen's skeleton to create a dozen more pairs, gripping and snapping, jutting from makeshift arms all over his body.

Shouting erupted from all corners of the little camp as wizards and thieves slid slowly from disbelief into hysteria. Follen did his best to rush to Silver's aid, hobbling to stand over the fallen man, an incantation on his lips. Nevin noticed that Grymon had maneuvered himself in front Belhurst and did likewise.

Without taking his eyes off the ever-changing form of the erstwhile Moxxen, Nevin called back to Belhurst. "What now, wizard?"

"I'm not sure, Nevin."

"What do you mean ...?"

"This has never happened before. We always theorized that it might, but our discussions never evolved beyond the argumentative phase."

"That's just lovely," Nevin spat.

"Perhaps if we ..."

The thought hung uncompleted on the thick air of the night as the being that had been Moxxen began to rise. Twice as long as an ogre stands, the multi-armed monstrosity used its newly formed tentacles to lurch into motion and cover ground faster than anything bred for speed. It was on Follen quickly, and a casual back handed slap sent him flying through the air to land akimbo at Nevin's feet.

"Nevin!" Silver, who had just struggled to his feet, was snatched up in the air before he could turn to flee and thrown skyward by the beast as if he were an empty rucksack, his limbs flailing like unfastened shoulder straps. He landed in an outcropping of dense brush, bruised and barely conscious, but alive.

From the other side of the camp, Grymon gestured furiously. No sooner had his first invocation, a fan of searing flames that erupted from his fingertips, proved ineffective than he had begun a second spell, a torrent of jagged hail. To the wizard's chagrin, this attack proved equally fruitless. From behind him, Diminutia had produced a pair of wickedly sharp daggers that he hurled into the maelstrom of fire and ice. The demon, anticipating such attacks, had constructed a chitinous exoskeleton over its bulk so the blades menaced nothing more than the ground.

"Belhurst, we're in trouble here," Nevin yelled. Think, man!"

"Retrieve the enchanted dagger!"

"And you propose I do that how?"

"I will distract the creature. Get the dagger to Silver."

"Truly?"

"Go now, Nevin." That being said, Belhurst pushed the thief into action. Nevin stumbled toward the dagger while Belhurst called out to the creature.

"Creature of the abyss, I command you to return thence!"

"By what ... right ... do you ... claim ... dominion ... over me, mortal?" the monster growled, using Moxxen's mouth.

Belhurst drew forth the obsidian stone from the depths of his pocket and held it aloft.

"Ah, yes ... give ... it to me ..."

In a blur of motion, the creature covered the score of yards to the wizard's side. With similar celerity, Nevin raced across the campsite, scooping up the glowing dagger as he passed its resting place. Then he made a headlong dive at the prone form of Silver.

"Silver! Get up man!"

"Nevin!" Diminutia shouted from across the campsite. "Get a move on!"

Looping his arm under Silver's, Nevin struggled to get them both to their feet. Diminutia rushed to their collective side to lend his own support, the third leg of a tripod.

Across the way, the demon had taken Belhurst in hand and raised him a dozen feet off the ground. Another one of the beast's hands was near the wizard's temple. Four of the digits on the hand were retracting into its "skin" as the middle one elongated into a flesh and bone spear, its intention to lance him apparent even through the excessive drool formed by its cackling. Belhurst did his best to keep the beast fully focused on him with taunting words, but the creature gave him intermittent squeezes, making prolonged speech impossible. Though the stone in the wizard's left hand was clearly the object of its desire, the demon seemed quite intent on making the wizard suffer unto death.

"Silver," Nevin said, "can you stand on your own? You have to stab that thing."

"I can stand, but wobbly. And my vision is a tad blurred."

"Right. Follen, can you levitate us?"

No verbal response came, but within an instant Silver and Nevin, locked together by their limbs, began to rise. Diminutia drew his dagger and watched as his friends took flight. Unnerved by not being able to contribute, he stood ready, his eyes bouncing from the creature to his sky-bound comrades.

"Not too high now. The goal is to break the creature, not us," Nevin called down to Follen.

A wry smile crossed Follen's crooked mouth, but still he did not answer, focusing on the spell. When they were in position, a man's height above the center of the beast, Nevin whispered to Silver, "Aim well."

"As well as I can."

"I see ... you ... up there!" the creature moaned, eyes forming from bubbling sores on its back.

"Lovely," Silver muttered.

"It matters ... little. As you ... can see... I have ... the stone!"

"And as you can see, demon, you are mistaken," Belhurst said. Gasping, he uttered a phrase and flicked outward a black powder he had hidden in his other hand. The wizard's corpulence dissipated, his body turning into a fine mist that slipped through the demon's hands. Belhurst escaped, taking the stone with him.

Seeing that Belhurst's maneuver distracted the demon, Follen released the two floating thieves from his spell and allowed gravity to work its own magic. In an act of self-defense, Silver put his hands below himself, still holding onto the dagger. As he impacted with the creature, the blade buried itself deeply into its flesh, searing its way even deeper until it was lost from his grasp. Nevin wrestled with the flailing arms and tentacles, hoping to give Silver the time he needed. The demon's skin peeled away in a frothing boil everywhere the blade sliced. Acrid smoke and death cries filled the air as the demon twitched and bucked spasmodically for several minutes.

"Well then. That was certainly entertaining," Diminutia said after the creature delivered its last twitch.

"Not now, Dim," Nevin said. He walked over to the sullen trio of wizards and asked, "What is our next course of action?"

Without moving his eyes from the fell demon, once his friend, Belhurst replied, "First, allow my brethren and me a few moments to mourn. Then we will do what we can to cast more spells to hide the stone's presence from the shadow demons and continue our quest. Morning comes, so we have nothing to fear from them at the moment."

Nevin turned to the horizon to see the rising morning sun and wondered how his fate fit into the new day.

TEN

BOGOSH WAS commonly referred to as a "creature town"—a town whose population consisted of more nonhumans than humans. However, Bogosh was hardly the nightmarish image many cloistered humans might envision. Certainly, there were far fewer cobbled roads, and nary could a domicile be seen that was not in a state of ramshackle disrepair. But appearance was subjective. Instead of a home built from tinder and twigs with thatching for roof, many inhabitants found comfort in a hollowed out hill or knoll, topped by wild grasses and heather. Many other houses were thick, clay domes that had one opening to allow the owners and visitors to enter and a second opening in the roof to allow smoke to leave. The insulation of such a structure was far superior to wooden boxes pocked with joints and windows that made heat preservation during the depths of winter a losing battle.

Main streets were lined with posted oil lamps, just as any other town, maintained by those who were elected to do so. Orcs and goblins and trolls were neighbors not nightmares, offering what they could for the community, including smiles and courteous conversations when required. Compliments were given about the state of a yard, mud not grass, or the progress of a garden, thistle-berry not rose. For an observer who could see beyond the bitter rind to the sweet citrus it covered, it was plain to see life in Bogosh was no different than the town in which they themselves resided.

The populous of Bogosh was not restricted to creatures other than human. However, any human living in a creature town had neither the riches of royalty nor the beauty of fable characters. Those who received scoffs and jeers on the streets of human-only cities received comfort or anonymity in a creature town if they so inclined.

One such human was the bard. With the facial features of a sloppy boar, the Withered Wart Tavern was one of the few public establishments where his appearance would not catch a discerning eye. He spent more than a fortnight huddled in solitude at a table close to the tavern's main entrance, nursing many an ale. He had a tale to tell, yet could not seem to find the right audience. Those who needed to hear the tale had to be born of adventuresome stock, with the occasional proclivity to turn a blind eye to better moral judgment now and again. The tavern seemed the logical place to start. Unfortunately for the bard, many of the clientele had noble motivations, like hard work and family, none who might bend in the howling winds of temptation.

As fate would have it, just as the bard contemplated settling up his tab and turning in for the night to dream of traveling to the next town at sunrise, four creatures entered, cut from the very cloth he wished to embroider. He could sense it. More specifically, he could smell it. The bard was a very well-traveled man, it would be impossible to be a bard and not have seen much of the world, and he recognized that smell. These four had recently been to the Fecal Swamps.

Bale Pinkeye, the ogre, Pik Pox, the hobgoblin, Zot, the orc, and Phyllis Iphillus, the satyr, entered the tavern. All eyes turned toward them, but at the speed of smell, all noses turned away. A few nearby patrons placed the appropriate coin, with overly generous tip, on the table and scurried away from the foul miasmas surrounding the four. Never passing up a gifting opportunity, Bale and his cronies immediately sat at the table. Not only did the serving wench assigned to the table offer to forfeit claim to the coin, she tried to convince, then plead, then argue with the other wench to take the befouled customers. Two pixies happened to fly too close to Bale on their way out; their wings shriveled as if an invisible flame had melted them. After a precipitous fall to the floor, they supported each other as they staggered from the tavern the way two drunken loons would. However, their night would continue at the apothecary and end at the nearest abbey.

His hope renewed for finding someone to do his bidding; the bard listened with vigor to their conversation.

"The Fecal Swamps!" Bale moaned. "Damn those thieves! And those wizardy guys! We can find the Fecal Swamps well enough on our own without those guys sending us there!"

Being easily duped is exactly the characteristic I was hoping for, the bard thought, unable to halt a smirk from forming.

"Yeah, it's really not as funny as they think," Pik said. The consoling tones of his voice were lost on Bale. "How did those wizards know to send us there anyway?"

Wizards? Thieves? the bard thought. *Could it be?*

Thinking about Pik's comment, Bale tilted his head to one side, then tilted it to the other as if trying to drain water from inside his head. "I still say the thieves told them to do that! I don't trust them. Especially that Nevin."

Great fortune! The bard could barely contain himself. Taking a closer look at the motley group, the bard realized he knew this group. Or at least he had seen them before ... at the tavern with the thieves. *His* thieves!

Phyl placed his hand on Bale's forearm and did his best to console the ogre, "Bale, it didn't seem like Nevin or the others knew the wizards. I don't think they told the wizards anything. How could they?"

The ogre's eyes fixated on Phyl's hand. For the life of him, Bale could not figure out the purpose of the gesture. He was so confounded, that he did not hear a single word the satyr said. Bale abruptly stood, taking his forearm with him, and said, "I'm gonna get an ale."

Almost giddy, the bard bided his breath as the ogre approached the bar, needing to pass by his table first. Waiting, almost lurking, he sat as the ogre came closer.

Closer. Closer. And like a spider whose web just snared a fly, he sprung.

"Ho, dear ogre," the bard called to Bale.

Bale stopped midstride and looked about only to find a grinning bard sitting at a table. Unaware that he was the lone ogre in the tavern, Bale pointed to himself and mouthed the word, "Me?"

"None other," replied the bard.

"Oh, sorry," muttered Bale. "I thought you meant me," he concluded before turning away from the mongrel-looking human.

"Wait, mighty fellow. Yes, yes, I meant you! Why, no other within these confines possesses the skills and attributes I see manifest in you."

Bale began to pat at himself nervously. "I'm infested? Infested with what?" he exploded.

"No, no, my humorous friend. I mean you are exactly what I am looking for."

"Umm, yeah, well I have a friend named Phyl over there who might intermingle such an idea. Who would have thought my good looks would be a curse?"

"Please, my colossal companion, have a seat. You misunderstand me. Let me get you an ale while you listen to a proposition I have for you."

"I think I understand you perpetually well. You think I'm dumb, but I know well enough what it is to be propositioned. And I want no part of it!"

"*What?* No! No, no, no. I'm not propositioning you. I have a job for you."

"I'll bet you do ..."

"All I'm asking you to do is listen to a story while you drink a mug of ale that I bought for you."

"You bought me a mug of ale? Where is it?"

"We're waiting for the barkeep to bring it."

"In that case, I'll sit down. But you have to buy me as much as I can drink while you talk."

"Very well," agreed the bard, motioning to the barkeep to bring another round.

The barkeep, very familiar with ogres and more so with this ogre in particular, brought Bale a bowl brimming with ale, watered down to decrease potential future hostility or inebriated clumsiness. He had learned the hard way that an ogre-sized hand was capable of destroying every single glass in the establishment.

While the bard told his tale of a mad wizard and five magical stones, Bale consumed first one ale, then another. He pondered over the difference in flavor between the first two bowls and decided that a third was required to formulate a true hypothesis. The ogre philosopher, Inebrious Frequentous once said, "Never judge one's ale, until the final draught is drunk ... and you are, too."

Soon enough, the bard's words begin to swirl and eddy like the ale in Bale's bowl. Bale had even taken to shaking the bowl or perhaps it was merely the unsteadiness of his hands. Either way, he stared, bemused by the sloshing liquid thinking, smiling in the manner of a dolt whose one clever idea left him thinking that he, too, would one day be remembered as a great, Ogrish philosopher. So wrapped up in his own thoughts, which were saturated with ale, Bale took no notice to the bard nor the map he unveiled.

The bard unfurled the map on the table, using Bale's bowls as weights for the curled corners. "As the map shows," he continued his sales pitch to the ogre, "you have to travel to Mount Pyrous. Near the base on the south side is a cave. Inside the cave you will find the stone. However, it is guarded by a dragon who ..."

"Dragon!" Bale blurted, the word acting like ice water poured down his pants.

"You have a problem with dragons?"

"Well ... they are kind of big and scary."

"*You* are big and scary."

"But not that big and scary."

"Sure you are! You and your companions are the creatures that haunt dreams!"

"He dreams about us?"

"Who?"

"Pyrous."

"Pyrous?"

"The dragon. You said his name was Pyrous."

"I said he lives in a cave on Mount Pyrous!"

"Well, I'm sure they named the mountain after him, don't you think?"

"I highly doubt that. Now, when you get there you will ..."

"Then what's his name?"

"Name? How should I know?"

"So you've never met this dragon?"

"Met the dragon?"

"Yeah. You know, talk to him, share a pint or two ..."

"Talk to ...? No! Dragons don't talk! They are foul beasts born from the very depths of the worst hell imaginable, whose sole purpose is to dash the life out of others, wanting only to rend every creature limb from limb and feast upon their souls! Attempting to talk to a dragon is certain death!"

"*Certain death?*"

"Oh, you *can't* be scared!"

"I wasn't until you said talking to a dragon is certain death!"

"Well then, it's a good thing I'm not going to ask you to talk to the dragon."

"Pyrous?"

"Yes, Pyrous. I'm sure he's much nicer than the other dragons."

"You're sure? And you think ... what? Just talk to him about the weather and how much nicer his cave is than the Fecal Swamps and all that, and he'll just say, 'Hey, how 'bout you take this stone I have here?' Is that about how you figure it?"

"Well, I'm not positive, but that's about how I figure it, yes."

"Then why don't you do it? Take him a few bowls of ale, and poof! You get the stone."

"Yes, well, the thing is, I can't make a journey that far. Bad knee, I'm afraid. Happened to me when I was performing at an inn. I got so caught up in my own story that I fell off a table. Hasn't been right ever since."

"Hmm ... too bad. Well, this Pyrous sounds like a mighty nice dragon, but I don't think it's for me. I have strict schedules for eating and drinking and breathing. Plus, you never said what was in it for me. Do I keep the stone or what?"

"No, no. The stone would come to me. And in return I'll immortalize your courage in songs that shall be handed down from generation to generation."

"So I get the stone," Bale reasoned, "but I give it to you, and then you'll sing songs to tavern crowds and make lots of money. Hardly seems fair."

"Well, my impressive friend, did I mention to you that there is another group looking for a similar stone? A group with whom you are familiar, I believe. They have failed to update me on their progress, and so I must either assume the worst or that they are of weak moral integrity and absconded with the stone."

The bard forced a neat little smile to settle on his lips as he wondered if the ogre was really dumb enough to fall for this change in tactics.

"The worst? You mean Pyrous ate them?" Bale asked.

"No. No dragons for them, but a desert. The thing is, I believe the three fellows who were working on this for me are friends of yours."

Bale turned his attention to the table from whence he came, the current locale of Phyl, Zot, and Pik. "When did those three trolls have time?"

The bard shot a glance to the same table. "Trolls? What? No. No, no, no. Not *those* friends of yours. The other three. The thieves."

Realization splashed Bale in the face like a bag of used fish scales as he wrinkled his oversized nose. "You mean Nevin and Silver and Diminutia?"

"Yes."

"I *knew* they were looking for some kinda stone! This map is like the map they have."

"Exactly. One of the stones from my tale."

Bale's attention quickly diverted to the seat of the bard's chair. "I don't see any tail."

"My *story.*"

"A story about a tail?" Bale asked as his eyes returned above the table's top.

For each throb that slammed into his temples, the bard clenched his teeth harder. "Not tail. Tale! Story. Epic. Saga. Recounting of past events done in a melodic, yet dramatic, way."

Glassy and empty were Bale's eyes. His attention had been lost while trying to figure out why the bard said he had a tail when he clearly did not. "I like rattails. Put them in a pan for a bit and they crisp up real nice."

"Okay. Forget the tale. Forget tails completely."

"Even rattails?"

"Even rattails. Here. Let's look at the map again," the bard said, relieved to finally get to the point he was trying to make. However, during the exchange, his hands clenched the map from utter frustration, crushing the center of it. Hoping the ogre did not notice, he attempted to flatten the creases with his hands.

"Why's the map so wrinkled?" Bale asked.

"It's old."

Before the bard could continue, Pik had made his way over to see what kept Bale from rejoining his friends. "My, my, my. What have we here," he said as sly as a spider talking to a fly. "A map?"

"Yes," Bale said. "To one of the stones that Nevin and Silver and Dim are looking for."

"Really? And this bard is giving us the map to the stone ... why?"

"Because he's not as brave as we are. And he wants to make a story about us. But don't talk about his tail, he's very sensitive about that."

The hobgoblin's shallow eyes mixed with his disseminating smile sent a chill rippling down the bard's spine. Hobgoblins were noted for their mischief, and this one was no different. "Well, he doesn't seem like a creature born with a tail. Did you happen to get one by skimping on a story to a surly wizard? Bed and run from the wrong witch, perhaps?"

The bard slid his left hand to his waist to keep close tabs on his coin pouch. "I fear your brutish friend may have misinterpreted an ill-formed comment I made earlier. I have no tail."

"So, dear bard, you wish to give us a map to a very powerful stone? No fee?"

"None needed. I have a personal vendetta against the very same set of thieves you do. I have had past dealings with those miscreants and wish nothing but ill will toward them."

Pik's long fingers danced across the map, sliding from landmark to landmark. His face twitched and turned between recognition and confusion. "I believe this map is accurate in its assessment of the surrounding lands, but how can we be assured the end treasure is correct?"

"The only way you can truly be assured of that is when the thieves find the stone they quest for before you find the stone this map leads to ... but that would mean the thieves have shown you up. And I'm quite convinced that yours is the more capable group."

"Well, Bale, he has offered us quite a tribulation. It's a chance to outdo that miserable Nevin and his cronies. Maybe we can even send *them* to the Fecal Swamps! Shall we talk to Zot and Phyl to see what they think?"

Bale's eyes lit up as his hand patted his belly, waking it up to let it know that it will be filled soon. "Do tribulations have tails?"

"No," Pik and the bard yelled in unison.

Disappointed, Bale slouched his shoulders. His defeat was short lived when he finally remembered this tavern served food. Slamming his fist on the table, small splinters shooting from its legs, he demanded, "Bar wench! A plate of rattails!"

"Well," a raspy voice came from beneath the table's horizon. "I can't speak for Phyl, but I'm in."

Being the only one at the table surprised that a voice would be coming from under the table, the bard leaned over only to come face to face with a rotund orc, finger wiping under his nose. "Hi. I'm Zot."

Again feeling the need to check, the bard's hand covered his coin pouch as he said, "Greetings, friend Zot. You have arrived at the conclusion of the business deal between myself and your associates."

Zot responded with a phlegm-filled snort, followed by fanning his hand in front of his face. "From my angle, I can tell that you have no tail. However, I can also tell that you need to cut milks, creams, and cheeses from your diet."

The bard's cheeks flushed from unbridled rage more so than embarrassment. The effects of his teeth gritting could now be felt in the bridge of his nose. Now that Pik had the map, the bard felt an all but insurmountable urge to dash through the nearest door, or even window, to escape the calamity. "Yes, well, I appreciate third party confirmation that I do not have a tail and ..."

Fighting back his own bile, the bard stopped his sentence when the barmaid delivered a heaping plate of fried rattails. Many nightmares would seem like a summer day traipse through a field of flowers compared to the sight of Bale Pinkeye devouring a plate of fried rattails. All the pain in the bard's head now relocated to the pit of his stomach. Especially when that smell was replaced by the smell of unkempt and weathered animal fur.

Curious by the new stench, the bard turned his head to find the source. His quest was a short one as the navel of a satyr eclipsed everything else from the bard's vision.

"Why would anyone think you have a tail?" Phyl asked, standing next to the seated bard.

His body starting to reject his mind's commands to stay cordial, the bard jumped from his seat, almost tripping over Zot as the orc ambled out of the way.

"Demons of the Dark Pit!" the bard shouted. His outburst caused such a shock, four pairs of eyes locked onto the bard; even Bale paused mid-slurp. Feeling the heavy gazes, the bard reminded himself that they were dupes, challenging and trying dupes, but dupes nonetheless. "I apologize for my reaction. Our satyr friend here startled me."

"Actually," Pik said, "most people react far more dramatically when they meet Phyl—usually with a little more screaming. Or sometimes laughing."

"Is that supposed to be funny?" Phyl asked. "Because I sure find no humor in it," he said, putting his hand on his hip.

"No," Bale chimed in, half chewed chunks of rattail covering his chin, "But what is funny is you're the only person in the tavern with no pants on."

"I am a satyr. Satyrs don't wear pants. How many times must we go through this same argument before you understand?"

"I just think it's uncivil, that's all."

Upon Bale's comment, anyone within ear shot stopped mid-conversation to look at the creature who made such a proclamation; a creature who had traveled from the Fecal Swamps two times within as many weeks, with no bathing in between, whose fingers were halfway in his mouth, shoveling in his dinner as fast as they could while a steady stream of drool and ale flowed freely from the corners of his grease-glossed lips. "What are you all looking at?" was all he could ask.

Viewing this as an opportunity to make his exit, the bard began his farewells, "So, my new friends, do we have a deal?"

"We most certainly do," Pik replied.

Confused, Phyl chimed, "Wait. What deal?"

"We got a map to a dragon that has a powerful magic stone we're going to steal," Bale sputtered, smacking his lips and licking the last remnants of his meal from his fingers.

"Dragon! Don't I have a say in this little adventure we're about to go on?"

"No!" Bale, Pik, and Zot replied in unison.

Phyl folded his arms and flopped down in the chair the bard had recently departed. "Fine. When do we leave?"

Giving another mischievous smile, Pik said, "Well, since we have our bellies full of food and ale ..."

"... And rattails," Bale burped.

"... And rattails," Pik continued, "there's no time like the present. Especially since Nevin and his cronies are after a similar stone."

"B'ah! I spit on that pompous elf!" Zot yelled, punctuating his thought by spitting on the floor.

"Yeah!" Bale shouted, jumping to his feet. "I'm tired of them making us look stupid! Let's go!"

The bard watched in disbelief as all four creatures gave a raucous cheer, causing the patrons of the tavern to cheer along in similar fashion. He might as well have been invisible as Bale led his three friends out the door into the night-ensconced streets of Bogosh. And after watching Bale accidentally step in a pile of manure, the bard could only slap his hand against his forehead.

ELEVEN

DEARBORN WAS scared. She didn't know why, but she felt emptiness in the pit of her stomach. It certainly was not the situation, for she had been through much worse before, and although in a state of disarray, all control had yet to be lost. Yet, something felt missing. *Iderion*, she thought. *How did I allow that fool Haddaman distract me to the point of forgetting my training and separating myself from Iderion?*

It was a rare mission that he and she were not side-by-side. Iderion recruited her into the king's army the day he saw her refining her archery skills with a bale of hay behind her father's blacksmith shop. From there, she vaulted into the Elite Troop and quickly came to know Iderion, becoming his right hand, planning every mission side-by-side. Being separated from him on the battlefield felt like two lovers sleeping in separate beds. She was not without her own resources, though.

While searching for the general, she had encountered three more cloaked creatures from The Horde, laying waste to them with ease. But the manner of creatures disturbed her. A mix of kinds, the three she faced and finished were human, goblin, and were-creature of some sort. What motivation would force a variety of creatures together as a band of well-trained marauders? Was a life with Praeker Trieste so enticing?

THE DEVIL'S GRASP | 109

To her surprise, a cloaked attacker dropped from a low-hanging tree branch. His chest slammed into her shoulder, knocking her askew, but due to her size, she remained on her horse. She wedged her arm between their bodies and wrapped her fingers around his throat, holding his gnashing teeth at bay. Legs flailing, his body writhed like a beheaded snake as his gnarled hands clawed at her armor, driving her off balance. She hoped to keep from falling by twisting her body and pushing him as hard as she could, but it was not to be that easy. She managed to push him off the horse, but with vicious swipes, he grabbed her shoulder plate and entangled his other hand in her hair.

With a thud, she landed on him. He squealed like stuck pig as she leapt to her feet, hoping to get a sword from her horse to finish this madness. As he had done during his first assault, he kept her off balance, thrusting his entire body against her legs just as her hand missed her weapon. Again, she hit the ground with a thud. Moist dirt and dead leaves squished into her mouth and nose, the taste of muddied decay coated her tongue. She twisted and kicked wildly with both legs, but the creature moved with such speed that she did not land a solid blow. He scurried up her torso, his teeth and claws sought out her face and jugular. She jammed her forearm into his throat, fending off its frothing mouth as she would a rabid dog.

The creature had the beady black eyes and snout of a rodent. Foaming saliva sprayed from its mouth, splashing on Dearborn's cheeks and chin, as it barked and growled, chomping at her. Then as sudden as the batting of an eyelash, it stopped. The creature seized and shuddered as the tip of an arrow erupted from its forehead. A second arrow popped from its left eye, stopping just before piercing Dearborn's skin.

Frustrated from never having the upper hand of that battle, Dearborn tossed aside the carcass and stood, wiping from her face mud, mucus, and gore. She spat the dirt and leaves from her mouth, ready to spit venom at whomever had loosed the arrows that made her feel weak and unworthy to ride with the Elite Troop. But when she saw who, all she could muster was, "You?"

Oremethus stood tall and firm, like a hero from the epic poems Dearborn read as a girl. The setting sun behind him created a glow about his body and a bold shadow before him as if the heavens emphasized their proudest creation. He eased the tension from the cord and lowered his bow. Dearborn knew that if he had released the third arrow, it would have hit the same mark as the first two. Going all but unnoticed behind the crown prince stood two men of the Elite Troop, sentries sent along to scout ahead with the prince for protection.

"Your Highness! I ... I ...," Dearborn said, choking down the anger she felt toward herself.

As any good prince would, Oremethus said, "I am hardly king yet, Sergeant, so no need for that title. I am more concerned about how you fare?"

Dearborn continued to spit the foulness from her mouth, cursing the circumstance in which she must act so unseemly before a prince. "Save for my pride and an acrid taste, I am unharmed."

Grabbing the reins of Dearborn's horse, Oremethus led it to her. Turning to his own horse, he fished through his satchel until he found a ragged cloth. He tossed it to her and said, "Judging from what I stumbled upon, I'd say there was an ambush while I was away?"

After she mounted her steed, Dearborn made use of the rag to wipe away the mud and ichor. "Not quite. As we were making our way to Balford's Bounty we spied an odd caravan. Upon investigating, the civilian gave away our position ..."

"I believe it was that same civilian who saved your life." All eyes latched onto Haddaman as he walked toward the crown prince while Glindos and Barrett flanked him on their horses. "Right before you cast him off like a sweat-soaked shirt."

The tussle with the strange creature was less painful to Dearborn than Haddaman's words. Then the situation worsened when the booming voice of Iderion came from behind her, "Is this true, Sergeant?"

He seldom called her sergeant, and never with the angry tone she had just heard. She wished she could remove the bitter taste of his disappointment as she rubbed her tongue over the rag. "After our troops scattered,

I needed to evaluate the situation. The civilian's horse had been killed, and I felt keeping him with me would have slowed the process. I placed him in competent hands with Glindos and Barrett."

"This is true," Haddaman said. "And their competent hands proved their worth, rescuing me from the clutches of an attacker."

The forest chilled as the waning day sun set, but Dearborn felt her face set ablaze by all the men staring at her. Embarrassment. Anger. Shame. Fatigue. She so desperately wished that the creature's corpse could shake off death's shroud so she may release her fury upon it. She'd even settle for a few witness-free moments alone with Haddaman behind a large tree.

Iderion's glare wore heavier on Dearborn's shoulders than her armor as he commanded, "Sergeant, the civilian is now your full-time responsibility until mission's end."

Not even trying to contain his smugness, Haddaman joined Dearborn on her horse, smiling the whole time. Sitting behind her he whispered into her ear, "I see we are partners again."

Watching Iderion turn his attention to Oremethus, Dearborn replied, "I do not understand your motivations, but understand one thing, you are *not* my partner."

"Don't be ridiculous. Your company has been the highpoint of this adventure. Plus, you need someone to pick the leaves out of your hair," Haddaman said as his fingers went to work.

"Do not touch me, you worm."

"See, that would be an impossibility. Once we go to gallop, I will need to brace myself. And since there is no other option ..." Haddaman's haughty voice trailed off as his hands slipped around her waist.

For a fleeting moment Dearborn welcomed the idea of a man touching her so, since it had been far too many years since the last time one did. However, the thought of *this* man making such an intimate gesture stirred within her gut a disgust that rivaled the refuse pile of any slaughterhouse. Keeping a watchful eye on her superiors, she leaned forward and threw her elbow back, connecting with Haddaman's nose. She hardly had the leverage to do any real damage, but a mild sense of satisfaction skipped through her body when she heard him say, "OW! My nose is bleeding!"

Before Haddaman could demand the drama he so craved, Dearborn threw at his head the filth-soaked cloth she had just finished using. As Haddaman fought with his gag reflex, Dearborn warned, "If I hear one more word of this incident, I will be certain that rag will be the last thing you ever eat."

"Well, this is just wondrous. I can't tilt my head back without holding onto something, and I fear losing an eye if I try. Is there a strap we can arrange somehow or perhaps a braid to hold? This is really gushing. Were you chiseled from granite?"

"Enough, Haddaman," she hissed.

"You would make a handsome statue ..."

"I'm flesh and bone, Haddaman. Never again suggest that I am otherwise."

"You know, it's a compliment. You could accept it gracefully."

She drew in a large gulp of air so she could launch a hostile and wordy retort, but before she could begin, Oremethus ordered Glindos to sound the horn signaling his command to regroup. The sound was taken up by several other horns, and within moments the company was assembled for inspection.

Normally Dearborn would join Iderion in the task of examining the troops and making sure every member gave account of himself, but after their recent exchange, she settled back, her pride pricked and wounded as if she wandered through a briar patch of emotions. Iderion did not tarry for her, nor did he look to her. If he took notice of the breach of conduct, he gave no signal as he set himself to the task of inspection.

"Two lost, Crown Prince. I request a brief moment that we may honor their valor," the general said.

"Iderion, take the night. The troop is weary. I scouted a path that leads to a well-traveled road. It is not a long ride, and if we leave at dawn, we'll reach the road by mid-morning."

"With all due respect, my Prince, you took a considerable risk scouting ahead. It would be best if we press the advantage immediately. We will be ready to ride before an hourglass would need turning."

"Very well. There is no need for a disagreement in front of the men, General. I'll take your counsel to heart. But there are three officers present, so we should vote and let the majority rule. Sergeant, what are your thoughts?"

Dearborn had been so engrossed in her own displeasure that it did not register at first that she was being addressed. Haddaman, not wishing to miss an opportunity to create indebtedness, roused her with a quick jab of his fingers to her ribs, then whispered the prince's question into her ear.

"If we stay, my lord, the loss becomes stigma. We are well prepared to ride onwards. And we will benefit from better ground upon which to throw our bedrolls."

Oremethus held her in his gaze for a long moment. Dearborn knew without doubt that he had included her in the decision to restore her confidence and save face with Iderion. Dearborn did not look away from his gaze, signaling her thanks.

"Consider it settled then. Take a few minutes to honor the fallen, then prepare to move." Oremethus moved off towards a small cluster of men who had taken up a prayer for the fallen. The man who led the prayer faltered at the prince's approach, unsure if he should allow the prince to take the lead, but Oremethus flashed him a quick gesture to continue talking as he found an unobtrusive spot in the back of the group.

Dearborn entertained the idea of broaching the subject of their journey with Iderion to assure herself that they were back on stable ground. But as she was about to urge her horse into motion, a phlegm-filled cough from Haddaman reminded her of his unwanted company.

Twenty feet away, Iderion sat impassively atop his horse, a roan that was massive in its own right, a head higher than her own mare. She pitied the beast as she watched its muscles jerk in reaction to the strain of Iderion's bulk. The thought filled her with a longing to feel his full weight atop her, crushing her down into a soft pile of leaves—pinning her back into a bed swathed with soft linens and pillows …

"So, you suggested that we move on?" Haddaman's voice was a clarion against the stillness of a serene night. "It's always been my experience that a thick forest offers a little more in the way of concealment than an open plain. Not to mention protection from the elements. You are exposing us to who knows what. Do you choose this path because it is wise to bridge the chasm between yourself and your superior?"

"Haddaman, *you* are the chasm between me and Iderion. Still your tongue—swallow it if you must—but do not interrupt my period of bereavement again."

"You call this grieving? You haven't even gotten off your horse!"

"Once again, you are my tether, Haddaman."

"There is no weakness in grief, Dearborn. You are like no woman I have ever known."

"Enough," she said with undisguised severity. "Now hold your tongue, or I'll help you to bite it off. We ride in silence."

Dearborn busied herself with tightening the flaps to her saddlebags and running through mental checklists of supplies. When it was time to make camp, she wanted to be prepared.

She could not see his face, but she imagined Haddaman smiling. Though he was not physically threatening, his mental perspicacity was sharpened to predatory precision. His insidious nature made him just smart enough to be dangerous. She could imagine him as capable of even the worst sort of betrayal, while being cunning enough to assume an innocent posture in the aftermath. She shivered as she tried to push his image out of her mind.

From behind Dearborn, Haddaman scanned his companions as they saw to last minute preparations. Despite, or perhaps because of, their recent display of fighting prowess, he felt that he could have done far worse for himself. If nothing else, he rode with a score or more of other potential targets. Yes, he thought, his odds of survival had vastly improved since his rescue from the cellar and those abhorrent scorpions. Just the thought made his very skin crawl, and he gave a slight shudder.

With an effort, Haddaman stilled himself and drew his thoughts back to the requirements of the present. He still had not quite figured out how to brace himself against the dual powers of inertia and gravity once the horse leaped into motion, but he was pretty convinced that holding onto Dearborn was not an open option. He resolved himself to the notion that he would have to lean back and hold the saddle as they rode, knowing full well that his reward would include pinched fingers and strained shoulders, but it could not be helped. Some precautions were necessary. Survival was often a fickle notion that alternated like the sides of a spinning coin.

Dearborn felt him shiver behind her. She noticed for the first time the slight chill in the air. *Good*, she thought, *let him be uncomfortable and catch a mighty cold.*

Dearborn tapped her heels against her steed's sides, readying it to move as she saw her comrades finish their prayers. She listened to Iderion as he barked out orders and announced plans, soaking in his every word with her entire body. As smooth as silk against satin, the Elite Troop reformed its caravan, this time with Dearborn taking rear flank and noticing that Iderion made no gesture for her to join him at the front, not even a stray glance back. She sighed with her whole body, not even caring how obvious she made her feelings in front of Haddaman, and settled into her mount. A rough and winding road lay before her, physically, mentally, and emotionally.

Twelve

NO LONGER DID the word "lines" sufficiently describe the deep furrows that assailed the face of King Theomann. They were trenches that stress had dug into his flesh. Though his father smiled at seeing him return, the effects of the strain were rapidly aging the king. This worried Perciless.

"Father, please forgive me if this seems pessimistic, but are you well?" Perciless asked. "Though your first concern is undoubtedly for your kingdom and your people, it would not do for them to be suddenly without a king."

King Theomann chuckled. "Perciless, I may never have raised my family in an overly religious fashion, but I certainly never gave any of you cause to fret over the natural cycle of mortality. Your mother died when you were but a year old. You were taught to mourn out of respect and to move on out of pragmatism. This is the way of things. The people will always have a king, so it is only right that they be my primary concern."

"Does kinship really bear such little meaning to you?"

"Do not mock my teachings. You know what my sons mean to me. You three are all I have left of your mother, especially Daedalus, whom she died bearing. I've often thought that part of her lives on in him. No more of this talk now, Perciless. Have you done as I asked of you?"

"Yes, Father. I have met with the logistics officers at the army camps by the border and scripted their needs. Tomorrow I shall meet with the craftsmen and see to it that they are able to supply the army with the required goods in a timely manner. I'm sure I'll need to assuage one or two ..."

"Well if anyone is more capable of persuasiveness than you, dear Brother, I'd be hard pressed to finger the individual," Daedalus said as he entered the room with the stealth of light breeze, startling both Theomann and Perciless. His words oozed thick and sugary, clinging to anyone who listened like molasses on sweetbread. "Is there any assistance that I might offer to you in your ... task ... what was it again?"

"Daedalus, dear boy, you have errands of your own to run. Perciless is quite capable of handling his own affairs," Theomann said while reviewing the requisition order he intended to give to Perciless.

"Father, never would I suggest otherwise. I merely wish to extend the additional vitality that my youth offers and ..."

"This is not the time for a family moment, Daedalus. There are matters of kingdom security ..."

As the praying mantis seeks to attack the soft underside of its prey, thus Daedalus sought out the weak spot in his brother's nature. "And since we are the ruling family of said kingdom, then any discussion we have collectively serves as both family time and kingdom security. Is this not necessarily so, Perciless?"

"Daedalus, I ..." Perciless spoke with difficulty; conflicting loyalties created a lump in his throat, making speech difficult. He did not want to offend his brother, but neither did he desire to disobey his father. Perciless, of all the members of the noble family, wished to appease everyone.

"Enough, Daedalus," Theomann said with a weary sigh. "I must insist that these meetings be held privately. Please retire to your chambers until your appointed meeting time. If you prefer, I can have Seneschal Wainwright or Chamberlain Joudry notify you at the appropriate hour."

"Thank you ... sire ... but no. I feel that telling time is well within my realm of capabilities. Until then, Your Majesty. Prince-Brother, good day to you as well."

With a halfhearted bow suggesting a disgruntled nature, Daedalus turned on his heel and strode from the room. Perciless watched him retreat from the room before turning his attention back to his father. He noticed the king shoot a dismissive glance after Daedalus, but the look he received had become much more scrutinizing.

"I wonder, Perciless," King Theomann said, "if your head completely rules your actions."

His father's eyes seemed cold and empty to Perciless. There was no familiarity in that gaze, only recognition. *Was this truly what it meant to be king?* Perciless wondered. At moments like this, Perciless thanked fate that Oremethus stood between him and the throne. He had never been as close to his older brother as he had been to his younger one, despite Daedalus's inveighing manner.

"Father, the commanders have requested a large number of goods. Will we issue credit to the craftsmen or pay them in coin?" Perciless asked.

"More than likely we will need to levy a tax on the landowners to keep the coffers from being depleted. And since the arms are for the good of the kingdom, we will request them at lower than standard price."

"Forgive me, Father, but if we levy a tax on the landowners, won't they only pass it on to the peasants? What of them? Will they not go hungry? Surely there is enough in the treasury to cover our needs."

"What good is food to a peasant who is not alive to eat it? A little discomfort is acceptable to ensure their safety. And we must do what we can to keep the treasury reserves high. We may pray that no war happens between Tsinel, but if it does, our prayers will do little good against their armies."

"If Oremethus is successful and no war happens, will we make restitution to the people?"

King Theomann pondered his son's question as he rolled the weapons requisition order parchment. He frowned as he poured a dollop of wax to seal the overlap and sighed as he pressed it with his insignia. "Perhaps. Perhaps not. One must always plan for the future. The people of this kingdom accept our rule, and they accept our judgment. They have prospered under the hand of our family, and now it is only just that they pay for that. Our goal is to see not only the kingdom survive this threat, but also for the untold misfortunes of the next several

THE DEVIL'S GRASP | 119

centuries. You have your mother's capacity for caring. Empathy is a wonderful quality, but you must show concern for the kingdom as a whole. To care for every individual is the concern of a priest, not a prince."

"Father, have I not completed what tasks you laid before me? Whatever my thoughts, I have always fulfilled my responsibility to the kingdom."

The king looked at the prince; he found both fault and perfection within the young man. He knew Perciless wanted to please everyone, but he could never seem to grasp that a horse could not be both racer and worker. Once more, the sigh of a frustrated father passed over his lips as he handed his son the sealed and stamped requisition order. "You have fulfilled your duties adequately, Perciless. Here are the requisition papers, and I know you will perform this delivery duty as well. It is obvious your studies go well, but I would see you spend more time on logic and critical thinking. You are several seasons too soft to rule, Perciless. In the meantime, I thank the gods for Oremethus's lack of naiveté. He will see our kingdom through these difficult times should it be required of him. I am tired now, Perciless. Leave me to my tasks so you may do yours. Think on what I have told you, and decide where your future lies. I have tried to be a good father to you, but I must always be your king first and foremost."

"I understand. As you wish, Father," the frustrated prince mumbled as he left the chamber, giving nary a glance back to his father.

Perciless fidgeted with the requisition order, knowing very well he would not complete his mission in its entirety. He strode down the stone hallway, stepping with alacrity, hoping to flee from the chills running down his spine. He knew he was being watched, could feel the eyes on him, throttling him like a cloak tied too tight. Then he saw the lone figure emerge from a shadowed alcove, his brother Daedalus.

"All goes well, Brother?" Daedalus asked, stepping into the light.

"As well as expected," Perciless replied.

"Very good. I see you're carrying the current weapons requisition order. Shall I assist you in this matter again?"

Perciless sighed, hating to break a direct order from the king. However, he hated to see his brother cast from governmental operations so often. Did the king want to protect the youngest of the brothers? Or did he simply not trust him? Either way, Perciless had never seen any justification for such treatment. Yet, he feigned protest, "You know, Daedalus, our father gave the task specifically to me."

"As he did the time before, and the time before that, and all the times since he entrusted you with the duty. Have I not delivered the order to the shops in a timely manner? Do the weapons not get made for our troops?"

"Well, yes, but ..."

"Perciless, I consider myself a self-aware individual. I know I should love the peasants as you do, but I don't. I find them dirty and unappealing, yet you revel in their company. I respect that and admire your ability to be so at ease with them. Father continues to burden them under taxation without satisfactory reasons, then sends a daft squire now and again to give reasons that are far too curt and fancy for their tastes."

"Daedalus, I ..."

"It is *you* who quell them, *you* who explains to them why they do what they must. You walking among them for a half day can do more good than ten squires in ten days. The more time you spend doing menial tasks such as delivering supply orders and routine communications with the army, the less time you can spend supporting the back bone of the kingdom—its people. That task is meant for you. The tasks of delivery and memorandum composition are for me."

Another sigh preceded Perciless's wry smile. "I cannot argue with such logic. Your wisdom surpasses your years, Daedalus."

"If only Father could see as such," Daedalus replied, accepting the sealed parchment from his older brother.

"I trust one day he will," Perciless said with confidence as he started back down the hall. "One day he will."

"Oh, he will, dear Brother, he will," Daedalus mumbled to himself on his way to his room. "As I plunge my dagger into his heart, he will know how much he truly underestimated me."

Once alone in his quarters, Daedalus cracked the wax seal and then crushed it in his hand, giving only minor relief from his frustrations. He then placed the wax pieces in the melting spoon cradled over a lit candle on his worktable. With the skill of an expert calligrapher, he changed the numbers on the work order, upping the quantity of every weapon listed, as well as the "Duty for the State" discount, keeping the bottom line the same. No extra coin from the kingly coffer would be needed.

Feeling more of a sense of duty to the monster known as Praeker Trieste than to his own father, Daedalus re-rolled the scroll and reused the wax from the melting spoon to reseal the order. From a secret drawer he grabbed the king's insignia and used it to stamp the warm wax. He chuckled to himself as he thought about how easy it was to steal it and convince the aged king that he misplaced it, having the smith produce another. Daedalus then laughed, for he had to pull the same scheme twice since he, himself, misplaced the first one he stole months ago.

Satisfied that his work would fool even the most stringent auditor, Daedalus exited his room, back to the task at hand. Until the walls wobbled and evaporated, the floor refused to remain flat, rippling like waves in a pond. The fires in the urns dimmed then brightened until they burned with the intensity of the noon-high sun ...

... The castle was gone, and he was outside. He looked around to see his brother Perciless at age twelve standing next to him in the fenced horse-training yard by the royal animal pens. The clucking of chickens, snorting of pigs, and the occasional cow mooing unnerved him. Then the smell. The smell that sent a constant churning through his stomach, the odor of baking animal waste. Daedalus remembered this day all too well.

Pendrick led two unbridled horses to Daedalus and Perciless. On the ground next to their feet were saddles and reins.

"Boys," Pendrick started, "Your father wants you two to learn about your horses. Riding them and taking care of them. Saddle up your mounts and ride them for four laps. The only rule is no helping each other. At all, for any reason."

Wanting to be any place other than there, Daedalus's eleven-year-old mind went off on its own tangents, leaving him to forget a buckle and improperly harness the saddle. His focus returned once he mounted the steed and gazed upon his observers. Peasant farmhands took pause from their chores, smitten with the visions of the two princes. Showing all the grandeur he could muster, Daedalus sat straight, stretching his spine to its fullest, competing for height against his older brother who rode next to him.

Among the observers were his sibling-cousins Tallon and Tallia, receiving training of their own. Daedalus looked down upon them as he passed by; they looked up and waved. They were where they belonged, beneath him, down with the peasants. However, the suns did seem to shine more brightly upon Tallia than any other. Even at such a young age, she was radiant.

But his superiority was short-lived, and his lack of dedication to doing a job proper caught him off guard. His shoddy strap work gave way, and with one less buckle there was nothing to stop the saddle from sliding off. Surprised by the shift, slow at first, Daedalus panicked and froze—his only action a look to his brother for help. Perciless watched, and out of reflex started to extend his hand, but quickly withdrew it, remembering Pendrick's rule forbidding assistance. Thanks to Perciless's inability to do anything but follow every rule to the dotted i and crossed t, Daedalus's saddle continued to slide, forcing him to fall victim to gravity's devilish prank.

Stone stiff, Daedalus fell, his ribs absorbing the force of contact with the wooden beam of the fence separating the riding yard from the pigs' pen. As fate would have it, there was sufficient momentum to flip Daedalus over the fence, landing him feet first into pig slop. That made the crowd gasp. But the windmilling actions of his arms and a face-first fall made the crowd laugh.

Fresh feces and rotten vegetables splashed his face, squishing up his nose and oozing into his mouth. His stomach's reaction to expel his breakfast was immediate. With spastic haste, Daedalus jumped to his feet and discovered his left ankle and right knee were not working as they should, sending him to his back, still deep in slop. The crowd laughed again.

There he lay, seeing nothing but bright-blue sky. He heard them laugh. And laugh. And laugh. His right leg throbbed hot while a deep shooting pain numbed his left foot. His ribs hurt, feeling as though a dagger stabbed his side with every breath. He couldn't move, his will to do so buried even deeper in the muck than he. But he still heard the laughter. His tears, the only hope to wipe away the filth, flowed down his cheeks.

After proper medical attention and much bathing, Daedalus was bed ridden from the myriad diseases he contracted from ingesting animal filth. For three days in a row no food stayed down, his stomach rejecting everything that touched it. His heaving fits would last an hour, painful and unyielding, made worse from the constant torment of a fractured rib. Five days following, his stomach no longer rejected the food, however, nature's natural process had been accelerated, forcing Daedalus to relieve himself every few hours, accompanied by the same abdominal contractions and the same hatred from his cracked rib.

His only joy came at the suffering of his cousins. They partook in the laughter during the incident, and that indecent action was simply not tolerated from royalty. As punishment, they aided in the attempts to comfort Daedalus. Tallon brought his food during his time in bed care, and cleaned up any messes the diseases forced Daedalus to make. Tallia assisted the nursemaids, even for his daily sponge bath. There was one reason why Daedalus fought so hard through sleepless nights of sweats, chills, and cramping to make it to the morn—to see Tallia, his angel, as he called her during his dire time of need. Every swipe of the cold, wet cloth over his burning body wiped away the pain, the misery. And he begged for the cloth to slip from her hand, for her bare fingers to brush across his skin. He begged for her touch. Her touch ... her touch ...

... Her touch brought Daedalus back to the present, huddled on the cold castle floor, his skin blistering hot.

"Cousin, you're having another attack!" Tallon yelled.

As the interior of the castle fully reformed into sharp, vivid clarity, Daedalus regained his wits. His eyes focused on Tallia's face as he savored the touch of her palm against his forehead.

"You're feverish," Tallia said.

A smile slid across Daedalus's face as he whispered, "My angel."

As if having a debilitating vision of her own, her mood darkened. She jolted to her feet, wrapping her arms about her, trying to fend off the invasive chill of her cousin's words.

"Daedalus?" Tallon asked, shaking him now.

Daedalus's face soured, a bitter tingle formed in the back of his throat as his eyes slid from Tallia to his shoulder, Tallon's sullying hand. As fluid as an acrobat, Daedalus smacked Tallon's hand away and arose. "Touch me again, and I shall wear your severed hand upon a chain around my neck!"

"I meant no offense, Cousin," Tallon said with a slight grimace, remembering all too well the punishments that Daedalus had meted out to him for both real and imagined slights. He had no desire to clean up after anyone or anything. Nor did he desire another false mission in the Fecal Swamps. But neither could he swallow the rising gorge of his indignation. "It was merely my overwhelming concern for your safety that prompted me to such action."

"And I should be grateful, I know; however, there is still the matter of your diction. You are my cousin." Daedalus, after pulling himself upright, indicated Tallon by stabbing his first two fingers like ersatz daggers. "I," he continued, patting himself on the chest with the selfsame digits, "am your prince. It's not difficult, so try to use what nobility runs through your veins and remember the proper terms for our relationship from now on."

"As you say, Prince Daedalus," Tallon said, his words grinding through gritted teeth.

"Good. And what of you, dear Cousin?" his voice softening as he spoke to Tallia. "Why do you shrink back amongst the shadows like a specter?"

"It is nothing," Tallia lied. Although there had been several times when she could have been counted as Tallon's accomplice in acts for which he had been punished, Daedalus had never ordered her to suffer anything more than his presence. But the blistering touch of his feverish skin was not something she cherished; the touch of his fingers left trails of disgust running across her skin. Despite myriad baths, she could still feel their tracks as though they had eroded chasms into her flesh. "I am merely taken aback at the frequency and the severity of these attacks. Have you seen a doctor?"

"I have no need of medical attention, dear Cousin. At least not while you're around. Fresh air travels with you to clear my thoughts and purge the pestilence in my mind." Daedalus regarded Tallia with eyes that threatened to absorb her. She was part of the bounty of this land and, in due time, he would have her in the same manner that his father demanded taxes of the peasants.

"Daedalus," Tallon began while casting furtive glances down the various hallways of the castle. "Pendrick is due to be making his rounds shortly ..."

"We should continue this somewhere more comfortable," Daedalus replied, his eyes never leaving Tallia. "As these are matters of the state, we can retire to my private chambers. It won't take long, so, Tallon, you can stand in the antechamber."

The prince's rooms never displayed a dearth of decorations, though they were ever changing. Daedalus constantly rearranged things to foil would-be assailants, hoping that a replanted divan or a newly nested plant pot would catch an unsuspecting foot should he ever find his life endangered. Tallia considered his tastes gaudy and rarely took notice of the fineries strewn about her, though she did notice the small gilt cages that stood against the far wall. That they contained some exotic creature she had no doubt, but her eyesight failed to penetrate the darkness of the corner where they rested.

When they reached his innermost sanctum, Daedalus offered Tallia a chair by pulling it out from the engraved table and turned it to face her general direction. The chair was made of a dark wood and bore elaborate engravings beneath the heavy padding of multiple cushions, made from the finest silks and brocade. He paced over to a small table and poured them each a goblet of pure wine. Though the descendants of many a monarchy insisted on a watered-down version to keep their mind from clouding, Daedalus relied on his brooding hatred to filter out the intoxicants.

"You should know by now that you needn't go through such efforts for a simple exchange," Tallia said as she stared at the full wine glass.

"No effort," he replied. "I'd be lying if I said I didn't enjoy some time for other pursuits."

To be polite, Tallia sipped a swallow of wine. Then as casual as a serpent, she slid her hand over the sealed weapons order. "Well, I hate to bare bad tidings, but Tallon and I must be on our way, so I'll just take the order ..."

As if springing a trap, Daedalus's hand clapped onto hers. "What plans could you two possibly have that would be more important or ... desirable?"

His touch cut an icy swath of disgust that started from her hand and ended in between her legs. His words covered her like soured vinegar. His coveting desire was obvious. But if she could keep her senses under control, as well as the bile in her stomach down, she could use it to her advantage.

With a slight lean forward, she saw his gaze fall from her face to her cleavage. She could not help herself from thinking back to the last time she pulled such a stunt; three months ago she distracted him in the same manner to steal the king's seal that he had stolen from his father.

"Nothing's more important than desire," she whispered, certain to allow her hot breath to massage his cheek.

Suppressing a shiver, she felt his hand on her knee; her cue to tighten her grip on the weapons order. As he opened his mouth to spew more filth, she stopped him by standing abruptly with weapons order in hand. "But ... even though we are neither prince nor princess, we *are* still royalty. And as such, we *do* have various duties to perform. Lest you wish us to forego those duties and give your name as the reason?"

Daedalus's scowl was answer enough for Tallia.

"Very well then, dear Cousin. Nay ... Prince," she continued. "We shall do your bidding and deliver the order to the Craftsman Guild. Good day."

She gave one glance back, feigning flirtation; she could hardly wait to crack the seal and change the weapons order.

THIRTEEN

"NO MORE," complained Phyl. "No more walking. For days on end we do nothing but walk. My hooves are killing me."

Phyl rested against a young spruce tree sprouting awkwardly from the mossy dirt. He looked back at where he and his friends came, down to the base of the mountain, lush with steep, meadowy runs to expansive, rock plateaus, only to climb through trees and brush to get to the next plateau.

"Shut up, and keep moving," wheezed Bale. "We have a chance to win. I want to see Nevin make that twisted, confused elf face that means 'you guys win' when we make him say, 'you guys win.'"

"These rocks are murder on my hoof polish. And my knees hurt from all this hopping. And I haven't ..."

"Shut up, Phyl," snorted Zot, emphasizing his disgust with expectoration.

"Fine!" said Bale. "Phyl, set up camp."

"We're stopping?" asked Zot.

"No, he's stopping."

"Wait, what do you mean I'm stopping?" asked Phyl.

"The bedroll's open, but the bugs are all dead, aren't they?" Bale mumbled to Pik as he jammed his meaty elbow into the hobgoblin's bony arm.

Agitated that the bumbling ogre all but knocked him off his feet, Pik hissed, "What?"

"I mean he's not too bright," Bale explained.

"How is anyone supposed to get that meaning?" asked Pik.

"Shut up! If you pay attention, it's obvious."

"Obvious to you, maybe, because you said it."

"Excuse me! What do you mean I'm stopping?" Phyl tried to interrupt.

"No," Bale continued with Pik, "I understood it because I pay attention."

"Bale!" Phyl yelled, stomping his hoof. "What do you mean by 'he's stopping'?"

"When are the rest of us stopping?" Zot could never pass up a chance to add to a confounding situation.

Bale sighed and pinched the bridge of his nose. He didn't know why he did such an act, but he had seen other smart people do it when confounded. "Phyl stops here, because he's complaining. The rest of us stop when we get there."

"Where exactly is there?" Pik asked. "And how do we know when we get there?"

"We'll know when we're there!"

"Ah! That's what I was afraid of. You have no idea where we are. Do you even know where the map is?"

"Of course I know where the map is. It's somewhere safe."

"Uh-huh. Bale, where's the map?"

"I, uh, it's all right here," Bale said, tapping his temple with his warped forefinger.

"Yes, but where is the *actual* map?"

"Well ... wait ... why do you wanna know?"

"Why won't you tell?"

"It's a secret ..."

"Bale!" screamed Phyl, his face puffed and wreathed in a shade of vermilion that he would have thought to be rather suiting had he the ability to see how fabulous it made him look. "Why am I stopping?"

"You wanted to stop!"

"Not by myself, I didn't"

"Shut up, Phyl!" yelled Pik. "Bale can barely hold one conversation, let alone two."

"I think I did quite well, actually. I talked to both of you while telling neither of you nothing!" At this, the ogre thumped his pride-swollen chest with one of his fists. "Since you all want to stare at me open-mouthed instead of hiking, then why don't we set up camp under those trees? It's hot here and those trees make good shade. Pik, the map is safe. It's ... well ... anyway ... the map is safe. Now, I'll go look around at those mountains and see if I can figure out where we should go from here."

After his speech, Bale stared at the other members of his monstrous troupe with his eyebrows peaked. The other nonhumans shifted from side to side while they tried to get their minds around the incomprehensible clarity from such an unlikely source as their ogre leader. As was befitting his race, Pik was the first to recover his wits. "Bale, I think I speak on behalf of the entire group when I say that we apologize humbly for any instance where we may have been condescending towards you."

Ever the quick wit himself, Bale responded with the trademark alacrity for which he was known. "Pik ... I ... uhhh ... what were we talking about?"

And with that, life changed from surreal back to normal for the little group. Those charged with the task of setting up camp set about passing their individual tasks onto the members who were lower in the group hierarchy.

Bale dropped his pack, large enough to hide a small family. Zot and Pik each had a pack as well, complete with bedrolls, a tent, and half-a-day's supply of jerky. Phyl had been relegated to carry the cooking pots and pans, since he demanded that he needed each and every one of them to cook properly. He also seemed to be the only one who could figure out the proper way to return them to the bag, or the only one fastidious enough to care about such things.

"Zot, take this bag and set up the tent," Pik ordered.

"Zot do this. Zot do that," the hunchback orc mumbled. "One of these days, hobgoblin ... Phyl, grab this bag and set up the tent while I find the frying pan."

Phyl huffed, "Why do you need the frying pan right this second? Why can't you help me out? You never help ..."

"Zot help Phyl," chastised Pik.

"You help Phyl."

"Somebody better get over here and help me," Phyl whined. "I'm sick of always having to do it all. Zot, stop making a mess. Look at yourself! You're dumping stuff all over the ground."

Zot slammed the frying pan to the ground. "You pick it up, Phyl. Pik stop looking at me like that ..."

"Pik, come over here and give me a hand with this tent."

"Phyl, I'm not helping you do anything. I'm busy over here getting some wood for a fire."

"A fire! It's summer, you dolt. And those sticks you are picking up are nothing more than kindling. You're just being lazy."

"Lazy? I'll show you lazy," shouted the hobgoblin as he began to throw sticks at the satyr.

Sneaking in from around the other side, Zot had a finger full of nose secretion and reached for one of Pik's shoes as Bale watched dumbfounded, more dumbfounded than his usual state.

"Um, I'm gonna go ... oh, forget it." With a wave of his hands, Bale left the rest of the group to their infighting. He was pretty sure they were unaware of his absence, but he didn't really care. He enjoyed a good fight and appreciated the doctrine of rule by strength even if he couldn't explain it intelligently, but when he was not involved, it tried his patience. And even as obtuse a creature as Bale Pinkeye knew he needed to be at his least aggravated if he hoped to survive an encounter with a dragon.

Bale stalked off from his friends and meandered at a slow pace. The ogre still covered a great deal of ground in a short period of time due to his huge stride.

"I wonder what the dragon will be like. Maybe I shouldn't have bathed. I should make myself taste really bad in case he wants to eat me. Maybe those wizards will show up and send me back to the Fecal Swamps. No ... wait ... that's a bad thing, because I hate it there. Maybe I'll just run and sweat a lot. I get pretty stinky, so I should taste pretty bad then. Stupid dragon. Oh!" Bale stopped to a dead halt, surprised to see he had found what he was looking for. Tearing into the sky like teeth, a small mountain range lay in the distance, just as the map dictated. "The mountains. Okay, Bale, look for a cave somewhere. That was on the map. A cave. It was marked with an X, a big X, so I guess I need to look for ... oh, wait, that's silly. Stop being stupid, Pinkeye, or you'll wind up being a dragon snack."

He stopped for a minute and stared at the mountains on the horizon. Not used to being smaller than anything short of a two-story house, for the first time in his life, Bale Pinkeye was in awe. Certain peaks stretched up beyond his view to heights he couldn't even imagine. However, before he could have an epiphany, he felt his attention wane.

"I wonder what those stupid guys are doing back at camp. Probably all yelling at Phyl while he's running around cleaning stuff up all nicey nice. Ha! Silly Phyl. Good thing those stupid guys aren't here. They'd make all kinds of noise and get us all eaten by the dragon. Still it would be nice to have some company out here. Oh, hey! A bunny. He'd make a great pet."

Bale reached down to scoop up the rabbit in his hands. However, the rabbit did not appreciate such a fate and hopped out of the ogre's reach. Bale tried again, but this time the rabbit ran, prompting Bale to give chase. So enthralled with his prey, the bumbling ogre never noticed that he ran straight back the way he came. Still hunched over, hands cupped together, he collided with Phyl, sending the unsuspecting satyr into the pots, pans, and bedrolls. Pik and Zot wanted to laugh, but upon seeing the rabbit zip through camp, they made their intentions known by yelling, "Food!" As if playing a game, the rabbit zigged to make Pik miss as he dove headfirst into the ground, then zagged to get Zot to commit the same act. All four friends regained clear vision just in time to watch the rabbit run into a large cave opening.

"Ummm, who put the cave there?" Bale asked, standing.

"You mean to tell me we set up camp and no one noticed a large cave right in front of us?" Phyl asked as he brushed dirt from his leg fur.

"Well, if you wouldn't be so damn difficult all the time ... hey! Look! The rabbit!" Zot said, pointing to the cave entrance.

All eyes followed his finger to the rabbit sitting on its hind legs at the edge of the cave's darkness. The rabbit then coughed into one of his front paws, "Ah-hem! May I suggest that you four vacate the premises?"

"Did ... did ... that bunny just say, 'ah-hem?'" Bale asked.

"Yes. Yes, I did," the rabbit replied. "Now, I must ask you again, please leave, for your lives are in peril."

Bale's eyes fell straight to the ground as he lifted his feet, almost dancing. "Perils? Where? I didn't see any."

Pik rolled his eyes. "'Peril' as in danger, not 'pearl.' And, Sir Rabbit, why, may we ask, are our lives in peril?"

"Simple. This is the cave of the Mount Pyrous dragon."

"It is?" all four friends said in unison.

Bale shoved his thumb between his bulbous belly and tattered pants. He pulled them from his waist, just enough to look inside. So confused by his actions, the spectators could only stare in horrified amazement, even the rabbit. But they all bellowed and fought hard to keep their breakfasts in their stomachs as Bale used his other hand to reach inside. Tensions eased back to horrified amazement as he pulled out the map and unfurled it, mumbling, "Okay, we started here."

As Bale talked to his finger while tracing their trek, his three friends turned their attention back to the rabbit as he hopped back into the cave. He reappeared. However, this time he stood atop the forehead of a dragon.

"Did we pass through a field of whistling willows?" Bale asked, unable to move his finger until he received a response.

"Yes," came in chorus from the other three as they watched the dragon's head emerge, blue scales shimmering, but glinting green in the sunlight.

"Hmmmm," Bale moaned, his finger gliding across the map again. "Did we pass through a forest where all the trees look like witches?"

"Yes," his three friends answered again, watching the dragon's saliva drip from its mouth, forming small pools on the ground. It smelled a great deal like lantern oil and the fumes caused the air to ripple. Taking an aggressive stance, the dragon stepped forward from his cave and raised his head high to stare straight down at the intruders. His upper lip snarled, exposing rows of pernicious teeth, and released a slow, deep growl.

Bale patted his tummy thinking the rumble came from within as he continued to follow their trail along the map.

"There, there, belly. I'll find you food soon enough. Did we pass by a stone that looks like a turtle?"

Dodging droplets of the dragon's flammable drool, his friends again answered, "Yes."

"Humpf!" Bale snorted. "According to this, we should be standing right in front of the dragon's cave. You guys think this cave is his?"

"Yes!" The three could do nothing more than quake in uncontrollable fits as the dragon opened its mouth, its serpent like tongue flicking towards its next meal.

Bale continued to study the map while massaging the tuft of hair atop his pointed head. "Okay then. Let's go inside and talk to him."

The dragon's breath was heavy and hot, close enough to frizz Phyl's fur. It was ready to enjoy a nice satyr snack until the rabbit yelled, "Wait!"

The dragon reeled its head back, confused. He growled, his frustration obvious. "Why?"

"Didn't you hear?" the rabbit asked. "He said they wanted to talk to you. I think they're looking for the ... the ... you know what."

"What?" Bale asked, finally prying his eyes away from the map. Of course, he had no idea that he would then be staring at a dragon large enough to swallow him whole. His natural reaction was to scream, and Bale was not a creature to fight nature, even if he knew how. "AAAAAAAAAAAHHHH!! Dragon!"

"Aaaaaaaaaahh!!" the dragon replied, taking a step back. "Why must my food always scream at me?"

"I always knew Bale was scarier than a dragon," Phyl whispered to Pik.

"Well, they're not food yet," the rabbit replied. "'Tis a formality."

"But it's part of the oath. You must put forth a riddle to anyone who asks. And since there are four of them, that means four riddles."

"Baaaah! They won't solve the riddles. None do."

"Excuse me?" Bale interrupted. "Riddle?"

"Yes," the rabbit answered. "Those who are looking for the ... ummmm ... those who wish to speak to the dragon must answer a riddle. If they answer correctly, they are rewarded. If not, then ..."

"Then what?" Bale asked.

"Well, two hundred years ago, I was the first to ask, and I did not answer correctly, so he turned me into a rabbit. I've been his herald ever since."

"So if I answer wrong, I'll be turned into a rabbit."

"Not exactly. Every person after me he'd simply eat."

"Let's do get on with this, please," the dragon moaned. "I am quite peckish."

Bale could only give a quivering whimper as a reply.

"Very well. I can be full, but never empty. I can be new, but never old. I can ..."

Bale stopped quaking, but his friends quaked for him, not comprehending how he could possibly stop. And they certainly could not comprehend how he thought it was his place to interrupt a large, salivating dragon. "Why are you talking about the moon?"

The dragon scowled, ready to strike the ogre dead, but realized what had happened. He rolled his eyes, trying to look at the rabbit sitting atop his head. "Does that count?"

"I ... I ... believe so?" the rabbit replied.

"He interrupted me!"

"But he did get it right. Try another."

"Oh, very well!" the dragon huffed, misting spittle and fumes. "I have three feet, but cannot walk. I ..."

"Now you're a yard stick?" Bale asked, oblivious to the blatant signs of agitation the dragon displayed, his drool flowing faster.

"I first walk with four legs, then two ..."

"Man!"

"I have eyes ..."

"Potato!"

"I ..."

"A three-toed, flat-billed, golden-spotted, Albathian field grouse!"

"Ah-ha! You're wrong!"

"I am?" asked Bale.

"How quickly the tables turn ..."

"A roulette wheel!" shouted Bale, raising one of his crooked fingers skywards.

"Stop that! We're through with riddles."

"Wait! He isn't wrong," yelled the rabbit, his nose wrinkling in confusion. "The answer to the last riddle is a three-toed, flat-billed, golden ..."

"It is not, Rabbit, I ... uh ... uh ...," stammered the dragon.

"It is too!"

"I changed the question."

"You can't change the question. It's part of the oath. And I'm here to keep you honest."

"You're here in case I get hungry. Now shut up!"

"No, *you* shut up, Dragon! Do you think it's so wonderful to be your herald?"

"Are you saying you're *unhappy?*"

"Hello! No one in the history of anything ever asked to be a *rabbit!*"

"Well ... hey, how do you know, anyway? It is very possible that the first turtle would have preferred something a little different."

"So do I! A small change would do us both good," said the rabbit. With that, he turned his back to the dragon and began cleaning his fur.

"Don't be like that. What can I do? I can change," the dragon began, his voice filled with regret.

Seeing that the dragon's attention was captivated elsewhere, Zot took off at an ambling run, his arms windmilling as though that might help him pick up more speed. Pik had quietly and discreetly crept away. Phyl hopped in another direction, his morningstar anklet tinkling, after he had picked up most of the necessary parts of their tent. Bale, scared as he was, stayed mesmerized by the exchange that was taking place.

"I'm not talking to you," the rabbit said. "You always assume your way is right and that everyone else is happy to follow your lead. I had plans once, too, you know."

"I'm sorry, Rabbit. I had no idea you felt this way ..."

"And my name isn't rabbit ... it's Lapin!"

The dragon sighed. "I know. I promise to always call you that from now on. And you were a knight! Your plans were to slay a dragon! Why you treacherous little ..."

"I was not a knight. I was *a thief*, and I had an eye for some of your treasure. The horse and armor were a disguise."

"A thief! Just like that no good Nevin," Bale muttered. "I should mash this little rabbit. Let me find a stick or a rock or something," he said and began trundling around in search of a suitable weapon.

"Oh, get over it, Dragon," Lapin said. "In the years since then I have served to keep your honor intact. I have been your footstool and your napkin. Just look at this fur! I still find bits of last month's meal in it. And your spittle gets it all nappy! How am I supposed to fluff this out?"

"Yeah, and you have it real bad," the dragon replied. "You get a place to stay and full meals every day. In fact, here ... have a carrot. Have all you want. There's some potatoes over there, too. Oh, and don't forget the celery. So you see," he mumbled around great mouthfuls of drool, "you don't have it all that bad."

Bale's search led him from one stick to another, all of which he discarded in favor of a heavier cudgel, but each was doomed to fail his "see-if-it-will-break-over-my-knee" test. Without quite realizing it, he had made his way into the cave that served as the dragon's lair. He huffed and puffed his way around the expansive area rooting through a heap of moldering clothing, then sifting through a massive heap of gold and silver coins. Finally, he stood with his hands upon his hips surveying the entire area, tunnel after tunnel, from as close to the top of the mound of coins as he could get, but still he could find nothing he considered suitable to strike a blow.

"Nothing here, Bale," he said to himself. "Well, I better get back before I miss the whole thing."

Resigned to the fact that nothing useful was lying about, he began his way back toward the cave exit.

"Hope that thief gets what he deserves," he muttered, his hands dragging across the ground as he walked. "Nothing worse than a thief. I hate thieves! Especially when they come in threes." Spittle flew as he gnashed his teeth on his words. Acting on its own volition, his right hand scooped up a stone lying about. It was smooth and tiny between his oversized fingers. He began to fondle it absently in his anger. "If I had the chance, I would just," he smashed his fist into his empty palm, grinning his rotted smile as he walked back towards the feuding dragon and rabbit.

"Oh!" said the rabbit, "so we're back to that are we? Well, you just go ahead and eat me, Dragon. I hope you chip a tooth!"

"Bah, you're barely a taste. There'd be more spit than meat!"

"Here," said Bale absently as he strolled back amidst the yelling. "Hit him with this, Dragon." He stretched out the hand with the stone between his fingers, still caressing its smoothness.

"I'm quite capable of handling this myself! And besides ... my claws are too big, you dolt!" He demonstrated by rearing up and waving his front claws at the ogre.

"Here we go again," said the rabbit. "You, you, you. You know best, you think better than everyone else, you fight better than everyone else. You never listen."

"Watch yourself, Rabbit. I'm losing my temper!" shouted the dragon, his sides stretching and expanding as he began to pant his words, rage inciting labored breathing. His chest heaved as his internal bellows stoked in time with his mounting ire.

"It's always about you! I'm sick of hearing about you, Dragon!"

Pik, who had slunk behind a boulder, kept a deft eye on the situation. Seeing Bale so close to the argument that threatened to foment into full-blown violence forced him into action. He dashed to the ogre's side and tried to forcibly pull him away, though he only added a few wrinkles to the ogre's stale outerwear.

"Smack him, Dragon!" shouted Bale.

"C'mon, Bale," pleaded Pik. "Let's get out of here."

"Shut up, ogre," yelled the dragon.

"Do you *ever* stop talking, Dragon?" asked the rabbit.

The dragon's fury boiled over and erupted in the form of a fiery snort from his nostrils. The small stream of flame licked the large patches of saliva that had pooled by his feet during the arguments. The eruption released great gouts of flame that completely covered the area, blasting Bale and Pik off their feet and hurling them no small distance away. Flames licked at the trees that stood near, dancing up their boughs and consuming their leaves. The scorched earth emitted a horrible smell, and smoke covered the surrounding area so thick that even the dragon couldn't lift his head high enough to see over its obfuscating effect.

Pik and Bale lay stunned for a brief time until Phyl loped over to them and dripped some briny water from his water-skin onto Pik's forehead. In a flash, Pik found his feet and chased the satyr back into the woods. Not wanting to miss this, Bale stood, then chased after them to the sound of Phyl's trailing explanation. "I thought you were unconscious."

"With my eyes open?" screamed Pik.

"This is gonna be good," the ogre laughed as he disappeared into the woods after his companions. "I wanna play, too!"

Before the smoke had cleared, the sound of coughing came from within the area of burning flora. The dragon, still not quite able to see, chuckled when he realized how mad Lapin would be.

"Was that absolutely necessary?" asked the rabbit.

"Apparently, I needed to remind you of your place. And I didn't realize how much saliva escaped my mouth. Besides, I imagine you don't need to clean your fur anymore. It's a good thing that part of the magic that turned you into the rabbit also makes you impervious to my fire."

"Don't kid yourself. It still hurts, Dragon! And fur doesn't grow on trees you know!" Lapin huffed and sat on his haunches. He crossed his front paws over his chest and surveyed the damage. "It's nice to know you still got it. What were we fighting about anyway?"

"Who knows? Now where's that miserable ogre and his friends?"

"Hey! He got all of your riddles right. What are we going to do about that?"

"I was thinking about that, Rabbit ..."

"My name is Lapin!"

"Don't start. If I tell them they can choose any one item from my lair, they are far more likely to take some shiny piece of gold or silver over a dull stone. I mean, they can't be complete morons, right?"

The dragon pondered his own question as he surveyed the scorched landscape. Nearby brush had been reduced to piles of ash, while the closest perimeter of trees looked like discarded lamp wicks. The black residue of burnt oil coated the ground, footprints of fleeing treasure hunters led to the forest.

"They did imply they were looking for the stone," Lapin reminded him.

The dragon turned and snorted a huff of discontent, a cloud of smoke billowed from his nostrils. He retreated to the comforts of his cave and followed the one path, of the dozens available, to his most prized treasure, to prove the rabbit wrong. That insufferable rabbit he should have devoured years ago must be put in his place! Alas, the rabbit was right.

Clawing through piles of gold coins and silver trinkets, the dragon searched his hoard. For the first time in centuries, the dragon felt the hollow-gut feeling of dread, of panic. His heart thumped in his scaled chest as he smashed open chests and shoved aside boulders. He couldn't find his most prized treasure. He could only choke out a whisper, "It can't be."

"It's not here, is it?" Lapin asked, still perched on his companion's shoulder.

"No. No, it's not," the dragon replied. Admitting to himself he was finally bested, his heart filled with reverence. "Amazing. He tricked us into arguing, giving ample time to find it, and then ensnared me with inescapable conversation, making time for my saliva to pool under me. Once ignited, the ensuing conflagration allowed him to escape. Simply brilliant!"

"Quite possibly the most ingenious scheme ever devised," Lapin added.

"Well, Rabbit, take a few minutes to collect a supply of alfalfa and sprouts. We're going after them," the dragon said, walking toward the cave's exit. He himself wanted to see if he could find a tasty stag to fill his belly before they began their hunt for the Spirit Stone.

FOURTEEN

LIFE REPRESENTS nothing so much as a collection of journeys. If only every journey could be neatly summarized and defined by a single purpose. If the point were simply to get somewhere or to perform a particular task or to learn some skill or to express one's deepest desires, no matter how secret, to the object of one's interest ...

"If only life were that easy," Dearborn whispered, completing her thought, then looked around self-consciously to make sure no one overheard. As she focused back in on her surroundings, Haddaman dozed in the saddle behind her. She believed that they deserved a little respite. The group had pushed hard, straight into The Scorched Sea. Haddaman knew the location of an oasis within the desert, and, counting on this, Oremetheus thought it was wiser to push through with as much haste as possible.

She stared again at the wall of stone that stood in front of her—The Dragon's Maw. Finding the crevice that the map had singled out had proved itself a tedious task. She had lost track of the number of times she had been called upon to scout, scaling some part of the cliff face in her search. But perseverance had won the day. Now she was reminded of her insignificance in the face of such an imposing natural creation, which was the source of her earlier flight of fancy. There was little in life quite as impressive as the works of nature, yet nothing was as full of humility either. No single creation was impressed with its own impressiveness, save one: man. Man simply refused to be impassive ...

Haddaman snorted in his sleep, yet again, interrupting her thoughts and yet again proving her theory. Even in sleep, Haddaman was anything but impassive. There was much to be done, and Dearborn urged her mount on. Overeager to wake Haddaman, she allowed a slight hint of a smile to ply her lips.

She guided her mount quietly to a tree with a low-hanging limb, then dismounted carefully so as not to disturb Haddaman. Looping the reins over a branch, which she judged to be right around head level for the unconscious rider, she tied them off. As she walked to the back of her mount, she planted a light smack on its rump, sending the mare several slow steps toward the tree and its impending limb. There was no need for her to turn around. The meaty sound of contact between flesh and wood reverberated deliciously in her ears as she walked away, quick to assist Mahlakore in the pitching of tents, lest her impishness be uncovered as something far less than good-natured.

"My head," Haddaman moaned. "Why didn't you wake me when you tied up the horse?"

"I did not wish to disturb you. Though you may be well unaware of it, you resisted sleep until it frankly overwhelmed you and even then you struggled with it. I was sure you were in dire need of its embrace."

"I sleep lightly on the worst of days. You know this. It is my preparedness for the unexpected shining through ..."

"Excuse me, Sergeant. There are other tasks to see to," Mahlakore said, his words hidden by the same upraised arm with which he concealed his smirk. His eyes, however, flashed with a mirth that Dearborn envied. With position and responsibility, sadly, came the need to water down convictions long enough to reach equitable resolutions. She sighed as she realized she simply couldn't wave Haddaman away.

"Move your hand, Haddaman."

He took his hand away from the spot of the offending pain to reveal a forehead-long expanse of purple that beat angrily with his pulse. She smiled inwardly, but almost felt a touch of remorse. Almost.

"Haddaman, I am so sorry. My thoughtfulness turned out to be carelessness. Can you forgive me?" she asked, trying not to trip over her own sarcasm. "There is a small jar in my saddlebag. The ointment should take away the sting, though I must warn you, the smell is slightly offensive."

Haddaman spoke between gritted teeth. "Thanks for your concern. There is no need, though. I am quite able to withstand a little pain. I leave you now to your appointed, menial task. I'm sure my proclivity for clear thought will be appreciated at the planning table. Good day."

He stumbled off, barely able to stay upright, much less walk a straight line. Dearborn smiled after him, all guilt evaporating in the heat of enjoyment. She knew her words rang falsely in his ear, but she also knew he was too proud to breathe a word as to the true nature of his injuries. Still, she wished he had used the ichthymous salve in her saddlebag. The thought of him with the salve of tarry black fish excrement spread all across his forehead would have been more laughable in person than in her mind's eye.

She strangled her smile and turned her attention back to the tent she was tying down. Still smarting from her last conversation with Iderion, she knew she couldn't let Haddaman have his ear for too long. *Iderion knows not to trust him*, she thought to herself as she worked to tie off the last tent. *Then again, there are some things best not left trusted to fate, and Haddaman is at the top of that list*, she concluded in silence.

After finishing off the last of her tasks, she moved with purpose to Prince Oremethus's tent. Even at thirty paces away, Haddaman's pompous voice came to her, and, from his tone of superiority, it was clear that Oremethus had asked the man's opinion on something. She quickened her pace.

"Yes, I agree," she heard Oremethus say once she arrived at the tent.

She had no wish to barge in unannounced and uninvited, especially if she did not know the argument she would be countering, but she was more than certain that if Haddaman had laid out the crux of the argument, regardless of the content, she would be opposed to it. She could barely contain herself knowing that the crown prince was agreeing so heartily with whatever was being set before him. Still she fought with herself to stay outside and listen. *Forewarned is forearmed*, a belief she never questioned.

"Well, since His Highness ...," Haddaman continued.

"Oremethus," the prince corrected.

Great! she thought, *my prince is on a first-name basis with the king of deception.*

"Forgive me. Since Oremethus is loath to ask another to place himself in peril and not be present himself, someone in charge will need to stay behind. Therefore, I will go in Iderion's place. My expertise in antiquities and riddles should make up for what the group loses without Iderion's puissance at arms. I think we will just need one more person to complement the group."

Unable to contain herself any longer, Dearborn strode through the tent flap. The prince's tent was larger than the rest. It was distinguishable not for any opulence, since it was unadorned and made of the same canvasses as the rest, but because of its shape. While the rest of the Elite Troop sported triangular tents that were meant only to serve its owner's most basic needs, Oremethus used a square-shaped tent that was roomy enough to accommodate small groups for strategic sessions, such as this.

With a sense of determination that had eluded her more often than not in the past, she strode into the meeting. Like something out of Dearborn's most hellish nightmare, Oremethus and Iderion sat facing Haddaman, hanging on his every word as if it were rapture. Haddaman, who had been about to say something else to his two companions, stopped himself short upon her entrance. He regarded Dearborn shrewdly for a moment, then broke out one of his most impish grins. The prince and the general regained their wits and seemed only to take notice of her presence after many awkward seconds of silence had passed.

"Dearborn," Haddaman purred, "how good of you to join us. I was just about to suggest that you accompany the pr ... Oremethus and I on this excursion to find the stone. Does that meet with your approval?"

"I ... yes. I would be honored to shield the prince with my life. I do, however, suggest that one other accompany us as well."

"Surely there is no need to clutter up the mission with excessive bodies. Speed and stealth are the trademarks of any successful plan and I ..."

"With all due respect," she interrupted, "there is always the possibility that someone will be injured or something else untoward befall one of us." She paused to stare at the huge bruise on Haddaman's forehead and rubbed her own forehead for effect. Haddaman blushed. Dearborn continued, "I think it wise that there be an extra person along to alert the rest of the troop in case of emergency."

"Surely you aren't suggesting that we can't handle ..."

"On the contrary, Haddaman, I am suggesting that we err on the side of caution. After all, my lord here is the crown prince of Albathia. Better safe than sorry."

"Oremethus," Haddaman began, his hands spread wide as if to show that he were harmless, "certainly you won't listen ..."

"Enough!" Iderion's voice rang out in a stentorian staccato. "Mahlakore will accompany you. My sergeant knows her business, and I trust her judgment. Whether I go or not, my reputation is as much at stake as anyone else. I don't plan on losing a king's son."

"Very well, it's settled then," chimed in Oremethus. "We leave at dawn. Prepare yourselves as best you are able. Haste will be our staunchest ally in this, and I'll not see any time lost on laggards. Sergeant, will you kindly inform young Mahlakore on your way out?"

"Of course, Highness. I'll see to it immediately," Dearborn said with a salute. When she received her permission to leave from Iderion, she spun on her heel and took advantage of her long strides to cover the distance across camp. *Why do they not see through that thin façade of his*, she wondered.

She played that thought forwards and backwards in her mind as she sought out Mahlakore. He had completed a wide assortment of tasks in the time since he had taken leave of her, and she found herself yet again impressed with the initiative that such a young recruit displayed.

Doubtless he felt that his youthfulness was viewed as a stigma by some of the more seasoned members of the group, but efforts were always impressive.

He was brushing down another soldier's horse when she finally found him. He seemed lost in thought as she approached him from behind. Dearborn couldn't help but notice that his own horse had already been groomed and was feeding. Again, she found herself impressed. As she took in the scope of the tasks that he had completed, he noticed her shadow and spoke to her without turning around. "I trust you found the merchant and spared us all from another of his ill-advised plans?"

"Oh, I found him alright, but I'm not so convinced that I spared us of anything. Mahlakore, you and I are to accompany the crown prince and Haddaman on the search for the stone tomorrow morn. Haddaman talked Oremethus and Iderion into splitting up. If something bad should happen, then the troop would not be left leaderless, though I suspect he has some other reasons for wanting to be near the prince. He wanted me to be the only other person involved in the quest, but I convinced the prince and the general that we should have another able-bodied person along in case something unexpected should arise. I hope you don't mind. You were the first one who came to the general's mind."

"I'm honored, Sergeant," he said as he stopped grooming the roan in mid-stroke. "I hope I don't let you down."

"Mahlakore, I've known you for only a short while, but I have a great deal of faith in you. And I need someone I can trust implicitly on this. I don't know what Haddaman has in mind, but I'm sure it can't be for the good of all. Plus, you're as strong as any two of the others. We truly might need your vitality if ... well ... if things take a turn for the worst."

"I ... thank you again, Sergeant. Your vote of confidence means a great deal to me. I'll not disappoint you in any way. And you can count on me to keep an eye on our 'friend' as well. At the very least, he's up to something self-serving. I have no doubt of that."

Chuckling, Dearborn turned to leave. "I agree. The day sun sets soon. I suggest you turn in early, for when the morning sun rises again, it will begin a long day."

Dearborn's words could not have been truer.

The morning sun peeked over the horizon to watch four figures climb rock and stone, pitfalled with juts and crags. For over two hours, it beat their backs, only relenting once they reached the cave; everyone thankful that they made it before the day sun could rise and add to the lashings. However, the cave offered only cold stone and stale air.

Being fair-skinned, Mahlakore despised the sun, both of them. The two hours of climbing affected him the most—he wore minimal covering since he did not wish to haul any more weight up the side of a cliff than he had to, and there were no opportunities for shade until he reached the destination. The near-frozen cave gifted relief at first, but his freshly ruddied skin quickly went clammy. He hoped for a shred of warmth once they lit their torches, but it seemed like the frigid walls devoured any possible heat. Shame became his traveling companion as he watched the steadfast Oremethus and statuesque Dearborn traverse forward with nary a hint of pain or discomfort. Even the weasel-like Haddaman seemed to be faring better! Of course, how could he not? Carrying a pack that had extra clothing he donned once inside the cave, as well as being strapped to both Dearborn and Mahlakore during their ascent, it was doubtful Haddaman did any work climbing at all other than to balance himself.

The uninviting cave did not appreciate visitors. Walls danced with each other, flowing in and away, creating narrow pathways with jagged rocks meaning to scrape and cut any who passed. The ceiling flowed like a snake as well, raising high only to set up for an unexpected drop, twice using surprise stalactites to smack Mahlakore in the head. But the ground was the cruelest trickster of them all: infested with stalagmites, none tall enough to use as support when passing by, the floor rippled with holes and cracks and pits ready to ensnare an unsuspecting foot with every step. Mahlakore lost count of how many times he had twisted an ankle or almost fallen. His heart beat hard and strong from his shins to his soles. Mahlakore cursed his luck for being chosen to go on this assignment—he was a swordsman!

However, he was surprised to see Haddaman prove his worth as a strategist. Many times when a fork in the cave appeared, Haddaman knew which path to choose, almost from instinct. A pernicious gulch almost claimed them, going unnoticed by Mahlakore, due to rock placement that caused a natural illusion, but Haddaman noticed it.

"The shadows from the torches did not act as they should have," Haddaman said, chest puffed, proud as a peacock. Surely the story of how Haddaman saved everyone's lives would be repeated at the camp—by Haddaman.

Mahlakore soon became sick to his stomach with every word Haddaman spoke. Thanks to him, they avoided every trap, dodged every trigger. Once he knew his importance, Haddaman pointed out even the obvious.

"See how the heads have been severed?" Haddaman said, investigating a mound of decapitated skeletons. "That must mean the trap is a set of blades, so we need to find the path these blades would travel along the walls, and we'll find the trigger point."

Even a child could see that! Mahlakore screamed in his own mind.

The trek became tedious. Mahlakore understood adventures would be long, but most were seen from the top of his horse, with a pleasant battle or skirmish breaking the monotony. He did not train to have his skin rubbed raw, or his ankles pained by following a man of suspicious history through a cave! Mahlakore's head throbbed harder than his feet every time he thought about the return trip through these caves, following the same paths to exit. He begged every god he could recall for an ending soon. He got his wish.

After thwarting one last trap, they came upon a wall, polished smooth, with a hole as wide as his shoulders. It glowed a pale blue. Without hesitation, Dearborn crawled through first. Upon her clearance, albeit from a shaky voice filled with wonder, Oremethus went next. Not giving the only person who could find their way back out of these caves a chance to leave them behind, Mahlakore stood angry and defiant, convincing Haddaman to go next.

Making his way through the hole, more like a tunnel, Mahlakore's hands became as sore as his feet. His curses overflowed his mind and uncontrollably slipped from his lips with every jab to his head or scrape across his shoulders. With one final tumble, Mahlakore made it to the end, flopping on the floor of the final room.

All four stood in amazement, unable to truly conceive what they saw. Mirrors of all different shapes and sizes lined every cragged wall, the entire uneven ceiling and floor. The room seemed larger than the mountain, an infinite illusion, but it might only be the size of an outhouse, as far as any observer knew.

"It's like being inside a diamond," Haddaman whispered as he looked around. Within each facet, within every flat surface of every mirror, was the prize they sought—the Satan Stone resting on a modest pedestal.

Oremethus blew out a lengthy sigh through pursed lips. "Try not to move too fast. We will need to be cautious. This could take hours."

Hours? Mahlakore shrieked in his own mind. That was not an option. They were too close to the prize to wait in this damnable mountain for hours. He decided it should take minutes.

With a quick step, he stumbled around the room, watching his reflection appear, or disappear, depending on how he moved or turned.

"Mahlakore!" Dearborn barked. "Get back here!"

The young soldier focused on the myriad mirrors. He watched and studied, turning left, then right, then right again, far from his superior's view. "'Tis simply a maze of mirrors."

"Nothing on this trek has been simple, young man. Let's all take a moment to catch our breaths and formulate a plan," Haddaman added, his words sounding sincere.

"A plan has already been formulated. And I'm executing it riiiiiiiiiiight ... *now!*" Mahlakore noticed a mirror the size of a melon by his head that refused his reflection, but happy to show the stone. Thinking there was no mirror there, simply the stone, he grabbed for it. The sting of jammed fingertips rippled through his arm and he realized the mirror was set back farther than he thought, with a slight angle downward.

"Damnation!" Mahlakore cursed, saliva frothing at the corners of his mouth. He turned to head back to Dearborn to take his well-deserved tongue lashing, but his hand did not move with him; it was still stuck to the mirror. Needing the use of his other hand, he pulled harder. His hand came away, but some of the mirror came with it.

Stunned, Mahlakore watched as strings of the reflective glass clung to his fingertips, a silvery web. The strings then tugged, yanking his hand into the mirror itself. Never once losing its reflective clarity, the mirror oozed past his wrist, creeping up his forearm, and then pulled him in some more, submersing him to the elbow.

"Sergeant! Dearborn!!" he cried, his voice showing his youth, cracking in panic.

By the time Dearborn, Oremethus, and Haddaman arrived, the entire left side of Mahlakore's body was consumed by the wall of mirrors and continued to be devoured. Without thought, Oremethus grabbed Mahlakore's flailing right arm while Dearborn wrapped herself around his twitching leg. Both prince and sergeant screamed as they pulled, using every muscle they could call upon. Despite their efforts, Mahlakore slipped from their grasp into the wall, leaving Dearborn with nothing more than the reflection of her tear-streaked face.

"Should have listened," Haddaman commented, looking around at the room for some clue how to get the stone.

Not appreciating the obvious, especially stated from Haddaman, Dearborn stood with fists clenched and the devil in her eyes. Not needing to be clairvoyant to see what was going to happen next, Oremethus diffused the situation, "Sergeant. Sergeant! Stand over there to collect your thoughts and say a quick prayer."

Dearborn picked up her torch and did as ordered. She prayed to have one hour alone with Haddaman. She prayed for him to find the same fate as poor, misbegotten Mahlakore. She prayed for everyone to open their eyes and see Haddaman for the treacherous snake that he was. She prayed ...

"Sergeant!" Oremethus said, disrupting her holy moment. "I have an idea how we can find the stone using a little more caution. Move about ten paces to your left."

Dearborn grunted in acceptance like a foot-soldier and did as she was told. Oremethus asked the same of Haddaman, then instructed him to alternately raise and lower his torch. The shadows, Dearborn thought. He's manipulating the shadows to understand the room and where the stone might be.

For over an hour, Oremethus orchestrated a three-person dance. Move to the right, stretch, squat. Flow to the left, bend, twist. Glide forward, spin once, twice, three times. They each moved around the room, often repeating paths they had already taken or moving to where another had once stood. The shadows danced with them.

Even with her heart in a vice, Dearborn felt impressed with Oremethus. The crown prince remained calm and focused, even though his spoken voice was worn raw. She often tried to guess which image of the pedestal perched stone was real amid the illusions, but she was overwhelmed. She had never in her life believed herself to be anything less than intelligent, but now she found herself floundering before this riddle.

Oremethus remained more patient than time itself. His eyes brimmed with determination, studying the slightest nuance of every shadow movement. Moving Dearborn here, moving Haddaman there, another step this way. Dearborn watched and obeyed, assuming his plan was working. He continued to experiment with the light and darkness, making sure he accounted for every contingency. Then, he stopped.

Dearborn watched as Oremethus stood before the stone. Or was it another illusion? A mirror ready to devour the crown prince for choosing incorrectly? She knew he thought this was the stone. "Prince Oremethus? Do you think you have found it? The real stone?"

His tongue slid across his parched lips as he wiggled his fingers, a snake ready to strike.

Dearborn moved from her position, walking toward the prince. "I do not believe you should reach for the stone. I'm sure Haddaman would be more than happy to try for it."

As if no one else existed in the room, Oremethus raised his hand, fingers still wiggling, as a smile, touched with a hint of madness, slid across his face.

Dearborn's pace quickened. "Oremethus! Please, don't!"

As fast as a viper strike, Oremethus shot his hand forward and plucked the stone from its pedestal.

Dearborn stopped in her tracks. She looked around the room, wondering what trap was tripped, what murderous device would befall upon them. Nothing, except the quickening of her heartbeat.

Oremethus smiled, wide and bright, showing every tooth in his mouth. As if just plucking an apple from a low hanging branch, he held it between his thumb and index finger and waved it above his head. Haddaman laughed and rushed over to the prince. He clapped him on the back, dispensing with the pomp and circumstance of being in the prince's company and shared in the celebration of an arduous task completed. Dearborn still looked over her shoulder, over her head, under her feet.

With Haddamn's hand on his back, the prince shined his smile upon Dearborn. "As you were saying, Sergeant?"

"I never doubted your abilities, sir. It would have eased my mind if you let either Haddaman or me reach for the stone."

"Allow someone else to claim the prize after I did all the work?" Oremethus asked, sarcasm dripping from his words. He watched Dearborn lower her gaze and decided to rephrase. "This may shock you, but I do enjoy hunting boar and bear without the watchful eye of body guards. Even ones as apt as yourself."

Dearborn smiled at the compliment and looked at the prince and Haddaman hanging from him like a river leech. Then a chill ran down her spine when she noticed the look in the prince's eyes—it was the same as Haddaman's.

"Now, let us leave this place," the prince continued. "I wish to give this stone to General Iderion for safe keeping."

As they left the mirrored chamber, a second chill ran down Dearborn's spine. Everywhere she looked, she saw Mahlakore's eyes staring back at her.

FIFTEEN

EVEN A MERE glance revealed the mountain range known
as the Dragon's Maw to be one of the most majestic sights
a mortal could ever hope to lay eyes upon. More than one
of its high perches had lanced a low-flying cloud as it tried
to drift by. Many a rain-laden cloud had dropped its cargo
on the other side of the range, and there was no lack of
forest. However, no forest dared to cross over the peak into
the desert side, giving way to a rocky soil unconducive to
many living things. However, as much as Nevin wished to,
he could not enjoy its beauty, only seeing the dire journey
that lay before him.

"Belhurst," Nevin said.

No answer. Once the wizards and thieves had made
their way through the winding foothills, narrow passage
ways, cliff faces, and one twisting cave to make it to the
other side of Halcyon Hills to the barren land that nature
scorned, The Scorched Sea, the wizards opted to rest on
this plateau. One final path down from their resting spot
through meager patches of pitiful brush and malnourished
trees, and they could walk upon the most fearsome patch
of forsaken land.

"Typical wizard," shot Silver, "selective hearing."

Nevin kept his chuckle to himself as he glanced at the
prone wizards. During the entire journey, Silver tongue-
lashed the wizards at every turn, admonishing them for
taking longest ways possible. He even went so far as to say

a team of motivated snails could have beaten them to the treasure.

It was twilight, though the gray had been removed from the sky, chased away by the waning day sun. Sunset was breathtaking here and Nevin had no qualms relishing it a bit longer.

"Belhurst," the elf tried again, this time shaking the man by the shoulder. For a man who proclaimed sleep was scarce, he sure knew how to become thoroughly absorbed by it. "Who are they?"

Nevin's acute eyesight had noticed a small encampment in the valley below. Only a handful of tents comprised the entire camp, though there could have been a few more under some low hanging branches. At this distance, the only certainty was that two of the tents were grand. And given their isolation from civilization, Nevin's calculating mind led him to a few assumptions he found none too pleasant. "Slavers?"

"I still don't think so," Silver muttered.

"Who else has money this far from civilization?" Nevin countered.

"You know, Nevin, clairvoyance does require a certain amount of concentration on my part and patience on your part," Belhurst replied at long last.

"Sometimes survival depends on a split second, so give up the goods, man. Who are they?" Silver snapped.

"Well, I'm afraid I'm not quite sure."

"What do you mean you aren't quite sure? What kind of wizard are you exactly?"

"Insults will nary get you the results you seek, Silver."

"Yes, well, neither will you," Silver said, his face reddening with each spoken word.

"Please open your lesson book to the chapter on patience, gentleman," Belhurst responded, words dripping with sarcasm.

"Look, this is getting us nowhere. I'm bored, and I'm going to take a look," Diminutia said as he walked past.

By the time his words registered with the arguing men, they were already staring at his back.

"Is he truly going down there?" Belhurst asked.

"Certainly looks as such," Silver said, letting his thoughts trail after his friend.

In days long past, Diminutia had divided his time amongst countless professions, trying new things in the continuous search to find the one perfect for him. He started by playing a street urchin in his youth, using his blond curls and sapphire hued eyes to pander to the pity of good folk offering free coin. He graduated to being a pickpocket, then one half of a con-man team, and then a flat out thief, though they all lacked certain elements he sought. He wished to be bold and debonair, yet clever and skilled, all while still maintaining his code of honor. He found the niche in life he so craved once he met Nevin and Silver. With these two he was able to display all of his talents, splash all of his colors upon the canvas, as it were, and paint a portrait of himself to which he could add more.

As he picked his way through the tall grass, trying to avoid the ruts that threatened to turn his ankles, it came to him in shocking clarity that he had never really done any true reconnaissance work. He began to sweat, from the heat he told himself, and that empty feeling in the pit of his stomach was merely a reminder that he had little to eat all day. He would never admit, not even to himself, that he was more than a little unnerved.

"Hunters, or poachers, or just simple folk out and about," Diminutia whispered to himself, descending to the dry desert floor. "Whoever they are, they're probably mere peasants and can't possibly be skilled. Don't even need to get that close, could just climb a tree and watch them from a distance."

When he figured he was within earshot of the few men milling about, he began to slink, like a great cat stalking prey. He stifled a chuckle once he realized that "reconnaissance" and "thievery" demanded similar skill sets. The smell of cooking meat reached him, though faint at this distance. He could hear two of the men conversing in low tones, though he could not make out any distinct words at this range.

Diminutia paused, watching the activities within the camp, studying each man in turn for clues as to their current duties and patterns. Several of the men were on guard duty, and Diminutia noted the arrangement of the perimeter they walked and the amount of time it took for each man to complete his portion of the circuit. Within the box-like shape that their footfalls created, several other men shuffled about aimlessly completing more urbane tasks. *Those are the more dangerous ones,* the thief reminded himself, always preferring the predictability of patterns to the erratic movements involved with random chores. Slowly shifting closer, he knew that his outfit blended with the taupe background as well as having the advantage of dusk's shadows.

Engrossed, Diminutia never noticed the guard until he suddenly appeared from between the squat trees a stone's throw to his right. Good peripheral vision was a gift, and he was thankful for it. He detected the movement early and was able to hold himself motionless until the man turned away, still oblivious to the thief's presence.

Well now, that was interesting. Nice one, Dim, he thought, scanning the low-hanging branches over his head as he contemplated taking to the trees for added safety. He spied a stationery man hiding in the shadows off a good bit to his left. The thief crawled on his belly to the trunk of a thick Joshua tree. He was skilled at climbing, and the branches above him might be thick enough to support his weight.

From the stealth that they displayed, Diminutia doubted that these men were slavers. Slavers tended to be coarse and not too concerned about giving away the location of their camp, believing that brute strength and sheer numbers would intimidate most would-be attackers. Nor would they have guards march a perimeter.

Tree, rocks, or brush? Tree, rocks, or brush? Diminutia thought. The tree might not support his weight, getting to the rocks might expose his position, and the brush was perfectly uncomfortable. But thanks to his careless self-debate, he found he no longer had a choice.

Within the crunch of dried grasses, the heel of a leather boot pinned Diminutia's hand to the ground. Petrified by the prospect of capture, the thief stilled himself solid, nary a breath, blink, or twitch; he would have stopped the beating of his heart if he could. Shifting his eyes only,

Diminutia followed the leg all the way to a man's rump, wide enough to hide the amber streaks of the sunset. The man let out a sigh of relief, followed by the familiar splashing and smell of used ale. The man sighed again, more relief, as trumpeting sounded from his posterior. First the noise, then the stench fell upon Diminutia.

By all the gods real and unreal! What manner of food could this man have eaten to produce such a rot? Diminutia yelled inside his head. The cascade continued far longer than the thief thought possible. Twisted images of needing to build a boat to survive the impending flood or life sprouting forth in the desert from this one lone drunkard danced through Diminutia's head. The flow slowed to a trickle, then to a stop. With a rumbling belch for final punctuation, the man strode back to camp.

Ire welled deep within the thief. Plans changed. What started as a simple reconnaissance now became a quest for pride. Diminutia was now going to steal something; something big, something that would be sorely missed once the suns came back above the horizon.

He skulked through the grasses and brush, careful to avoid the newest man-made lake, creeping within spitting distance of the camp's first tent. This tent sat farther away from the others, aloof in design as well as distance. Thicker than the others, Diminutia could barely see the glow of a lit oil lamp as opposed to the full silhouettes he saw through the thin cloth covering of the others. *Treasure tent?* he wondered. *Naah. Too foolish a placement. I'll move over ... whoa!* He interrupted his own thoughts once he finally got a good gander at his surroundings.

Even though the day sun had now set, the campfire shined quite a bit of light on Diminutia's situation. Swords. Shields. Bucklers. Quivers choking on arrows. Armor of all kinds. And the king's insignia touched them all. Soldiers. The men milling around the fire, tearing their dinner from its bones, were all heartier than the average soldier.

Run away, Diminutia thought. *Run away now.* Just as he thought to shift, he was almost stepped on again. By the same boot. Attached to the same rump. *How can a man the size of a horse move as a mouse?*

Were he more of a bandit and less of a rogue, he'd have slit the large man's throat! However, he was more of brain and less of courage to act upon such a foolhardy impulse. Plus, intrigue demanded he watch the theater play out before him as the soldier stopped in front of the tent's entrance.

Curious, Diminutia thought as he watched the soldier. The large man looked as nervous as a schoolboy, anxiety seeping from his eyes. He ran his hands through his tangled hair and bushy beard in what looked like attempts to either comb or shoo rodents from their nests. Rapping on the tent's post, the man sucked in his prodigious gut, which did little for appearance, and whispered, "Sergeant? Dearborn? You awake?"

"Yes, General?" Dearborn replied from within the tent.

General? This fattened ox is a general? And a woman is sergeant of such a fiercely armed group of soldiers? You sure know to chase a rabbit into a serpent's pit, don't you, Dim? the thief chided himself. However, he could not see the sergeant from his vantage point, only the nervous general. He stretched his neck as best he could, but saw nothing more than a hand flip open the tent's flap.

"Sergean ... Dearborn. I've ... I've been on edge this mission. More so than usual, because of Prince Oremethus. I am a professional, and his being here should not affect me so, especially in the forest when we were attacked ..."

"General, please. I acted inappropriately," Dearborn cut him off. "You should have said nothing different."

"Be that as it may, my words filled me with regret. You are my best soldier, even more."

"More?"

Diminutia rolled his eyes. The implications of the conversation were obvious in the tone of their voices. The stumbling of his words, the hope held within hers. How either of them remained oblivious to this seemed impossible.

"Uhhhh ...," Iderion stumbled. "Friend. You're my best friend. Other than my wife. And dog. But not like either of them. Neither of them. Definitely not the dog, at least. More like ..."

Wife? Diminutia thought as he rested his chin on both palms. *Ooooh, this is getting good.*

Dearborn forced a polite chuckle. "You finished most of the ale yourself tonight, didn't you?"

"Yes. Yes, I have," Iderion replied. "Which is why I'm here. To give you this, the Satan Stone."

"The Satan Stone?"

The Satan Stone! Diminutia's focus returned. Again, he craned his neck, able to see Iderion hand a small pouch to the mystery woman in the tent. *Ha! Not only shall I get revenge on this bloated fool for befouling the earth before me, but I also save us the hassle of trekking to an empty cave.*

"Aye," Iderion replied. "As you mentioned, the ale has cast quite a spell upon me. I fear I am the least qualified to guard it. Lest I awake tomorrow with no memory of where I may have stashed it."

"Iderion, I ..."

"You, Dearborn. I trust you. A trust like I have in no one else. No one."

Diminutia watched as Iderion turned and ambled away, giving Dearborn no chance to retort. Then he heard the tent flap close.

Making less noise than a breeze, Diminutia crawled to the back of Dearborn's tent. He watched the dull, orange glow cast from within the brown tent hide, wondering what a female sergeant might look like. *Rounder than the general*, he thought. *And possibly more hairy.*

The glow faded, and Diminutia counted to one thousand, thinking that would be plenty of time for the sergeant to drift into slumber's realm. As careful as reassembling a shattered eggshell, he rolled the back flap of the tent. Once he created a sufficient opening, he dug his elbows into the dirt and used them to slide his body across the ground, his head poking into the tent.

Dearborn had not extinguished her oil lamp; she merely turned it down. As she lay on her back contemplating the Satan Stone, Iderion, and her life in the Elite Troop she heard a minor rustling from behind her at the back of the tent. Thinking it a rat looking for food or warmth, she rolled over—just in time to see the blond head of a different type of rat poke through.

Reflex dictated she grab his wrist. But once she saw the way his blond locks played against his boyish face and the depth of his blue eyes, her senses took flight. A handsome man had never attempted to sneak into her tent before. The soldier in her soul fought with the woman in her heart, the desperate and lonely woman. Reason won over emotion when she deduced this man could only be one thing.

"Thief," she hissed, her grip on his wrist tightening, ready to rip his arm from his body.

Diminutia's hand throbbed from her tight grip. But he didn't care. So taken aback by her being the complete opposite of what he expected, he forgot why he was there. Finding and bedding bar wenches was second in nature only to breathing, but never did he imagine finding the most exquisite woman tented at the edge of a desert. With her face, she seemed more suited for the king's concubine than his army.

"Beautiful," he whispered.

Her face shifted from anger to surprise; her grip loosened. He wanted to stay, to speak, to talk to this lovely angel, but his instinct as a thief freed him from this ambush. Her hand no longer throttling his wrist, he wrenched himself free, jumped to his feet, and ran.

She chased.

He scrambled away from her tent, away from the noisy brush, toward the myriad jagged rock edifices.

She followed.

Surprised that he heard no sounds of alarm during the length of time he ran, he took a pause near the precipice of a rugged ridge to acquire his bearings. His breath eluded him as he saw what chased him. Her size confounded him. Never, never, had he beheld a woman so large, but her shape and movements, the sinewy grace of a wildcat, mesmerized him.

Leaping and bounding up the side of the rocky knoll, she questioned her motivation. *Why am I chasing him?* she thought. *He's probably a desert nomad, too scared to try a second attempt.* But upward she went, closing the gap between herself and her prey.

He reached the top, but realized the edge of the small plateau dropped into an abyss the moonlight was unable to explore. He had to jump across the chasm, the length of three men from head to heel, to another plateau that had a much more reasonable grade down and plenty of tall grasses for an appealing escape route. The sounds of pebbles and stones giving way indicated that his pursuer grew closer. Concentrating, he sprinted the length of the plateau and sprung right at the edge. Out of fear, his legs continued to churn even though there was no ground beneath them. He leapt just far enough to land right at the edge of his target. Momentum allowed him no balance as he stumbled, tucked his head, and rolled as his shoulder hit the ground. Coming to a full stop as his legs flopped over his head, he panted like a rabid cur, then kissed his hand and patted the ground. He sat up in time to see her spring across the gap between plateaus and land with the softness of a feather.

She stood as a statue and his heart seized. She only wore a ragged shirt to sleep in, and it barely kept her modest. Sweat coated her arms and legs, shining from the moonlight, accentuating the tone of her muscle. Her hair flowed over her body like a cloak, a dark mist that seemingly crept across the ground to him, wanting to pull his heart from his chest. Then she was gone.

Unaccustomed to such abuse, the ledge of the plateau gave way from under her feet. He scrambled to the ledge hoping beyond hope she did not fall. On his knees, he saw her hands and fingers sliding across the dirt toward her doom. Certain she could conquer any demon she faced, he still refused to let this angel be swallowed by the dark maw of hell.

He grabbed her wrists and pulled. She outweighed him, and he had never attempted to lift anything heavier than a stolen sack of gold. Digging her toes into the side of the edifice, she scaled the rock wall and gave one final thrust as her foot hit the plateau floor. The thief and soldier twisted and tumbled onto the ground. She landed on her back, he on top of her.

She saw only his face above hers; sweat matted random strands of his hair to his forehead. A bead of sweat slid around his cheek to the tip of his chin and broke free, dropping to her chin. She gasped.

Supporting himself with his left arm, he was still chest to chest, hip to hip with her. Every woman he could remember was softer, but none had the body control. She inhaled as he exhaled, she exhaled as he inhaled, a perfect rhythm formed. Locks of her hair covered the left side of her face. Dizzy with anticipation, he slid them aside. Her breath ceased as his fingers glided over her skin. His knees slid across the ground, closer to her body. Her feet followed, her thighs sliding along his. They exchanged desperate breaths, as if breathing for each other; his lips descended toward hers.

"Dearborn!" rippled through the still night air. And the thief was gone, stealing something after all; the one thing Dearborn was never able to give away. She sat up and watched the tall grasses ripple and wave as he ran through them. Only when she saw no more movement did she reply.

"Here, Haddaman!" Standing, she dusted herself off as she saw the dark figure of the civilian she despised the most appear on the other plateau, one chasm away.

"What happened? What are you doing all the way over there?" he asked, huffing as if he had never climbed before.

"I thought I saw something," Dearborn said, looking back toward the tall grasses. "So I followed it. It was just a deer."

"I hardly think so," Haddaman huffed. "A desert deer, indeed."

Dearborn snapped her gaze back to Haddaman. "It was a deer. And what exactly are *you* doing here?"

"Due to your raucous cohort, I could keep my eyes shut for no longer than a blink. Since I couldn't sleep, I figured some fresh air would help. I saw you running up this plateau and thought I'd check on you. I do care about your well-being, you know."

"I hardly think so," she said, taking one last look at the tall grasses, cursing her luck; the man she wanted to be with was a dream, while the man stuck to her side, a nightmare.

SIXTEEN

PHYL LIFTED HIS small tankard of ale, his trembling hand causing frothy liquid to splash over the sides and run down the length of the mug. By the time his beverage reached his mouth, the metal rim chattered against his teeth and foam shot up his nose. Frustrated from only garnering a sip of froth and unable to control his quaking, he placed his mug on the table. "It's the stone. It has to be."

"That's ridiculous," Pik replied. He considered the circle of events that led him and his companions back to the tavern in Bogosh to await a bard who, so far, might as well have been a figment of their collective imagination. No one in Bogosh had seen the bard, nor even vaguely recalled his presence on the day Pik and his friends were given the stone-finding quest. The light from the oil lamp slid across his pursed lips in slick strokes, while his furrowed brows and taut cheeks caused shadows to fall and tumble in a terrifying dance. His eyes held such anger that it was no wonder why humans considered hobgoblins things found in nightmares. "How is that even possible?"

"I agree with Phyl. The stone is cursed," Zot offered, watching the flickering flame as if it held the answers.

"*Bah!* Curses are for parents cajoling a child or washed-up witches pilfering a few coins from gullible tourists."

"Zot was just saying," whimpered Phyl.

"The only curse right now is having to listen to the two of you come up with explanations for what's happening."

Pik's words were enough to make Phyl try for another sip of ale. He used both hands this time, but found the results to be twice as disastrous. He returned the mug to the table. "You're not the only one who lost someone close, you know. Zot's brothers and sisters disappeared one at a time while he had the Spirit Stone. And I just lost my best friend and hunting partner."

"Hunting partner," Pik snorted, as if the words were offensive. "If it were possible to be a worse satyr than you, it would be him. You'd bend our ears with tales of hunting women with him, but after three ales you two would spend the rest of the eve singing like drunken fools."

"Still," Phyl said, slouching as if each word deflated his soul. "He's dead. And so is your sister."

"She could still be alive!" Pik's words gnashed at Phyl as sharply as his razor-like teeth. "She ... she ... she's missing. Maybe ran off. But she's not dead."

"They're all dead," Zot whispered. Unblinking, he stared at the oil lantern's flame, slowly rotating his mug with his stubby fingers. "My brothers and sisters. My cousins. My parents. Their parents. Ever since we came back to Bogosh with that stone. And it's my fault for wanting to carry the thing. Now it's Bale's turn."

Pik leaned forward and growled. "It's not the stone."

He leaned back again peeking over his shoulder. All eyes in the tavern were trained on Pik, Zot, and Phyl. *Everyone else thinks we're cursed, so why can't I?* Pik asked himself.

It started subtly. Pik and his friends returned from finding the Spirit Stone—after one more accidental trip through the Fecal Swamps. They spent the night in revelry, recounting the embellished tales to any soul who would listen. The ale and grog and mead and wine showered the town like no rainstorm ever could. The next morning, one of Zot's brothers went missing.

Zot's siblings were known throughout town for being excessive in their drinking, and a second thought about his whereabouts never crossed anyone's mind. The following night, one of Zot's sisters disappeared. However, the local authorities found her trussed up by her own entrails from a tree at the edge of town.

Fearing a legitimate scoundrel lurked parts unknown of Bogosh, children adhered to curfews mandated by their parents while the town witches placed spells of protection and good fortune on Zot and his family. Then Bale's sister disappeared.

To the untrained eye, Bale's sister bore a striking resemblance to her brother—including the knot of orange hair upon a pointed head, crooked yellow teeth, and placement of various warts—the only noticeable difference being her lopsided breasts: one tight and firm, the other flouncing with every step, as if it were trying to escape her all too revealing chemise that she always wore. The woman was of mountainous proportions, even by ogrish standards. From another town, she had heard rumors of Bale's recent dalliances with disaster and decided to visit him. Upon arrival, she burst into the tavern, sharing her brother's zeal and force, joining him and his cronies as Phyl shared a story in which he embellished, exaggerated, and downright lied about hunting female prey the prior night. During the story, Bale noticed his sister swoon and saw her send a wink Phyl's way.

Dismayed by the ramifications of his lies, and sickened to have an ogre woman flirt with him, Phyl excused himself from the tavern to retch in an alleyway. He walked with hastened step, gulping the fresh air as if it were a waning commodity; the stench of one Bale was harsh enough, but two was downright insufferable. A stray thought of Bale's sister's clammy, pockmarked paw stroking his leg fur slipped into his head. He retched again. Finding no other recourse, he went to see his best friend, Mungus.

His friend was a tall and lean satyr, leg fur the color of warm tar. His horns had perfect placement and an upward curl to accentuate his devious smile, extending it through his whole face. Once Phyl arrived to bellyache about his night, his friend offered spiced wine and a full-face smile. Through two bottles, they bragged about the human women they could conquer, no set of bloomers strong enough to stop them. Standing in front of an open window, his friend offered Phyl another smile. The window shared the same dimensions as a saddlebag, but large enough to allow the moon light in, making a halo around his friend's whole body. Then the halo disappeared.

Within two blinks and one heartbeat after the moonlight's extinguishing, Mungus's hooves left the ground as his haunches wedged themselves in the window. Something relentless and determined outside pulled his tail. Before he could react, a second tug forced his hips through the window. Mungus screamed. His hands flailed along the wall for support, but a third tug doubled him over. His bones popped and cracked, his hands flopped like headless fish, and his hooves wiggled like snake tails. Blood erupted from his mouth on his final exhale, splattering the floor. One last tug, and Phyl's friend disappeared out the window.

Even though Bogosh was a creature town, it had just as much gossip as any human town. Word spread of the killings and startling disappearances surrounding members of the community. By the time authorities could react to one of Zot's siblings dying, one of Pik's cousins went missing. Rumors plagued the town, ranging from these four adventurers being cursed, to insidious schemes of them attempting to gain power over the town through murderous fear. Conversations would stop anytime they entered a building. Their mere appearance turned average citizens into guarded sentinels, eyes watching, probing, observing every last minute detail and movement. Even in the tavern where three of the four sat contemplating their predicament. And the stares became more stifling as Bale entered.

The tavern shook with every step, but Bale's mouth was closed, no laughing, no boisterous barbs. He sat with his friends, his chair groaning for mercy.

"Any luck finding your sister?" Pik asked.

Bale turned his head, between slouched shoulders, and stared at Phyl through accusatory eyes. "None."

His soul heavy from the loss of his own friends and family, Phyl met Bale's stare. "Bale, you can't be serious. You can't think I had anything to do with this."

"I saw the way you two were looking at each other that night. Just because I can't find any indiscriminating evidence, doesn't mean you're incoherent."

Taking pause to muddle through the misused words and translate what Bale meant rather than what he said, Phyl replied. "I told you where I went that night. To a friend's house."

"Yeah. Your hunting partner. And my sister was probably on top of your list. A beautiful woman like her would have a hard enough time resisting one satyr. But two? She never stood a chance!"

For fear of spontaneous laughter, vomiting, or crying, Phyl fought hard to keep the images of himself sharing a romantic tryst with Bale's sister far from his mind. But no matter how hard he tried, he could not coax himself to hurt Bale's feelings by revealing that she was not as attractive as her brother thought. In fact, Phyl heard a rumor that a Dungbeast from the Horrid Mountains died from one look at Bale's sister. His best strategy was to block and deflect. "I think the greater mystery is why we haven't seen the bard? He told us to come back here, and here we are! Well, where is he? How come no one has seen him? And how come no one remembers seeing him the last time?"

"He set us up," mumbled Zot, unblinking. "He knew the stone was cursed. Had us get it, so he didn't have to face the curse."

"And that's exactly why we're gonna be ready for him when he shows up. Smart guys like that don't expect much from the likes of us, so we have to plan this out and play it smart," Bale said. He pushed himself from the table and stood up in slow motion, tapping a finger against his temple, his efforts filling the tavern with a dull, hollow sound.

"Where are you going?" Pik asked.

"Shopping," grunted the ogre in the general direction of his companions. "You guys stay here and keep an eye on each other."

"What about you," Phyl asked. "Will you be okay?"

"Don't confuse me. I might forget something. If the bard shows up while I'm gone, make him feel real comfy. And don't do anything awful to him until I get back," Bale finished his statement, wiping some drool off his chin with the back of his oversized hand, leaving only a wicked,

tooth-gapped smile. As he walked towards the door, he
hitched up his pants with his left hand. "Don't forget a
belt," he murmured to himself.

"Well, what exactly are you going for?"

"You'll see," Bale promised, still holding the waistband
of his tattered pants in his hand, and promptly
disappeared out the door leaving a trail of silence in his
wake.

The little group sat staring at each other for no short
time. They fumbled with their plates or stroked their mugs
pensively or stared intently at several bugs scurrying
across the ground. None seemed quite able to break the
silence, until Phyl cleared his throat.

"Did anyone happen to notice Bale's pants?" he
whispered.

As one, the other two members of the group wailed in
disgust.

"Aww, c'mon, Phyl!" moaned Zot.

"Well, he holds them when he walks now," said Phyl in
an exasperated tone as if trying to make the conversation
take a redeeming turn.

"Only you would notice something so miniscule," said
Pik, rubbing the condensation off his mug with his thumb.

"Um, there's hardly anything miniscule about Bale's
pants," the satyr said, flinching his shoulders as his
comments elicited a new chorus of groans.

"Guh," mouthed Zot as he stood, repulsion evident on
his disgusting face.

"Where are you going now?" asked Phyl.

"To find something to get this awful taste out of my
mouth, thank you very much," shouted Zot as he trundled
in a semi-straight line towards the bar.

"What did I say?" asked a dejected Phyl, his eyes
lowered toward the dirt he felt like.

Without a word and without even lifting his eyes from
his mug, Pik slapped the satyr in the back of his round
head, the meaty smack drawing a roar of applause from
every creature close enough to hear it.

"I just thought that someone should notice that Bale is
losing weight. No matter what the circumstances, Bale has
never been concerned enough to miss a meal. Until now.

He hasn't been sleeping, either." The satyr turned large, watery eyes toward his hobgoblin companion in the manner of a pleading child. And his silent entreaty was met with the compassion for which hobgoblins were known —another meaty smack to the back of the head. This time, however, Pik hit the satyr so hard that Phyl went flying from his stool. Shaking the numbness from his hand, Pik rose from his chair with a shout of pain that he quickly turned into a yell for more grog lest the other creatures see him as weak.

"I hate you, Pik! If it weren't for all of these strange happenings," groaned Phyl as he struggled to his feet, picking several bugs from his leg fur and straightening his right fetlock, "I'd leave these guys on their own. Now where did Zot go?"

Dinnertime neared, and the custom in Bogosh, as with many towns, was to go home for dinner. Creatures began to stream out the doors in twos and threes. The satyr scanned the thinning crowd until he found the misbegotten orc half sitting on a stool at the bar, his longer leg fully extended. Zot was miserable as he used both hands to cradle his cup towards his lips. He shook so badly that Phyl noticed even at some distance. Sentimentality was an emotional nadir to an orc, so Phyl knew that fear caused him such tremendous distress.

"It *is* that stone! I know it is. And if we don't stay together, we'll wind up getting picked off one at a time. I have to keep everyone happy until Bale gets back." Phyl sighed as he watched Zot dig a finger deep into his nasal cavity. "Why is it always up to me to make the peace?" With quick strokes of his hands, Phyl straightened out his leg fur as he hopped his way towards the saturnine orc.

"Zot, I'm really sorry I upset you. But you're totally right—it is the stone. We just have to stay together and ..."

"Phyl, leave me alone," Zot spat, spraying grog all over the satyr.

"I'm trying to apologize here," Phyl whined.

"And let me commend you on doing such a superlative job, too," yelled Pik from across the room. "Though I would remind you that 'butt-kissing' and apologizing aren't completely synonymous."

"Wha ...? I'm doing no such thing! I'm telling him that I agree with him. I mean, it all makes sense. I had nothing to do with the disappearance of Bale's sister and ... wait! Zot, where are you going?"

"Somewhere else, obviously. Don't wait up," Zot said, standing from his stool.

"Way to go, satyr," Pik said with disdain. "You've managed to do the exact thing that you charged yourself not to do. Oh, and by the way, I really liked the way that you disguised the effort to 'clear yourself' under the thin veil of an apology. Nice touch."

"AGH! I've had just about enough of you, hobgoblin!"

"Oh, really? Fur in a bunch, is it?"

"Yeah, something like that! And it's all because of you!"

"Me? Phyl, did you hear any of the words that were spouting out of your lips? For once, Mr. Perfect, you have no one to blame but yourself."

"I, uh ... oh, I suppose you're right. Pik, what are we gonna do? We can't just let him wander around out there. Where do you suppose he went?"

"How should I know, genius? You're the one who chased him off. Guess you should have thought that part out before you enacted your master plan."

Phyl pulled up a stool and hopped up on it, sitting with his shoulders hunched and his head down. He balled up his fists and dropped his head on them.

"What are we gonna do?" Phyl asked aloud, though he knew the only answers he would receive were the ones he gave to himself.

★ ★ ★

Zot shuffled down the main street of Bogosh, disturbing the dust with his shorter leg. "That stupid Phyl! What does he know anyway? And curses on Pik and Bale, too! Curses on that bard and his stupid cursed stone! I better find Bale. I'm sure whatever his brilliant idea is, he'll need some help with the shopping. He needs help, whether he admits it or not."

On cue, Bale strolled by Zot. The ogre still held his pants up with one hand while carrying a bag in the other. Oblivious, Bale continued past the orc.

"Bale!" Zot snapped, taking great offense to not being noticed.

Bale turned around. Then again. Well into his third rotation, he finally decided to look down. "Zot?"

"I see you made your purchases."

Bale held up the bag and smiled. "All of you are in for a surprise of epic propositions!"

"And what might be in the bag?"

"A ball of twine!"

"Obviously a wise choice on your part since you still haven't gotten a belt."

Confused, Bale looked down at his left hand holding up his pants, genuinely surprised that he had no idea what his left hand had been doing all day. "Damnation!"

Zot laughed. "Head back to the tavern, Bale. I'll fetch you a belt."

In a daze, Bale mumbled a thanks to Zot and continued his trek back to the tavern. Zot shook his head, his heart heavy with sympathy for his friend, for all his friends for that matter, and himself. They had returned home from their epic journeys only to have their families and friends die or disappear. Was it really the doing of the Spirit Stone? Was it cursed? Zot shook his head again, this time to shake away such distracting thoughts, lest he become as oblivious as his ogre friend.

As Zot ambled to the store, he was oblivious about one thing—the rabbit that had been following him. Never less than ten paces away at any given time, Lapin skulked in alleyways, bushes, crevices, and any nook or cranny in which he could hide. Distressed, the rabbit watched the orc, wondering if he should make contact. But what would he say? Not to mention the last time they met, the orc wanted to eat him followed by Lapin's dragon friend wanting to eat the orc. And just because the dragon spent centuries regaling Lapin with stories of how the stone was cursed didn't mean it was true. Did it?

The rabbit watched from across the packed dirt road as the orc entered the small general store. As he readied himself for another stirring round of internal debate, he noticed a slight fog roll in. So wispy, it went unnoticed by everyone else on the streets, except for Lapin as it stayed

low, hugging the ground. Then he watched as it slid
beneath the door of the store.

He ran across the street. Halfway to the store, he heard
the screams. Once he made it to the door, he saw why. The
dragon's stories were right. The stone was cursed.

The fog had divided into half a dozen trails of mist. And
each trail shifted between mist and demon. Skeletal ribs
formed sharp points while twisted and knotted bone made
long arms that led to clawed hands of white.

Even though the patrons of the store possessed
nightmarish looks and gnarled features themselves, none
could compete with the flying demons, silent as death's
whisper. Goblins stood little chance against claws that
flayed flesh in a flash. Troll guts splashed to the floor, the
carcasses soon followed. Those who had their wits about
them fought back, but every swipe of their hands yielded a
fistful of mist, only to have the smoke reform into demons
with spiked features.

Intelligence was a burden Zot never had to bear. But he
had enough to realize this was what had happened to his
family and his friends' families. These demons moved as
mist and struck as steel. Every ounce of ire in Zot's stumpy
body flowed to his fingers and feet. With a phlegm-filled
yowl, he launched himself at the nearest demon, grabbing
its arms. The bones turned to smoke leaving Zot with
empty hands and a burning heart. The demon escaped the
orc's grasp only to reform and attack. Ten claws, a foot
long each, drove through Zot's chest.

Pain shot through his short body, from the top of his
round skull to the tips of his stubby toes. In a cough, Zot's
mucus and blood splashed the demons smiling face. Zot
smiled, too, and grabbed the demon's hands. Putting the
force of his death spasm into his hands, Zot snapped off
the demon's wrists from its arms.

The demon screeched, its pain carried on its putrid
breath. Zot fell to the floor and gurgled one final laugh,
finding it amusing that the fetid disgust of the shrieking
demon mixed with the stench of his own gurgling ichor still
smelled more pleasant than Bale's feet.

As the handless demon writhed through the air, it
caught a rather unassuming creature from the corner of its

eye. A rabbit by the door, watching the horrors befall the patrons of the shop. Nothing deserved to live, especially the picture perfect puff of innocence like a rabbit! Despite its pain, the demon attacked. The rabbit ran.

Lapin fled as fast as his furry legs could move. The demon followed, riding the air the way a shark slices through water. Refusing to turn to mist until it caught its prey, the bony demon gnashed its crooked teeth, catching nothing but stray fur from Lapin's tail.

Scurrying from the town into the forest, Lapin hoped to lose his adversary in the brush. No such luck as the demon's bones shredded the thicket like slashing swords through dry thatch. It lunged, again snapping its jaws near Lapin's haunches. Adrenaline aided the rabbit, picking up speed while zigzagging, putting some distance between himself and the demon. He just needed to run a little farther, to a small clearing that lie at the other end of the briar patch. There!

Lapin burst through into the clearing and the chill of terror melted from his spine. After a few more leaps, he stopped and turned to his pursuer. He smiled with confidence and trust. The demon burst from the brush, twigs, and leaves exploding as the creature rushed forth. Jaws wide, teeth ready to rend its victim. Then with one crunching gulp, the demon ... was gone!

Lapin sat in the soft, warm grass and looked up to his long-time friend and companion, the dragon. The dragon looked down at Lapin while digging demon bone from between his teeth. "Lucky he was solid."

"Eh, I knew you'd be quick enough," the rabbit replied.

"Now do you believe me that the stone curses anyone who takes it from the cave?"

"Yes. Yes I do."

"This is going to be difficult."

"Yes. Yes it is."

"So, how are we going to do this?"

Lapin shifted his weight to his haunches and patted his face with his front paws. "Well ... I hate to say it, but we should enlist the help of the very trolls who stole the stone from us."

"Oh, this is going to be difficult. Very difficult indeed," the dragon mulled, sitting back on his own haunches. He felt a headache coming on.

SEVENTEEN

TALLIA CLUTCHED Tallon's hand. She tried to show no
fear, considering the company they kept, and, for the most
part, she had created a rather apt façade, a wall of stoicism
behind which all other emotions hid. But the snake around
her ankle started to crack that wall. She knew she should
be thanking this vile serpent; it ate the fist-sized spider on
her foot a moment ago. After a quick swallow, the arachnid
eating snake decided to explore, wrapping itself around
each of Tallia's ankles, creating a slithering set of shackles,
finding the scent of her perfume curious on its flicking
tongue.

Presenting a strong and unified front in these
negotiations was paramount. Tallia knew this. She and
Tallon needed to appear as stringent business owners, not
the spoiled nobility she often felt like. Damn this snake to
hell! She bit her tongue and tasted her own blood.

Tallon knew. He knew very well why his sister fretted.
Impressed with her strength of composure, he held her
hand tight, low, and between them. They sat knee to knee,
hip to hip on a tiny bench, making it very easy for him to
lean forward and rest his elbow on his knee, a sign of
intense passion for a particular point in negotiation. A
perfect time for Tallon to say, "Touch nothing in the
castle."

Across from the twins sat Praeker Trieste, staring at
them with hollow eyes. They had just delivered a batch of

weapons, the *fourth* batch, and wanted to firm up the price for them. Praeker leaned forward himself, looking at Tallon and not caring why the girl had such a problem with a rogue forest creature hugging her legs. "I find it difficult to tell my troops such specific orders when it comes to pillaging."

"They can kill everyone they want, save my sister and myself, and there are plenty of other treasures in the kingdom," Tallon countered.

"Why should I ask them to do this for you?"

"Not for us. For you. How can we run a fiefdom in your name without proper resources? Every smith in the city holds gold and silver in exchange for notes. The royal treasury is not in the castle. The head of every family around the castle itself is a prominent businessman. There is more gold from those sources than your men can carry. Just leave the riches in the castle where they lie."

Praeker leaned back and took a moment to admire the two youths for delivering the weapons themselves, walking them right into his encampment. In the thickest part of the forest small tents and tarps made from assorted furs and skins hung, draped over branches and alcoves. And those were just for Praeker's soldiers that cared—most found satisfaction within a patch of dead leaves or the nooks of large trees.

This battalion of nightmarish creatures numbered close to one thousand, but seemed like so much more through their acts of cruelty and hatred. None bathed. Ever. Some to the point of leaving an inky trail behind them wherever they walked. Bits of tattered and filth-saturated clothing would break off and fall from the festering skin of these putrid soldiers. They ate any animal that crossed their paths, leaving moist carcasses lie where they finished them. Latrines were unheard of, these monsters only moving far enough from where they slept to find relief. Sometimes they moved too close to where another slept, leading to the occasional skirmish quickly followed by a gathering crowd chanting and placing wagers. These creatures found a way to slice the belly of nature itself and then revel in the gushing entrails.

Tallon heard that Praeker formed this militia from leftovers and cast-outs from the society of Albathia. Citizens, both human and nonhuman—though the population tipped in favor of the latter—disgruntled, homeless, jobless, made the ranks. The Horde welcomed all who had a heart crafted by hatred and cruelty, ready to serve Praeker Trieste for the feral freedom of viciousness he offered.

A creature flanked Praeker on either side: a goblin examining a short sword, and a gaunt rat standing and acting like a man learning the nuances of a pike fashioned of iron. Praeker cast a sinister eye to the goblin and said, "What do you think, Captain? Tell the men to leave the castle's gold and jewels be?"

The goblin laughed. "Or what?"

"Or no more," Tallon replied. His impetuous response led to crushing glares from his audience.

The goblin, tall and the color of vomit with random locks of greasy, black hair sprouting from his wart-encrusted head, stepped forward, close enough to place the tip of the short sword under Tallon's chin. "No more, did you say?"

Focusing his eyes on Praeker only, Tallon said, "We're in this together. Kill us or refuse us, our weapons supply stops. And Daedalus will surely do the math if we go missing, meaning his supply to you will stop as well. Do you really want to risk angering a prince who can enlist an army to set an ambush for you? It's a small price we ask."

Praeker waved his hand to the goblin, ordering him to leave their guests alone, as he laughed at Tallon's bluff. He knew of Albathia's rising tensions with Tsinel and that nary a king's soldier could be spared at the precipice of war. But he liked this arrangement and sparing a lone building was an acceptable sacrifice to have his plans continue forth smoothly.

The goblin snorted in contempt, but did as instructed. He looked at Tallia and smiled, parting his thick lips to expose browned teeth, gnarled and half-missing. His fat tongue slid across his bottom lip. In one fluid motion, he stabbed the ground with his sword and brought it to Tallia's eye level, showing her the snake. The blade went straight through its skull, forcing its mouth closed as its body spasmed and tail flailed, smacking Tallia across her chest and lap. Just as the twitching subsided, the goblin took a hearty bite from the snake's side, blood and meat falling to Tallia's feet. The goblin turned and ambled away, the rat-creature with the pike followed, ready to barter or fight for a piece of the snake.

After the creatures left, Tallia's grip on Tallon's hand relaxed for the first time during this trip. Tallon slid his fingertips to her palm where he gently stroked it. She curled her fingers overtop his, caressing his knuckles with every stroke of her palm, creating a loving rhythm. And a warmth through Tallon's body. Emboldened, he asked, "Do we have a deal?"

Growing bored with his guests, Praeker responded. "Yes, yes. Keep the weapons coming, and your castle's lucre will go unspoiled."

Praeker stood to dismiss his audience, but before he could say a word, a gaunt soldier, looking much like a mummified man, interrupted the meeting. "Sir! Our reconnaissance has found a stone nearby. They said the town of Bogosh was decimated by demons."

Praeker turned to the twins, growling, "Our meeting is over." He grabbed the mummified soldier and dragged him deeper into the encampment.

The thought of spending any more time than they had to in this encampment of horror sent chills down each of the twins' spines. Once they made their way back to the horse-drawn-cart, Tallia flung her arms around Tallon's neck, buried her face in his chest, and sobbed. "That was horrible, Tallon. Simply horrible."

Tallon wrapped his arms around Tallia. "Then for the next meeting, you stay home."

"I won't hear of it! There is no way I will let you come here alone," Tallia said, pulling her head back.

Tallon looked at Tallia's tear-streaked face. Her eyes sparkled, the pinkness brought upon by tears, accentuating the shimmering blues. Tallon touched her cheeks with both thumbs, each erasing a tear-traveled path. He then stroked her cheeks again, this time his fingers unfurled to slide through her hair, his palms cupping her chin. He slid his fingers across her forehead to tuck a stray lock of hair behind her ear, causing her to gasp and part her full lips. Using his whole hand, he caressed her face again, his thumb gliding across her bottom lip. He stared at her as if they were the only creatures in the forest. Two people. Man and woman. Brother and sister. A chill tripped down his spine, forcing him to acknowledge his surroundings. "We must be going now."

With little effort, he assisted her to the driver's bench of the cart. He then hoisted himself up next to her and took the reins. With a quick snap of the leather strips, they began their journey back to the castle.

During the ride, Tallia had snuggled close to Tallon, placing her hand on his inner thigh and her head on his shoulder. The day had left her drained, a mental emptiness that accompanied a physical exhaustion. Asking her to use any form of mental faculty at this point would have been fruitless and, in Tallon's mind, cruel. So they rode in silence, despite his overwhelming desire to talk. He yearned for opinions on how the meeting went and what their next move should be, but it could all wait as he took a surreptitious look at her face, his movements minimal so as not to disturb her. Her face was pale and had the pinched look that spoke of recent terror. He decided again not to press her.

The ride back to the castle was long, but not altogether unpleasant. They had timed this journey, as with all the previous trips, to allow time for them to circle around and ride into the capitol from the direction that Daedalus would expect. The twins both knew he was the suspicious type and would certainly watch for their approach. Tallon had no desire to lengthen the actual trip on this day. Instead, he found a place to stop the horse and pulled out a simple meal of dried fruits and nuts and a small jug of wine he had stashed in the saddlebags.

"The wine will help you sleep," he assured Tallia when she looked at him with doe's eyes, relief flashing within them from his words. She accepted the cup from him with shaking hands. With that small gesture, she validated him as a person, as a brother, as a man ... so many feelings stirred inside him. From the embers of empathy within him, he knew a full spectrum of emotions awaited release. He watched her stretch out to lie down in the back of the cart for a brief nap. His eyes never left the prone beauty of her form. He drank it all in, more intoxicating than any alcohol he had ever known. Taking several slow, deep breaths to clear his mind, he stepped away.

"I must protect her from the monsters that stalk our world. Let Daedalus and Praeker Trieste have each other and be damned by their own insensate furies. We should tell the king. Play all sides. Preserve our peace. How I would love to see Daedalus in chains asking his father how he could possibly have known of his son's treachery and me stepping from the shadows to enjoy the disbelieving stare of a prince-turned-prisoner. What delicious irony," he whispered to the horses, patting their snouts, as if wrapped within another separate conspiracy with them. He took several deep breaths, slowing the wayward torrent of thoughts that escaped him. When they were safely dammed up inside him again, he returned to watching his sister's slumbering form and a more reasonable series of thoughts. "Soon this will be over, and we can slip away. I wish no more games, no more betrayals, no more danger. Only sanctuary, a little slice of perfect land for such a perfect beauty. And I'll be by her side."

The smile that played across his lips had grown steadily in size and intensity until it was at last full-blown and not even the cover of darkness could conceal it, entranced by a blurring kaleidoscope of visions of Tallia as queen. His favorite part replayed itself several times over in the theater of his mind: Tallia speaking to peasants assembled in the courtyard, the weight of her words carrying down the throng of milling bodies, their meaning returned by the smiles of the commoners. His face shone like a beacon in the night, and his skin felt feverish—all at the thought of Tallia in full regalia speaking to her subjects from on high. Then, in his vision, she reached backwards with one hand, touching him firmly on the chest. Her hand lingered there, clearly indicating that the placement was no accident. The acuity of his vision and the shame of such illicit thoughts startled him back to awareness, and though he tried to suppress the urge, he found himself checking under his shirt to see if he had in fact been singed by her imaginary touch.

His physical form boasted no such marks, but his psyche bore them indelibly, and it took him several minutes to recover. When his head finally cleared, he realized that the night had deepened, and he would need to make haste or face interrogation by Daedalus as to why their journey had taken so much longer this time. Tallon hurried back to the cart and woke his sister gently. After a few minutes of stretching, she joined him at the reins and then he set the horse forward. Still a bit groggy, she wiped the remnants of sleep from her, lest Daedalus notice even so small a detail as incongruous of their previous trips. They raced along the road to the castle. Tallia lit the side candles on the wagon to illuminate the crest it bore. By their light, the gate guards recognized their livery even at a distance and allowed them admittance without forcing them to slow their pace. They raced through the gate and headed straight for the stables. Leaving their steed and wagon for the stable boys to care for, the twins raced for their rooms and a quick bath before meeting with the prince. With any luck, the quickness of their entrance had shielded them from prying eyes.

From the balcony of his apartment, Daedalus watched as the cart approached the castle. With growing interest, he noticed the speed of the wagon and the haste its occupants made for the interior of the castle proper. Surely they had a tale to tell worth hearing.

EIGHTEEN

DEARBORN WAS packed and ready to go. The tip of the morning sun peeked over the horizon, not yet awake from its own nightly slumber. The chill in the air dictated the need for a blanket or heavier clothing, but Dearborn was warm and irritated. She hated how this mission fared.

The mottled men of the Elite Troop muddled through their routine. Some moved more slowly than others, paying the price for how easily ale and mead slid down their throats the night before. A few even swigged the remains from any mug they found, searching for the hair of the dog that bit them last night. Some drank in celebration of completing their mission; others drank to the loss of three comrades along the way.

Dearborn had not drank at all last night, nor slept a wink. She felt disappointed in the general and their men—she knew very well that no mission ended until they made it back home. She gazed to the rolling hills where she chased the mysterious and handsome—she could not help but use that adjective every time she thought of him—thief mere hours ago. Then another frightening chill ran down her spine, forcing her to look over her shoulder to the cave in which they found the stone. Eyes watched her. She knew it. She *felt* it! But she could say nary a word to anyone without feeling like an irrational harpy.

Blankets were rolled, fresh jerky and stale bread eaten, and canteens filled from a tiny stream that trickled between the mountains. And Dearborn watched, still staring at the cave where they found the stone. Then her horse shifted from the extra weight of another person jumping on its haunches.

"Good morn, partner," Haddaman said, his voice filled with a certain upbeat happiness, either from assisting in finding the stone, or anticipating the joy that came from annoying her. Dearborn could not guess why he seemed so happy, nor did she care, so she simply grunted in response.

Still smiling, Haddaman followed her gaze up to the mouth of the cave. "Quite an impressive climb, huh? But we did it. Just you, me, and the *future king*. Spectacular! Have you thought about your plans after the Elite Troop? I was thinking since you and I make such good partners in treasure hunting, we ..."

"We are not partners," Dearborn hissed. She thought of Mahlakore and the gruesome way he died. That man, that *young* man, was a good soldier and a good person. His parents still lived, and she would be the one to give them the news of their son's demise. "The very second this mission is over, I never want to see you again. And if you ever call me partner again, I will cut your tongue out and wear it as a necklace."

The other soldiers finished their packing, securing straps, looking over their steeds, checking their weapons and armor. Just as the rising suns started to chase away the morning chill, Iderion finished his own packing and approached Dearborn. "Good morn, Sergeant."

Dearborn looked down from her horse to the general. The *only* time Iderion seemed small was when she was on a horse and he was not. She hated when he called her by her rank, but she did love this smile that accompanied the words. She returned his smile with a fake smugness, as if they shared a joke only they knew. "Good morn to you, General."

"I trust our package is secure?" Iderion asked.

"Yes, sir," Dearborn replied, still smiling.

"Wonderful. I knew I made the right decision last night." As a social gesture, he placed his hand on her thigh. Surprised by the smoothness, he let his hand linger, and even indulged in the slightest of squeezes. His smile twisted to shock as he realized the gross breech of protocol.

Dearborn gasped. Images of throwing Haddaman from her horse so Iderion might join her so they could ride to a secluded nook in the cragged mountain base and throw each other around flooded her head as quickly as a flush filled her cheeks. His hand was rough, but warm, and felt like heaven on her skin.

Her eyes darted from his hand to his face. She hoped that her eyes conveyed the mix of love and lust that pumped through her veins. They did not. They showed shock and surprise, just as his did when they looked at her. He removed his hand and mumbled, "Ummm, I'll be out front. We'll keep the prince in the middle of the group. You stay toward the back. May our journey be blessed. Farewell."

As Iderion strode away, Haddaman all but laughed, "You two are pathetic. Any particular reason you two are hiding your love for each other? Afraid workmates shouldn't be bedmates?"

Dearborn hesitated, only because she could not decide which option to choose: break his nose, crush his windpipe, slap him, gouge his eyes, throw him from the horse. However, she would not get to do any of those, because Prince Oremethus interrupted her rage.

"Good morn, Sergeant," the prince said, directing his horse next to hers. "You look tired." The prince was not his usual picture of perfection. He seemed a bit disheveled: his hair not perfectly coiffed, hints of purple crescents under his eyes, a bit of a slouch to his posture. However, his handsome regality had not been diminished.

"Good morn to you, Your Highness" Dearborn replied. "I'm fine, thank you. For today's journey, the general has suggested that you ride ..."

"Actually," the prince interrupted through a gleaming white smile, "that's not why I'm here. I'd like to carry the stone, please."

"Excuse me?" slipped from Dearborn's mouth. She wished no disrespect, but his request caught her off guard, causing an unsatisfactory tone.

The prince's smile faded. The sunshine in his eyes gave way to dark storm clouds. He extended his hand and repeated, "The stone."

The warmth from Dearborn's face disappeared, leaving only pale, clammy skin. Her entire career, she had only taken orders from Iderion, *never* anyone else. She never felt more confused. "But ... the general ..."

"Is not the ranking officer. I am. And I *don't* remember opening the subject to debate. The stone. Now."

Reason forced its way into her mind, allowing her to accept her position. *Simply give him the stone and discuss it with the general*, it told her. So she did.

The prince's personal storm clouds parted, and the sunshine returned to his demeanor. His smile was back and twice as bright. He rolled the stone around his palm and fingers. "Sorry for seeming so demanding. Since I found it, I simply thought I should carry it." With a nod of gratitude, he rode away.

Haddaman fought every urge to vomit. Dearborn had carried the stone. She had had *the stone!* It was on this horse with her, which meant it was on *this horse with him*. And he never knew! Visions of him stealing the Satan Stone danced through his head. He could have waited for a particularly boring part of the journey when her mind would be all but asleep and he could have taken it. Or if he slipped an arm around her waist to distract her, he could have taken it. Or he could have engaged her in philosophical debate, forcing her to focus on grand ideas, and then he could have taken it. Oh, what a bargaining position he envisioned for himself as holder of the stone and a world bowing to him ...

Dearborn noticed a sudden shift in Haddaman's demeanor. He seemed to be sulking? She was going to ask, but enjoyed the silence far too much. She counted her blessings and kept her mouth shut as well.

The Elite Troop moved out.

Dearborn swept the area one last time with an all-encompassing glance. It was hard to believe, but there was nary a sign that anyone had camped in this area, let alone such a large group. All evidence of their stay was completely eliminated and in the matter of only an hour.

Even the holes from their tent stakes had been filled in so completely only a trained and gifted eye could spot them.

Haddaman picked up on her quick head movements, and, typical of a man, he could not help but say something. Typical of himself, he could not help but say the wrong thing.

"Who saw to Mahlakore's duties?"

"You no longer get under my skin, so say what you will."

"What? No, no, no. I was simply marveling at the astounding job your troop does. They make a comfortable camp in minutes and pack up, leaving no trace, in half the time one would suspect—all of it without effort or word. It's like watching a colony of ants. Every job is seen and attended to. I was just wondering how the, uh, recent 'vacancy' was handled."

"It is an honor to cover for another member. If anything, his duties were seen to several times over. No one here is selfish like you."

"How interesting. This selflessness that you all display ... how deeply does it run? Would you go hungry or lay down your life for another?"

"To a person. Without hesitation."

"I see. Does that extend to fame and fortune as well?"

"None here are interested in either."

"Really? So the members of the troop who have families to provide for would allow their children to go hungry whilst they empty their pockets for the benefit of their comrades?"

"What sort of twisted thinking is that? No one would ever ask, nor expect such a thing."

"But the nature of selflessness is to act without regard, quite prior to expectation and quite independently of being asked."

"You may appear to be a 'human' outwardly, but you reek like a kobold. Do you think up these ridiculous scenarios when you should be sleeping? Certainly there are better ways to occupy your time."

"Your avoidance of the issue is the only answer I require. I was merely trying to show you that your answers sound good, but hardly represent the reality of the human condition. Your back may be safe with these friends of yours, but your purse strings still require watching."

"Never again suggest that there is a thief amongst these men."

"Dear lady," Haddaman continued, "whether one filches coins or hearts or the credit for your deeds, a thief is still a thief."

Dearborn found Haddaman's smugness repulsive. His smile belonged on a barracuda, not a human being. And the actions he suggested ... such things may take place in a merchant's guild, but among this group such reprehensible behaviors could never be manifest. He toyed with her mind again. He sowed seeds; a malcontent spreading his wayward gospel: a reaper of the disillusioned. She could not wait to be rid of his taint, though she feared her skin would bear the putrid reek of his association forever.

"Haddaman," she said, "you would do well to quell your tongue, or you'll be ducking tree branches for the remainder of the trip."

To emphasize her point, she urged her mount towards a small hazelwood tree that sported a particularly low-hanging branch. The smell of it caught in his nose and lingered as an unpleasant reminder. Unconsciously, he raised his left hand up to his forehead and stroked at the bruise that was visibly imperceptible, but forever impressed upon his psyche.

Dearborn felt his reaction to the tree and allowed a smile to run rampant across her lips.

Several moments of quiet passed between them. She added them together in her head until the skeins could be woven into a tapestry of silence. When she was quite satisfied that Haddaman would remain reticent for a while, she reached out with her instincts to the surrounding landscape of brush and small trees trying to attune herself to their surroundings as the troop left the desert.

Only the sound of their horses' hooves broke the stillness as the troop rode in their customary column. Before today, she had marveled at the cohesiveness of the unit, despite the addition of two outsiders into their midst.

Haddaman would forever be an interloper into their world, but Oremethus was like an indigenous element.

Up to this point, she had been impressed with him the whole trip. She had expected something far different from a member of the royal house—stale emotions and manicured manners, perhaps. Someone who could barely handle a horse and rode with a weak back, like a tree growing on a hillock, bowed at the middle from its search for sunlight. His balanced posture was owed to his youth, she allowed, but that same trait belied his charisma and critical thinking skills. He was anything but indecisive, she thought, watching him ride in solitude.

Now he seemed a bit different—aloof, standoffish. He hunched his back. He wasn't well integrated with the riding column; the pace of his mount was uneven. He was keeping the horse from settling into an established pattern, constantly expanding the distance between himself and the men in front of him. In response, the riders behind him found themselves having a difficult time keeping a steady pace. On occasion he would turn around and cast scathing looks at them until they dropped back. The remainder of the formation made the adjustment without realizing it, but as she scanned ahead, she soon realized that the front of the column started to outdistance them.

She urged her own mount into a quicker pace, allowing her to draw even with the next rider. She whispered a quick message to the rider and watched as he mimicked her actions, spreading the missive through the back portion of the line. She watched the pair of guards receive their orders and respond by trying to close the gap between themselves and the crown prince.

Curious to observe his reaction, she watched as Oremethus took notice of their actions. The intrusion into his established personal space became apparent, and his response was immediate. In disbelief, she heard him snap to the nearest rider, "I need not be coddled like a muddled dolt!" before digging his heels into the horse's ribs to catch up to the front half of the train, leaving the back half behind in a cloud of bewilderment.

Dearborn took it upon herself to find what might be stuck in the crown prince's craw. She rode ahead, and her men changed the jumble of horses to an evenly spaced line. Communicated with grunts and pointing, the soldiers lined their steeds twenty paces apart, the rear held by Oxton, one of the troop's grizzled veterans.

Oxton's appearance often led the newer, younger members to believe the older man to be downtrodden. Little did they know the silver-haired man's muscles were twisted like rope, weathered and tightened to tense cords over time. Many a young buck walked away from challenging old Oxton to an arm-wrestling match with bruised hands and sore wrists. But in the Elite Troop, veteran status held the privilege of being a messenger.

Oxton had recently returned from a meeting with another messenger, receiving news that tensions with Tsinel were on the rise. Once Dearborn saw to the crown prince's mysterious needs, Oxton would ready himself to ride ahead thirty miles east and meet another of the troop's messengers to have him deliver the news of finding the Satan Stone. He just had to hold the rear long enough for his commanding officer to soothe the royal child. He never expected to hear a branch snap from behind him.

Oxton stopped his steed and stroked its mane to sooth it. Damn fool creature. He couldn't have his horse prancing around causing too much noise, or he'd look like a neophyte. The gnarled old soldier watched the chest-high patch of thicket behind him, wondering what he was looking for. *Damnation,* he started to wonder why he was even looking.

He considered calling out to his companions, but stopped himself, recalling the jabs about his 'advancing age.' He wasn't ready to be forced into retirement and wouldn't have himself appear addled. He could surely handle a rogue rabbit or a stray squirrel, determined to catch a light snack for the campfire later. Drawing his sword, he guided his horse to the brush. The foliage was surprisingly foreboding, as if light itself were too scared to touch it. The gray hair running down his neck and arms stood on end as his grip on the sword tightened. Oxton poked the thicket and brush with his sword, chills shooting through his body with every poke. Nothing. A smile slid across his face while he silently congratulated himself for keeping his demeanor cool. He sheathed his sword with a light heart and tugged on the reins, indicating to his horse to turn about so he could join up with the group again.

Before he could turn, the darkness gave way to glowing eyes, gleaming horns, and glistening teeth. One set would have turned his spine to jelly, but thirty pulverized his soul. Beset with the urge to flee, the horse whinnied and turned. But not fast enough. Claws of all shapes and sizes reached from the brush and pierced every part of horse and man. Not a scream, cry, nor even the slightest yelp could be formed. No twitch, flinch, nor parry could be made. Oxton tried to fight or flee or yell a warning to his troop mates, but muscles didn't move, and words couldn't form. Once he felt his own blood gush over his arms, chest, and legs, he realized he was being dragged into the darkness. ...

NINETEEN

DIMINUTIA SAT fidgeting, unaware that his foot tapped or his right hand ran up and down the back of his neck. He never could handle interrogations well. A decade ago he had worked with a different set of partners; however, he cracked under the pressure of the authorities' questioning and sold them out for his own freedom. Never forgiving himself, he vowed that he would be more steadfast in his moral conviction, never letting his weakness compromise Nevin or Silver. But now the pressure was on. Ten eyes stared at him as the campfire danced its wild dance, casting restless shadows on the world around him. He was about to crack; the need to surrender or run boiled deep within his gut.

"So, she was very beautiful, but built like a man?" Silver asked.

"No," Diminutia replied, his foot tapping faster. "I mean … she was certainly beautiful. But not like a man. She was very tall, taller than anyone here, and sinewy. But not round and … and … bumpy … like a man. Smooth and sleek."

"Did … you just describe her as … sinewy?" Silver asked, leaning forward. The fire's shadows altered his face to look more sinister than the devil.

"Ummm … yes?"

"Could she throw down anyone and everyone around this campfire?"

"Undoubtedly with ease."

"Did she have big, bountiful breasts?"

"Ummm ... no."

"It was a *man!*" Silver emphasized the word by pointing at Diminutia while a smile crept across his lips.

Not able to grasp the reasons behind ridiculous chiding among humans, Nevin often stayed out of those types of conversations. But tonight, he could not resist this opportunity. "Did Dim just say she did *not* have big, bountiful breasts? I thought that topped his list of 'must haves' when it came to women. Actually, are there even any other features on that list?"

Foot tapping even faster now, Diminutia's hand began to play with a few stray hairs from the back of his head. "She was beautiful. Beyond beautiful. And there was a connection there, between us. A spark I've never felt before. Maybe ... maybe that's why I've never found true love ... I'm always looking for big, bountiful breasts. Maybe I was looking in the wrong direction all this time."

In unison, Silver and Nevin pulled their eyes from Diminutia and looked at each other. A fit of uncontrollable laughter then consumed both of them. "Love! He said, 'love.'"

Their jocularity ended with the clap of Belhurst's hands and his agitated whisper, "Enough!"

He waited until all three thieves looked his way before he continued. "You three possess the stealth of a herd of drunken elephants. It amazes me you haven't been caught. While focusing on the dithering of Diminutia's crotch, you've glossed over the important part of his story—the king's Elite Troop."

"Elite Troop?" Silver asked, now scowling from having a good laugh interrupted. "What makes you think it's the Elite Troop?"

Belhurst rolled his eyes. "Do you know nothing of what goes on in the kingdom around you? Diminutia said they had the king's insignia on everything, and they had completed a mission to find one of the stones. Do you think the king would trust a regular troop plucked from his army to handle such a task? And, the most obvious clue of all, the Elite Troop has a female sergeant."

Diminutia gave a placating smile. "Belhurst, we are thieves, not spies. We're known for robberies, not espionage. We don't *care* about the king or his army. We focus on the local authorities and *their* routines."

"Never the matter," Belhurst huffed, dismissing Diminutia with a wave of his hand. "We must pack, douse the fire, and be on our way."

"Now?" Silver asked. "It's the middle of the night."

"Yes, now," Belhurst replied. Heeding the command, Follen and Grymon stood from the fire and prepared their trappings.

"Wait," Nevin said. "Wizard, we need our rest. We've been through more than we could have ever imagined since meeting you. We've been to parts of this land that we would have never ventured to otherwise. We witnessed an entire village razed by a horde of unholy creatures. We now know that demons are real. We need to rest."

"The Elite Troop is too close, and we're begging them to find us with your wanton rabblerousing."

"They completed their mission. I hardly doubt that they would care enough about some miscreant thief to search for him."

"Why wouldn't they? As you just said, they completed their mission. They have plenty of spare manpower now. Soldiers without a fight can become very restless, especially if they notice a campfire accompanied by raucous laughter. Besides, we still need that stone."

"We failed, wizard. It happens from time to time. When it does, we get a good night sleep and come up with a new business plan in the morning."

Belhurst stood, the shadows created from the fire made him ominous and unnaturally tall. "We cannot fail, thief. And your tiny little mind is missing the obvious."

Never one for succumbing to insults, Nevin discovered he did not like it when the wizard hurled one at him. Standing and puffing out his chest, Nevin stared Belhurst in the eye. "And what exactly is that?"

"We know where they will be going, you dolt. They are the *king's* Elite Troop. They report to the *king*. And where does the *king* live?"

"Phenomere, the capital of Albathia."

"I'm impressed you know that much," Belhurst said, turning his back on the other thieves, their hindquarters still planted on the ground. The old wizard moved off to help the other wizards pack.

Silver and Diminutia both looked up to Nevin, seeking his opinion. The elf could not take his eyes off Belhurst.

"See," Silver whispered. "I told you he was an ass."

With no shift in his emotionless expression, Nevin replied, "I agree. But let's pack. I'm inclined to travel with them to Phenomere. I want that stone. *And* the one they're carrying as well."

After they stood, they walked to their bedrolls in unison. Diminutia still fidgeted with the back of his neck. "The stones? Let's think about this. There are demons guarding *this* stone, the Shadow Stone. I can only assume there are demons guarding the other ones as well. And that one is called the Satan Stone. Much more ominous, don't you think? Why would we want that burden?"

Focusing only on travel preparation, Nevin replied, "Did you not just try to steal that very stone mere hours ago?"

"Well ... yes. But I was mad for almost getting urinated on."

"There you have it. Has Belhurst done any less to my honor ... our honor ... with the intonations of his words? I want to do the same thing for the same reasons."

Shrugging, Diminutia said, "Sounds like a good enough reason for me."

Silver rolled his eyes. "Waking up is a good enough reason for you to explore any and every possible shenanigan placed before you."

"You know how to cut a man to the quick." With the back of his right hand he made a pronounced pantomime of wiping a tear from his eye.

At this, the three friends shared a quiet mirth that left even Nevin twitching with the effort to restrain himself. They stood around waiting for the wizards to finish packing up their "damnable cart," as Silver had named it some time ago.

"Um, at the risk of disturbing our uncomfortably fraternal moment, Nevin, what *exactly* do you have in mind?" Silver asked.

196 | CHRIS PISANO and BRIAN KOSCIENSKI

"How many times do you remember tricking Bale into giving us something of value?" Nevin answered with his own question.

"More times than I can count."

"Same concept. Dim, do you want to keep one of his friends busy while I spend some special time with Belhurst?"

"With pleasure. Finally! A little skullduggery." Happy that the focus of attention had shifted from the story of his early evening encounter and stayed elsewhere, Diminutia hauled himself to his feet and sought out the most congenial of the wizards.

With minimal effort, a plan came together. Such was the reward of working with the same partners for such an extended period of time. Nevin afforded himself a slight smile as Diminutia went to offer Grymon whatever aid he could. The smile transformed into a wolfish grin when bits of casual conversation between the wizard and the thief floated back to him.

Nevin then turned to see Follen working on packing the bedrolls. "Silver, care to keep this one occupied?"

"I would love to."

"Excellent. I'll see if I can catch Belhurst's ear."

Silver smiled broadly. "Yeah, good luck with that."

Nevin sought out the head wizard, but something in his gut defied digestion. What could the wizard possibly be thinking? Did he truly expect them to take part in something that might end in a conflict with the king's Elite Troop? The very idea was ludicrous. The thievery part might not be difficult, but more than simple chains would greet them if caught. Odds favored someone getting seriously hurt or killed. Pure and simple, these were soldiers, not militia or law enforcement. They'd more likely kill the thieves first, then force Belhurst to perform some necromancy to interrogate them later. The thought chilled him through.

Nevin found Belhurst well outside of camp. Strange that the chief wizard secluded himself while the rest prepared to leave and could have greatly used his help, but Nevin was thankful for the opportunity it presented. Grymon was still chatting away in Diminutia's ear when

Nevin had last seen them while Silver kept Follen ignorant to Nevin's whereabouts.

Nevin climbed the slope of a rocky little knoll and stood next to Belhurst, clearly trying to meditate.

"What do you want?" the wizard groused.

"Just seeking the opportunity to coordinate. You have a plan. Or do you mean to take the Elite Troop on in a fight?"

"Nevin, I don't have the time to explain this to you. And even though I don't particularly care what your thoughts or opinions of me are, I wouldn't have you see me as disordered and impulsive. But we must get that stone. If that requires a fight, then so be it."

"Belhurst, that's madness," said Nevin, procuring some jerky from his hip pouch and tossing it into his mouth. "Surely you can't mean that. And more surely, you can't expect us to help with that."

"Nevin, believe me. If diplomacy and reason stood a chance, then they would be my first choice. The stone they carry has immense strength and perverse effects. Whoever carries that stone will be well beyond the capacity of rational thought when we get there. He or she will have set themselves up as godlike in their mind. Paranoia will cloud their judgment, and even their own friends will have cause to fear physical harm from them."

Here the wizard paused, lowering his head. His shoulders sagged, and he seemed suddenly frail to Nevin. In a moment, all of those months without sleep had caught up to the mage. Lines he was hitherto unaware of etched themselves deep into his brow and around his eyes and mouth.

"Of course, I will give you the opportunity to leave if you so desire, though I would greatly appreciate it if you and your men would try to steal the Elite Troop's stone. I would prefer to avoid bloodshed if possible. I will recompense you in whatever means I can, and do what I can to extricate you from the situation, though if things get tense you will have to fend for yourselves."

Nevin regarded the wrinkled wizard with a suspicious gaze. He held no contempt for the man, yet he had zero trust in him either. The wizard hid his true desires well, but Nevin knew they were there. Even the most generous of men acted for selfish reasons, they craved the feelings of enlightenment that performing good deeds brought. Nevin had never felt such feelings, but he knew they existed. Just as he knew every man and woman never acted without some form of personal gain.

Nevin's mind raced, visualizing various scenarios that could be brought about by certain word choices. He and his thieving partners wanted to swindle the wizards, but not to the point of evoking their wrath or leaving themselves in a situation of dire peril. However, Nevin realized the latter of the unsavory options could not be avoided as commotion from their campsite commanded his attention.

Screaming. Growling. The clanking of supplies getting hurled around. Belhurst and Nevin glanced at each other and then back to the site. They knew these sounds meant an attack.

Nevin ran back to the campsite, the old wizard a few paces behind, to see the commotion. His stomach sank, and his spine grew cold. He expected to see the Elite Troop, fearing they discovered the campsite. What he saw gripped his heart and squeezed all hope from it. The shadows moved.

Nevin and Belhurst ran to join their friends in the center of madness. Diminutia and Silver slashed at random movements. Follen and Grymon uttered nonsensical phrases as small bursts of fire flashed from their hands, enough to push the shadows back for minor reprieves, but not enough to keep them at bay.

"Where's the camp fire?" Belhurst cried, looking around the ground as if it had simply been misplaced.

"The thieves extinguished it!" Grymon answered.

"What? Why would you do something so asinine while the suns are gone?"

"*You* were the one throwing a fuss about being discovered by the Elite Troop! Especially worried about the fire!" Silver shouted in defense.

Nevin assessed the situation. It was dire indeed. They had set up camp on a plateau, high enough to prove fatal should they decide to jump, that could only be accessed by a small alley of difficult rock. Shadows swirled in front of the only viable escape rout while black mists rolled onto the plateau edge. And the thieves and wizards were caught in the middle of an ever-constricting perimeter of darkness.

Calculating the odds of survival, Nevin listened to Belhurst and Grymon exchange possibilities of spells to ensure escape or survival. They lacked necessary ingredients for every spell suggested. The odds diminished in Nevin's mind with every failed suggestion, until there were no suggestions left to be made—except one.

Nevin turned to Follen and watched with amazement at the fluidity of the wizard's movements. During any other situation, the aged wizard would twitch and fuss, but when it came to plying his craft, he possessed the skill of a dancer. Nevin drew his dagger and approached Follen.

"Enchant this," Nevin said, grabbing Follen's arm.

The wizard scowled, wondering if the thief believed the task to be enough for escape. He then looked into Nevin's eyes and realized the thief knew very well an enchanted dagger would be nary enough. With a quick nod, Follen took the dagger and stabbed the ground. He removed it from the dirt and sliced Nevin's hand. Finally, he forced Nevin to wield the dagger with his bleeding hand. "Babba Eyooga Dellat!"

Nevin watched as a bright, yellow flame engulfed his weapon. Looking at Follen, he said, "You better get ready to push that damnable cart."

As smooth and silent as a shadow himself, Nevin slid to Belhurst. Belhurst noticed the thief's wry smirk and pursed his lips, ready to spew forth insults and profanities at the thief for smiling during a time of despair. But he was interrupted by a simple gesture, Nevin holding up the pilfered Shadow Stone in his fingers. The wizard reached for it, but the thief was gone.

Nevin ran toward the blocked escape route and waved the stone for all demons to see. He then sprinted along one side of the perimeter of undulating blackness toward the plateau's cliff. The demons followed, uncloaking the escape route like a falling funeral veil.

Follen and Grymon took immediate advantage and pushed the cart to the exit. Belhurst needed to restrain Silver and Diminutia.

"Nevin!" Diminutia cried out. "Don't be a fool! Drop the stone and run!"

His friend's words fell on deaf ears as Nevin faced a wall of rippling ink. He slashed at it with his blazing dagger, but missed. Feeling enough time had passed for his companions to stage an escape, he turned to retreat. Bars of flowing darkness stopped him. He cut through them with ease, releasing shrill screams of pain as dark tendrils flopped along the ground. He ran toward his friends amid a chorus of, "Come on! Run!" but he soon found himself getting no closer.

Dark mist held the elf in place as the ink oozed over his shoulders and down his chest. His waist and hips disappeared. Blindly, he stabbed at the wall of black that held him, but did little more than elicit more screams. He could no longer see his legs and feet. The black was cold, ice touched every inch of his skin. But he endured the chilling pain by the warmth in his chest. Had he ever felt the graces of nobility before, he would have done it more often. As threads of frozen agony wove their way to his bones, he tossed the stone back to Belhurst. The shadows covered Nevin's face.

Silver and Diminutia both raised their daggers and screamed. However, the black mists disappeared into chasms and crevices as quietly as they had came. Belhurst pocketed the stone and put his hands on the thieves' shoulders. "Come. We must hurry. Their appetite has been sated, and they will need some time to heal their wounds, but they still might try to return tonight. We must move."

Silver spun and placed the tip of his dagger under the wizard's chin. Tears streamed down his face as he spoke through gritted teeth. "If you ever imply that my friend was nothing more than a diversionary meal again, I'll slice you and feed *you* to those demons!"

With a huff, Silver sheathed his dagger and walked past Belhurst. The wizard turned to Diminutia and stammered, "I didn't mean ..."

"Shut up," Diminutia whispered, still staring at the spot where his friend sacrificed himself. Diminutia's evening began with him running from an angel and ended with his friend running to the devil.

TWENTY

DEARBORN FACED three pairs of angry eyes, all of them bloodshot and trapped behind eyelids swollen from exhaustion. She imagined hers must look the same since they burned and watered with every blink.

"The horses can't take much more of this, Sergeant," Glindos stated, his eyes saying more. "And neither can we."

"He's right," Barrett joined in. "We all feel that way. Why don't you?"

Dearborn never liked her authority challenged. But in this case, she deserved it. "I do feel the same way. I do. However, there has never been a time when Iderion gave an order ..."

"Iderion?" Klandor snorted. "Iderion hasn't given an order in days. It may be his mouth moving, but we all know it's the mad prince's words coming out."

Klandor was young, a few seasons older than Mahlakore had been, but still young. His youth fueled the fire in his belly, and it would be some time before it mellowed to the point of discretion. A young dog always ready to fight, Klandor often barked and growled in the wrong direction. And like an unruly dog, he needed discipline.

Catching him off guard, Dearborn took a step toward Klandor and shoved her fingers between his leather armor and neck. She took the same step back, pulling down. Klandor dropped to his knees with a grimace. Dearborn then knelt herself and pushed, forcing Klandor's shoulders toward his heels, arching his back to provide continuous pain.

With her face close enough for her breath to move the hairs of his unkempt beard, loud enough for the other two to hear, she said, "Your opinion of the prince doesn't matter and should not be expressed. Remember, he is still the prince. If you can't remember that, then remember who your general is: a general who has *never* led you astray. And if you can't remember who your general is, then remember who *I am*."

To show her true dominance, she gave one last painful push against Klandor's chest, then stood, bringing the young pup to his feet with ease.

"Do either of you two care to express your opinion about the prince?" she asked Glindos and Barrett. "Care to start an open forum? Maybe a rousing debate?"

Neither Glindos nor Barrett could pull their eyes from the indents in Klandor's leather armor caused by Dearborn's thumbs. Wide-eyed, they simply shook their heads.

Dearborn exited the tent and looked around camp. Less than half the tents they started with lined the perimeter of the small, forest clearing. And their construction was less than perfect. Most of the men slept in the tents. The others chosen for guard duty or chores slept where they stood or sat. They were losing the battle against sleep; very few remained awake. She thought of rousing them, shaming them for passing out mid-duty. She then immediately thought of sneaking into a tent and closing her eyes herself. It was a tempting thought. She decided the best way to avoid temptation was to give in to it. Just as she started toward the closest tent, the general and prince emerged from it.

"Sergeant," Iderion said. His voice, though still deep, lacked the impressive boom that commanded attention. His gnarled beard and mussed hair seemed to converge, hiding his eyes. If he shut them to slumber, no one would notice. "We're moving."

She made no attempt to hide her exhausted frustration. "What? We made camp mere hours ago, and now we need to break it?"

"It is the best course of action. They'll never expect it," the prince huffed, his breathing shallow and erratic. His eyes matched, darting from treetop to underbrush, never focusing on one thing for more than half a blink. A rat's nest had more order than the prince's hair, dirty and poking in all directions and slicked to his forehead, glistening with sweat despite the early morning chill.

Pushing the dread thoughts of how disrespectful she must seem in front of the general, if he was even awake, Dearborn pressed on. "We've been doing this for a week solid, never more than two hours rest on any given day. The men are passing out on their feet. I beg of you, please let us rest until the sun is completely over the horizon."

"But The Horde ..."

"We have encountered them once and have not seen them since."

Out of new instinct, the prince placed both hands over his breast pocket containing the Satan Stone. Slightly hunched, he took a step back. "We are being pursued, Sergeant. Make no mistake of that. Unpredictability is our ally. If we head straight home, we'll be caught."

"Your Highness, we truly don't know if The Horde is pursuing us ..."

"I fear it to be much, much worse, Sergeant. *Something* is chasing us!"

"Then let us find out. This is all I ask. A few men. Everyone else can rest."

The prince's jittery eyes focused on hers just long enough to show he understood. "Very well. No more than a few hours. And send Haddaman to me for counsel."

"Thank you, Your Highness." She emphasized her gratitude with a slight bow, then she glanced at Iderion; even though his eyes were hidden, he gave a thanking nod.

Dearborn strode off with hastened pace. Despite the fact that Oxton had mysteriously vanished more than a week ago, she doubted that anything or anyone followed them, and she relished the opportunity to sneak away from camp. It was odd she got a renewed sense of vigor thinking about stealing a couple hours of sleep. And she knew just who to take.

Whipping open the flap of the tent from which she came, she saw Glindos, Barrett, and Klandor, all still dissatisfied with their last conversation with her. She gave them a smirk and said, "Come on. We're going on a mission. Mount up."

The men grumbled and groaned the whole time they prepared their horses. Dearborn had recruited two more men, Frewhar and Raynen, who had been falling asleep as they brushed their steeds. Despite the change of scenery, Frewhar and Raynen joined in the griping. Once the horses took them far enough from camp, Dearborn gave them the details of the mission. "I have heard less complaining from school girls with pigtails! I convinced the prince to allow me a reconnaissance mission, giving me 'a few' hours. I take 'a few' to mean five, so we shall ride a half hour out, take much needed naps in shifts and then head back with news that we saw no pursuers."

All five men smiled.

The half-hour ride passed quickly, the time eaten away by made-up songs praising the wisdom of their sergeant. Jokes were told at the expense of those who could not escape the maddening clutches of camp. Glindos even leaned forward to hug his horse around its neck and said with relief, "Did you hear that, my sweet? Beautiful, beautiful slumber soon. I have missed you so!"

"There," Barrett yelled, pointing to the base of a tree. It was actually two trees that had grown so close together they merged into one, forming a rounded alcove, the perfect size for a man to take a nap. "There is where I shall sleep! And I will run anyone of you through if you try to take it."

Dearborn and the four other men laughed at Barrett's zeal. She felt relaxed and gave the order to dismount, ready to discuss sleep rotations. She would take first watch, of course—until movement in the distance caught her eye.

With a quick flash of her left hand, she brought silence to the entire group. She had been in a similar situation once or twice previously, and she wondered for a moment if the sudden quiet acted more as a warning to the other party than as anything beneficial to her and her companions, but it was a force of habit.

Whatever she thought she had seen proved to be elusive at this juncture. Left hand was still raised; she tipped two of her fingers and pointed to the left. Wordlessly, Barrett and Glindos slipped off in the direction that she had indicated. After she was certain that they had moved out, she tipped her head to the right, and Frewhar and Raynen moved off to complete the perimeter. With a flick of the wrist and a wink, she commanded Klandor to guard the steeds.

Dearborn allowed both groups a few seconds before she strode directly toward the movement that had caught her attention. Knowing that she was completely out in the open and had no chance of sneaking up on anything, she decided that speed would be her only advantage. Hastening her pace, Dearborn neared the cluster of trees that had served as obfuscation for the mysterious movements in the woods. Just as she prepared to duck around a tree a noise from above drew her attention. She jerked her head upwards but could see nothing immediately and loathed being distracted from the potential hiding spot directly in front of her. Tensing the muscles in her legs, she sprang to her right and did a tuck and roll around the little cluster of trees. As she followed her roll through to fruition, rising to her feet in one fluid motion, she took notice of what appeared to be the backside of a raccoon. Its face was still buried amongst the trees, but its brindled gray fur and long tail seemed to hint at its identification.

Strange that a wild animal doesn't run, Dearborn thought. With her left boot, she kicked some dead leaves in the direction of the animal. It reacted as if in slow motion. Withdrawing its head from the vegetation with a pronounced slowness, it then hesitantly turned its face towards her. The muzzle was skeletal in nature, as was half of the face fixing her with a baleful stare. Shrinking back within itself, the creature gave a hideous hiss, revealing row after impossible row of spiked teeth.

In some deep, recessed part of her mind, it registered to Dearborn that this creature simply didn't have enough mouth to house this many teeth when she became aware of the fact that its jaws and muzzle elongated right before her eyes. She watched in horror, rigid with fear and disgust.

206 | CHRIS PISANO and BRIAN KOSCIENSKI

Despite her revulsion, she simply couldn't tear her eyes away from the spectacle. Until at long last she heard the shouts of her companions.

She refused to break eye contact with this gruesome creature, instead backing away. The shouts that seemed to start out as a warning escalated in both volume and pitch, finally turning sour with fear. A chill raced down her spine, and she drew her sword from the scabbard at her hip just as the animated carcass prepared to charge.

"Sergeant!" The cry came from several rows of trees away, but she recognized Barrett's voice through the fear that distorted his normal tone.

"I have one here, too," Dearborn yelled. "Status report! Everyone!" The ringing of steel carried the only audible answer she received. As she eyed her opponent, she could hear the dull thrumming of her pulse, feel the blood pushing through her veins. She was acutely aware of the sweat on her clammy skin. She continued to back away from her adversary, but a sudden shift in its hips suggested that a lunging attack was imminent. She braced herself despite its lack of bulk. As she predicted, the little beast charged. But as it loped at her, it mutated and grew, continuing to gain bulk and size. It was larger than an average man by the time it crashed against her armor. Dearborn fell back, staggering under its weight.

The beast stood over six feet in height, and she judged its weight to be twice that of an average man. The left side of its body sloughed off its form and onto the ground, an undead version of molting, revealing even more of its skeletal framework. The shadowy insides left Dearborn unsettled. Instead of putrid entrails, there was a swirling mass of ichor that coalesced constantly, each facet a human face struggling to break free of its tenuous confine.

If those be its victims, she thought, *I'll not hasten to add myself to the collection.*

Summoning her strength, Dearborn pushed her assailant away. The mottled beast took a few slow steps backwards, glaring at her with dead eyes. It seemed to be pondering its next maneuver as if overbearing its opponent was a tactic that had never been thwarted previously. After eyeing her for a few seconds, it simply charged again as if signifying its lack of rationality, something Dearborn hoped she would be able to use against the monstrosity.

Even as the beast ran at her, she was aware of the sounds of continued skirmishing around her, so at least some of her men still fought. Her labored breathing sounded loud in her ears. She noticed the stillness of nature all about her for the first time. She sidestepped the beast's attack and watched with interest the amount of time and space it took to come about. The beast was far from nimble, nor was it gifted with celerity. As it hobbled around to get her into view again, Dearborn charged, swinging her sword straight at the top of its hideous skull. The blade glanced off ineffectively, though the clash resounded and a shockwave rippled up her forearms, leaving her hands tingling.

The fiend began to shift and amble again turning its bulk towards her. Dearborn chose that moment to rush at it it again from the other side. This time she stabbed at it with the point of her sword. Due to her great size, Dearborn carried a broadsword, a blade far more suited to hacking and pounding on an opponent. Her attempt at impaling the creature was defeated by her own blade, which glanced off two ribs before careening off the beast. With a gnarled paw, the monster backhanded Dearborn, knocking her to the ground.

Stunned, she didn't move. The hit from the creature left her cheek and chin throbbing, but she remained still for tactical reasons. The creature was top-heavy and Dearborn reasoned that if it attacked while she was on the ground, it would have to come down on all fours. She deduced correctly. Rolling to her right, she avoided the heavy claws, now sinking deep into the forest floor. With adrenaline fueling her actions, she leapt to her feet and swept her blade through the creature's neck. A decayed tongue drooped from the decapitated skeletal head while its body twitched itself still.

Sacrificing only enough time to validate the lifelessness of her adversary, Dearborn ran toward the small clearing where she had left her comrades and horses. She pushed all fatigue from her body and soul, her legs churning with such speed her feet scarcely touched the forest's blanket of dead leaves. Honing in on the clearing ahead, Dearborn flew through the underbrush. *Surely I'm mad,* she thought once she saw what awaited her as she burst through the tree line.

The clearing had been transformed from a tranquil napping place to a battle-stained killing-field. Glindos lay in bloodied pieces at the base of a tree, his dripping entrails dangling from low branches like macabre decorations. Frewhar's corpse also rested at the base of a thick tree, pounded and pulped with his armor shredded; he looked no different than an over-ripened pumpkin hacked by butcher knives. Dearborn assumed the legs with no torso wearing army issue boots were all that remained of Raynen. Stabbed, butchered, and decapitated monster corpses blanketed the forest floor, three of their corpses for every one of the soldiers'. Klandor and Barrett battled in the center of the gory arena, each locked in combat with a monster.

Dearborn rushed to aid Klandor since his foe was largest. The monster matched Klandor in height, but had the girth of a mature bear. Its skin was red and corded, nothing more than twined muscles knotted together. Its head formed a dome from shoulder to shoulder and displayed nothing but a vacuous mouth lined with rows of teeth. Each of its powerful claws equaled half the size of its sinewy chest. With speed unbefitting its size, the creature's claws sliced through the air as it lumbered toward Klandor. But the young warrior kept moving, parrying every one of the demon's thrusts. Once he learned the movements of his adversary, Klandor struck. With two quick slices, the demon's hands fell to the ground like sides of beef being cut from a butcher's block. Klandor stopped to assess the new situation and formulate a plan. What he didn't factor into his plan was the monster shaking off gobs of gore to expose maws of gnashing teeth at the ends of his wrists. Too surprised to react, Klandor's body was torn to meaty ribbons by three sets of teeth.

Screaming from the frustration of arriving too late, Dearborn drove her sword through the back of the monster's bulbous head, the blade looking like a bloodied metal tongue. Putting her full weight into it, she used the base of the creature's neck as a fulcrum, her sword a lever cleaving the monster's head in half. With the grace of a dancer and speed of a sprinter, she spun herself and sword as one, the blade sliding through the creature's head as if it were freshly churned butter. The two halves of its head fell to the ground like a split melon.

Sword primed, Dearborn turned to aid Barrett. Even though a layer of blood coated him, Barrett needed no help, his sword finishing off the last of the monsters. His whole torso moved with every breath, gulping air as if he had forgotten the taste. "This ... is ... madness!"

Sheathing her sword, Dearborn ran to her steed, thankful harm found none of the horses. She fetched Barrett's as well while removing the tethers of the others. "We have to leave."

Not even aware that his Sergeant offered the reins of his horse to him, Barrett continued his intense stare at the gouged carcass. "They ... The Horde ... came from nowhere. Glindos had no chance ..."

"This was not The Horde. These were *monsters*. Demons. We have to go now."

"Th ... three of these ... these monsters tore through him and his armor like he were but a fattened pig in a sack ..."

"*Soldier!*" Dearborn snapped. She waited for Barrett to look up before she handed him the reins. "We *will* mourn for them. *Later*. We *have* to warn the others!"

The two survivors mounted in haste and jabbed heel to rib. Filled with just as much fear and confusion as their masters, the horses obliged with full gallop. However, they could sense what their masters could not. There were more.

The soldiers rode side-by-side, but within a blink, Barrett's chest exploded in a crimson spray. Still pushing her steed forward, Dearborn looked back to see squirming tentacles reel Barrett back to the blood saturated clearing. A dozen more monsters, horrors even her nightmares didn't dare to imagine, stepped out from the trees. Hungry teeth and impatient claws awaited the prize of a fresh kill. Tears streamed from Dearborn's eyes as she drove her horse harder.

Ar'drzz'ur, legs of a bull, torso and arms of a man, horns affixed to a frightening face, watched the woman warrior ride away. His demon brethren, slave to the Satan Stone, had been following her and her party for too long. The slaughtering of her comrades was nothing more than a teasing taste of things to come. The Satan Stone had called upon Ar'drzz'ur, General of the Demons. He smiled and salivated with anticipation.

TWENTY-ONE

PERCILESS PACED his chamber. He frowned so deep and so hard that his forehead throbbed. His right hand massaged his left, until he spun to walk the opposite direction. Then his left hand massaged his right. Three months. Three months he had been gone. Disappeared with nary a farewell and zero explanation. His gut knotted itself at the thought of telling his family why.

Four months ago Perciless began to see the world for what it was. That is, he stopped *allowing* himself to be so naïve. His brother, Oremethus, went on a mission with the Elite Troop searching for a mysterious and powerful stone. Shortly after their mission started, one of their message riders brought news that the town of Freeman's Way had been decimated by The Horde. Upon hearing that, Perciless had felt something stir within. But the wake-up call came with the next message rider of the Elite Troop—they stumbled upon a small Horde contingent outside Balford's Bounty.

To this point, Perciless had been living the life that peasant children hear about in fairy tales. Much to his embarrassment, he had believed those tales, including the ones that began with knightly heroes dashing off to adventure and ended with them returning home unscathed, treasure in hand. It never dawned on him that there were middles to these tales, hardships between beginning and end. Especially when he took it upon

212 | CHRIS PISANO and BRIAN KOSCIENSKI

himself to tell the families of the fallen Elite Troop members what had happened. Indeed, it was no fairy tale.

During the sleepless nights that followed, he tossed and turned under sweat inducing furs, trying with little success to shake one terrible thought from his head—one mishap for Oremethus, and Perciless would be crown prince. Then he received the letter.

Early in the morning, less than a week after the Elite Troop messenger arrived, a messenger from Balford's Bounty reached the capitol. The horse, gaunt and frothing at the mouth, delivered a rider who looked no better. Tending to his own horse, Perciless was at the stable to greet the messenger. To hear the tale and see the agita coursing through the man, Perciless felt sheltered, a foppish prince in an ivory tower. He took the letter from the man, made promises, and gave him coin for a meal and roof. But Perciless did not know what to do about the letter —give it to his overburdened father? The Seneschal? A general? Or deal with the matter himself?

That morning the world looked new, bigger. He felt as if he had wandered through life with horse blinders on, only seeing what lay directly in front of him. This new world was far more menacing, but replete with hope and opportunity. But to get to the hope that lay ahead, he had to first focus on what lay in the periphery he had never allowed himself to see before. And there was none better to guide him than his brother Daedalus, who hid in the peripheral like a hermit.

The day after his epiphany, Perciless went to his brother's quarters, hoping to recruit him as a guide to maneuver him through the dangers and pitfalls of this new world. Perciless could not help but feel he stepped into a crypt. The room was a perfect blend between dungeon and library, with a gaudy, oversized bed against the one wall.

Perciless always knew his brother was odd. Anger followed Daedalus like a shadow. But to Perciless, Daedalus was incapable of malfeasance. He had heard the lurid whispers behind backs from those who came in contact with the youngest prince but never gave them credence—until now.

He thumbed through the books on the floor-to-ceiling shelves, none striking at his worrisome inner voice.

Mostly, these books were histories of Albathia and the surrounding lands. A few works about the natural wickedness of man, but upon further review, they were merely fiction and fable. Handfuls about sciences stating the works of nature were nothing more than mechanics. No comedies or plays or anything for the eyes of a child. Again, nothing more than evidence of the pragmatism of his brother with a dash of darker entertainment. However, the desk was another story.

Parchment papers stacked in one corner, candle and wax cradle in another, ink and quill off to the side; the desk was meticulous. Perciless debated about leaving well enough alone, but something caught his eye from a darkened alcove created by the bookcase extending too far past where the wall jutted back. Despite the small windows, the ligth from the day sun spilled into the room, eliminating the need for candle or oil lantern, yet he could not make out what lay within the alcove from where he stood. Movement, he saw movement.

With tender step, as if navigating through a field of broken glass, Perciless slid from behind the desk. As he moved closer, he saw small, metal bars—rows and columns of metal bars. Tiny cages, stacked almost to the ceiling, were shoved into the alcove. Then Perciless heard clicking, the clicking of hardened little legs scampering across the metal floors of the cages. The clicking grew faster the closer he came. Then it came to a sudden stop as he stood within inches of the cages. Scorpions, dozens, all looking at him with their claws open and tails curled over the tops of their bodies, pointing at him and ready to strike.

Perciless found himself struggling to catch his breath from the unnerving sight. He backed away, but jerked around when he bumped into an object behind him. Fists clenched in reflex, he spun to see a monolithic obscurity covered in heavy blankets. His heart throbbed at the base of his throat as he grabbed the blanket. Covering his face with his other hand, he tugged.

Noise and flurry surprised him, forcing him to cringe back and use the blanket as a shield. But within one heartbeat, he remembered the tiny, caged arachnids behind him, all too happy to strike him dead if he ventured

214 | CHRIS PISANO and BRIAN KOSCIENSKI

too close, then he jumped back toward the cacophony. Feathers floated before him. Once he saw those, he focused on what he uncovered—more cages, but these held a score of beautiful white falcons.

Perciless stared at the birds, flitting and jumping about, angry that he took their darkness away. He bent down and scooped the feathers from the floor, sliding them into a cage. Still confused, he finally threw the blanket back over the cages. The bird noise ceased.

Stunned, he redoubled his efforts to find answers, but he found only mere clues. He returned to the desk and opened one of the drawers, shocked to find the king's stamp. His heartbeat now pushed the insides of his ears as he picked up the metal press engraved with the king's insignia. *Why?* He returned it then flipped through the stack of papers. None looked auspicious, save one. It was mostly blank with faint streaks of ink. Perciless examined it closer and realized it must have been underneath one Daedalus had written on, the streaks of ink being what soaked through the parchment on which Daedalus had written. Perciless held the paper close to his face and deciphered the whispers of word and numbers, resembling those on requisition orders.

Perciless stood confused, piecing together the scraps of words and numbers he could make out. The further he studied the parchment again, the more words and numbers he could decipher—the more puzzle pieces he discovered and put together.

He changed the numbers! Perciless deduced. *He has blatantly lied to me and committed treason against the kingdom! But why?*

Like a madman, Perciless searched the room. Every corner of every nook felt the touch of his curious fingers. Every carpet and curtain rolled and unrolled. Every piece of furniture overturned, searched and returned to its exact position. He found nothing incriminating. But what he did find was a sense of self, of purpose. His brother had lied to him about getting the weapons orders to the craftsmen; did he lie to him with the speeches about Perciless being the prince of the people? No! Perciless knew he was the prince of the people, and this was how he was going to prove it—

by going to Balford's Bounty himself to aid them in their rebuilding efforts.

"Perciless?"

Perciless snapped from his vision of the past, from his memories of rummaging through his brother's chamber, from the indelible images of horror he had seen at Balford's Bounty, and turned to see Daedalus. He found the role reversal irony of Daedalus snapping him from a memory spell rather charming. "Good eve, Brother."

"You're home?" Daedalus asked. No relief or concern found in his voice.

"Yes, dear Brother."

Daedalus's face contorted into a sneer at those words. Perciless knew he detested such tender acumen, but tried anyway to break down the wall around his brother's heart. He had to try. He worried that his younger brother was in a situation with limited solutions and needed help. Perciless was the one who walked among the peasants, the one who understood people in dire straights. Too many times he had families approach him with concerns of a member in trouble, usually gambling debts. And they became desperate to stay ahead of the consequences associated with the debts they owed, practically becoming different people. Often the debtor felt compelled to do illicit acts to obtain the money, or else do "jobs" for those they owed the money.

"Not like you to leave for months without a word," Daedalus said with marked slowness as if forcing the words past his teeth. "We were all so ... worried. That was why I entered your chamber just now. I have been keeping a vigilant eye on your belongings." Daedalus allowed his eyes to sweep over his brother's form. He made no attempt to disguise their purpose. He sought clues as to his brother's condition and previous whereabouts. Perciless appeared lean and unkempt, slightly pale and unrested. Despite his wishes to the contrary, Perciless had always worn the trappings of the proverbial do-nothing noble. His brow had always been clean and smooth, in part a credit to his youth, but more indebted to his lack of real responsibility—no wide-eyed children would go hungry as a result of his lack of initiative. The image he cut before

Daedalus's discerning eye was a far cry from the brother he had known his whole life. The person who stood before him now was swathed in mystery and had known hardship as a companion.

"Apologies, my Brother. I am exhausted and in need of a bath. Excuse me for the nonce," Perciless said dispassionately as he attempted to push past his brother towards the exit. He had not taken the time to properly prepare himself for such an encounter, had not ordered his thoughts, nor crafted his responses to the obvious questions. He did feel the desire to discuss with his brother what he had discovered in his chamber, but now was not the time, lest his rising anger get the better of him.

"No, Brother, my apologies to you," replied Daedalus as he deftly moved to impede his brother's progress. "You definitely have the look of a man who needs to eat. And you are marked by the scent of hard work ... or is that fear?"

"Daedalus, please ... I must be allowed to go." Perciless could no longer keep up the evasion game, and his eyes locked on Daedalus's. With their callused look, Perciless implored the younger man to allow him to exit the mounting confrontation. But Perciless now knew better, knew his brother would keep pushing. And he did.

Daedalus held his brother's gaze for a few seconds, then looked to the ceiling as if granting clemency by removing his harsh stare. "What, may I ask, shall I tell Father? He assumed you had left for the border of Tsinel to tend to the needs of our burgeoning army. Alas, his feeble mind knew enough that if his assumption were true, you would have returned weeks ago. It was almost more than he could bear to face the possible loss of *two* sons. At least allow me to ease his feverish imagination."

"You wish to put Father's mind at ease? You wish to know what to tell Father? Fine. Tell him why you have changed the requisition orders for the weapons."

Daedalus shrunk back from Perciless's fiery gaze like a moth's wings shriveling from a torch's flame. Visibly confused, Daedalus muttered, "What ... whatever do you mean?"

Pressing his advantage, Perciless said, "Come now, Brother, I am neither of our lackey-like cousins. I know the deed, but not the reasoning. Tell me."

Taking a moment to straighten himself, Daedalus indignantly brushed away wrinkles from his chemise, an obvious stall tactic. Perciless allowed him to indulge. Finally, the younger brother looked up and said, "Yes. Yes, I did change the orders. Do you know the details of the changes?"

"Some."

"Well, then you know that I increased production."

"At the cost of the craftsmen!"

With a huff, Daedalus snapped back, "Do you not believe that shaving off some of their robust profits is worth the extra armament? How can it be wrong to give soldiers *more* weapons?"

Perciless's only rejoinder was a quiet, "Why?"

"Why? Well, it is certainly nice to see that you and Father share your distrust in me. I *do* have tactical skills, you know. No doubt you have been rummaging through my room, so I can only assume that you have noticed the volumes of books I possess on strategy. Why, you ask? Because the numbers Father suggested were *wrong!*"

Even though his guts twisted like agitated worms, Perciless kept his face as unflinching as stone. "Even though your claims are admirable, your actions are not. Remember, your actions have consequences, and I seem to be the one who pays them."

Lips pulled tight, Daedalus almost appeared humbled. Pushing the words out of his mouth, he said, "I apologize."

Relaxing his expression, Perciless saw a glimmer of what he had hoped to see in his brother with this request for redemption. "Very well. I feel that has been settled. I am off to see Father, to let him know that I was at Balford's Bounty and the horrors I saw while tending to the needs of our people. I will also let him know that I will be leaving immediately for the border of Tsinel to tend to the needs of the troops."

"Truly? Leaving so soon after just returning?"

"The world is a cold and hard place, Daedalus, and one must remain ever cautious, ever vigilant. One can never drop guard for an instant. *You* have taught me this lesson," Perciless replied. Content with the look of surprise on his brother's face, Perciless left the room.

TWENTY-TWO

BALE STARED AT his mug of ale, using both hands to spin it. He didn't see it, though. Memories of Zot skittered across the ripples of ale. They had met in this very tavern about a decade ago. Bale had been drinking, as usual, and didn't know when to stop, also as usual. With blurred vision, Bale had mistaken Zot for a stool and tried to sit on him. It had been friendship ever since.

Zot and Bale shared many good times in this tavern. There were plenty of other taverns in Bogosh, but this one was where Bale had met Phyl and Pik as well. This tavern possessed the comfort of home. It only seemed fitting that he meet here with Phyl and Pik to mourn the loss of Zot.

"This place seems so empty without him," Bale blubbered.

"That's because it is empty," Pik replied.

As if just waking up from a long nap, Bale lifted his head and looked around the place. Pik was right, they were the only ones in the tavern, except for Munty the tall gnome, proprietor of this establishment. Despite the fact that he was tall for a gnome, he still needed a step stool to see out from behind the bar. His red, pointed hat could be seen any time the tavern was open; no one ever tried any form of shenanigans when the red hat floated about the crowd or behind the bar. However, it was rare to see his red hat as the only hat in the bar. Yet, there it was, on top of Munty's head, the only other head in the bar. He stood on his stool, looking with hawk-like eyes over the bar at his only three customers.

"Wow," Bale mumbled. "We must be early."

Pik snorted, his anger over the loss of his friend apparent.

"We've been early before," Phyl said. "And there always seemed to be people here."

"Maybe it's a holiday?" Bale offered.

"Yeah?" Pik snapped. "And maybe the king himself is visiting. Care to interrupt our mourning time to discuss it some more?"

Even with a frightfully low intellect, Bale understood Pik's hint and went back to staring at his ale. This time he took a sip. He thought of the time he and Zot spent a week wooing the Wartpus sisters. Bale smiled at that memory and took another sip. Then there was the time a rogue roc flew into town, caught Zot, and tried to feed him to its hatchlings, so Bale rolled in for the rescue. And he sipped his ale. He could never forget the time Zot had drank himself to near blindness, fell smitten for a female centaur, and aggressively pursued her. This led to a hoof kick to his kneecap, giving him his noticeable limp. Bale drank to that memory. He remembered when he and Zot tricked Nevin, Silver, and Diminutia into wandering to the Fecal Swamps. No ... wait ... that was the other way around. Bale reflected with fondness anyway and sipped again. After a few more memories, Bale found himself out of ale.

"Munty! I need another," Bale barked. No response. He lifted his head again to look around. Still no other patrons. No Munty either.

Knowing Pik would spew forth insults and Phyl would turn a simple question into headache-inducing, empty rhetoric, Bale took matters into his own hands. Well, his own feet, as the ogre stood and ambled to the bar itself. Still no Munty.

"Odd," he mumbled to himself as he inhaled a few times through his nostrils. "I smell fire. And rum?"

Leaning over the bar, he looked to the left and saw a spitting spark eating away at a line of black powder. He looked to his right to see that the trail of black powder led to twenty stacked cases of rum, three of them spilled and flowing along the floor. Once he had watched the disastrous effects of Zot lighting a pipe after a long night of sloppy rum drinking—Bale was finally wise beyond his limited intelligence. He knew what would happen once the sputtering flame reached the rum.

Moving faster than his girth would suggest, Bale turned from the bar and ran to his friends. Despite Pik's cursing and Phyl's questions, Bale snatched them from their seats, one under each arm, and barreled toward the closest wall. Having no other means, Bale decided to use the hardest thing he could find as a battering ram—his head. Lowering it, he plowed forward just as the flame reached the cases of rum. The fire flash explosion propelled the ogre and his friends through the wall, tumbling and rolling along the dirt roads of Bogosh outside.

Bale awoke to the sounds of arguing. He knew that Pik had to be involved, but he swore he could hear dozens of other voices. Rubbing his sore head, he sat up and opened his eyes to see what his ears heard. Phyl cowered behind Pik as the hobgoblin argued with dozens of townsmen. And half of them held shovels, pitchforks, or lit torches.

"What ... happened?" Bale moaned as he made his way to his feet.

Phyl ran to the larger of his two friends. "They're kicking us out of Bogosh! They set us up in the tavern, that's why we didn't see any other customers today!"

"What? They blew up Munty's tavern?"

The tall gnome sidled up to the ogre and waved his finger in fury. "You bet we did! It was my idea!"

"You blew up your own tavern?" Bale repeated.

A random voice from the crowd of creatures yelled, "We'll help him build another one!"

"Plus," Munty continued, "it was the only way to get rid of your stench! Why is it every time you come from the Fecal Swamps, the first place you come to is my tavern? Ugh!"

Heart hurting beyond words, Bale sniffed and asked, "But ... but ... where will we go?"

With rage like a boulder rolling down hill, Munty blurted, "Who cares? Just get out! If you're looking for some place to fit in, why don't you go live in Grimwell?"

As if Munty had blasphemed, a hush swept through the crowd. Both Phyl and Pik stared at the tall gnome in disbelief, wondering how someone they had known for so long could say something so hurtful. On the verge of tears, Bale whispered, "Grimwell scares me."

"As it does everyone," Pik said.

"But it's not as frightful as that curse you three brought here," Munty replied. "Please. Just go."

With a snort, Pik turned and started down the road leading south out of town. Phyl shook his head and followed. Confused by all the emotions swirling around in his chest, Bale lashed out the only way he knew how. He stole Munty's red hat. However, Munty's white hair came with it. Bale looked at the cap, long, white hair stitched into it, and then to Munty, the tallest, baldest gnome he had ever seen. Not knowing what else to do, Bale shoved it in his pocket and ran after Pik and Phyl.

By the time he caught up with them, Pik was well into another diatribe. Bale was used to the scene that spilled out before him, but it was only his accustomedness to such things that upgraded the display from disturbing to disconcerting. Many times had Bale stared at Pik, convinced his limbs were tied to puppeteer strings and well beyond the hobgoblin's control. Pik's arms, long and spindly, seemed akin to spider's legs as they flailed about him, moving in rhythm to his griping. In fact, the only thing that could move faster than his arms was his mouth. Once that was set into motion ... well, it was like a ship at sail with no port to call home. "Who needs nonhumans anyway?"

"Pik, in case you haven't noticed, we're the only friends we have right now, and our own number just dwindled," Phyl muttered. His face had taken on that ashen look of someone who had seen death. In life, the satyr had not been very close to Zot, but in death they were bound to one another.

"Bah! We sell the stinking stone, and then we can buy friends! In fact, I'll bet the human king himself is looking for this stone ..."

"Pik, stop talking about it," Phyl said, casting anxious glances over both of his shoulders in turn. "You can never be too careful about who hears."

"Who cares? It will only up the market value. More potential buyers means more profit for us," Pik stated. Surreptitiously, he peeked at his friends to see if his speech was having any effect on them. The key to persuasion lay in convincing Bale. Get the ogre agreeable, and the satyr would acquiesce to selling his own family. The satyr was pale from worry, and his brow was lined with deep furrows. No great surprise to Pik.

He continued to spew meaningless drivel at a rate that was surely incomprehensible to even the most erudite creatures. Keep them off balance; convince them before they knew what they were agreeing to; that was the hobgoblin's wont. Now to see what reaction he was getting from Bale, but, as luck would have it, a blank stare was all that met him when he looked at Bale. No great surprise he realized, but he was disappointed nonetheless. His reasoning should be met with accolades, not the silence of stupidity!

Exasperation seized Pik by the shoulders, a crushing grip that threatened to compress his spine. In that instant, the hobgoblin had an epiphany. Ogres are a moving mass of destruction, an injustice at best. In the case of Bale, it was an utter waste of flesh. Was his brain even large enough to cramp occasionally?

"Ogre," Pik yelled, "what do you have to say? What are you thinking?"

"Pik, I, uh ... do you see that bunny?"

"Bunny! Bale, you're a walking monstrosity. Nature trembles at your approach ..."

"That's because nature has a nose," posited the satyr with a smirk.

"Four hundred and thirty stones' weight worth of stupidity! That's what you are, Bale! You moronic mass of muscle ..." The hobgoblin swayed in irritation as his lithe form was whipped into a frenzy of motion by his rage.

"And would it be too much to ask for you to bathe once in a while," asked Phyl, his offended nose wrinkled. "And how about buying a decent pair of pants?"

"How is it that you even speak? *Why* is it that you speak? Words are wasted ..."

"We may be creatures, but we can still be civilized ..."

"Words are affronted when you use them."

"Noses are offended when he walks past."

"Trees understand the rules of argument better than you."

"Trees understand the rules of fashion better than he does!"

The verbal abuse continued for several more minutes as the hobgoblin and the satyr unleashed every insult they could muster. The witless ogre merely walked without blinking. Perturbation seemed a concept he simply couldn't grasp with his meager mind.

"Bale, even stupidity is offended by you ..."

"Colors are offended when you wear them."

As if an inharmonious chord had finally been struck, the ogre reached out with both hands and gripped the shoulders of his companions. Without discernible effort, Bale lifted both of his companions from their feet and shook them until all of the words had spilled from their mouths and silence reigned.

"Pik, do you see that bunny?" Bale asked after getting the hobgoblin's attention.

"I ... uh ... guh ..."

"I think that bunny is whistling."

"Phyl," Pik grunted, "I think ... uh ... we should ... guh ... reconsider our statements."

"I ... uh ... agree! Bale, you're mussing my hair!"

"You guys are dumb," said Bale, lowering his companions back to the firmament.

"We're dumb? You're the one who thinks a rabbit is whistl ... wait! A whistling rabbit?"

"Oh, Pik," whined Phyl. "That can only mean one thing!"

"*Dragon!*"

Phyl and Pik began to run in wild circles looking for a place to hide. Finally, the need for distance outweighed the notion of concealment, and they both took off at full speed in a straight line.

"It's not a dragon," Bale said. "It's a bunny. One that whistles, too." He was oblivious to the flight of his companions. Their voices began to fade with the distance, though snatches of their conversation drifted back to him.

"Phyl, go the other way!"

"Right! He can't catch us both if we go opposite directions."

Before him on a stump sat the rabbit, merrily whistling a tune that Bale recognized as a drinking ditty. Or at least he would have recognized it if he were capable of more than one thought at a time. But he was too preoccupied with catching the little critter to think or hear or speak or do anything more than drool. Bale stared at the bunny, not wanting to risk any sudden movement that would send it scampering off.

"Hey there, little bunny. It's okay. I won't hurt you. I think I have a carrot here ..."

"Bale!"

"That's right, Mr. Bunny. My name is Bale. And your name is Bun ..."

"Bale," said the rabbit. "It's me ... Lapin!"

"Rabbit ... right. Yes, I see that you are, Mr. Bunny. I'm an ogre ..."

In an effigy befitting a talented mime, Lapin's jaw dropped. This ogre displayed true talent with riddles. He'd shown a remarkable facility for languages. He'd bested a dragon! Lapin had always doubted the assertion that the intelligent lacked common sense, but here was undeniable proof.

"Perhaps recruiting you isn't such a wise move after all."

"No, it's okay, Mr. Bunny. Recruit me."

Bale used two fingers to hold his pocket open.

"Here's a nice hole for you to stay in while you do your recruiting."

"Bale, we need to talk."

"We are talking. But I could hear you better if you were snuggled up in this pocket."

"Oh, for crying out loud! If I get in your stupid pocket will you just go where I tell you?"

Bale offered the smile of a simpleton as a response. Lapin felt he had no other choice, so he leapt into Bale's cavernous pant pocket. "This is so revolting. Okay, let's ..."

"Wait!" Bale shouted. He reached deep into his other pocket, digging around for an object. Lapin winced with every clack of metal he heard, not wanting to think about what he heard or how it managed to fit in the ogre's pocket. Bale stopped rooting and let out a rumbling chuckle. He found what he was looking for—Munty's hat.

With the care of handling a ceramic flower, Bale placed the hat, with long, white hair still attached, onto Lapin's head, his ears snug together inside the point. Bale recognized the disgust in neither the rabbit's contorted face, nor his soured voice. "Follow the road and veer into the forest by the second boulder."

Bale walked to the boulder as instructed, but stopped, not knowing what the word "veer" meant. Too proud to ask, he did whatever came to mind, hoping one of his actions was right: first, he sniffed the boulder, then he licked it, then he did an arm-flailing jig. Fearing for his own safety, Lapin yelled, "Go into the forest here!"

A bit ashamed, Bale followed the order. Lapin ducked and dodged the whipping twigs and leaves, as Bale opted for the most direct approach.

"Left!" Lapin barked, blowing white hair from his face.

Again, Bale listened, walking right into a clearing.

"Stop," Lapin ordered, keeping his instructions short and easy.

Not having to wait long, Bale saw why the rabbit directed him to go to the clearing—the dragon. The monstrous reptile stalked around the perimeter of the open space, never taking his eyes off Bale. As a primal form of expressing dominance, he tossed clods of dirt with his claws and gave occasional snorts of smoke. Bale didn't know much, but he knew that if he was capable of eating creatures smaller than him, then creatures larger than him were capable of the same. And this dragon was much, much larger than him. And probably still upset by the fact that Bale stole the stone from his lair.

"Ogre," the dragon gruffed, eyes locked on Bale. "You are brave to face me. Much more brave than the hobgoblin and satyr hiding behind the trees."

Knowing their cue, Pik and Phyl poked their heads out. With tentative steps, they made their way next to Bale in the clearing, trembling before the circling dragon.

"Fear not," the dragon continued. "I am not here to seek vengeance. As befuddled as I am about the fact, you claimed the Spirit Stone rightfully. But I know of its curse, know of the demons killing your families and friends. I'm here to offer my help."

"Help?" Phyl squeaked out, the fur of his legs keeping his knocking knees from being audible.

"Yes. Lapin and I will accompany you to the human capital city of Phenomere. The world's greatest wizards reside there, and we shall seek their council in this matter."

Pik, Bale, and Phyl stopped trembling. Having no home, no town to call their own anymore, and no discernable plan, the trio found no other alternative than to accept the dragon's offer. Upon doing so, the dragon smiled and turned to his partner, Lapin. He wanted to congratulate the rabbit for executing such a brilliant plan, but instead said, "Are you wearing a gnome's hat? With long white hair attached to it?"

Lapin retreated farther into Bale's pocket, fearing whatever might be lurking in there far less than the shame he felt.

CWENCY~CHREE

"THIS IS MADNESS!" Dearborn screamed.

"Dearborn!" Iderion bellowed.

Dearborn's heart ripped into two. She stood inside Prince Oremethus's tent with the prince himself and General Iderion. She *hated* arguing with the general. But he was wrong about this. She knew it, and he knew it. The prince was mad! Insane! Reason and reality had vacated his senses! Did Iderion not see this? Or not wish to admit it?

"She is wrong!" Oremethus shouted back, pointing to Dearborn. His face glistened with sweat as he paced the perimeter of his tent. The fingers on his right hand rolled as if he played an invisible instrument. "We have to do this! Have to! They want the stone!"

"Prince Oremethus," Iderion said, his voice even and calm. "Though we know you are a master tactician, we must give credence to the sergeant's suggestions. She and I have more battlefield experience. That is why the king has an Elite Troop to begin with."

"Wrong!" the prince shouted, the word exploded from his mouth with such force he stopped pacing and forced his eyes closed.

Iderion and Dearborn exchanged glances, allies again in this struggle. But the prince continued pacing, his right hand still strumming, and his left waved wildly in the air. "Don't you see? Surely you do! They have been picking us

THE DEVIL'S GRASP | 229

off one at a time. We started with forty plus myself, and we picked up Haddaman. We are down to twenty-seven. If we run, they will get us. Get us all! One. At. A. Time."

Iderion turned to Dearborn, and she knew she lost her ally again. Before he could say that he agreed with the prince, Dearborn barked back. "You didn't *see* them! These aren't men. These aren't animals. These aren't even those hideous creatures of The Horde! These. Are. Monsters."

Oremethus continued to pace. All form of decorum had diminished. Pomp and circumstance no longer mattered. Spittle flew from his mouth, and his face reddened as he rebutted, "Yes, monsters! Yet, you yourself stated that you and your men had *slain* them. If you can slay one, you can slay a dozen. If you can slay a dozen, you can slay a *hundred!*"

Dearborn turned back to the general. "We are frightfully outnumbered. And thanks to our delusional prince, we have scant enough rest to keep moving, let alone wage a frontal assault."

"General!" Oremethus snapped, his pacing getting faster. "You must do this! You must do this! You must do this!"

Frustrated beyond words, Iderion growled and stepped toward Dearborn, stopping within an eyelash of her face. With a guttural whisper, he commanded, "Our job is to fight while outnumbered and win unscathed. We shall rest when we are dead. And the prince, no matter how close it may be to truth, shall never be insulted. Prepare the men."

"Then I fear we shall be resting sooner than either of you realize," she whispered back. Before the general could retort, she turned on her heel and marched out of the tent. Two dozen sets of weary and worried eyes greeted her.

"We're making our stand here." Her voice cracked and crumbled as if she ate gravel. "Prepare yourselves."

The men grumbled and griped and groaned from the news. She allowed them; it was hardly proper, but she couldn't bring herself to chide them for something she herself did as well. She did plenty of griping under her breath as she went to her tent to prepare herself for battle. She adjusted her armor, tying extra pads and plates on her arms and legs. She found ways to strap every sword and dagger she owned to her body, all the while formulating a plan.

Demons were brainless beasts, not well-trained soldiers. Their previous tactic was to charge and keep charging. She didn't assume they knew no other way, she just chose the most logical scenario. Half of her troop was very young and agile. She would order these men to climb into the trees. Hopefully when her men dropped from above, they could surround the monstrous attackers. An ambush, no matter how small, always yielded favorable results. But if the battle turned for the worse and the demons killed the prince, the self-appointed keeper of the stone, she would immediately order her men to scatter and retreat, with orders to reconnoiter at Phenomere.

After she finished preparing for battle, she drank an entire bladder's worth of Pallarian root juice. The sugary syrup burned all the way to her stomach, but her heart rate increased to a nice strong rhythm as the liquid fire spread through her entire body. She exited her tent, proud to see that her men were ready for battle.

Barking orders, she had half of the Elite Troop in the canopy of the thicket in front of the camp, ready to pounce. The other half stowed what little food they had left and tied the horses to trees at the back of camp. They would be spooked by the demons and too ornery to ride into battle, but they had to be close by ready for retreat. The men hid weapons in strategic places, perfect for feigning retreat only to draw the enemy close enough to finish them with a surprise strike.

Twelve men formed a line, each standing four paces to the left or right of any other man. Dearborn and Iderion stood in the middle. They planned to draw the monsters in and steadily pull back. The men closest to them would pull back as well in an effort to form two sides of a triangle. Finally, her men from the trees would fall, cutting the enemy off from behind, forming the third side of the triangle. The sole task remaining was to wait.

Dearborn stood steadfast, a guardian statue. Iderion fidgeted with his battle-axe, unhappy with the sergeant's silent treatment. She might have been a sergeant, but she was still a woman, and as such, needed nary a single word to make a man squirm. Iderion could take the silence no more and whispered, "I know you disagree with this course of action, and I know you believe the prince to be touched in the mind, but this is the right thing to do."

"They're coming," was her only response.

Iderion was at a loss. Not for the first time in his life, he realized, but it simply didn't get any easier. If he expressed his true concern for Dearborn, he knew he would be undermining the confidence he had in her abilities. He was loathe to give her pause shortly before battle. But to say nothing would pull at his heartstrings should something untoward come to pass. He was no poet, he knew, and had not been blessed with a gilded tongue. His mind understood tactics and the balance of a weapon, but even one as obtuse in the ways of women as himself knew that he had a miniscule window here to make a statement that she would carry with her for life.

"Dearborn ... I ..."

His stammering was as effective as wind-milling one's arms to keep from falling. She turned to look at him. Confusion was clearly etched on her face as their eyes met. Reaching, digging, her eyes bored into him as though searching for the source of his very soul. For the first time today, Iderion allowed himself to be drawn into her eyes; tourmaline blue, and as clear as the most perfect specimen of that gem, even in this moment of tension and stress, her brow was smooth and unmarred by worry. If only he could lend voice to any of those thoughts. She took his breath away, and he wished to fill her sails with it, but was unable to do anything more than stare and create an uncomfortable moment.

"Be careful," he mouthed. So blank was his mind that even those words failed to register sound. If she had asked him to repeat himself, he would have been hard pressed to remember them.

"Protect the prince," she responded and turned away from him in a haste that caused her black hair to swirl about her.

Iderion stood up straight, arching his back. To an independent observer, it would have appeared that he was stretching. In truth he was listening to her. Her words held disappointment, the disappointment of one who had hoped for more and not received it. He sought forgiveness from his lame apology, but felt foolish for not receiving it.

"General, what would you have me do?" Haddaman. No one had considered Haddaman, or how to effectively protect him. This was not his fight. Nor could he be allowed to participate. But what to do with him? He was a forgotten man, a lost trinket, its value forgone, which suddenly found, no longer served any purpose.

"Haddaman, I am reassigning you. You have a new partner." Iderion lacked agility when it came to improvisation. He drew out his words hoping a plan would coalesce in the lacunae of his mind. Not much came forth, but he knew the civilian needed to be sent far away from the killing field.

"Can you use a khopesh?" Iderion reached for the hooked blade that was strapped across his back.

"General, I am ... ummm ... quite skilled with ... throwing ... weapons. In fact, I was once ..."

As Iderion suspected—no bravery was present in Haddaman's voice. He gave up reaching for the weapon and used his other hand to pull a dirk from his boot, then shoved it at the erstwhile antiques dealer. It wasn't much, but his impromptu plan depended on speed and avoiding battle. This way, at least he could shield himself from guilt while reminding himself that Haddaman wasn't totally defenseless.

"Go with Siempre."

Beneath his finely constructed façade, Haddaman was scared to death and was hoping to be sent as far away from a fight as possible. He would puff his chest and then accept the task of messenger with an air of disappointment. Or at least that was what he hoped would happen. That was the point of talking to Iderion in the first place. Oremethus would send him in front of the front line. The prince would do anything to place distance between himself and the encroaching danger of being separated from the stone he carried. And Dearborn ... she would have tied him to a tree and used him as bait. While Iderion was no genius, Haddaman was far from average in that department. He chose his mark wisely and would dupe him with ease. "Siempre? With all due respect, sir, he's a messenger—a glorified page."

"Haddaman, history teaches us that many wars have been lost due to lack of communication. The king must be informed of what happens this day. Reinforcements may be required. Our lives are in your hands. We need a hero. It is a role suited to you."

Haddaman you are a gifted actor, he acknowledged silently, his plan worked perfectly and gave himself an internal nod. Time was of the essence. He should protest once more, briefly, and then accept the gracious gift he was offered. The Elite Troop would do all the work—provide the sweat, tears, and blood, yet he would emerge the hero. It suited his ego and his mantle.

"General, I fear I must protest ..."

"I will not be swayed, Haddaman," Iderion said, wondering if Haddaman heard the sarcasm in his voice. "I cannot afford to risk failure in such a vital task. It must be you and your skills that see this done. If Siempre is attacked on his trip, the kingdom could be placed in jeopardy. Avoid the prince at any means. Now go. Mahlakore's horse is young and light. It will be among the fastest steeds."

"General, I ask that you remember my protest formally. I'll not be dishonored by ignorance later. I will do as you bid ..."

Screams filled the air. It was the kind of agonized noise that no human throat could produce even under the direst of circumstances. The demons charged, and Haddaman watched the general's eyes widen then glaze over with the adrenalin rush of a seasoned warrior. Haddaman recognized that the conversation had ended, and he ran. He knew where Mahlakore's horse stood, and he wasted no time seeking him out. Siempre was to leave at the first sound of battle and had been chosen for his role as messenger because of his mindset and loyalty to his orders. Even Haddaman understood that it took a special sort of individual to leave his companions in a crisis, regardless of the importance of his task.

As he reached the horse, Haddaman cut the fetters with the dirk Iderion had given him, hoping a few seconds saved would spare his life. He leaped into the saddle and had the horse under way before he was properly seated. From his left he heard the sound of hoofbeats and knew that Siempre had started out. *Yet another perfectly executed plan*, Haddaman thought as he galloped away.

Iderion barked orders as the demons attacked. Dearborn and the men that formed a line next to her moved back with perfect pace and launched arrows with elegance. The monsters certainly took more arrows than any other creature to fall, but fall they did. And they continued to advance at a pace the Elite Troop dictated.

The demons had rushed the line like the brainless brutes Dearborn hoped them to be. Once in range, every member of the Elite Troop line fired shaft after shaft. The monsters slowed, but persisted. Leading the way, Dearborn ordered the center of the line to fall back, forming the point of a triangle. The demons followed, but not to the perfection Dearborn had hoped.

So dumbed by bloodlust, the demons tore after the closest men as opposed to the ones firing the arrows, the men on either end of the line. The young men fought with the vigor all soldiers dreamed about, but soon fell. In a flurry of muscle and claw, the soldiers' bodies twisted, their insides spilled out.

Needing to keep the monsters corralled, Dearborn and Iderion barked a simultaneous order. Before the end of their breath, the men in trees dropped. With the deft placement of a watchmaker, the soldiers landed with perfect precision, the Elite Troop now surrounded the demons.

Bringing the fury of hell with them, the demons in the middle of the godless pack of roiling flesh squirmed and squealed, trying to claw their way out. The monsters at the edge sliced and bit at the Elite Troop soldiers. The soldiers were too well trained, and the monsters' ranks dwindled.

An occasional claw dealt a critical wound, shredding armor as easily as flesh, leaving torn steel and strewn entrails. Wild tentacles snatched a young recruit, yanking him to the center of mayhem. Nothing but a yelp and mists of blood lent to his legacy. The demons did mortal damage to members on the perimeter, but not enough.

Dearborn threw knives faster than arrows could fly, then never wielding less than two swords. She saw slicing fangs rend plate-mail to scrap and deemed her shield useless. Plus, it took twice as many cuts and stabs to kill one of these monsters. And kill she did, lopping off heads and cleaving skulls, she used ichor and entrails to paint a portrait of fearful rage. Her shoulders burned past the point of feeling, her arms swinging and hacking as if they were possessed by the very demons she killed. She felt nothing, not the sweat streaming over her body, not the blood and guts spraying from every kill, just primal anger. It devoured her heart and gnawed her soul, reminding her that the prince demanded this, and the one person she trusted—loved—agreed with him.

Iderion's humanity disappeared as well; it served him little good in combat situations such as this. A civilized human might feel compunction for the twitching, beheaded bodies of the enemy. An upstanding member of society could never tolerate a face full of vomit after stabbing an opponent in the belly. The general could hardly afford such compunction leading his men to imminent death. And the warm ember that tried to ignite his heart every time he glanced at Dearborn had to stay extinguished—for now.

The general and sergeant led by example, being more monstrous than what they fought. The mob of flesh shrank, the numbers diminished. A soldier would fall, mutilated beyond any form of recognition, but the circle shrank, the noose tightened. Finally, the last dozen warbled death knells came from slit throats of monsters.

Falling to their knees or sliding against a nearby tree, the Elite Troop collapsed, every iota of heart and soul spent for their victory. Twelve remained, eleven men and one woman, gasping and wheezing, coming up for air after almost drowning in horror. Fatigue froze every inch of every body, only their eyes could move. All gazes shifted to the pile of carcasses. Two hundred bodies, severed and cut and stabbed and ruined, formed piles—huge piles. Dismayed and in awe of the force of their collective will, the remaining twelve stared slack jawed at the carnage they created. Then came a laugh. And a second. Unable to contain any form of emotion, the twelve let out all they had

236 | CHRIS PISANO and BRIAN KOSCIENSKI

with laughter and tears and screams. Concerned, Prince Oremethus exited his tent. As stiff as knotted wood, the soldiers ordered themselves to stand in recognition of the prince. But before any questions could be asked, ideas thought, or orders made, a noise came from a hundred footfalls away. Then another, more terrifying sound.

Every soldier felt their soul turn to ice once they realized their tactical error. The demons weren't buffoons—they were chess masters. The Elite Troop wasted time, ammunition, and energy on the pawns while the king and his court casually approached.

TWENTY-FOUR

THE TRAP WAS SET. Daedalus felt it, knew his cousins cavorted with deception, knew they participated in clandestine dealings. With whom, he did not know, but he had every intention of finding out. He stroked the Nessian Valley constrictor slithering across his lap, admiring the black diamond patterns in its tan scales. While it certainly couldn't be listed as a strong point of his, patience, it seemed, *could* be counted among his virtues when a long-term goal demanded it.

Daedalus still felt the adrenaline course through his body—the anger, the agitation—from Perciless discovering his ruse. His brother dug into him like a woodcarver with a virgin block and discovered the truth. Now he intended to do the same with his cousins. Two Southland adders slid over his shoulders and over the constrictor. Daedalus ran his fingers over each as they slithered across.

The snakes were meant to give him an advantage in the impending conversation. Tallia was the smarter of the two cousins, and Daedalus hoped to diminish that cunning she had with the snakes. He knew what secret meaning the snakes held for her.

Then came a rap at the door.

"Enter," Daedalus commanded.

Tallon and Tallia strode into the room; Tallon staying at the threshold of the antechamber, Tallia glided to him like the angel he knew her to be.

As soon as he saw her and felt the serpents across his skin, his mind slipped. His room blurred and melted away to the forest just outside the castle ...

... He was fifteen years old again, holding Tallia's teenaged hand as he led her through the trees and brush. He held an oil lantern with his other hand to fend off the approaching twilight.

"Where are we going?" she asked.

"I want to show you something," he replied. His heart swelled with pride and excitement; he was able to feel it throb within his fingertips.

"It's dark and getting cold, Daedalus."

"Almost there. I'm ... I'm very proud of this. It took me years to create this."

Tallia sighed. "Very well. How much farther, though?"

Just as she finished her question, they stopped. "Here. We're here."

Tallia looked down and saw a large circular pallet. Daedalus bent down and moved it aside to reveal a hole, larger in diameter than a man was tall. Confused, Tallia peered in and only saw movement. Squirming? Then Daedalus moved closer, the light from the lantern showed Tallia what was in the hole. She screamed.

"What?" Daedalus asked.

"Snakes!" Tallia shrieked.

"Yes," Daedalus replied, puffing out his chest, proud of his accomplishment. "There are over a hundred in there from various nonpoisonous species."

"Snakes? Why would you think I'd want to see snakes?"

"But, my angel, while you were nursing me back to health after my riding accident, you had suggested that if I understood the animals and people lower than me, then maybe I wouldn't have as much contempt for them. After that, I started with the one animal with which I felt a kinship."

Tallia barely heard a word as her eyes refused to look anywhere other than the hole. Daedalus sought the approval of his angel, hoping to win her heart and her love. He had hoped this moment would bring them closer, show her that he wanted her to understand him and love him. Instead, she stared into the pit and mumbled, "Snakes. So vile."

THE DEVIL'S GRASP | 239

Daedalus set the lantern down and realized one thing—
if she wouldn't give him her love, he'd have to take it.

Tallia watched with rapt unease for what seemed like
hours, unable to remove her gaze from the very thing that
disgusted her. She finally turned to see Daedalus standing
before her naked, his erection pointing at her like a
poisoned dagger. The dim lantern flame mixed with the
forest's darkening shadows cast a sinister pall upon her
cousin, his skin as white as a corpse. His eyes revealed he
was just as lifeless. As swift and quiet as death, he lunged
at her, reaching for her, his lips stealing hers. She wanted
to scream and vomit, but could do neither as her instinct
to back away took over. Too close to the pit, she teetered
on the edge. Daedalus reached out to save her. So filled
with angst, she recoiled, landing her in the serpent pit.

Everything she ever feared congealed in her heart. An
infernal squirming mass moved about her, over her,
around her. She lay in a bed of moving scales, blanketed
by perverse lechery. Snakes moved through her blouse
until it no longer covered her, her skirts and bloomers as
well. All her body allowed her to do was breathe, and at
that moment, she sincerely wished not to.

She felt Daedalus squirm about as well; his skin far
more chilled than any serpent slithering around her. His
hands stroked her hair, but it could have easily been tiny
ribbon snakes weaving their way through. His tongue
found hers, only to be replaced by a serpent blacker than
the looming midnight sky. The snakes crawled across her
body just as Daedalus did. She couldn't distinguish scales
from skin, motion from stillness, soft from hard, what was
on her or in her. She could no longer differentiate the
hissing of a hundred snakes from one lone viper
whispering, "I love you. I love you. I love you ..."

"... I love you," Daedalus whispered, mind back with his
body in his chambers. His body slouched down in his
receiving chair. Sweat streamed from his forehead, and his
tongue dried. His lustful panting was that of sexual
release, the same release from his memory, as he stared at
Tallia. However, her reaction was not one that he imagined.

Tallia watched Daedalus's demeanor and knew exactly
what memory he relived.

And she snapped.

Like prey turned predator, she strode to him and snatched an adder from his lap. While gritting her teeth, she used both hands to twist the snake's head. It hissed and twitched, its tail flying about wildly, until its eyes bulged and tongue flopped free. She dropped the snake carcass at her cousin's feet and returned to her brother, who tried to hide his shock with a stone expression, but couldn't stop his eyes from widening in surprise.

Incensed more than ever in his life, Daedalus's sweat froze and the ripples of pleasure turned to waves of ire. He sat up in his chair bellowing, "How *dare* you!"

"Shut it, mouse. Your words are worth less than pig slop," Tallia yelled, spittle glistening her lips.

Daedalus stood from his chair. "You unappreciative little *whore!* I'll ..."

"Do nothing," Tallon interrupted, charging into the room from the antechamber, ready to protect his sister. It was now Tallia's turn to be surprised. "Because you can't. You can never be king of Albathia, so you pretend to be king of your own little world made of feces and filth. You fancy yourself a great tactician, because you intend to stab your father in the back, however, you have the strategic ability of a four-year-old snit. You're willing to bring down an entire empire to get Daddy's attention, because he doesn't love you as much as your brothers."

No sooner than the words left his mouth, Tallon took Tallia by the arm and turned their backs on their cousin, leaving before he could react.

Daedalus moved from anger and hatred to a primal rage. He could no longer form words, only harrowing howls as he dropped to his knees from his chair.

Panting, he stared at his door. Had he gone mad? Was this another of his fantastic visions of the past? Foul magic? A temperamental dream? He turned to his snakes, still squirming over his chair, and saw the dead one on the floor.

The world was a place rife with possibilities. Daedalus reached out with his right hand and picked up the limp form of the dead snake at his feet. He stroked its body at length.

He rarely knew defeat from any other side other than that of the victor. They were his kin, so Tallon and Tallia should have, by all rights, been capable of such clever trickery. No, not defeat. Tallon and Tallia had just hit him with surprise, but that was a one-time deal. His plans were still intact and with their trump card played, they could never one up him again.

Still, he needed to know with whom they cavorted. Who knew what treachery he preached? Who could have emboldened the twins to the point of such blatant spurn? Clearly this person or persons had to be dealt with swiftly and with harsh reprise. Who could it be? Certainly, if his father knew, Daedalus, his status as a prince notwithstanding, would have been imprisoned for the good of the kingdom. That ruled out the king. Oremethus was preoccupied with other tasks and had been gone for some time. It was unlikely that he would have gleaned such knowledge from any of his companions; simple fighters that they were. Perciless ... well, he had certainly gone rogue, which was out of character for him. He had, however, shown little interest in their cousins, and Daedalus, to be sure, had monopolized much of their time. It seemed very unlikely that Perciless would have had any opportunity to foster such a surreptitious relationship. Certain parts didn't seem to fit, though he scrutinized the facts as he spun them to and fro in his mind looking for possible connections. Clearly, though, he could not rule Perciless out. And what of Praeker Trieste? He was an eldritch figure with a largely unknown power base at his disposal. Ahhh, he represented the obvious choice. Daedalus had learned early on never to be too comfortable with the apparent; a fixation that often led to unexpected failure; an acceptance of mediocrity; a pair of blinders that he chose not to wear.

Action was called for, and he strained to keep himself under control. Anger caused his adrenaline to surge, and his muscles rippled with a compulsion to act. But purposeless movement would only open him up to further attacks. He needed a plan. He could ill afford to be rash, though he relished the challenge of exposing a double cross. Improvisation said a lot about character, and Daedalus loved to dare himself impromptu-style.

Daedalus wove his way through secret corridors and seldom-used chambers, moving like the spiders skittering along the cobwebs found in every corner. However, the dust and dirt of the unused rooms forced him to pull his cloaks tight to his skin, lest they attract the impurities. Finally, he reached his destination.

He found the stables just as displeasing, even his own private one cleaned thrice as many times per day as any other. No matter, he had a task to complete. Once he finished preparing his horse, he rode off.

The bright day sun stung his eyes, such a contrast to his dank world. He cursed the brightness the entire ride, until the sun approached the horizon. Most people would view the twilight reds and oranges as breathtaking. Daedalus viewed them as less annoying. He pushed his steed well into the forest until it began to tire. However, the horse reared and fretted as they made their way deeper into the forest. Frustrated and angered by his horse's fear, Daedalus tethered the foul beast to a tree and continued the remainder of his journey on foot, cursing the rest of the way. His destination—Praeker Trieste's camp.

The motley soldiers sang and shouted, whooped and hollered. Jowls flopped as they ate, or fists flew, trying to steal the food from the neighboring soldier's greasy mouth. Such conditions repulsed Daedalus, but he flexed his muscles to keep his riling stomach from rejecting its contents and strode to the edge of the madness, finding the one he sought.

"Praeker Trieste!" he shouted. What was he doing? This was madness! He should turn and leave while he still laid claim to his life. But the words of his cousins echoed through his head. "Mouse." "Pig slop." "Snit." Were they true? No! They could not be! And Daedalus was bound and determined to prove them wrong!

With the wave on one hand, the monstrous general commanded his troops to remain at bay. The armor made of emerald, shelled scorpions danced and fussed and hissed, their fervor reflecting their master's mood. His bloodshot eyes beheld the waif-prince and weighed the options of killing him now.

"How dare you!" Daedalus snapped, spittle spraying from his mouth. "I gave you everything you asked for. Every weapon you needed. Only *one* road leads to Albathia, and that road goes through *me!*"

Mouse.

Pig slop.

Snit.

"Mark my words, General, if I find you're working with anyone else, it's over. If you have other dealings behind my back, all supplies shall cease! You will be cut off!"

Mouse.

Pig slop.

Snit.

"And don't think for a second that I need you! I've been financing your expedition, been paving the way for your destruction for over a year. With no results! This is your final warning!"

With a final snort of discontent, Daedalus turned on his heel and strode from camp, walking among wide eyes and dropped jaws. All noises ceased, too afraid to announce their presence, save for the chattering scorpions. Once Daedalus made sufficient distance from camp, every soldier turned in stunned silence to their leader. How could he have taken such verbal abuse from such a spoiled fop? And then let him leave with his life? Without so much as a retort?

"We attack Phenomere in three days."

With those six words, Praeker Trieste returned to his tent, leaving behind the throng of celebratory shouts.

TWENTY-FIVE

BLOOD SPRAYED into the sky and rained back down to the ground, flowing like rivers through the forest. Men battled demons—swords clashed with claws while teeth challenged armor. Arrows whistled and bucklers whined. Howls and growls ripped through the trees; the forest trembled.

Through the din, orders from both sides of the battle could be heard: "Flank here, fallback there, press the formation now! Bend, never break! We have trained for this, men! We always knew hell had a place for us, and now it's *here* to take us! Brethren, these mortal fools befouled the sacred stone we were meant to protect! Cleanse the world of this filth!"

Men turned to animals, and demons turned to flesh and bone. The stench of gore turned the air to warm broth, overbearing to any not locked in combat. Every creature fighting wore the blood and the sick and the ooze of their enemy, bathed in the merciless hate.

Dearborn battled with a ferocity she hardly thought capable. She knew she could rise to any challenge, but protecting an enchanted stone from a horde of hellspawn? Never in her most ghoulish of nightmares. She finished her melee by driving her long sword through her combatant's chest, and her short sword through his skull, via its jaw. Releasing the carcass, she turned to aid Iderion, but he forbade her.

"The prince!" he shouted.

Hating to leave him and the few remaining soldiers in battle, she knew her place, knew her duty, and sprinted to the tent where the prince hid. She slaughtered two smaller demons along the way, but it did little to quell the nausea roiling around like anxious worms in her stomach. Before entering the tent, she scooped up a smoothed pebble the size of her thumb and clenched in it her palm.

The prince jumped and screamed as she burst through the flap of his tent. He swung wildly with a dagger no larger than a common steak knife. A sight she must have been: her long hair slick, clumped, and matted from various coagulated fluids. Her skin the color of whatever dripped from it. Chunks of meat and strands of sinew clung to her body. A coating of oozing mucus sheened her entire person.

"My lord, the battle does not fare well. It is time for you to go," Dearborn said approaching.

"But the stone?" the prince replied, clutching a small bag in his other hand.

"That is why you must leave. To protect it." To emphasize her point, she snatched the bag from his hand and emptied it, the Satan Stone falling into the palm of her hand. The prince's eyes fixated on it, hypnotized by a beauty only he could see.

"Yes, the stone," Oremethus repeated. "Protect the stone."

"Prince!" Dearborn snapped, causing him to move his gaze from the stone to her eyes, white islands tipped with blue in a repulsive sea of crimson and brown. She slid the plain pebble into the bag and shoved the bag into his hand. "Go. Now!"

Little argument was needed to make the prince acquiesce. Especially when the tent wall split in half, replaced by countless rows of gnashing teeth in a vertical mouth. After rending the tent to rags, the demon roared, lashing out with its tongue of squirming snakes.

Thanking the gods this monster had no more intelligence than that of a field mouse, Dearborn cleaved through its skull with her long sword. The body twitched, and its flailing tongues wrapped around her waist as she wiped its brains from her sword.

The prince had escaped. Dearborn watched his steed gallop away with every ounce of speed it possessed. Unfurling her fingers, she looked at the Satan Stone in her palm. She wanted one last look at what damned her, her soldiers, and possibly all the lands to hell. It glowed orange and yellow as if it captured the flames of the netherworld itself. Spitting blood from her mouth, she put the stone in a small pocket and buttoned it. The battle for this thing would end *now!*

Dearborn raced into the fray. Five figures remained: herself and Iderion, the only survivors of the Elite Troop, and three demons. As she charged, one of the demons confronted her, a serpent hybrid. The creature had the tail of a giant snake, but chest and arms of a human, while its head was of an alligator. With no weapons in hand, it slithered toward Dearborn and attacked with its teeth. She easily dodged the frontal assault, but not the tail. Cracking like a whip, it snapped her across her chest plate, knocking her off balance. Possessing a speed she had never before witnessed, the serpent creature pressed forward. Dearborn avoided its teeth and claws, but the tail proved too much, knocking both short sword and long sword from her hands. In one fluid motion, the creature wrapped its tail around Dearborn's legs and waist. In an effort to halt the assault, she grabbed the tip of its tail with both hands.

From the corner of her eye, she watched her general, her Iderion, finish off one more demon, leaving only the demon-general, Ar'drzz'ur. Holding his massive shield and a broadsword larger than the right leg of most men, Iderion stood before the demon twice his size. Built like a man with the skin of a molded corpse and teeth of a crazed shark, Ar'drzz'ur had two horns sprouting upward from his temples; one shorn off from a battle before history even began. Iderion wanted to circle his opponent, size up his stance and movements, but the corpses of the fallen cluttered his path. Ar'drzz'ur snatched the largest sword he could find from the fallen. He then tossed aside or used his cloven hooves to kick away the bodies of man and demon alike.

Pools of blood welled around their feet, Iderion and the demon-general, as they circled each other. Every step ended with a splash—the dirt saturated with ichor and bile, entrails kicked aside. Iderion bellowed a promise to send the demon-general back to hell. Ar'drzz'ur laughed and attacked.

The demon swung with the force of every soul he had sucked the marrow from; Iderion blocked it with his own sword. Fissures of pain ran through his arm. He swore as if all his bones exploded. The demon's second swing connected with Iderion's shield, knocking the large man to the ground.

Taking his time, Ar'drzz'ur sliced downward, but Iderion displayed a speed disproportionate to his girth, rolling out of the way. The demon's blade stabbed the ground as the human-general jumped to his feet. He hacked at the demon's arm, but Ar'drzz'ur deflected the sword with his monstrous hand.

The demon and human continued to exchange blows. Iderion continued shouts of bravado as Ar'drzz'ur responded only with patronizing laughter. Inspired by Iderion's unwillingness to forfeit, Dearborn gathered what little air she could muster in her lungs and spat in the face of the serpent demon that constricted her. Angered, the demon opened its jaws, saliva dripping from its jowls, and lunged for Dearborn's head. Wrestling with the tip of its tail, she shifted it while moving her head aside as best she could. It worked! The demon's jaws clamped shut and severed off the tip of its own tail. Hissing and howling, it loosened its grip on Dearborn to grab its tail, its own blood cascading from its mouth. With a somersault and spin, Dearborn procured her sword and lopped off its head. A final spit to clear the filth from her mouth was all she left for the twitching creature.

Dearborn ran toward the man she loved, short sword in one hand, long sword in the other. Iderion succumbed to his warrior rage, swinging his broadsword with inhuman speed. Ar'drzz'ur blocked each attack with his own sword, but fell off balance with each blow. Watching her general turn the tide of the last battle to his favor gave Dearborn the strength to run to him faster. With the vigor of a pup half his age, Iderion chopped at the demon, driving him to his knees. Ar'drzz'ur held his sword as a shield with his left hand while his right disappeared into the piled organs of fallen soldiers on the ground for support. Dearborn smiled, knowing the demon-general faced imminent defeat. Iderion raged against the demon. Panting like a whipped cur, Ar'drzz'ur dropped his sword. Dearborn's heart almost burst with joy, until she saw the demon's right hand. Iderion raised his sword one final time. Ar'drzz'ur twisted his body to his left, his right hand, holding a sword from one of the fallen soldiers, exploded from the offal on the ground that hid it.

Iderion was run through, his gut and sternum doing nothing to hinder the demon's attack, the entire sword driven upward and out through his neck. Ar'drzz'ur wore the twitching Iderion like a sleeve. After one final spasm from Iderion, the demon flicked the corpse from his arm like a discarded rag.

Dearborn screamed the pain of a million dying worlds. Miles away towns heard her, but none knew what it meant, many citizens taking the wailing howl as a divine sign or start of a legendary ghost story. None knew where it came from or by whom, lest they beat their own breast or rip their own hair out deep from the root as a grand gesture of sympathy, knowing no living creature should feel the loss of Dearborn Stillheart.

Mere feet from the man she devoted her life to, *her life*, Dearborn froze from disbelief. Never taking her eyes off his corpse, she dropped her swords. She undid all her buckles and buttons, removing all of her armor. With the kind of strength the demon possessed, it would be useless. Dearborn knelt by her precious Iderion, stroked his hair once, let a tear fall from her cheek to his, and kissed his blood-soaked lips for the first and last time. When she stood, she took his broadsword with her.

Ar'drzz'ur laughed.

Dearborn charged, sword raised high and a heart full of hate. The forest shook with every strike of her sword against the demon's. Not since its birth in the days of endless volcanoes had the world known such fury. And never had it heard thunder and seen lighting start at the

THE DEVIL'S GRASP | 249

ground and move to the sky. With every swing of the sword, sparks threatened to burn the forest, but the battlefield liquids soon extinguished any flame started.

Ar'drzz'ur laughed.

Dearborn slashed. And hacked. And cut. With every movement, she released a vicious noise that made a lion's roar seem like a mew. Sweat washed away the blood, threatening her hold on her weapon. But she held tight, held hard to every memory, every smile she shared with Iderion. She lashed out with steel and profanity, cursing and yelling to every painful beat of her heart.

Ar'drzz'ur laughed. And grew tired of this game. With one flick of his arm, his backhand sent Dearborn sprawling backwards.

Every fiber of Dearborn's being ached, begged her to stop. Her arms felt like boiling jelly as her legs turned to spoiled butter. Every nerve recoiled into a ball of hot razor wire. Her bones were made from thin porcelain. But nothing compared to the torment of her heart, a cyclone of butcher's knives in a cathedral of silk. It demanded she stand, demanded she fight, convinced her to die later. Not sure how, she did just that—stood and gripped Iderion's sword.

Ar'drzz'ur smiled a smile of broken daggers as he sauntered over to Iderion's corpse. Mimicking a scholar, he examined the body. As if making a grand discovery, the demon picked up the shield and looked it over. Determining it was sturdy enough for his needs, he turned to the wobbling Dearborn. "Little girl, you and your … heh … warriors have been most entertaining. But I grow bored, and I want the stone back. Because I think what will happen next shall be amusing, and it saddens me to think I'll leave a battle without at least one scar, I offer you this. You have one unfettered attack. I shall not move or dodge or parry. Then I shall kill you and rape your corpse for one hundred years."

The demon-general, still laughing, held Iderion's shield. He used two hands, one on either side of the shield, so large it blocked his entire chest. Little of the creature was exposed, only from his eyes up, his fingers, and his legs. But Dearborn did not even consider any of the exposed parts a target.

Loving Iderion meant loving him completely and utterly, everything about him, down to the soles of his shoes. She loved his shield, because it was his, and because she loved smithing. She loved how the weight of the shield had always striated his left shoulder, adding to his already immense size, transforming him from a man to a god simply by holding it. The shield transcended craftsmanship, moved beyond the magnificence of artwork, to something Dearborn could not articulate, only admire. Loving the craft, she knew a shield of this size could never be made with one single sheet, but two sheets soldered together. And it took an artist to hide the seam from view. Loving the man who had owned the shield, she knew *exactly* where that seam was.

Dearborn focused on the shield, staring at the seam, anticipating how the demon might jerk or tighten his body right before impact. Wrapping both hands around the hilt, she held the sword point out. With one final mountain-cracking roar, she charged. The sword slid right through the seam, right through the breastbone of Ar'drzz'ur. Smiling as the demon's laughter faded, she felt his heartbeat vibrate the sword. The demon-general looked down and then back at Dearborn. His smile returned; he would live. But before he could move, Dearborn put every iota of pure hatred into one twist. The shield cracked in half and fell away. The demon's ribs split, his heart turned sideways, and a geyser of blood erupted from his chest.

With his last effort, Ar'drzz'ur stared Dearborn in the eye, smiled, and toppled forward. Having nothing left in her soul, Dearborn could not move fast enough, falling backwards, still holding onto the sword. The weight of the demon was more than she could ever hope to move, even when well rested. With a squish, both bodies hit the ground, blood pooling around Dearborn.

The demon's fetid final breath nauseated Dearborn. But she no longer cared. She stared into the demon's dead eyes, his face frozen in a twisted, sinister smile. Her fate was to die trapped beneath the monster that killed the man she loved. She accepted that fate. Now she could follow Ar'drzz'ur to hell and kill him again.

TWENTY~SIX

LOST. DIMINUTIA was lost. Not with respect to the journey, though. He knew very well where he was— traversing through the thick forests that surround Halcyon Hills. He was lost on the inside, in what little soul he had.

He trudged next to his partner in crime, Silver, but nary a word had been spoken between the two for the good part of a full day. It had been like this ever since Nevin died over a week ago. They both lost their best friend and brother in trade. Thoughts of good times, better pilfers, and narrow escapes danced through their heads, as did questions about why he acted so bravely and what would possess him to sacrifice his life. Did either Silver or Diminutia possess the depth of soul to reach deep and pull forth a sacrifice such as their deceased friend? Neither wanted to know the answer, be it yes or no. Either way chilled them to their bones.

In front of the thieves, the three remaining wizards, Belhurst, Grymon, and Follen, led the way, pushing their greatly depleted cart of magical ingredients. They walked in silence as well, out of respect for their partners' fallen comrade. Nevin might not have held the wizards best intentions in mind with his sacrifice, but they benefited from it as well and, thus, were thankful. Plus, they knew Diminutia and Silver well enough to know if they did speak when not welcomed to, then that would be the last thing their tongues would ever do.

The five men headed toward Phenomere Castle. They had no horses, but hoped they got a head start on the Elite Troop, undoubtedly heading to the same destination after procuring the Satan Stone. Realizing that idea was futile, the five men simply trudged forward, three pushing a squeaking cart, two searching their souls, but all five cloaked in silence.

Able to bear the pains of silence no more, Belhurst whispered to his cronies. They whispered back. All three peeked over their shoulders to the thieves, both of whom continued to keep pace, heads down. Since neither of them drew their daggers to flay the wizards, Belhurst assumed their level of talk to be acceptable for today.

The wizards kept their words accurate and sentences brief. They made nothing more than a list of ingredients they would need from the wizard's guild as well as others they could recruit to their cause. Despite their losses, they still guarded the Shadow Stone and knew that the Satan Stone had been found. They needed more help.

Diminutia heard the wizards whispering but didn't care. Their words were just empty noise as far as he was concerned. They didn't annoy him. His own silence did. The lack of laughter and jocularity. The lack of Nevin.

"I miss him," Diminutia mumbled as he did each day since Nevin's sacrifice.

"Me, too." Even though Silver only mumbled two words, his anger dripped from them.

Diminutia smirked, the gears of his mind grinding away. "Remember the triplets?"

Even though immersed in anger, Silver couldn't stop a smile. The one time Nevin acted more reckless than Diminutia. Of course, Nevin had one too many tankards of ogre ale, but armed with a boldness never before seen, he approached three sisters in a tavern. Both Diminutia and Silver assumed he would introduce them to the lovely girls and all six would have a salacious time. Not in their wildest dreams did either Diminutia or Silver expect Nevin to leave the tavern with all three sisters. That memory brought a tear of pride to Diminutia's eye.

A chuckle escaped from Silver. "Sure do. Do you remember him running through town the next morning in his britches because their father came home early?"

Diminutia rubbed his jaw. "Yeah. He ran right up to me and punched me square in the face. I told him my lifestyle wasn't suited for everybody."

Both thieves shared a quick laugh, until a familiar stench wafted under their noses. They looked at each other with disgruntled frowns. Diminutia yelled to the wizards, "Hey. Any of you smell that?"

"We all do," Belhurst replied. "It smells of death."

Pushing their emotions to the side, Diminutia and Silver unsheathed their daggers and joined the wizards by their cart. They continued at a slow pace, but all five sets of eyes watched the forest, shifting from tree to tree, examining every movement, even something as simple as a falling leaf. Silver's squinted countenance twisted as the smell thickened. "Notice there are no animals? Not even a bird."

"Yeah," Diminutia replied. "That can't be good."

The five men with a cart pushed on a bit further, until Diminutia noticed a figure on the ground. "Over there."

Their eyes turned as one, following the direction indicated by Diminutia's pointing finger, though the scene they beheld was incomprehensible. For several long seconds they stared in bewilderment at the carnage that stretched out before them. After a silence devoid of any form of thought or understanding, Belhurst spoke.

"Demons."

Though it was but one word, two mere syllables, it was pregnant with many emotions. The wizards recovered their wits first. A sharp hiss rent the still air as Follen drew an abrupt breath. His stance shifted from unnerved to wary, and his eyes danced about the surrounding area. Grymon took Follen's cue and allowed his eyes to roam the other side of the scene. When no immediate danger was revealed to either wizard, they fanned out to their respective areas, moving slowly as they continued their search.

Silver and Diminutia couldn't pull their eyes from the carnage. Nor could they display more than an inkling of recognition. The bodies, if they could be referred to in such

254 | CHRIS PISANO and BRIAN KOSCIENSKI

mortal terms, were strewn about, hacked and hewed to pieces.

"What happened? Who could do such a thing?" Silver mouthed, displaying the numbness of uncertainty.

"Isn't it clear?" Belhurst asked. "Only the king's Elite Troop could have killed so many demons. We cannot be far away from them, assuming they survived this battle. We must hasten to catch them or their attackers and retrieve the stone that these gory corpses once protected."

"Demons? Like the ones following us?"

"Worse. Much worse. Each stone is protected by a different set of demons. Dark and lightless demons born from the great abyss itself haunt the stone that we carry. You can only imagine what kinds of demons protect the Satan Stone."

"I don't have to imagine," Silver mumbled as he saw a severed head of mandibles and horns.

"If that is true, we should leave." Diminutia looked to Silver as if he were a river rat scrabbling to stay afloat in a torrent.

"Don't be a fool! We have a great opportunity. The item we seek waited for us. Don't give that back." Belhurst strode off into strewn out carrion, searching for clues as to who survived the battle and in which direction the survivors went.

"What do you think?" Silver asked.

"That this is crazy!" Diminutia said rolling his eyes, exasperated with himself for even considering risking his own hide against more of these demons. Yet, consider it he did. He wasn't sure where the wellspring of philanthropic ideals came from, but he had never been one to place the good of humanity before the good of Diminutia and yet here he was, poised on the precipice of benevolence, and he was having trouble backing away.

Silver took a good look at Diminutia. Watched the way he rolled his eyes when he spoke. Caught every nuance and syllable of his body language. He knew very well that his companion's mind was set, and there would be no changing it. If there was no talking him out of it, then at least he could go along as damage control.

"Well then," Silver replied, "since we've both just enlisted ourselves into the service of certified lunatics, shall we begin?"

"After you," Diminutia responded with an embellished bow, indicating that Silver should lead the way.

"Right. Let's check over here," Silver suggested, pointing towards the side of the grisly scene that was fronted more by open grassland and seemed the least likely place for them to risk being ambushed.

The battlefield was huge and stretched before them like a lake of gore. They picked their way through the remnants of melee participants, careful not to touch. Both had come to the conclusion that whatever demons were made of, it certainly wasn't the flesh of any creature birthed in nature. Many of the cadavers oozed or began to melt away, like a gelatinous mass set out in the heat. "Ugh, the smell!" Silver said, pulling his shirt over his nose.

"I know," Diminutia replied, doing the same.

Neither of them was exactly unaccustomed to the smell of rotting flesh, but if this battle was as near its end as Belhurst suggested, then it seemed a bit early for such charnel smells to pervade the air.

Silver tapped Diminutia on the shoulder. After he received the other man's attention, he pointed to their left. A tangle of corpses laid piled a few paces away. As the thieves moved closer, they found all of the evidence they need to confirm Belhurst's theory. The uniform of the king's Elite Troop, though not intact, was identifiable on the body of one young man. His body was bent at horrible angles, and while Diminutia turned away to fight a spell of retching, Silver silently thanked the fates that the man's face was buried in the ground. He was certain that had he faced the grimace that must accompany such apparent agony, he would end up on the ground heaving.

"Dim, this guy was too young to be entrusted with the stone. I'm not gonna mess with this one. I'm going to search over there a bit." Silver spoke in mellow tones as though his words might disturb the air enough to cause his comrade further discomfort.

As he walked, Silver noticed that the ground itself seemed to recoil from the waste that had been spilled upon it. Grass had withered beneath the mess of demon flesh. Rocks melted, and the dirt was pockmarked as though pulling away in revulsion at what had been laid to rest upon it.

In all directions he could see more soldiers or remnants of soldiers. Mixed in periodically were horses, too, though they had been shredded and feasted upon and often the parts he found were too indistinct for his brain to immediately recognize them. It was odd that horses were in such a state, but given what appeared to be the massive numbers of slain demons, it was possible that they had overwhelmed the humans with such impossible odds that many of the attackers simply had no fighting targets and spent their time on other diversions.

Confounded and disgusted, Silver trod forth regardless of his roiling stomach. His right hand pinched his shirt over his nose, while his left handled the occasional satchel or checked a lumpy pocket with gossamer touch, afraid of offending the items he handled. Repulsed by his own actions, he reverted to testing the effects of the human corpses with the tip of his boot first, all the while mumbling his discontent. Until he heard a moan come from behind him.

Silver's spine petrified as his muscles froze, a defense mechanism employed by small game. He even held his breath, but decided that if it rarely worked for the rabbits and rodents, it probably wouldn't work for him. In one fluid motion, he spun, crouched, and produced his dagger to face more unmoving corpses.

Just then, he saw movement. A foot. A leather boot twitched. Then came another moan, a woman's.

"DiiiiiiiiiiIIIIMMM!" Silver yelled as he watched the foot twitch again. His friend ran to him, as did the three wizards. Slack jawed, they all stared as the foot jerked again. It took some doing, but they made out two legs, the rest of the warrior hidden by the half mound of slaughtered demons. A very large one on top trapped the soldier. Another moan snapped the five onlookers from their stupor.

Surprising even themselves with their act of selflessness, the thieves joined the wizards in aiding the soldier. All five men gathered on one side of the monstrous demon, four times the size of a normal man. Positioning themselves between its shoulder and hip, they pushed. Hands slick with the demon's gore, they all released shouts at various volume and intensity. With a unified thrust, they rolled the demon aside.

Pulling in a large gulp of air, the soldier coughed a thick gurgle. Then she sat up and spat.

Diminutia recognized her. Even though malachite-hued blood masked her face and matted her hair, causing the other four men to mistake her for a fellow male, Diminutia knew who she was. His angel. "You?"

Dearborn paused from spitting and retching to look up at Diminutia. Stunning the other four men with her feminine voice, she replied, "You."

Their eyes locked, their hearts grappled, neither knew what to say or do. Each wanted the other to speak first, not caring what the words were, just wanting some indication of what to do next. Their silence was as boundless. It truly would have lasted an eternity had Belhurst not kept his wits about himself. With the slight-of-hand of a street magician, Belhurst removed a cloak and handed it to Dearborn. "Here, madam warrior, use this to rid yourself of demon filth."

With great difficulty, she pulled her eyes from Diminutia and accepted the cloak, using it as a towel to wipe away the larger chunks. She stood and felt four pair of eyes widen at her height, taller than anyone there. Only Diminutia was not caught unaware. Attempting to cover for the rudeness, Belhurst removed another cloak and handed it to her.

"Thank you," Dearborn offered as she accepted the second cloak, dropping the first one to the ground with a goo-filled slosh.

"Madam Warrior, what happened here?" Belhurst asked.

Dearborn told them. Of the successful mission. Of the maddening of Prince Oremethus. Of the demon ambush. By the end of her story, Belhurst offered her a third cloak for her to wear and made introductions. Silver did a double take with the wizard, noticing that less three cloaks, he still seemed to be wearing just as many as when they first met.

"So you are in possession of the stone?" Belhurst asked as nonthreatening as possible.

Dearborn turned to Diminutia. "Why? Are you going to attempt to steal it again?"

Diminutia begged his mind to produce a clever and savvy answer, but nothing came.

Belhurst replied for him. "No, Dearborn. We are going to attempt to destroy them."

Dearborn looked to the old wizard as he held out his hand. In the center of his palm rested a stone blacker than the hole to hell. Her eyes widened, mesmerized, only able to break from her trance when Belhurst closed his hand. Feeling a rudimentary sense of trust with this small group due to them rescuing her, she reached into a small pocket and produced the Satan Stone. Crimson, orange, and yellow swirled together like the flames to the hell whence the Shadow Stone led. Before the men could become entranced, she placed it back in her pocket. "It's cursed. It brought ... *this* ..."

For the first time, Dearborn looked at the battlefield. To her, it seemed to go on forever, littered with bodies. Most were demons, but the rest was comprised of her friends, men whom she called family. One she wanted to call lover, even husband. Her gaze lingered on Iderion long enough for Diminutia to recognize the large man. He wanted to comfort her, put his arm around her, but felt it to be inappropriate. Again, Belhurst became the voice of reason, "Madam Stillheart, all of us have lost someone close because of these stones. None as fathomable as what you had to endure. I suggest you travel with us to Phenomere where we intend to meet the wizard's guild and devise a way to destroy these stones and send them back to the hell they came from."

With her eyes still scanning the battlefield and her mind half-wondering how she survived, she heard enough of what the wizard said to reply, "Yes. Yes, that would be a good idea."

After rounding up the four horses that remained alive, Diminutia offered to share his steed with Dearborn. She accepted and jumped on the horse; the horse groaned, not happy that it had to carry such a large passenger. Dearborn wanted to wrap her arms around the handsome, blond man in front of her, but opted for the less presumptuous choice of gripping the back of the saddle for balance. With one last glance over her shoulder, she wondered her fate, wondered how she planned on telling more than thirty families that a member would not be coming home, wondered how to tell the king that the mission failed, wondered about her future in the army. She closed her eyes and swallowed the lump of guilt in her throat as she wondered how, after days of riding, the man in front of her managed to smell so good.

TWENTY-SEVEN

PHYL WALKED OUT of the stable where they had stayed the prior three nights and greeted the late morning sun with a yawn, stretch, and a few excited flickers of his tail. Even though nonhumans enjoyed the same freedoms as humans within the country borders of Albathia, they were not always well-received by the human residents. Although Prince Perciless pushed for, and upheld, all forms of affirmative action, not all business owners adhered to such principals. When Phyl, Pik, and Bale first stumbled into the capital city of Phenomere, they had great difficulty finding a room. They knew very well that any time an inn owner said, "No vacancy," he secretly implied the finishing phrase of, "for you." It took some time to find an inn run by a fellow nonhuman, one owned by a centaur. However, the centaur was of limited intellect and even more limited business skill, opening a stables-only inn, since he, as a centaur, enjoyed stables.

Phyl, Pik, and Bale hardly minded, having endured worse conditions in the past. And they certainly enjoyed the company of other nonhuman creatures who also found closed doors at many of the human-owned inns. Although entertaining, especially one particular minotaur who was a never-ending source of raucous haiku, none could replace the void left by the death of their dear friend Zot.

After Phyl finished stretching away the prior night's sleep from his body, he noticed Pik stumble from the stable holding his palm over his bruised eye. Earlier in the morning Pik and Bale had gotten into an argument regarding a mysterious note found attached to Bale's pants three days prior. Bale said the note was from the bard instructing them to wait. After three days of waiting, Pik demanded to see the note. Bale said "no" the only way he knew how—with a punch to Pik's face.

Phyl offered only a tsk-tsk and said to Pik, "About time you decided to join the land of the living."

Shooting Phyl a glare with his good eye, Pik walked past him and growled, "Let's get to the tavern to see if Bale is making money or spending money."

Phyl walked along, unable to stifle a silly smile. "That rabbit is something else."

Upon first arriving in Phenomere, they decided to spend their last silver pieces on grog. So distraught with the unpleasant turn in his life, Lapin decided to join them in their revelry and began whining about how they had to leave Dragon hiding in the forest that neighbored Phenomere. Pik and Phyl found out quickly that the tavern patrons were more than happy to pay to see a talking rabbit. However, they were a bit dismayed to discover that Bale was also more than happy to pay to see a talking rabbit. After a few pints of ale, the patrons were privy to a singing, dancing rabbit. And so it went for days, a flask of alcohol never out of Lapin's reach.

Pik and Phyl entered the tavern and paused to let their eyes adjust to the dark gloom of the room. It took no time to find Bale, probably the largest creature in Phenomere, straining the joints of a bench while seated at a large table enjoying a plate of rattails. Much to their surprise, they noticed the bard sitting at the same table. With his eyes glazed over. And his fingers massaging his temples. Visibly in pain. There, in the center of the table, sat Lapin, drunk and bending the bard's ear with the epic tale of how Bale and crew found the Spirit Stone.

"... and then ..." Lapin paused to lap some ale from the shallow bowl he nursed. He wiped his mouth with his left paw. Swaying, he pointed to the bard with his right paw and continued. "... and then, you know what he did? You know what this dumb, stupid, dumb ogre did? Do you? He licked it! He licked the rock! Licked it!"

In between lip-smacking slurps of fried rattails, Bale tried to defend himself, "He used big words on me!"

"Veer!" Lapin tried to glare at Bale but couldn't figure out which blurry ogre to focus on, so through crossed eyes, the rabbit yelled at all four. "The word was 'veer!' How do you not know what veer means?"

The bard felt his own eyes cross. He assumed they turned to look at the inside of his head, hoping to see the hammer that pounded against his brain. No such luck. He then looked outward to the rest of the bar, hoping to find a sympathetic patron willing to rescue him. Instead, he found something better—Pik.

Jumping out of his chair, the bard greeted Pik and Phyl with open arms and a wide smile. "My friends! It is so good to see you!"

"And what makes you think we're happy to see *you?*" Phyl started. "We've been waiting for three days. Three days for you. It sure seems like you've been here for more than a day. Couldn't leave messages for us at the local inns? And don't tell me you couldn't find us. Seriously, how hard is it to find an ogre? I mean, you should have the common courtesy to try to find us to let us know you're in town. And, sir Rabbit! Are you drunk again? So early in the morning? You should be ashamed ..."

The bard stood rubbing his temples again as the flustered satyr moved past to cajole his traveling partner. Pik made his way next to the bard and said, "Now you know how I feel. I have to deal with that all day, every day."

"My condolences," the bard groaned. But his smile returned as brightly as the day sun slipping out from behind passing clouds. "I hear your little cadre found the stone in question?"

"Yes."

"May I see it?"

"No."

"Why not, may I ask?"

Pik made his way to the closest empty table, his lanky limbs giving the impression of him walking against the wind. The bard followed and took a seat. The hobgoblin's

eyes blurred, his vision leaving for far off lands to watch
unspeakable horrors. "It's not with us," he lied. "We have it
some place safe. Away from us. It is cursed."

The bard laughed as if Pik told a joke. "You jest,
spinning a silly tale to bemuse yourself at my expense."

Pik cast a hard glare to the bard. The laughter ceased.
"I assure you, Bard, it is no joke. Or have you not noticed
one missing from our fold?"

The bard's gaze fell to the table in shame. "Aye. The
short one. But ..."

"It was the stone." Pik emphasized his point by slapping
the table's top.

The bard kept quiet, letting Pik fume in silence. A bar
wench delivered two mugs of ale and Pik drew hearty gulps
from his. The bard cleared his throat before attempting to
speak. "I know where the Sun Stone is."

"No," Pik replied, staring off into a deserted corner of
the tavern.

"I don't have a map, but I have reasonable assurance ..."

"I said no, old man. We lost a dear friend. We've lost
family members. We've been *banished* from the town we
once called home. All because of the first stone, the Spirit
Stone, you had us seek. Now you *dare* ask us to find a
second stone? You are indeed mad, Bard."

The bard threw himself back against his chair,
wondering what strategy would work best. Before his
thoughts drifted too far into the rash and excessive, the
tavern door opened again, and in walked six figures. The
bard smiled.

Weary from their journey and simply looking for a room
to sleep away the rest of the day, Diminutia and Silver led
Dearborn and the wizards to a tavern that offered rooms
and had an owner who owed them a favor. Diminutia
convinced Dearborn to remain in their company until the
following morning. She agreed, needing some time to rest
and regroup her thoughts. What would she tell the king?
Would he view the lone survivor of his Elite Troop as a hero
or a failure? How could she possibly explain the
disappearance of his son? She would love to tell him the
truth, tell him that Oremethus's sanity abandoned him,

but could not put a father through such misery. And it was doubtful that he would even believe her.

Dearborn had a home, had her own room, but after everything that happened to her, she doubted she would find any comfort there, and she doubted that she could make it there without being seen by someone she knew. After a battle, she found it necessary to be with those she fought with rather than spend the time alone. Being in the Elite Troop brought the benefit of camaraderie, and that was something she craved right now. Even though these thieves and wizards did not fight by her side, they still fought similar battles, shared similar victories and losses. She needed them right now and followed them into the tavern.

How wickedly wonderful, thought the bard. The bearers of pain, the victims of his farce—the brainless, the gullible, and the noble—here they were and all under one roof. If the stones stayed in several hands, it was as bad as them being lost, after all. Now to play upon their suffering, their sense of duty, their simpleton nature. His eyes sought out a buxom serving wench, while his mind formulated the best way to use her.

Silver, having panned the room as they entered, found an empty table suitable to accommodate his group. He quickly noticed the presence of Pik, the hobgoblin, herald of Bale Pinkeye and his terrible troupe of monstrous misfits. Silver led the way toward the empty table ahead of them, but allowed the wizards to pass him by until Dim pulled even with him. His back to Pik, Silver pointed toward his own chest in the general direction of the hobgoblin for the benefit of his partner.

"Hobgoblin company," he muttered.

Without breaking stride, Diminutia responded to his partner. "Satyr at high noon; Ogre at mid-dusk. No sign of the living footstool," Diminutia warned with a worried look that changed to a pleasant smile when Dearborn drew even with him. "Does this table suit you, milady?" he asked, punctuating the question with a sincere, though foreshortened bow, in an attempt at good humor that he did not feel. His actions came across as practiced, but not callous. Dearborn could understand if not fully appreciate the philosophy behind the "yet life continues" attitude. A smile, as fleet as a leprechaun, touched at the edges of her lips, an evanescence of hope, an emotion that was briefly contemplated but had never formed.

"Anything with four legs that can support me will do." She had the haggard look of loss about her. It seeped into her skin, strung itself through her clothes as if it were thread, settled at the bottom of her glance as if steel. She reminded herself not to allow grief to eradicate cordiality.

Silver stared at her as she passed him, awash in the waves of her despair. Though he had suffered his own loss, he marveled at how she must have willed herself to remain standing through such anguish. He had lost a dear friend, and his world seemed clouded over, but Dearborn had clearly lost so much more. What, then, must be driving her to continue on? Duty? Maybe. Honor? Possibly. Ambition? Not likely. Self-loathing? Revenge? He shuddered inwardly and physically. With her skills and size, he could only imagine the utter destruction she might leave in her wake if she harnessed such caustic purposes allowing them to goad her towards action. It was a scary proposition he decided, in no small part from watching the tendons and muscles in the back of her arm stand out huge and horseshoe-like when she drew her chair under herself.

Silver moved over to the bar to ask for service for the table. No one in his group would be in the mood to wait for drinks. After a short and guttural exchange with the barkeep, he showed up with a tray full of mugs to deliver in person.

"Drinks for all," Silver announced sullenly, without looking up from his distribution of beverages. He assumed as he moved them from tray to table that they would be passed about, but quickly realized that they were, in fact, piling up in front of him. "Belhurst, you want to share these ..." he began, looking up at the wizard finally and realizing he was already drinking from a mug. They all were, in fact.

Diminutia looked at Silver and said, "The barmaid," he hesitated over the nomenclature, clearly struggling with himself not to call her a "beer wench" in the presence of Dearborn, whom he feared would react harshly to what he considered a statement of fact, not an indictment or passing of judgment, "showed up with them as soon as we began to seat ourselves."

"So, who ordered them?"

"She didn't say."

"Bale! I'll bet Bale noticed that Nevin wasn't here, and he's rubbing our noses in our own mess. He'll pay for this. That son of a bitch! If it's him, Dim, I swear ..."

"Yes, my friend, you do need respite it seems" the bard said, approaching the group. "And you draw a lot of unwanted attention to yourself, as well. Forgive me for not announcing myself sooner, but I noticed the ... ah ... difference in your group and thought it best to give you a few moments to dedicate to your thoughts."

"You!" Silver growled, pivoting around to greet the bard. "What are you doing here?"

"Was this not where we had agreed to meet at the journey's end?" asked the bard assuming a stance of innocence that stood falsely in Silver's mind.

"I ... no, actually, I don't think it was," Silver said starting to rise.

"I paid for the drinks, my friend. Let your mind find ease. Merely an opportunity to show a little courtesy to those who so rightly deserve it," said the bard.

"Do you have any idea what we went through? Do you know what you put us through? Do you have any idea ..." Silver fumed, puffing himself up, adding the mass of his fury to his already weighty words. But the bard interrupted him.

"Yes. Yes, I do. I know what you left behind. Each of you," confessed the bard, lowering his eyes from the burning stares he received from across all corners of the table. "May I procure a chair and join you?" he asked, already grabbing one without an owner from a neighboring table.

"No, I don't think you should," Silver snarled.

"Silver," Diminutia said, touching his friend's arm. When he was sure he had Silver's attention, Diminutia continued. "This is it. This is the end. This is where we can leave things. Find a resolution, a completion."

"Oh, we'll end things, all right. I'll see things ended on the end of my dagger," Silver seethed.

"That won't solve things. We all wanted to do this, and it's done. Let's move on, Silver," Diminutia urged, his voice even and reasoned.

"Are you saying we quit?"

"No, Silver. I'm saying this is how we can ... can bury Nevin."

"There is much to what they say to you, Silver. And I can offer you something more yet," the bard said, "something of what you are looking for to aid you in your struggle of the spirit. There is yet a way for you to recover what has been lost. All of you. All who work together in this task stand to profit from a reversal of fortune."

"No more, Bard. We'll have no more of your riddles or tasks. And no more of your stones ..."

"The Sun Stone can grant life, Silver. And it beckons from a spot not far from here ..."

"Damn you! How dare you dangle another trinket in the face of our loss?" Silver shouted standing up, shining poniard glinting dully in his hand.

"Silver," Belhurst said mildly, "what he says is true."

"Belhurst, no more," Silver pleaded, falling back into his chair. "Let it end here, please."

"You have two stones already, wizard," the bard said seductively. "Seek it out or our hope of redemption will be lost to the swirling depths of evil that is The Horde."

"The Horde?" Silver asked. "Better them than the demons. Let's end their threat here and be done with this. The king and his army can handle The Horde."

"With the Sun Stone, Silver, The Horde can regenerate their numbers. All hope will be lost in the face of their ever-replenishing numbers. To end this once and for all ..." His words trailed off, but Belhurst made the meaning known to all at the table. Their work was near an end, but far from finished. If it was ever truly to end, then all evil must be eradicated. Despite their wish to be free from the stones, the companions at the table found themselves drawn yet again into the maze of events that men call destiny.

"Tell us where we can find the stone," Silver whispered.

Though their conversation had been lost in the ebb and flow of all of the other goings on in the tavern, the other patrons were certainly aware of some of the events that had transpired. Pik, in particular, had seen enough of the action to recognize Silver and the wizards who banished him to the Fecal Swamps. And now the bard sat with them. His eyes glinted with malice, or was it purpose, as he gathered up Phyl and Bale and led them to the table with the bard, Silver, and his friends. "I see your journey for the stone has brought you loss as well."

Silver scowled at the hobgoblin, but understood the meaning when he realized why Zot was not with Pik. His face started to soften, until another realization hit him. "You have one of the stones?"

"Yes. And this charlatan here tried to trick us into finding yet another."

Silver glared at the bard, not attempting to hide his hatred. "Funny. He's trying to trick us as well."

The bard smiled. The snare was baited, now to trip the trap. "Well, I guess it's of no circumstance to anyone standing here that the Sun Stone is in Grimwell."

Nostrils flared and brows furrowed. Gasps and grunts escaped from unsuspecting throats. Fists clenched as feet shifted. The reactions were different, but everyone who heard the bard's words had one. Some reacted to the news that the Sun Stone was close. Others reacted to the town name of Grimwell, like a child uttering a profanity, hoping no adult took notice.

In a daze, Dearborn's hand slid atop Diminutia's. "Do you believe the Sun Stone can resurrect our comrades?"

Not knowing what to make of the physical gesture, Diminutia moved with it and placed his other hand on top of hers. "If it does, do we *truly* wish it to?"

Her eyes sinking into a pool of tears, Dearborn turned to Diminutia, trying not to lose herself in his sky-blue eyes. "I watched almost forty of my closest friends, each and every one of them I'd call family, torn to shreds by ... by monsters."

Trapped by Dearborn's beauty, Diminutia's heart spoke faster and louder than his mind could comprehend. "We'll do it. We'll go to Grimwell and get the Sun Stone."

"*What?*" Silver shouted.

Anytime Bale heard the word Grimwell his stomach shifted. His mother scared him with bedtime tales of the monsters lurking in that town. What kinds of creatures would willingly live in a city of mud and feces, squalor and filth? Not kind ones or nice ones, Bale believed. But a lone spark of suspicion ignited inside his mind. Then a breath of rational thought fanned the flame. Soon realization blazed through his skull—if Diminutia and Silver found the Sun Stone, they'd be one up on him and his friends. "We'll go. We'll go, too!"

"What?" Pik shouted.

"I agree with our odoriferous friend," Belhurst chimed in. "We should all go together."

"What?" Silver and Pik shouted in unison.

"It will be an arduous journey, and it wouldn't hurt to add more to our party. We should all get some rest tonight and reconvene here tomorrow. Follen and I will go to the wizard's guild at first light to replenish our supplies."

"No!" Silver and Pik shouted, again in unison. They paused and sneered at each other, sickened to their stomachs that they agreed with each other.

Belhurst frowned. "Stop thinking with your egos or your broken hearts. Use your heads. This is the best course of action, and you know it. We need to rest and resupply, not argue like disruptive children."

Rest and supplies would not come to anyone, even if Pik and Silver weren't formulating their arguments. The far side of the tavern creaked then crashed forward. The wall of dark boards and thick logs cracked into popping splinters, collapsing part of the roof. Confusion reigned as patrons screamed and ran, many unable to escape, reduced to bloody sacks of pulp. Silver, Pik, and their friends readied themselves for an attack while searching for an escape route. However, Silver couldn't help but notice that the bard had mysteriously disappeared.

TWENTY-EIGHT

POETS AND ARTISANS pontificated that there was no greater beauty than watching the sunrise over Phenomere. Many would agree that the actual event would render all their works nothing more than scribbled words and splashed paint. The sight inspired pauper and politician alike and always gave the hope of a new life emerging from the darkest of nights. But today the sunrise brought a foreboding chill of death.

The early morning red rays cast a murky pall upon Praeker Trieste's armor, turning it from green to brown. He stood motionless upon the tallest hill beside Phenomere and watched as the morning sun's red turned to orange, glinting an amber brilliance off of every window. He almost felt pity for what he was about to do to the city.

Behind him his troops grew restless, quarreling amongst themselves, pushing and shoving for the best position. Every one of them wanted to be first into the city once the general gave the command.

Praeker smiled as he listened to the snarls and grunts and howls from behind him. More beautiful music he had never heard, save for the retched cries of anguish from the innocent. But he remained patient until the horizon no longer hid any part of the sun, its bright yellow rays chasing away early morning shadows. Praeker Trieste did not want any moment of his glory to go unnoticed. He wanted the entire world to see what he was about to do. He wanted the world to know that he could raze it all with one simple word: "GO!"

The lands rumbled as Praeker's squalid army charged down the hill's side. Men and non-men alike rushed forth with hatred in their hearts and death on their breaths. Centaurs galloped and satyrs hopped, ogres lumbered as best they could, while lycanthropes tossed clods of ground into the air with every stride. Wings flapped and scales slithered and claws protracted for a better grip while racing to a bloody glory.

The only obstacle between the hilltop and the city was a small farm. Many of the creatures ran past, not wanting to waste their time. But an ogre and a cave troll made a wager to see who could do the most damage as they barreled through the house, reducing it to tattered tinder. They bickered the rest of the way down the hill as to who won. A small contingent of cat-creatures succumbed to the lure of fresh livestock, taking but a moment to bloody their muzzles on fresh pig while three rabid satyrs raped the farmer's wife, a way to tease themselves before the carnal gorging they expected from within the city. They laughed as the farmer himself perished underneath the pounding hooves of a half dozen centaurs.

The army caught Phenomere completely unaware. The first wave of the fastest creatures reached the suburban streets and shops before a single scream could be wailed. Morning chores ended with evisceration. Those finishing breakfast soon became breakfast as a sick twist of fate descended upon them. Gargoyles used the baker's own bread to sop up his blood as they snacked. Ghouls retched at the sugary smells of the tart shop, more content feasting upon the tart maker and his apprentice. The tulips of the garden shop were barely a garnish as a minatory minotaur tore the shop keeper and her customers to shreds.

In an agonizing instant, the streets were covered in a creeping carpet of blood. A few of the slower moving creatures in the rank and file army, realizing there would be little enough slaughter for them, turned their dim-witted focus towards herd animals setting about their grazing and the shepherds who tended them. The shepherds didn't last long against their assailants, and the only protection the flock offered was the time it took to be slain and devoured.

A pair of bugbears ran a ring of sheep in circles until they fell dizzied to the ground. Then each set upon the hapless creatures in a sadistic race to see which could kill the most. The shepherd had run off towards the woods, his shrill screams crying out his location. When the bigger of the two bugbears had endured enough of the unyielding shrieking, she caught the shepherd and ripped him open at the navel, peeling back layers of skin as though it were an orange.

Praeker Trieste had given careful orders to his lieutenants not to discourage any act of vandalism, fornication, or murder, unless an actual skirmish line developed and bodies were needed in the front lines. Demoralization was often the key to victory he acquiesced, mentally reviewing the timeline he had established. Everything was proceeding according to schedule; he smiled, watching his legion make friends with the locals. How important and gratifying it was to be good neighbors.

Agitated and excited all at once, the scorpions that made up his armor skittered across his skin. It glinted with unusual beauty in the sunlight in an odd parody to the death and destruction that it heralded. The charisma of his magnanimous presence had been used to cull the minds of hundreds of creatures, creating an army that was impressive in its array, if not for its head count. His appearance inspired fear even in the dumbest and biggest of creatures, but his understanding and tolerance of mayhem kept morale high. His army was not comprised of specialists, nor of extremely intelligent beings, though his officers had been handpicked for that trait in particular. Yet the world of men would be hard-pressed to stem the tide of his advance.

The citizens of Phenomere fled their homes and businesses, but to little avail. When a few stragglers began to outdistance the army, a wave of harpies swooped out of the clouds to lift them from the firmament. They carried the screaming victims several hundred feet into the sky, the creatures torturing the humans with random talon rakes or attacks aimed at their most tender parts. When the skin had been sufficiently torn and enough blood let, they dropped the sufferers to their deaths.

Within the walls of Phenomere castle there was disarray as word of the insurgence slowly leaked through the outer bailey. Several guards stationed atop the highest turrets, who witnessed the harpies and other flying creatures, passed word to their sergeants who deduced the meaning of it all. War had come to their very doorstep without a vanguard to announce it.

"Lower the portcullis," one sergeant yelled at his men, moving quickly to complete his appointed task.

"Nay, nay. Belay that order! We must leave the portcullis raised so that any survivors have egress," a young sergeant, barely able to sport stubble, shouted.

"There will be no survivors, and you'll only add us to the number of the fallen. We must close the gate," came the response from a grizzled veteran.

"What if we send a contingent of men out there to help fight off the creatures? Then we can do a fighting retreat to cover them," suggested the young man, clearly not willing to write off the lives of so many of his countrymen.

"That's suicide! Don't you see how much ground there is to cover? Plus, we'd have to defend against an aerial assault as well," chastised the veteran leader. "Drop the portcullis. Cut the losses. Fight them on our terms."

Random orders streamed in from all directions as officers shouted directives to men they couldn't even see amidst the confusion.

"Ready the ballistae!"

"Turn the catapults."

"Prepare the pitch."

"Fetch quivers and water skins."

"Archers to your posts."

Shouted orders replaced birdsong. Hatred strangled serenity, and fear mangled tranquility as the world spun out of control. All seemed lost in a wave of confusion as the moment of theory and application merged with disastrously disorganized results. To the eyes of those few who had seen fighting in their lifetime, all seemed lost. Then a calm and commanding voice rose above the tumult. The penultimate moment replaced by the promise of rebirth.

274 | CHRIS PISANO and BRIAN KOSCIENSKI

"The portcullis shall remain open, by order of the king of Albathia."

Noise ceased to the point that even breathing stopped. All eyes turned to the near turret and beheld Daedalus, Prince of Albathia, resilient in gleaming cobalt-colored mail. The young prince stood on the deck outside his apartments, several stories above the maelstrom of men in the outer bailey.

"We will not abandon our people, nor betray their hopes of salvation. They look to us in their time of need, and we shall arrive to them as saviors. Commanders, form up your men. Take this war to our enemies. Let them know that the very streets of our city are armed to repulse them, wave after wave, until their lines dissolve, broken. Go forth with the blessings of your king. Return with the salvation of our city held aloft."

The confusion and panic of a seemingly unwinnable situation melted away as the world suddenly came back into focus. Purpose took direction in hand, and resolve was born. Sergeants barked out orders with authority, and men fell into rank as if this were merely another routine drill to be played out with precision before one could return to the comfort of his feathered bed. Within a score of minutes, men were armed, ranks were formed, and divisions marched out the raised portcullis, leaving only a handful of their number upon the walls and two dozen, at most, left standing upon the grass inside the outer bailey. Those who remained in the sanctity of the walls watched their comrades march out into the streets of the capital.

From his perch, Daedalus watched them march out as well. Watched them march to a grim and certain demise, he thought to himself smugly before setting his feet to the task of walking the escape route he had devised for himself.

Praeker laughed as he watched the king's guard pour out from the castle gates into the city streets. They offered little resistance. However, it never ceased to amaze him that the first of his army to attack were the humans. Nothing hated a human more than another human. Sure, other creatures in his army plunged headfirst into the throng of armor and weapons as well. Most of those creatures ate their kill, toying with it a bit on a primal level. But humans were different, willing to turn on each other for a few coins and shiny baubles, or for immature notions like revenge and a sadistic need to prove superiority. Whatever the motivation, Praeker's troops had it.

A dozen members of the hellish army, hefting a blend of wooden-hafted polearms and steel blades of high quality, loitered near the gate as the guard spilled forth. Despite the thrills found in their individual acts of carnage, they stopped and unified with the smoothness of flipping a switch. The guards slammed into a wall of flying fists and feral fur. For every strike The Horde felt from a guard's sword, they delivered three, often more critical, with their hands, teeth, and claws.

At this juncture, though, the guards had numbers on their side, especially since those leading the charge pushed their way into the streets enough to allow the battalion behind them through. However, The Horde reacted in kind. The guards shouted orders to form flanking formations while The Horde issued their own form of commands through barks and howls. From rooftops, from between buildings, from the skies, The Horde's members lacked the crispness of training, but they congealed nonetheless.

With frothing fangs and terrible talons, The Horde showed the guards that their numbers were meaningless. The creatures of The Horde tore through armor and tossed it aside as a child would while looking for a favorite toy within a filled box. Shields crumpled like foil and pikes snapped like used toothpicks. From fine mists to gushing gobs, sprays of blood painted the streets. The guards were finished.

Whooping and howling, the remaining Horde battle participants crashed through the open castle gate like a crimson-covered tidal wave. A bevy of riches awaited those who desired wealth. Most of the humans in The Horde chose to continue the slaughter of aristocrats and bureaucrats. One group even found the tax collector and chopped him to bits, one inch at a time, using hot coals to cauterize the fresh cuts. Any time the tax collector passed out from pain, he'd be awoken to streams of fresh urine splashing against his face.

Even those who feasted on the flesh and bones of the rich did so with zeal. Some argued that the wealthy offered a better taste. Others argued that since the rich were nothing more than hot air, they were less filling.

Praeker walked through the gate, straight for the castle. He had business to conduct and was less than amenable to the lone figure who stood between him and the castle. The figure displayed a twisted smile that he felt everyone should love, a smile only a bard could possess. "Good day, sir."

Praeker drew his emerald sword, its blade so sharp it seemed to slice away layers of air with every flick of the general's wrist. "Shall I assume you possess a litany of reasons why I shouldn't flay you?"

"Just one," the bard said with an easy smile. "You need an advisor."

Nonplussed, the general strode forward, the tip of his sword level with the bard's eyes. "I appreciate you not boring me with a long list. However, I have lieutenants to advise me, if I deem advice is needed."

"Oh yes, lieutenants. Would these be the same ones you've had in employ for years who have yet to get you a single stone that you so covet?"

The tip of the blade stopped before the bard. Were he to examine it, his eyes would go cross.

With a snarl, the general lowered his blade and glared pure hatred. "If you know where one is, tell me!"

"Not one. *All!* Better yet, as your advisor, I will guide you to them."

Praeker raised his sword again. "I don't have time for this! Tell me ..."

"On the contrary, my General ... nay, my *King* ... you have nothing but time. Take a moment of it for your conquest. *Their* king lays dead upon the cold stone floors of your new castle, and now you need to establish your presence here. Promote lieutenants to governors. Divvy up the lucre to your soldiers. Send messengers to the lands letting the sovereignty know who the new king is. With no sleep, it should take but a day. Of course, if you had an adept advisor, the necessary time would be mere hours."

The general, soon to be king, growled. The restless scorpions skittered around his body, mimicking Praeker's fiery mood. He leaned forward, and the stench of death wafted over the bard's face. "One misstep, Bard ... nay, advisor ... and I shall feed you to my armor."

For dramatic effect, the bard placed his palms together and offered a slight bow. "Fair enough, my liege."

Without further ado, the bard led Praeker to his new castle.

TWENTY~NINE

THE CITY WENT UP in smoke, fire turning years of labor into smoldering ash. Tallon watched from his window and felt the same thing happen to him. *Dealing with a monster, one could only expect the promises made to face a similar demise,* he thought. He knew Praeker's hordes had invaded. But he didn't know which monster was truly responsible—Praeker or Daedalus?

They should have run away three days ago after their outburst with Daedalus like Tallia suggested. Tallon said to be patient and simply avoid Daedalus for a time. She was right, but there was no time to worry about that. They had to go. Now.

He turned from the window, expecting to see his sister put the finishing touches on their packing. Instead, she sat on the edge of his bed, crying silent tears. Confused, he asked, "What are you doing? Have you finished packing?"

Trying to choke back a gurgled sob, she replied, "It's over, Tallon. It's all over."

Tallon strode to the bed and pulled her to her feet. "No. No, I believe ..."

"Believe we can make it out of this with our lives? These castle towers are on fire. Praeker has no intention of keeping his promise to us. And if we make it out unscathed, then what of the streets? And if we make it past Phenomere's borders, then where? We have no friends, no connections. Daedalus always made sure of that."

Just the mention of his cousin's name made Tallon cringe. "We ..."

Tallia cut him off again, "Have nothing. Except each other."

She stepped forward and wrapped her arms around him, burying her tears in his chest. He returned the embrace, feeling a twisted knot in his stomach over his sister's emotional malaise. He tried to think of ways to talk her out of this situation, give her hope that they could escape the stifling influence of their cousin. But the mere thought of Daedalus led his memories down a dark and twisted path, to a time when he and Tallia were teenaged. A dreadful night when Tallia had followed the young Daedalus to his snake pit. Tallon watched from his window as she returned, alone and in a staggering stupor, her soul stripped away leaving only a moving corpse. Concerned, he ran from the tower to the back of the castle. Just as he made it outside, he saw her walk to the stables. Wondering what she could possibly want with a horse at that time of night, he skulked over. Then he saw.

She stood in the doorway to the small nook where the stable boys slept. The castle's stable needed a dozen adolescent men for all the daily duties. Most were fast asleep except for a few exchanging bawdy jokes to fend off slumber. But their tongues fell silent when they noticed a member of the royal family standing in their doorway. Confused, those awake tapped and shook those asleep, hoping someone knew the proper procedure for this. All twelve sat, unsure of what to say to Tallia, just standing there, staring at them with empty eyes. Confident she had their undivided attention, she disrobed.

Still in awe, the stable boys sat frozen. Until one slid off his shirt and shed his pants. Seeing no recourse from the young man's bold move, another followed suit. Then the rest. Certain this was the only way to erase her memory, Tallia threw herself onto the laps of twelve naked, young men.

The stable boys snapped to attention. Some attacked like hungry dogs; some remained more patient, seizing any opportunity that presented itself. All were sated.

Tallia writhed and wiggled, enjoying the ebb and flow of the endless waves of flesh rolling over her, around her, in her. Smiling, she reminded herself that these were examples of men, not that lecherous creature who stole her virginity. She felt Daedalus's slime within her and prayed that the essence of these young men would mask it, conquer it. Using every man as a scrub, she washed away the dirty memories of her cousin. They filled her with confidence as they filled her with semen, each explosion rocketing her away from her cousin. She replaced the fetid taste of Daedalus with the tastes of satisfied, young men.

Using whatever means necessary, her loins, her hands, her mouth, she took each man twice. Some even three times. And one exceptionally vigorous stable boy five times. She remembered his name for future reference.

Tallon watched. His sister was lost in a sea of sweaty sinew. He knew he should run to tell someone, but his legs refused to move. To his surprise, he watched, with his hands down the front of his pants.

Tallia's sobs, rather the cessation of her sobs, snapped Tallon back to reality, back to a crumbling world, trapped in a tower under siege. Wondering why she stopped crying, but not wanting to ask, he continued to hold her. Then she shifted in his arms, her thigh purposely rubbing against the erection he was not aware of until now.

Still unsure of what to do, he kept his arms around her, his heartbeat quickening. Then his vision blurred as he felt her hands slide between his thighs and gently fondle him. She pulled away and looked into her brother's eyes.

Just outside, a weapons cache of oil and alcohol exploded, strokes of fire streaking the air. Neither sibling needed to look out the window to know what happened. They didn't need to watch the fiery fingers tickle the rooftops leaving trails of flame in their wake. They knew these were their last moments. And they knew of only one way to spend them.

Their lips rushed together as their tongues tussled in a fit of primal urge. Hands clawed at clothing, desperate to reveal hidden treasures. Stripped clean, Tallon pushed Tallia away, to look at her. Tears trickled from his eyes, enraptured by the beauty before him. His body begging for release, he rushed to her again, his lips devouring hers as his initial thrust lifted her from her feet. Holding her buttocks with a death grip, he secured her on him and thrust again. And again, faster, harder, as twenty years of desire he could never act upon, twenty years of hating nature for such a cruel prank of loving the one person he shouldn't, coursed through his body. The explosion from within him, into her, rivaled yet another eruption from a compromised weapons cache outside. But Tallon didn't stop. He couldn't.

With three forceful strides, Tallon guided them to his bed, both bodies flopping on the fur blankets. Again, he pumped hard and fast, her hips moved in rhythm with his every thrust. Tallon climaxed again. And again, he couldn't stop, still showing his sister how much he loved her.

The heat in the air was palpable, moving over both of their bodies. Were either of them able to tear away from their kiss, they would have seen vapors rippling through the room. And smoke. The heavy curtains caught fire, spreading to nearby chairs and wall tapestries. The ceiling creaked and groaned, attacked by the blaze in this room as well as the inferno in the room above it. The fire spread.

Tallon broke the kiss, shifting Tallia's ankles to his shoulders, allowing for a deeper embrace. They looked into each other's eyes as he pounded into her, her body quivering with spasms.

The bed burst into flame, but all either of them saw was love. Embers drifted through the air like searing little moths, landing on their skin. The fire spread to their feet while burning chunks of ceiling fell onto Tallon's back.

Unable to sustain the weight of the falling rooms above it, the ceiling screamed and collapsed. Tallon leaned into Tallia for one final kiss as crushing planks of burning wood blistered away his skin, eating deeper. The wooden floor shared a similar fate as the ceiling. Weakened from the fire, it too gave way, falling into the room below. Yet Tallon still thrust into his sister for one final release.

Across the courtyard, Daedalus watched his cousins' tower fall. The roof caught fire from a weapons cache explosion and collapsed, undoubtedly taking every floor with it, gutting the structure from within. He sneered, hoping that both of them were still inside when it happened. Let those who would betray him be taught the lesson of their lives. Or, more aptly put, *with* their lives. It was obvious that their betrayal led Praeker Trieste to invade the capital ahead of schedule. Not being inflexible, Daedalus shifted his plans as well. He knew that if Praeker had attacked ahead of schedule, then whatever contractual obligation he believed they held was now rendered void.

After Daedalus had offered his brave posturing on the castle parapet, he fled back inside, disposed of his armor, and sought out his father. The old king slouched in his throne as withered as a sun baked prune, gasping for breath after dismissing his council with orders to be completed with haste. Daedalus went to his father and held him, gliding his fingers over his stringy hair. Leaning in, the youngest son whispered into his father's ear a rash of obscenity-laced words of disdain, ignoring whatever blathering his father attempted, and then slit the old king's throat. As Daedalus walked away, he actually felt he might have done his father a mercy.

Daedalus wound his way along a seldom-used path away from the wreckage. Never one for superstition or prayer, he did count his blessings since his escape route was ignored by Praeker's conquerors. Even though Daedalus controlled a lot within the castle walls, he had no friends, only tenuous allies at best, and they were few in number as well. As he skirted from the castle walls, he followed the refuse gulley all the way out of the city, thankful no one else had thought of the idea. As he used his robes to cover his nose and mouth to ward off the stench, he came to the sudden realization that all of his plans would come to an end once he hit the nearby forest. Until a voice came from behind, freezing the blood in his veins. "Fine day for a stroll, hmmm?"

Daedalus spun, wielding a knife he procured from his robes. He looked around seeking the source of the voice, catching sight of a portly man in tattered robes. The man paid no heed to the weapon Daedalus brandished, nor the feral manner with which he was regarded by the prince. Like Daedalus's knife, the man seemed to appear out of nowhere. "Who are you? State your business!"

Holding his palms out to signify he meant no harm, he took a step forward. "I am but a humble bard, here to help you."

Daedalus squinted. Never thinking himself one who succumbs to base notions such as fear, he did feel a certain unease from a man smiling in front of a backdrop of a city engulfed in roaring flames and billowing smoke. Daedalus could still feel the heat from the fires, yet the bard's smile was so pleasant that it seemed he had no inkling as to what was happening behind him. "You know who I am, I assume?"

The bard chuckled so demurely it could be mistaken for a titter. Even though his voice was as soft as rose petals, his words cut like thorns. "I know who you are, Prince Daedalus. I know all about you. I know your dealings with Praeker Trieste. I know your desire to posses the stones."

"Humble bard, indeed! Even though I have been banished from my home, I would rather no one know of such things. Prepare to lose your tongue, or worse if you struggle," Daedalus growled as he advanced with his dagger.

Unflinching, the bard simply cleared his throat. When the dagger was close enough to his face that he could fog the metal with his breath, the bard said, "I know where the Sun Stone is."

Daedalus froze in his tracks. His eyes flitted back and forth, weighing the validity of the statement. Tensing his arm as if to strike, he asked, "Where? Where is it?"

"Grimwell."

Again, discomfort touched his senses. He sneered as he stepped back and lowered his weapon. "You jest."

"I do not."

"Why tell me? Now that I have the information, I could still kill you."

Smile never once wavering, the bard took a step forward. "Because you need me. Do not forget, I know you have no friends. Do you see that large fir tree?"

Daedalus looked behind him. "I do."

"Go to that tree. From there, head north fifty paces. You will find a boulder that looks like it does not belong in these woods. A faint footpath from it will lead you to a safe

284 | CHRIS PISANO and BRIAN KOSCIENSKI

house of mine. Use it as if it were yours. Clean yourself. Eat whatever jerky and jarred foods you find. I will meet you there a half day from now, and we will begin our journey together."

Confused, Daedalus looked back to the bard. "A half day?"

"I have one last bit of business in the burning city."

The prince didn't care to know, so he asked, "What if I don't wait?"

"No one knows a better path to Grimwell than me, I assure you."

"Other than being a concerned citizen doting upon his prince, what is it that you seek?"

The bard chuckled again, this time with more substance. "Power, My lord. After you get the Sun Stone, you will be able to retake the kingdom and be its king. I merely wish to be your advisor, enjoying all the riches and accoutrements that come with the position."

It was now Daedalus's turn to chuckle. The rewards of power. He wanted the entire nation, but the cretin only wished for finer clothes and richer foods. Even though Daedalus wished not to enter into yet another allegiance with a dubious character, he did feel there was some substance behind the bard's promises, and the price was but a pittance in the prince's mind. He also yearned for a cleansing from all the sweating he had been as of late. "Very well, advisor. I agree to your terms.

The bard smiled and bowed. "Thank you, Your Highness. Now, off with you. Be on your way. Just because there are no members of The Horde here now, doesn't mean there can't be at any moment."

Seething, the prince could find no reason to argue. He gave the bard his blessing for his mysterious task and then continued toward his safe house. Daedalus found himself in a position that was not one of control, certainly a position he disliked very much. However, he found little choice but to follow along with the plan. But he planned to be as guarded as possible.

CHIRTY

SILVER WATCHED as half the tavern disappeared, its walls and roof reduced to tinder and dust. Striding through the debris came the cause of the wreckage, a cave troll and an ogre. Each as tall as Bale, they shoved each other and argued about who caused more damage. They paused when they noticed that they didn't scare everyone out of the tavern then smiled as they wagered who could kill the most. And they had quite the selection to choose from: three wizards, two thieves, a warrior woman, a quivering satyr, a hobgoblin, a rather dim looking ogre, and one drunken rabbit staggering his way into the ogre's pant pocket.

"Bale?" Diminutia asked, wielding his dagger. "You don't happen to know them do you?"

Bale stood straight, indignation rippling through his spine. "All ogres don't know each other. I didn't ask you if you knew the bartender just because he was human!"

"You pick now to be logical? Just go talk to him before he and his friend squash us!"

Bale scowled at Diminutia and advanced to greet the other ogre and the cave troll. But the only words he could get out of his mouth were, "Hi. I'm Bale ..."

With a ground-shaking thud, the ogre punched Bale in his bulbous gut. The cave troll delivered an upper cut that lifted Bale from his feet. Bale fell into a pile of splintered rafters and shreds of what was once a thatched roof. The ogre and cave troll turned their attention back to the devastated tavern's remaining patrons.

Dearborn drew her sword and grabbed a nearby chair as she calculated ways to use it as a weapon. Diminutia, Silver, and Pik wielded daggers, planning strategies based on speed and avoidance. The wizards backed away, scrabbling for food scraps, wood flecks, candle wax, anything to use as makeshift ingredients for any kind of offensive spell. Phyl fainted.

Follen found enough ingredients to release a weak fireball at the cave troll just as Dearborn threw the chair against the head of the ogre. Both monsters laughed. Even though they were only two feet taller than their prey, they looked down at them as if they were puny insects, begging to be stepped on. They laughed so loud they didn't notice Bale make his way out of the pile of rubble.

Diminutia and Silver saw Bale mad once. Really mad. It was the only time he didn't act like a bumbling lummox, the only time he truly inspired fear. When they saw the veins in Bale's jaundiced eyes bulge and saliva flow from between his brown and broken teeth, they knew he was really mad.

"Time to leave," Diminutia said, grabbing Dearborn's hand, getting ready to seize any opportunity to run. Silver gestured at the wizards to prepare to escape as well. Despite loathing to touch him, Pik scooped up Phyl in his arms.

The cave troll and ogre laughed at their prey, finding it amusing they thought they were going to escape. Their laughing ceased as Bale slammed their heads together. Anger reduced Bale's already limited vocabulary to growls and snorts as he pounded his adversaries with his fists. A crushing blow to the troll's head. A devastating punch to the other ogre's jaw. While the troll was dazed, Bale grabbed his head, twisted, and spun, lifting the monster off his feet. After three revolutions, Bale released the troll into the other ogre. They collided with enough force to level the rest of the tavern down around them.

Huffing and puffing, Bale stood in a hazy daze. Still carrying Phyl, Pik approached his ogre friend and asked, "Bale? Bale, you okay?"

"Uhhhh. What happened? I remember everything going black, and I saw sparkly stars and ... why are you holding Phyl?"

Through groggy eyes, Phyl looked up and replied, "Because he cares."

Pik dropped Phyl.

"We have to leave. Now!" Silver yelled as he witnessed the devastation around him. The once majestic scenery of Phenomere now burned and smoked with streets stained red from blood.

The dilemma between fight and flight was never further from anyone's mind. They simply ran. Smoke, pungent and acrid, billowed upwards from over a dozen places just within the area directly around them. Shouts hung thickly in the air suspended by the screams that rose up from human throats. There was very little actual combat, and what small patches of it that could be seen by the fleeing group was horribly one-sided. A pang of guilt touched several of them as they ran through the streets, an effigy of the once-proud and clean cobbled visage.

To the humans in the group, it was like hearing their own death knell. A symbol of freedom and strength crumbled before their very eyes. A sense of hopelessness pressed in on them.

For the nonhumans, it was a stirring moment as well. Though they had no sense of being bound to this place or its terrified and hunted inhabitants, there was still a feeling of a community in need, and though they were outwardly and inwardly not human, they still had a communal sense that was left without placation by their seeming cowardice. Bale was deeply affected by the sights and sounds as they rushed to meet him.

When a woman or child stumbled into their midst, they did their best to provide a direction, dodging debris and conflict with a purposeful determination known as avoidance. A baker met them with an upraised rolling pin and a half-burned apron that had the look of being only recently extinguished. He implored them to lend a hand against his plight. Still they ran on.

A schoolteacher staggered into them, her arms straining with a load of supplies and dusty tomes. She asked them to

288 | CHRIS PISANO and BRIAN KOSCIENSKI

loan her the use of their strength to carry away the remainder of the school's books. Panicked and fearful as she was, her request was more of a command, and Phyl had to stop Bale from doing the woman's bidding, such was her presence and determination. But still they ran.

And when a shepherd ran to them wringing his hands and expelling his tears over the demise of his defenseless flock, they continued to run. They ran through the fields and into the forest, not stopping until the sounds of battle had been left behind. But they knew their memories were forever stained with the sights of this day. They stopped to catch their breath and figure out a plan, but for some time no one spoke.

Gone from their minds were the humorous happenings of daily life. Diminutia no longer thought about women and their supple curves. Silver lost all track of money and fame. Phyl couldn't give a hoot if the others liked him or not, nor did he look for their opinions about his current hairstyle. Bale didn't mind being thought of as the "dumb one." Their personal needs had changed, mutated by the events around them, powerless to effect changes upon the world around them.

They panted, heads down and sightless for many minutes. The thieves and nonhumans, their groups ravaged by attrition, were simply unable to comprehend how their ill-tempered but jovial disputes had led them to such a bloody end.

Belhurst, knowing that it would take a directed effort to lead this group onto their necessary next step, was the first to recover his wits and, thus, the first to speak. "Thoughts of hopelessness trudge through our minds like a homeless leper searching for his last meal. But we must stave them off. Phenomere will rebuild, lives will reconnect. We know the reasons behind this disease, and only we can stop the contagion from spreading. The monster behind the attack on the capital of Albathia wants the same treasure we seek, and with it he could raze the entire world. We *must not* allow that to happen! We must retrieve the stone from Grimwell."

Catching her breath, Dearborn hunched over, her hands resting just above her knees. Trying to clear her mind of the recent horrors, she fought hard to ignore Belhurst's speech. But haggard gasps turned to sobs and what dripped from her face to her feet was no longer sweat, but tears. "The stones. The stones! All I hear about are these damnable stones! I've pledged my life to a man I could never love, a troop long since decimated, and a kingdom burning as we speak. All stripped from me, all taken. I have nothing left but my very life, and I refuse to give it to those stones!"

Pik and Silver wore the same expression on their faces, brows furrowed in pragmatism as they glared at Belhurst. Even a witless fool could see the dissention roiling below the sweat-slicked surfaces. Even Bale saw it and knew he had to speak before they did, because they would use fancy words to confuse and manipulate him. But not this time! He strode to the wizard's side and faced the opposition. "I'm with Belhurst."

Phyl squealed, and Pik snorted. "Bale ..."

"It's a chance to save the world," Bale said, trying to stifle the excitement of an ogre attempting to fulfill an adolescent dream.

"Bale ..."

"Zot would have done it."

Amazed and dismayed that Bale played the friendship card so well in this emotional game, both Phyl and Pik sighed. Seeing little recourse, the satyr and the hobgoblin stood by their friend.

"Madness," Silver said as he turned to Diminutia, ready to suggest they leave. Before either could converse, Pik added his thoughts.

"There goes Nevin's merry band of cowards. Saving the world will certainly be an achievement never to be one-upped."

Fire ignited behind Silver's eyes. Diminutia put his hands on his friend's shoulders. "Silver. He does have a point. Could you live with yourself if Bale saves the world?"

Silver cooled from blind rage to sorely irritated as the cogs in his mind ground soundly. Weighing his options, he deduced it would be much easier to steal and fence in the current state of the world than a demon inhabited tyranny. "Fine!"

Diminutia's lips wrung into a wry smile. He turned to Dearborn, arms crossed over her chest and cheeks still glistening from used tears. Approaching her, he extended his hand. "Dearborn. You have not lost everything, you have simply yet to find more. And I certainly would be interested in aiding you in that quest. No matter how long it may take."

Dearborn took Diminutia's hand. But their moment was ruined by footfalls, shuffling leaves and snapping twigs, phlegm-filled snorts, and prodigious belches. And a gruff voice laughing. "Awww. Ain't that sweet?"

The band of wizards, trolls, and thieves turned to see a contingent from The Horde, blood soaked and weapons ready, making their way through the forest. Everywhere one of the heroic party turned, they witnessed yet another creature reveal itself, as if the trees gave birth to the retched beasts. Weary and broken, but still the humans and trolls readied what weapons they had to face the patrol party.

Whooping and laughing, the salivating monsters encircled their prey, taunting them with verbal jabs, promising slow evisceration. Diminutia and Dearborn still clutched each other's hands as they found themselves back to back. Muscles tensed and nerves electrified, they waited, readying themselves for the monsters to pounce. Until the sounds of cracking timber distracted everybody.

Echoing sounds of trees splitting approached. Thunderous noises of whole trunks snapping while the cacophony of tens, dozens, hundreds of trees falling into each other filled the forest. Then the familiar smell of oil wafted into the nostrils of Lapin. He smiled.

A rippling gush of horizontal fire flowed over half a dozen monsters, crisping them in an instant. Those left standing trembled as a maw full of teeth let loose an ear-splitting roar. With a few well-placed chomps and quick slices of his claws, Dragon disposed of the immediate threats.

"Dragon!" Lapin squeaked from Bale's pocket. Then hiccupped. Then pulled a swig from his flask. Then hiccupped again. "I knew you'd save us, buddy!"

"Lapin? Are you drunk?" the dragon asked.

"He has been since we arrived to Phenomere," Belhurst answered.

Dragon shook his head. "Be that as it may, you must go. The forest is crawling with scouting parties, and I'm sure this fiasco attracted some attention."

As if on cue, screeching from above the tree line revealed circling griffins and harpies.

"I'll take care of them," Dragon continued. "Where shall I meet up with you?"

"Grimwell, brave Dragon," Belhurst said.

Even Dragon winced at the town's name. He looked back to Lapin and said, "Do your best to protect them, Rabbit."

Lapin lifted his flask in acknowledgment. "That, I will do."

Within a blink, the dragon launched himself from the forest, frying a griffin and shredding a harpy. With heavy hearts and sore bodies, the stone-searching party continued on their way. Though, Dearborn's and Diminutia's fingers remained entwined.

Thirty~one

"I'M SCARED," Bale whined.

The others, except Lapin, felt similar feelings of dread walking through the ominous forest. However, none of them expected such sniveling to come from the largest creature of the group. This was, after all, an ogre who could scare sunlight and mere days ago fought to victory against another ogre and cave troll, both of whom possessed superior physical prowess.

Lapin, thoroughly pickled and still imbibing from a stolen flask while lounging in Bale's pant pocket, gave no thought to the ogre's words of cowardice. With every sip of an unnamed, wicked whiskey, the rabbit's emotions flipped from numbness to concern. Having done nothing more than consume amounts of alcohol that would knock Bale to the ground, Lapin simply couldn't feel anything other than numbness at the moment. However, if he noticed the lack of his long-time companion, the dragon, he wondered where he might be. It had been days since they fled from Praeker Trieste and his Horde as they attacked Phenomere, thanks to the dragon facilitating their escape. *Where could he be?* Lapin would ask himself. *Maybe flying ahead to clear our path?* Then he would take another swig and erase his mind of all thought.

"Shut up," Pik said to Bale. The hobgoblin's voice held a false bravado as chills ran down his spine with every step. How could anyone not be afraid? The scarcely used foot path even seemed frightened, twisting and turning through the black trees, as if trying to flee from the forest itself. Branches reached for the travelers like hungry fingers trying to scoop up a snack. They appeared everywhere, as if from nowhere, making it impossible to determine which tree held what branch. The black wood of the angled branches stabbed the sky as if trying to scrape away the light. The trees created perpetual night even though not one held a single leaf.

Diminutia and Dearborn walked side-by-side, neither very comfortable with the twisted trees. The black and knotted bark flaked and curled in such ways that anyone who looked at the trees swore they saw screaming faces. Diminutia saw yelling guards and angry victims always in pursuit, always one step behind him knowing one day they would catch the slippery thief. Dearborn saw the anguished grimaces of her fallen comrades, each screaming in pain, each falling to death's clutches way too young.

Silver watched Belhurst, only letting the ragged wizard out of his sight to blink or to glance at the other ragged cohorts. The thief knew how the wizards thought now, knew why they fussed and jumped over the sound of every breaking twig or tree trunk creek. Not only did they not have enough time to supply their cart, the cart itself was lost during the attack of Phenomere. Each wizard possessed a few ingredients, stuffed in the myriad pockets of their robes. But judging from their perpetual state of paranoia, Silver knew they did not have enough to fend off the demons of the Shadow Stone. Nor the demons that guarded the Satan Stone or Spirit Stone, if the stories from Dearborn and the trolls held truth. Silver approached the lead wizard and asked, "What do you fear the most?"

Belhurst chuckled from the question. "Too many choices, my friend."

"The Shadow Stone demons?"

"Yes, for they are near. As well as the Spirit Stone demons that decimated our nonhuman companions' families. Praeker and his army may be faster, but even he wouldn't raze Phenomere and leave it. He needs to stay to restore order to his sick liking. Dearborn and her troop vanquished the Satan Stone demons back to hell. But from the stories of our smelly friends, the demons attached to the Spirit Stone are swift and stealthy."

Grip tightening on his dagger, Silver asked, "How much farther to Grimwell?"

Before Belhurst could answer, the trees curled inward. Those who had daggers or swords cut and sliced at the furling branches. Dismay filled their hearts as they cut nothing.

"What manner of trees are these?" Pik screamed, waving his dagger around as if trying to stab a fly.

"It's not the trees," Belhurst yelled. "It's the Shadow Stone demons!"

Snarling, Silver grabbed Belhurst by his robes. "Then make light, old man!"

Belhurst slapped away Silver's hands. "With what?"

Follen produced weary words and waved withered hands. He used the only ingredients he could muster from his robes to produce a handful of flaming moths. With jerky flits, the fire-winged moths swarmed one tree, crashing into its bark and disappearing into fiery puffs. The dozens of moths were enough to ignite the peeling bark of a blackened tree. In seconds, the tree popped and crackled like a giant torch. Dearborn and Diminutia broke branches from nearby trees and tried to ignite them from the wizard-made inferno. To no avail.

"Why aren't they lighting?" Diminutia asked.

As the others ran to the light of the burning tree, Belhurst explained. "The fire will only burn this tree, nothing else."

"Splendid," Diminutia mumbled as he tossed the branch at the undulating blackness. "Now what?"

"We have to push through," Silver said. "The fire may not burn anything else, but it certainly won't last until morning."

"And the forest is so thick, we have no way of knowing when morning is," Pik added.

Before anyone else could participate in the debate, high-pitched whistles split the air. Everyone paused, no longer fearing the rippling blackness. The whistling grew louder, bolder, closer. Hands tightened on hilts when they

realized that what they heard wasn't whistling at all. But
laughing.

The wind whipped near the travelers, confusing them.
Turning in circles, Grymon stepped too far away from the
others and the burning tree. Before he could right himself,
he jerked. And jerked again. His chest heaved in then out,
as did his abdomen. Blood cascaded from his mouth. His
severed left arm fell to the ground. He looked to his friends
for help as his torso slid from his waist, making a
sickening thud as it hit the dirt. Like an unbalanced stalk,
his one leg leg fell away while his wooden leg remained
upright, planted in the forest dirt. Behind where Grymon
once stood, three snickering demons appeared as misty
wisps at first, until the smoke congealed to form bone
white monsters. The Spirit Stone demons. Bale had not
seen these demons before, but recognized them as the ones
who killed his friends and relatives and got him banished
from his home village. He knew that they killed Zot from
the harrowing descriptions given by witnesses. He no
longer felt fear.

"No more!" Bale screamed as he grabbed the burning
tree. Bending his knees and hugging the trunk, he
uprooted it with one tug. "No more!"

Surprised by the bold move, the laughing demons failed
to move fast enough as the top of the flaming tree came
crashing down on them. Two of the demons survived and
went back to their smoky forms. Spinning in circles, Bale
continued to swing the burning tree, his companions all
dropping to the ground for cover. Except for Lapin, who
enjoyed the twirling ride in Bale's pocket as he continued
to drink. "Weeeeee! Woooooo!"

Noticing that the darkness moved away from the
whipping fire, Silver crawled to Pik and Phyl. He nudged
them and pointed. They too noticed that both the Shadow
Stone demons and the Spirit Stone demons retreated from
the burning tree. "Can you guide him?"

"With some help," Pik said.

The three raised themselves to a crouch, waiting for the
right opportunity. As Bale spun and the rabbit squealed,
Silver, Pik, and Phyl rushed the ogre. They timed their
attack right, pushing the ogre, guiding him. Still waving

the tree like a madman swinging a fiery club, Bale ran, cutting a swath through the blanket of darkness. Staying close to Bale, the rest followed as he continued to scream, "No more!"

The slashing and swinging continued well past the wall of shadow, but no one dared to interrupt the crazed ogre. He only stopped once they broke through the forest perimeter into a clearing of mud and filth bordered by haggard trees, dismal swamp land, and jagged rock croppings. They found Grimwell.

Even to the group of nonhumans within the party, Grimwell often represented anathema. Today, however, its warped walls and rutted roads meant sanctuary. Despite the need of the unlikely companions to cover mileage, there was a noticeable pause upon reaching the entrance to the monster town. An unspoken relief passed through the group leaping from member to member like a jolt of electricity.

The tree that Bale hugged to his body had burned and charred until it resembled a spent wick.

"Read your future for a silver, lord?"

The majority of the group stood paralyzed as if in an apoplexy of fear, for the creature huddled on the ground before them was a twisted effigy of life. Her skin was black as a nightmare, and her lank hair hung in greasy waves like a measure of despair. The woman's body was bent and twisted, her limbs wrenched at impossible angles as if by hell's own fury. With colorless eyes, distinguishable from the rest of her face only by the barest trace of moisture and the lavender colored pupil that marked their precise center, the woman leered up at them. When she spoke, a waft of decay brushed over them as her reedy voice intoned its way past the decomposing ridge that seemed to serve as her upper teeth. From her bottom jaw protruded two fanglike teeth, perfectly fitted into the center. They gleamed ivory-like up at the group with a palpable malignancy that suggested only the basest aspects of night.

"Come, Prince ... it's only a silver! And quite a steal at that price!"

"Belhurst," Dearborn asked, "what is that?" Her hand straying to the pommel of her sword.

With a stifling gesture, Belhurst stopped the warrior woman before she could make any menacing movements. In a quiet voice, he named the creature before them.

"Night-hag."

"What does it want?" Silver asked.

"Very dangerous. No hostile moves."

"We don't have time for this, wizard."

"We do now, thief."

"We could certainly push aside a haggard old woman," Silver queried.

"Few could. At a betting tent, I wouldn't lay my gold that none in this party could."

"What?" Silver asked in a voice that was far louder than intended. Without realizing himself, he spun about to face the wizard, but blackness overwhelmed his senses, and he was on the ground without even feeling himself fall, the night-hag perched upon his back. Her move was so sudden that even Dearborn, inured as she was for the unexpected in battle, had no opportunity to react.

Diminutia, ever quick to gather his wits, made a move to help his friend, but it was met with a sound so maleficent it would have paled an ogre's bellow and muted a dragon's roar. A gaze of hideous intensity transfixed Diminutia. Spasms of pain rippled through his musculature dropping him to his knees. His head swam until he would have been hard pressed to utter his own name, and his only possible response was to lie down. To his friends, he appeared to have drunken himself into a stupor so deep that even falling down posed difficulty.

With a movement as distinct as a mumble, the hag moved again, leaving her perch atop Silver's back for the spot where they had originally encountered her. A visible distortion in the air over Silver's back, like rising steam, was the only evidence of her passing. Dearborn knelt slowly towards him, her eyes never leaving the crone.

"He lives," Dearborn reported to the others after searching his neck for a pulse.

"Had she meant for him to be dead," Belhurst said, "he would be beyond all of our power to save. Look there." He indicated the spot above Silver's back with a directed finger. "That isn't heat you see rising. It's his will to live. In

298 | CHRIS PISANO and BRIAN KOSCIENSKI

time it will return to him, but he will not be of much use to us for a while."

A moan rose from the mass that was Diminutia's sprawled form.

"And him?" Dearborn asked. "What has befallen him?"

"A mind cloud," the hag cackled. "Nightmares that not even the light of day can chase."

"Let's not see them," Phyl suggested mildly. "We have our own nightmares as is."

"Agreed," said Belhurst. "The trick now is to appease her. She seems to be interested in your pithy friend, Bale."

"Bale?" several of the members of the group asked incredulously, turning toward the wizard.

"But she said 'Prince,'" stated Phyl dumbly. "She called him 'Prince.'"

"Yeah," said Bale. Then, as he noticed that several of the others present had begun to shake their heads as though clearing away a stray, but unpleasant memory, he, too, began to shake his head slowly. He watched the others through narrowed eyes, not wanting to be the odd man out when they all stopped.

"Bah! Prince!" snorted Pik.

"Yeah," said Bale again, still shaking his head as though the mystery would shake itself out.

"It is weird, Belhurst. Isn't prince more of a human term?" Dearborn asked.

"Yeah," said Bale again.

Belhurst cleared his throat before answering. "Well, no, not really. As most nonhumans lack the, um, taste for a more complex political structure, they tend toward monarchies. Though as I understand it princes don't ..."

"What!" snorted Bale, now clearly perturbed. "What do you want?"

"I'm not sure I take your meaning, Bale?"

"You all keep calling my name then don't say anything when I answer you.

"No one has been calling your name, Bale," Belhurst stated.

"I mean, it's rude. In case your moms never told you," finished the ogre.

"But no one said your name, Bale," Belhurst complained, clearly upset at allowing himself to be drawn into an inane conversation with the immense creature. He had seen what destruction Bale was capable of when perturbed and would have preferred to skirt the issue, but the big lummox intrigued him.

"Yes. You have. You've been saying, 'Prince. Prince. Prince.' But whenever I answer with, 'Yeah,' you just keep on talking."

"Your name ... your *real* name ... is ... Prince?"

"Yes!"

Silence befell the group, none could register the concepts set before them until Pik started laughing, a hard belly-cramping, tear-forming laugh formed from a violent mix of comedy and insanity. Unable to stop himself from doing anything else, Phyl joined with a knee-shaking guffaw. The wizards laughed along as well but hid their zeal by turning their backs. Dearborn found no energy to laugh, sitting on the ground with Diminutia's head on her lap and stroking his hair. "Need I remind everyone here that we just got finished fleeing from demons only to stumble upon a nightmarish hag who felled two of our own."

Incensed, Bale reached into his pant pocket not inhabited by Lapin and pulled out a silver coin. He handed it to the night-hag. "I agree with Dearborn."

The hag smiled a gnarled-tooth grin and accepted the coin. "You, sir Prince, are the strongest and bravest of the lot. But it is your intelligence that will guide you to greatness."

Despite the wretchedness of the bare ground, both Phyl and Pik fell to it, their laughter unstoppable. Dearborn twisted her face in disgust at their behavior, longing for the discipline of her lost Elite Troop; she turned her attention to Diminutia. She never gave much credence to the felonious career of thievery. Yet, observing Diminutia for this journey, getting closer to him, she recognized some of the same qualities within the field as she saw within the army: life-depending trust; bravery, albeit in a different form, but bravery nonetheless; and a deep bond with associates that transcends mere friendship.

Dearborn stroked Diminutia's hair while replaying the events in which he demonstrated these acts. She then stroked the soft skin of his face. Chuckling to herself, she knew that softness could have only come from using the same lotions housewives of wealthy men would use. That detracted from his manliness, but certainly not from his handsomeness. Stroking his square jaw and chiseled cheeks, she could not resist leaning in to kiss his inviting lips. To her surprise, he kissed back.

Dearborn pulled away to see sapphire-blue eyes staring deep into hers. A wan smile formed. She then looked to the night-hag, standing near and watching the display. "I thought you said he would not be joining the waking world for some time?"

"I guess some fairy tales are true," the hag snorted and turned to walk away. "Now, follow me."

Still confused, both Dearborn and Diminutia looked to Belhurst who flashed a grin and mouthed the word, "Love."

Blushing, Dearborn and Diminutia helped each other to their feet. After kicking sand on Pik and Phyl, still on the ground, they aided Silver to his feet, now semi-conscious and wobbling like a drunkard. They all followed the night-hag as she led them into town.

The streets were indistinguishable, bare footpaths etched into the ground. The structures could hardly even be called hovels, mere openings formed in the rolling knolls of the landscape. The rippling land, devoid of any form of vegetation, held both the color and stench of rot. The entire town looked as if the neighboring mountains had defecated it into existence.

Belhurst looked around, catching movement in every shadow, every nook, and every ravine from the corner of his eye. As he turned to focus, he saw only filth and waste, mired by rotting leaves. But no movement. At times, the ground itself seemed to ebb and flow. After a few more futile glances, he realized he witnessed the town's inhabitants. Watching him. That was when he also realized the night-hag had to be some form of mayor. "Good mistress, we need your assistance in ..."

The night-hag interrupted with laughter, course and unnerving, the noise of a cat being strangled. "Wizard, I assure you, there is *nothing* good in me, or Grimwell. And I know why you're here. You can't have it."

"How ...?"

"The only reason why we ever have visitors. And all visitors are unwelcome."

"Praeker Trieste is on his way here as we speak."

The hag stopped walking. The arcane movements that avoided detection even stopped. With a glare in her milky-black eyes, the hag turned to Belhurst, the stench of her breath befitting the anger of her words. "*You* bring him here? The one creature that fears nothing, even Grimwell itself?"

"*We* did no such thing! Housing the stone is the *only* invitation he needs."

Without another word, the hag turned and continued to shuffle through town. Belhurst and his companions saw no other recourse than to follow. Through sand and silt, they walked to the center of town, marked by a hole in the ground no larger than a man's fist and gaping like a stab wound.

"No!" a voice coughed from the ground.

"We must," the hag replied.

Just as Belhurst was ready to question whence the voice came, the ground shifted as if unhappy about what lay beneath it, offended by the hideousness it hid. Offal earth slid away from a dozen points, forming a circle around the hag and the visitors. Unfolding from out of the forged flaps came twelve creatures more hideous than the hag. Some held faces scarcely more than covered skulls, many missing lips and cheeks. Few had two eyes; most either sported empty sockets seeping noxious fluids, or had shredded flaps of skin stretched over malformed cranial bone. No noses to speak of, pocked pimples or jagged slits were the best any creature could offer.

Once unearthed, the twelve stood, as best they could, in judgment of the visitors. Gnarled bodies wracked with generations of malevolent mutation, knees bending improbable ways, arms split and shooting like spears escaping torsos that looked like clenched fists, backs twisted like knotted hemp. No clothing among them, all wearing the filth of the ground that birthed them, ungrateful miscarriages refusing to discard mother's placenta. "We are the elders of Grimwell, and we forbid it."

Phyl retched, and Pik felt his stomach weaken. Dearborn closed her eyes while Diminutia turned his head downward, offering only furtive glances. Even Belhurst and Follen would have admitted to never seeing such befoul monstrosities. Bale slid the back of his hand across his nose, hoping no one thought he was doing more than scratching an itch. He then looked down as he felt a stirring in his pocket to see Lapin poke his head out. Even though Lapin was a rabbit, Bale could tell that his eyesight was blurred.

"What's goin' on?" Lapin asked. "Why's everyone look so nauseated?"

"Don't know," Bale replied. "Some of Grimwell's inhabitants are arguing with each other."

The hag neared one part of the circle. "We are *descendents* of the first demons released from hell by the wizard Wyren. It is our birth burden to make sure the stones are never to be used again."

Mucus flowed from the rotten pores of the town member who countered. "And this, to you, means handing the Sun Stone over willingly? To strangers?"

Belhurst stepped forth and replied, "We assure you, we will not use the stones. We are looking for ways to *destroy* the stones."

Senses addled by alcohol, Lapin found it difficult to understand the conversation. He looked up at Bale and whispered, "One of the stones is here?"

"I think it's in that hole," Bale whispered back.

"Huh. Really?" Lapin whispered to himself. With his heartbeat thrumming in his ears, he found it impossible to hear the spirited discussion among the wizards, the Grimwell inhabitants, and everyone else. His vision was blurred enough not to know how many people were actually arguing, but he was pretty sure everyone was talking at once, but lacked the knowledge to do so in a logical manner. No matter. He was bored of the conversation he couldn't hear and didn't understand and sought the means to end it. He burrowed back into Bale's pocket.

He reemerged with a ball of twine he had discovered a few days earlier. Tying one end around his waist, he tapped Bale on the hip. When he caught the ogre's attention he handed the other end to him. "Here. Hold this."

Blurred as his vision may be, he hopped from Bale's pocket to the filthy ground. He approximated where Bale had pointed earlier. Sure enough, he saw five holes. As he ran closer, the number of holes decreased to two, then only one. The stench emanating from the hole would have surely knocked any other animal over, maybe even killing it. But *all* of Lapin's senses were dulled, and he was sure Bale's pants smelled even worse. With little thought, Lapin jumped in.

Not sure what to do, Bale just stood there holding the one end of twine as the ball unraveled. Within a few blinks, the ball unspun and the line of twine was taut. A little concerned, Bale began to pull the string. He felt the weight of Lapin as he pulled the string. With every pull, his heartbeat quickened, especially because the overcrowded conversation became louder and faster with every breath.

"You must listen to me!" Belhurst yelled.

"We must do nothing you demand!" one of the elders yelled back.

"I have seen their souls," the hag argued.

"I find it impossible to believe their souls are any more pure than this town," another elder said.

"I'll kill you for what you did to me," Silver slurred as he became more conscious.

"Greater have tried and failed," the hag hissed back.

"This is for your own safety. The safety of the entire world," Belhurst said.

"Our people are in charge of their own safety," one elder said. As if on cue, the grounds behind them slithered while figures emerged from huts and holes. The inhabitants showed themselves, showed they were no less disgusting and disfigured than the hag or elders.

"What the hell is going on," Silver shouted, finally coherent enough to stand on his own.

"Give us the Sun Stone!" Belhurst yelled.

Finally, one elder tilted his head back and released a shriek that sickened every nerve in everyone's bodies.

When no one had the wherewithal to utter a single noise, the elder stomped his foot and bellowed, "The stone *stays!* That is *final!*"

Despite his new headache, Bale continued to pull the twine. With one final tug, Lapin popped from the hole holding the stone in question. With a slurred smile, he presented it for all to see. "Found it!"

CHIRCY-CWO

THERE WAS NO ROAD between the Kingdom of Albathia and the monster city of Grimwell by design. In fact, not even seldom used paths existed in most places. The walk was arduous, and the conditions were heinous to the average traveler. In one area, the conditions were dusty, and dry soot hung all about in a thick cloud, the grime permeating even the densest clothing, lying on the skin causing it to sweat, then caking in the moisture. In an odd twist of fate, it was only several miles beyond that a vast expanse of moisture-rich soil laid. Not fully a swamp, but bearing many of the same characteristics of this geographical feature, the soil was damp and the air thick with humidity. Scores of pestering insect species sought out life within their demesne and then proceeded to make that life wish it were somehow something less than living. Again, even the densest clothing provided little relief to the stinging, swarming, eye-seeking, aperture-exploring insects. Nestled within the inviting arms of a small forest, this mire lasted for several miles, lying invisible beneath a lush carpet of loam that gave way easily under foot, causing the walker to slip as the bugs attacked his ears, eyes, and nose.

Daedalus dropped to his knees for the thirteenth time that he could recollect, though, by his own admission, he wasn't sure when he had begun keeping track of the ignominious acts nature had wreaked upon him during this journey. It wasn't until his "walking companion" had disappeared, his parting words an offer to run ahead and act as the prince's herald to the citizens of Grimwell.

"It simply wouldn't do for the human prince to show up uninvited and unannounced," the knotted little bard had said with a lopsided smile that carried no mirth.

At first, the prince acquiesced. Were it simply one of his brothers making this trek, then such frivolities could have been overlooked. But someone of his stature and standing, soon to be named king ... certain etiquettes could not be ignored. But after walking through the muck for several hours, his mood had soured considerably, and Daedalus decided his first act upon reaching his gods-forsaken destination would be to choke his erstwhile companion until the little fellow's face turned livid with pent up life. The herald would beg for death in front of the assembled natives of Grimwell, and Daedalus, the Merciful, would oblige his sad wishes. His first meeting with the indigenous members of the nonhuman city would be notable, and he would be remembered as a sanguine individual even as they placed a crown upon his head. *Let previous plans burn in great plumes of smoke,* Daedalus thought, salivating at the thought of becoming king. He would claim this city of wild things as his subjects, as was only right, falling as it did well within the established borders of Albathia. He would be coy at first, he decided, pushing them to the limits of their need until they verily begged him to be their king, uniting them against the thronging Horde and delivering them from the evils of Praeker Trieste. Surely tales of the scorpion-clad general's bloodlust must have reached even the most remote pockets of civilization, no matter how rudimentary.

He smiled to himself, despite the pressing concerns of his present situation and for just a moment allowed himself to forget that he was on his knees and sinking in the hungry mud while flies and gnats barraged his skin until red. Welts and white, pus-filled abrasions too numerous to count surfaced like so many remote island chains upon the globe of his skin.

It was an unusually virulent sting upon his oft-blistered foot that brought him out of his vision of coronations and coquettish speeches. He seethed in silence; let his anger vent in ragged panting, the white clouds of hatred almost discernable against the backdrop of humidity. In time, the humidity would be replaced by humanity, still grouped and overlapped one upon the next, the necessity of their existence palpable, though not entirely palatable. It was at that moment that he would unleash his boiled-over rage, his antagonism reaching where sight could not. A gleaming spotlight of zeal crowning his head, like no circlet of no man-made forging could deign, would be the only herald he would need, though he would allow himself the normal courtly pleasantries lest the dignitaries of other states who would prostrate themselves at his feet be at a loss to express their humility in the presence of his greatness.

And so Daedalus had slipped from one vision to another suffering the ignominy of nature yet again. But his fervor was redoubled, so sure he was of his course of action. At some point, though he was quite unaware of it, he had become mobile, moving with somnambulistic grace through the muck that grasped at his feet, his sandals having been lost and forgotten some time ago. In his mind, though, it was easier to walk without them. Right up to the point where he stumbled through the brush, erupting onto the dusty scratch of land that served as the main road of Grimwell. So sudden was his departure from the nightmare of his nature walk that the change failed to register in his mind. His daze continued, carrying him amongst the residents of the nonhuman city who rose up in twos and threes like fangs in the maw of some great beast. He was fully ringed by monsters, his forward progression impeded before his dream faded. And when true sight returned to him and he beheld himself circled as he was by the bestial inhabitants of Grimwell, he mistook this moment for the moment he envisioned, standing expectantly for some offspring of the elders to seek him out, bearing his crown.

He did not attempt speech, so moved by the moment in which he found himself. The nonhumans puffed and grunted, nudging each other and raising their eyebrows in a lewd manner, saliva pasting their chest hairs as they considered wordlessly how to consume the meal that had walked so willingly into their midst.

"Oh, you're here! Let me through," rang the familiar voice of the bard for all its unctuousness. "This is the human prince I told you all about."

They know their king, Daedalus was tempted to retort, but good fortune touched his fevered mind before he could form the words, and he fell limp where he stood, collapsing in an unimpressive heap.

As with so many points in his life, Daedalus had no recognition of the happenings that passed around him. When he awoke, he lay upon a crude bed. Before his stomach protested its hunger, before his eyes grew accustomed to the filtered light, before he had even stretched his cramped limbs, he was acutely aware of the fact that he had not been bathed. And that simply would not do.

"Bard! Herald! Manservant," he shouted, repeating as necessary until the bard appeared at the entrance to the hut in which Daedalus found himself. Upon recognizing his form, Daedalus greeted him.

"Where am I? How long have I been here? And why have I not been bathed?"

"My lord, we feared to move you much. You had suffered from a dozen maladies and a severe infection where something injected you with its toxin. You are in Grimwell. And it's a good thing I went ahead of you. Or you would have been spitted."

Daedalus knew very well the bard's words were merely a euphemism for "you owe me your life." The young prince sat up and looked around the cramped room. Two beds, poorly constructed, even for peasants, and one oil lamp on a small table. He noticed no sunlight, even though he knew both suns were up, which meant no windows. With a sneer, he said, "Who could possibly live in a squalid home such as this?"

"Home?" The bard chuckled. "No, my liege. This is the town's hospital."

A million worms squirmed in Daedalus's stomach at the thought. He stood, looking for the exit. He found it, a hole at the end of upward sloping dirt. "What madness is this?"

"Madness? Why, sire, this is Grimwell. Have you heard none of the stories?"

"I have. But there is a difference between hearing a story and living it." Remiss at the weakness of his own words, Daedalus took a step toward the exit.

A worried look in his eyes, the bard stepped in front of the prince. "Sire, I must insist you return to the bed and rest."

The prince's face ignited to a red matching the fire behind his eyes and the heat of his words. "Listen, old man, be blessed that I haven't killed you yet for leading me through, and to, such indignation. I have *never* been so humiliated and befouled in all my years in this life, and *you* are the reason for it. Were you not as filth ridden as these surroundings, I would merrily wrap my hands around your wretched throat and crush your neck with mine own thumbs! Unless you have the stone which I seek hidden in one of your pockets, I *suggest* you remove yourself from my intended path!"

The bard regarded the prince. Finally, he offered a slight bow, then stepped to the side, allowing the prince free access to the exit.

Once through, Daedalus began to think that the bard was actually trying to protect him from the horrors that waited outside the horrid hospital. The buildings nestled themselves underground, only ravaged holes served as entranceways. No roads. No signs of *any* form of civilization.

With every step he took, his feet sunk into the sandy ground. The land sloped and curved, roiled like the bubbling of a witch's brew frozen in an instant. When the mother world was young and giving birth to Albathia, Grimwell was stillborn and yet to be discarded. As he walked, he felt eyes upon him, but every time he turned to meet them, there were none to be found. Daedalus changed his mind—once he assumed the throne, he would dispatch his army to Grimwell and raze the entire town.

Daedalus continued to walk, doubting his judgment in shunning the bard, the only one who might know how to procure the stone that he sought. However, he heard noises, voices, and followed.

Knees and ankles throbbing from navigating the unpredictable terrain, Daedalus did his best to find the most direct path to the noises. Trudging up the slope of a slime-flooded gully, the prince discovered the source of voices: thirteen nightmarish townsfolk, two wizards, three creatures, two men, and a large woman dressed for battle.

Knowing he couldn't make it any closer without being noticed, Daedalus stayed low, clinging to the gully's lip. The humans looked like lone roses growing in a field of dung. Even the three creatures seemed foreign. There was a reason for them being here, and the only way for Daedalus to ascertain the reason was through stealth.

Fighting every urge to vomit from the squalid surroundings, the prince listened. He soon discovered that they too sought the stone. *Did they have any yet?* he wondered. How many? What were their plans for them? He heard Praeker Trieste's name mentioned. The town elders refused to give the adventurers their stone. Then he noticed something odd with the ogre, he was not part of the conversation, opting to play with a string instead. Daedalus watched the ogre pull the twine, reeling it in. At the other end was a rabbit. Holding the stone, the Sun Stone!

Unable to resist any longer, Daedalus scrabbled from the gully and approached. Standing tall and regal, he puffed his chest out as he joined the commotion. "I trust you all know who I am?"

Jaws dropped. The prince's presence only added to the confusion. Why was he here? Unescorted? And covered in the same filth that covered everyone present? Such a shock to see royalty appear from squalor, no one made any effort to bow. Coveting the stone as he did, the prince chose to forgive them for their base indiscretion. So with stately acumen, he struck a princely pose, legs straight with best foot forward, the back of his left hand on his hip and right hand extended, waiting for the stone to be placed in it. "The stone, please. In the name of the king."

Nothing. No reaction from a soul. Even Lapin found the situation sobering.

Frowning, Daedalus tried again. "In case you did not understand me the first time, I demanded the stone. And in case your senses have abandoned you, fleeing from such hideous surroundings, then let me remind you there is no higher decree than mine."

The night-hag approached, every step a painful conflict with her own mangled body. "I assure you, dear Prince, the laws you pen to paper do not apply here. This is a Grimwell matter, which does not concern you. I suggest you take leave before you get involved."

The brazen contempt added another blow to the prince's already fragile sanity. He turned to the humans and appealed to their senses. "Obviously, none of you are denizens of this muck-ridden village. My flag flies over your heads, and I expect you to act as such. Now, one of you fetch the stone and give it to me."

Diminutia and Silver reacted to his demands with scowls. Belhurst stepped forward and said, "Your Majesty, I assure you we are acting in the best interests of the kingdom. This stone, and the others like it, are cankers upon the flesh of your kingdom, which need to be burned away. Please allow us to do that."

"It is not up to *you* to decide what is best for *my* kingdom. That is for *me* to decide. The stone. Now!"

Never recognizing the king's rule to begin with, Belhurst found it very easy to reach down and scoop up Lapin within his hands. He took the stone from the rabbit and handed him back to Bale. The wizard then turned his back on the prince.

Ire exploded within the prince's chest. He no longer smelled the offensive odors or felt the grime caking his body. He felt only pure rage. Turning to Dearborn, he snapped, "You! You wear the insignias of the king's Elite Troop. *You* must obey me! It is your sworn duty! Your oath to *me!* I own your *very soul.* Now, you must fetch me the stone!"

Tears rolled from Dearborn's eyes. What would Iderion have done? The general sacrificed his life, the lives of more than thirty others for the whim of one mad prince. Even when the prince was wrong, the general followed orders, obeyed the prince. And this prince knew very well who she was, but offered no sense of recognition. His wits clearly left him if he could not recall her name. She could, *should,* take all four stones with ease, hand them to the prince, and escort him home to Phenomere. But back to what? The city lay in ruins. She knew that, she was there, witnessed the horrors of the city's destruction, impotent to save it. She knew what Iderion would have done, and could make no other choice but to honor his memory. "No."

She expected a lashing retort, a string of discredits to her ancestry, some physical abuse, but the prince merely displayed the smile of a slow child. It was as if they spoke differing languages, and he was merely reacting to the roll of tears down her cheek in a calm, beneficent manner. For his part, Daedalus was dumbfounded. He knew of the word she spoke, but it existed only for his use, and it did not register into his vocabulary for any other usage. For a moment, his mind was as shaky as his body. No action held any certainty for him. If there was a path leading through this dilemma, he was powerless to discern it. But he had never been a man of action, and plan be damned, he launched himself into motion.

"There are no options for you to weigh, wench!" he said lunging past her. "It was not a suggestion, but a demand!"

She slipped one chiseled arm about him, as though steadying a drunkard and spun him about.

"Forgive me, my lord, but you are not well."

Her touch infused him with fury, its red bloom rising in his cheeks and flushing his neck amidst the cords of muscle that twitched there like so many squirming vipers. His breath came in quick pants, small plumes of white heat rising up from his parted lips as he regarded Dearborn with more malice than could possibly be harbored within one heart.

He regarded her with steely eyes and used his thumb and forefinger to gently remove her hand from his person, then wiped his offended flesh upon his ragged shirt. Despite his fevered madness, his eyes were clear and focused as he finally recognized who she was and words were welling up in his throat awaiting a torrential release. But suddenly a great clamor erupted on the far side of town, and the denizens stumbled off towards the shouting, so the coup-de-grace of his words died as Dearborn turned her back on him to follow the action.

"I claim this town. Kneel and accept me as your master." Before all like a god, his presence eclipsing even that of the prince of Albathia, stood Praeker Trieste.

A morbidly disfigured centaur, clad in the black strips of cloth signifying one of the elders, trotted up to the newest invader and stated, "You are known to us, Praeker Trieste, as a demon. Here you are a monster even among monsters! You can expect no succor here."

"I'm not one who disappoints easily, and yet you have succeeded in doing so. I wonder," Praeker began, using one hand to grip the neck of the centaur that addressed him and with a quick contraction of his arm drawing the beast close to his person, "if the sentiment will remain the same after you have expired." A sickly noise followed an imperceptible movement, and Praeker released the centaur to fall lifeless to the ground his head lolling, neck bent at an impossible angle.

Dearborn and her companions left Daedalus to survey this new development. Her training taught her that she should never turn her back on anything as desperate and deadly as the maddened prince, but one death looked very much like another to her at the moment. And there was a part of her mind that would sooner have this lunacy at an end than sit through the playing of the final card.

Praeker's voice rang out to every corner of Grimwell, his tone creating a void within every living creature. The hollowness did not last long as fear crept into those empty spaces. "Harbored within your midst is the Sun Stone, goodly creatures of Grimwell. It will remain hidden for only as long as it takes me to reduce your populace to nil. My army lays outside your border available upon my command. Though, looking at the pathetic resistance about me, I wonder if it will even be necessary."

"There are none here who will help you, Praeker," said the night-hag.

"So be it. Then choose amongst yourselves the order in which you'd like to be martyred."

"Belhurst, does Praeker stand a chance against the night-hag?" asked Silver.

"She is formidable. But Praeker Trieste is no mere mortal, Silver. There is nothing here that can oppose him."

"So you led us here hoping to avoid him? Or was all of this chasing around pointless? What of your magic, wizard?"

"Only the combined power of the stones can defeat him. As you well know, we are lacking in that area. The citizens of Grimwell will attack him en masse, and we will need to use their sacrifice as a cover for our escape."

"You would let them die so that we might live?"

"If we fail, there will be no living as you know it. Is it pointless to preserve hope?"

"Is it any less a slaughter?"

"Fate works in strange ways, Silver. Not all of them will satisfy you."

Belhurst never took his eyes off the scene of Praeker challenging the citizens of Grimwell as it played out before him. Whatever their chance of success, it depended on his ability to react to the nuances of the events that were in motion around them. He continued, "There is little time, be ready, all of you. We run as soon as he loses sight of us."

During the length of their discourse, the denizens of Grimwell had grouped and massed around the solitary figure of Praeker Trieste. Like a spire amidst a ring of stone, he loomed over them, motionless, a creature sensing the air before a storm as it filled with electrical current. They stood about him a grim resolution mantling them. But before the wave could crash upon the strand, a lone figure approached. Huddled and hunched like any of the other creatures before him, this one approached with a defiance the others lacked.

The hunched man pulled all eyes toward him. He hobbled to the center of everyone like an actor building suspense for his soliloquy. Daedalus approached, recognizing this man as the bard. "Where have you been?"

Without even acknowledging the uppity prince, he removed his hood. Those who had met him could never forget the unsightly face of the bard. Perplexed, everyone watched in silence, even Praeker. The silence was broken once the bard held out his hands, one toward Belhurst, the other toward Praeker. A small clap of thunder accompanied the brilliant bolts of electricity snapping from his hands to the men at which he pointed. Like a violent slight of hand, both Praeker and Belhurst soared backward, hovering in their stead were the five stones; four where Belhurst had been, one where Praeker had stood.

No one could move, from fear, from shock, from amazement. Reflexes dulled due to the awe of the sight they just witnessed and watched as the five stones floated toward the bard. Once they fell to his clutches, he cackled, the sick sound of salacious satisfaction itched every ear. And his skin melted away.

As warts bubbled and pockmarks gaped then fell away, the bard produced a walking stick with a pommel carved into the shape of an open hand, small cup-like indents carved into the tip of each finger. Cackling at his still-frozen audience while his skin continued to slide away, he placed one stone in the cup of each fingertip. Like a starving man clutching for meat, the fingers curled shut to form a wooden fist. He held it over his head in triumph.

Once he finally shed the last layer of skin, the bard was no more. Only Belhurst knew the man who stood before them now. "Wyren!"

The mad wizard cackled even louder, his eerie laughter echoing around everyone. After imprisonment in hell for hundreds of years, he had some revenge to exact.

Thirty~Three

PRAEKER TRIESTE gasped for the first time in sixty years, since he first laid eyes upon this continent only to see his naval fleet had been launched from his native lands of Irabel decimated by Belhurst and his band of wizards. Trieste had been transporting the Shadow Stone upon the boat he captained. Capsized and dashed to flotsam and jetsam, his boat was lost with the treasures, including the stone. Crawling upon the shore, just as broken as his ship, he swore he would get the Shadow Stone back, as well as its four other brethren.

Trieste had done some fell research, learned nefarious incantations and soul-blackening recipes to thwart the effects of aging for the scores of years necessary to obtain the power and knowledge of the other stones. He even culled together a band of outcasts that the citizens of this continent named "The Horde." Through patience and a crushing fist, he finally obtained the Self Stone. He spent many decades tangling with the residual demons who protected the stone, ultimately destroying them. He used its power to control the scorpions that form his armor and mold the weak-minded to do his bidding.

But now the stone he worked so hard to find and keep floated with the other four to the mad wizard, becoming part of the devil's grasp. "Impossible."

"Ha!" Wyren laughed. "Everything is possible. All you need is enough time. For example, it takes a cunning wizard four hundred years of bribery and promises to escape from hell."

"Troops! To me!" Praeker bellowed. Behind him, the forest of black and twisted tress that bordered parts of Grimwell rustled with life. Even though the number was less than two hundred, the armor-clad and weapon-wielding human and nonhuman troops of The Horde still looked menacing. They formed a semicircle around Praeker as they growled and spat at everything not a part of their army.

"What in the name of every god great and small is he holding? It's merely an old man holding a bejeweled staff," Pik whispered. "But he has the power to frighten Praeker Trieste?"

"That's what happens when a madman holds the world's most powerful weapon. He frightens fear itself," Diminutia whispered.

"That staff," Silver said, hoping to alleviate his fears by verbalizing them, "if the stories he told us are true, has the power to open doorways to hell itself. The wielder can summon as many demons as he'd like and control them all."

"If the stories he told were true?" Dearborn asked.

"Yes," Silver answered. "As the bard he told us the tale of the first time he ... as Wyren ... possessed the staff. A band of mercenaries defeated him, casting him into hell. They removed the stones and hid them."

"The stones we so deftly found." Dearborn frowned as a knot twisted in her stomach, realizing she had been duped, tricked into destroying her life and possibly the world as she knew it. "However, it does explain the demons attached to each stone."

"True. I doubt very much any of them would want to go back to hell or stand to be someone's puppet."

"Now what?" Pik asked.

"It seems we are now a part of Praeker's army," Dearborn said, noting the actions of the creatures within Praeker's control. Griffins and harpies glided in cautious circles over Wyren. Weapon-wielding men and monsters shuffled slowly toward the threatening wizard. Praeker himself tightened his grip on his sword's hilt, an action the general so rarely needed to do.

"This world. This world is now *mine!*" Wyren screeched as he threw back the flap of his robe to expose filled bladders tied around his waist. Before anyone could blink, the cragged wizard snatched one from his belt and flung it to the ground. It burst, splattering globs of crimson blood. With the tip of his staff he connected a line of blood into a circle. Even as Praeker gave the order to attack, Wyren broke two more bladders on the ground and formed a grave-sized oval. By the time anyone or anything could even react to Praeker's command, Wyren ran toward an outcropping of rocks just outside of the town's border. He slammed more bladders against the flattened surface of one of the jutting rocks, twice the height of a normal man. Wyren's staff traced a circle on the rock's surface just as large. He brought forth hell and ruled it like a god.

From the smallest hole, swarms of pinching, stinging insects erupted forth. The ground vomited vicious clouds of them. Undead and rotting pixies and imps, craving flesh to rend, quickly followed them. Hundreds of them followed the angry noises of the insects into the skies, focusing on Praeker's winged warriors. Griffins snapped their jaws and slashed with their claws, but did nothing to diminish their attackers. Harpies screamed and tried to flee. None could escape. The demonic insects flooded mouths, bloating stomachs and lungs, as well as stung eyes. The fetid faeries wasted no time as they tore through gobs of flesh to sink their teeth into still-beating hearts.

Mutated vipers and enlarged scorpions slithered and scuttled from the second of Wyren's doorways. Praeker's soldiers found them substantial enough to slay, but were not fast enough to press forward or give chase to Wyren. Swords sliced through scale with ease. Wriggling bodies flopped across the grounds. Many of Praeker's men swung their weapons back and forth, back and forth, as if reaping fields of bloody grains. But fangs and pincers found their marks as well, massive waves of hell's living bile engulfing those in its way.

The ground trembled as the demons emptied from the doorway formed on the boulder. Monstrous creatures strode forth, abominations to nature. Torsos of trolls sprouted from bodies of enormous spiders. Raptor talons replaced legs of mammoth millipedes. Fangs and claws twisted onto perverse bodies of corded muscle and rippling sinew flowed forth from the hole, every creature larger and more fearsome than the prior. Finally, the stentorian commander followed, chest out and back straight, the fires of victory burning within his eyes and clouds of death billowing from his nostrils. Ar'drzz'ur.

"No," Dearborn whispered, tears streaming down her face. "No. No. It's ... it's not possible. I killed him. *I killed him!*"

Belhurst turned to the others and said, "Follen and I will work with the Grimwell wizards to stave off the masses. The rest of you, stop Wyren. At *any* cost!"

As they ran off, Belhurst and Follen did as promised and followed the Grimwell mayor to a nearby mud hut that served as their magicians' guild. The two wizards and a half dozen magic wielding citizens stood firm. Ten other citizens, the least encumbered by physical deformities, acted as runners, simply bringing everything from the inside of the hut to the outside. The Grimwell witches needed only seconds to make brews that bubbled into noxious clouds, killing demon insects by the thousands. The falling bodies seemed like an endless shower. Carcasses crunched with every footstep as the crusaders continued. Follen and Belhurst sent blankets of azure flame across the ground, turning every viper and scorpion to dust upon contact, yet leaving all other battle participants unharmed. The swarms of small creatures dwindled. But the larger creatures attacked.

Within a few short strides, claws and teeth shredded the runners. The sorcerers retaliated as best they could with devastating spells, turning the monsters to mist or setting them ablaze with inextinguishable flames. But jaws devoured a Grimwell witch and claws shredded another. For every two of the larger monsters that melted into a pool of ichor, one spell-caster was lost.

Seeing the dire situation for what it was, Follen knew of only one solution. One that Belhurst would not like. As his colleague fought, sending lightening to strike as many opponents as possible, Follen grabbed the necessary ingredients and a cauldron. Despite the war raging around him, he mixed the ingredients with impeccable precision. Once complete, he lifted the cauldron and poured the thin liquid on himself.

"Follen?" Belhurst yelled, whips of fire snapping from his hands. "What are you ... *No!*"

Before his friend could protest further, Follen spoke an arcane incantation, a spell that would end this skirmish.

"No!" Belhurst yelled again, powerless to stop his friend.

But it was done. The spell was complete. Giving one last smile to his friend, Follen dissipated, turning into a cloud of black smoke, living death. The spell only lasted for seconds, but that was more than enough time for Follen. Still maintaining control of his now nebulous body, he glided through the air in many directions, black wisps touching those he wanted to kill. Scores and scores of demons fell upon contact. The spell worked. But it could only be performed once.

Belhurst wept as he watched the black smoke fade away on the winds, leaving only memories.

Angered that he lost an entire battalion, Ar'drzz'ur turned to Wyren and said, "Master!"

Wyren was running up the side of the nearest rock face, a jagged path leading three stories above the battlefield. He paused when he heard his lackey. The war was not going in his favor. But that was easily remedied as he paused and emptied a few more bladders of blood to create more doorways.

Hideous beasts erupted through the planet's crust from within the circles of blood.

The clash was titanic. Praeker did his best to rally his army, though his calls and commands were lost in the cacophony of death. Rage and hatred became palpable entities.

"All is lost here if we do not stop Wyren," Belhurst yelled.

When Pik and Bale stared at him openmouthed, he resorted to pointing in the direction Wyren had taken, hoping his nonverbal cues would be understood. Pik nodded and grabbed at Bale's elbow, steering him off at a loping run in the direction the wizard had suggested, dodging combat wherever possible.

Belhurst, surveying the carpet of carcasses before him, began a nefarious incantation. He had never approved of the necromantic arts and so had rarely used them, but desperation drove him. His allies were dwindling in number, and exhaustion was a terrible concern. When his hands waved in the final gesture and the last syllable had escaped his lips, he turned and ran after Bale and Pik, evading combat with a nimbleness none would have guessed he possessed. In his wake, the dead began to twitch spasmodically, shaking and jerking themselves to their feet. They would not fight with the same puissance they displayed in life, but they would be tireless in their efforts, and their numbers, Belhurst hoped, would buoy the flagging spirits of their living counterparts.

On the other side of the rising dead, Dearborn fought with tremendous ferocity. Flanked on either side by Silver and Diminutia, she cut a swath through their enemies, leaving a corridor of death behind her. It was an inexorable march towards an opponent she dearly sought to avoid. She had thought never to look upon the twisted face of the demon-general, his ragged lips coming together with great effort over his crooked, dagger-like teeth to form a sneer of satisfaction. He was presently engaged in combat, though she could not see his opponent through the sea of bodies and hoped to take advantage of the situation, perhaps catching him unaware and while she had two bodyguards to fend off other interlopers.

With deep but ragged breaths, she sought to exhale her exhaustion. Slowly she made her way to the towering spire of flesh that was the demon-general she thought she had banished forever. At twenty paces away, he was unaware of her as Dearborn summoned all her strength. His back was to her, shielding his opponents from her view, though he fought multiple opponents from the way the sword and axe he wielded were swung as with independent thoughts. Soundless, she charged the remaining distance between them, seeking to skewer the demon upon her blade. But as her sword-point drew near to impacting the base of his

322 | CHRIS PISANO and BRIAN KOSCIENSKI

skull, a face formed on the back of his head, and a new pair of arms sprouted, weapons in hand, to fend off her charge and repel her without even losing any ground. In frustration, she screamed a stream of profanities. Silver and Diminutia drew to her flanks and fought equally hard to keep other attackers from interfering with her battle.

It was a game of hack and slash, parry and riposte, each seeking for a break in the other's defenses. Within the first few seconds of the clash, Dearborn bore three cuts, none of them deep, though blood ran freely down both her arms, threatening to make her hands slick. Ar'drzz'ur also bore several slight nicks across his abdomen and chest, but nothing that might compromise his grip on his weapons. With a sword and bardiche, he continued his onslaught on the female sergeant.

She was getting nowhere. She was loathe to move too far, lest it disturb her comrades in their defense of her. But deciding to change her tactic, she began to circle the great beast. As she moved, her eyes darted to and fro searching for an opening in his defenses. The demon-general's other opponent held his ground as she circled, and she was startled by the alien-green armor bristling with swarming scorpions that stood with her. Her movement was halted as the arachnids menaced her with an uprising of claws and stingers alike, though their master paid her no heed. Praeker Trieste, then, was her accomplice in this, at least for the moment, though she feared his help almost as much as she did his opposition. Then, with fading hope, she realized that even his huge stature was dwarfed by that of the demon. Suddenly, to her eyes, the legend appeared vulnerable. The three-sided battle raged on.

Bale lumbered forward, Pik at his side. Though their gait was strange and hardly graceful, still the results were undeniable—the bent and gnarled wizard was within their view at long last. Wyren cast a strangle-mouthed gaze in their direction and paused only to spill blood and draw another circle with the butt of his staff. Before more demons could crawl from the depths, he was moving forward again. He reached the top of the plateau where in a stone alcove he had stashed two urns of dragon's blood. He had only to reach it, and this whole battle would become but a fleeting struggle, a tale none would hear.

A new contingent of demons sprang up from the area he innocuously anointed, twelve wild–looking, lupine forms howling and slathering in a charge at the would-be heroes. Bale met the force with his own headlong charge, refusing to lose the power of his momentum. They were upon him in a flash, but even their insane rage paled against his own. Teeth clenching, he ignored the pain of their bites. He focused his fury on his opponents, one at a time; his balled fist pounding one, then another of the creatures straight into the ground, crushing their heads like melons. Pik, who slowed up initially knowing that his slim form would be swept away in the tide of the charging frenzy that faced him, came to Bale's aid within seconds of the skirmish's start. Suddenly, the two friends wished they had paused long enough to gather a few more allies in their chase of the crazed wizard.

Amidst a background of howls, snarls, and scrabbling claws, Bale and Pik stood tall, withstanding the furious onslaught of their attackers. Bale continued to pummel his opponents, but as he raised his left arm, two wolf-demons lunged at him. One of them found purchase and attached itself neatly to his huge bicep, and, refusing to relinquish its hold, grinded its teeth together, rendering his left arm useless. Growling in pain, Bale used his other arm to squash another skull against the unyielding rock beneath him.

Pik danced and whirled in an attempt to evade his attackers. He knew he needed to kill a few of the beasts before Bale was swarmed under, but he dared not risk taking the full brunt of a leaping attacker, or his own slight frame would be knocked down, exposing his throat to the snarling mass that stood before him. But the demon-wolf burst into flames, giving a blood-curdling yelp as it burned.

Pik leapt to his feet and spun around, seeing that he now owed thanks to Belhurst. However, he doubted the wizard would accept it, or even notice it, for he continued shouting spells and spraying arcane liquids that diminished the pack of demon-wolves into howling streamers of distended flesh. The hobgoblin smiled as he saw Bale, now unfettered, advancing toward Wyren as the mad wizard tipped one of the blood-filled pots, the river of red arcing down the cliff face. One lone demon-wolf loped past, hunger in his eyes. Pik almost let him go until he saw what prey the creature sought. Pik gave chase.

Silver and Diminutia attempted to aid Dearborn as best they could against the now four-armed Ar'drzz'ur. Their skills seemed childish against a warrior who trained for millennia. The demon-general laughed as he fought both Praeker and Dearborn like an adult scolding impetuous children. For a glimmering second, the demon-general focused on Dearborn. Praeker saw this as an opportunity to withdraw from the battle, leaving his two opponents to determine a victor between themselves. As he watched, he backed away, closer to the forest that edged the one side of Grimwell. When he was within the tangle of ebony branches, he scowled. He had lost. There was only one thing now to do—he turned and fled.

Physical fatigue crashed through Dearborn; her legs quaked, and her arms shook. The shock of blocking Ar'drzz'ur's blows proved too much for her joints to handle, and she flopped to the ground like a freshly caught fish. Fueled by passion, Diminutia ran to her aid, an unholy scream raging from his throat—which did little good as Ar'drzz'ur used one arm to lift the blond man from the ground by his throat. Feeling extra sadistic, he turned Diminutia's body toward Dearborn. Ar'drzz'ur gave one last laugh as both humans shed tears. Then his laughing stopped. His body trembled. And all were surprised to see his freshly severed head drop to his feet and roll along the ground.

As the demon-general's decapitated body fell, reduced to a limp sack of organs, it released Diminutia, who immediately ran and held Dearborn. They and Silver looked to see who could possibly wield the power to kill a demon. They saw Phyl dropping a freshly bloodied broadsword as he pulled both hands to his mouth to stifle a quivering squeal.

Diminutia wanted to thank Phyl from every corner of his soul, but instead pointed and gave shout, "Behind you!"

Phyl turned to see the salivating maw of the last demon-wolf's razor-sharp teeth. But the wolf never struck. Pik tackled it midstrike. Growls and curses shot forth as the two rolled along the ground. The wolf bit and clawed, while Pik hacked away with his dagger. The growling stopped. Pik lay on his back and pushed the fresh carcass off of him. With labored breath, he rested his sweating head on the cool ground and coughed out a burst of blood.

Sobbing, Phyl ran to his friend and dropped to his knees, pulling the hobgoblin onto his lap. "You saved me?"

Pik frowned. Through hacking coughs, he asked, "Why'd ... you save ... them?"

The satyr turned to Dearborn and Diminutia, then back to his dying friend. "Because they love each other. I'm such a sap for love."

"Well," Pik coughed. "It's known that ... I hate everybody. But you ... you I hate the most."

Through tears, Phyl smiled as he watched his friend go. Silver, Diminutia, and Dearborn each limped over and put a hand on the satyr's shoulder. But their grieving would have to wait. The trembling ground reminded them that greater issues were at stake.

Wyren succeeded in overturning the second urn, the blood ran down the cliff side and crossed the first stream at the base. He had created a doorway tall enough to dwarf most buildings. The world quaked as the encircled rock fell away, creating a hole leading to hell.

Bale lunged toward Wyren, but found himself frozen, suspended midleap. The wizard cackled as white energy flowed from his left hand to the ogre, keeping him in stasis. The energy tingled, enough to aggitate Lapin.

Confused, the rabbit poked his head from the burrow of Bale's pant pocket and looked around. He noticed that he was high off the ground with a tumultuous battle raging at the base. And some withered old man was holding a staff in his right hand while crazy light flowed from his left.

Wyren laughed harder, drunk with impending power. He peered over the edge to watch a massive hand emerge from the hole in the cliff face. He cackled knowing the supreme demon would soon tear itself free from its womb, born to destroy all that the wizard commanded. "Yes!"

Wyren shrieked. "Yes! Come forth! Centuries of waiting! Years of calculating and searching for the stones! Finding stupid fools to fetch them for me and a dragon to supply the blood! Finally, it will be mine! The world will be mine!"

Dragon to supply the blood? Lapin asked himself. Realization struck him like a lightning bolt. The dragon blood the wizard used was fresh. Fresh enough to come from his friend who had recently gone missing. Anger rippled through every strand of fur. When he first met the dragon, he had lied about being a knight, but now honor raced through him. He jumped from Bale's pocket and attacked.

Lapin's diminutive body did little good. He went for the wizard's throat, but left nothing more than a nick as the old man slapped him away. It did, however, distract him enough to lose the focus of his containment spell, dropping Bale.

With one meaty blow, Bale cracked several of Wyren's ribs. Unable to stop himself, the wizard dropped the staff. And Bale picked it up.

All fighting ceased. The eyes of all combatants focused on Bale holding the staff. Diminutia and Silver were not exactly sure who the more menacing threat was, a power-hungry wizard, or a dimwitted ogre.

Bale stared at the staff in his hands. He tried to think logically, tried to weigh his options, even though he was fairly certain he didn't know what his options were.

"*Miiiiiiiiine!*" Wyren screamed as he jumped to his feet and charged. Out of reflex, Bale held the staff in front of him with both hands, implying he would snap it in half. The wizard froze midstep, not wanting to do *anything* that could harm his staff. Then Bale had an idea. And with a very muddled thought, his unspoken command came to fruition.

The giant hand protruding from the gaping wound in the mountain wall reached up and plucked Wyren from the plateau ledge. The wizard screamed a noise that would haunt the nightmares of all who heard it as half the bones in his body snapped. The hand slowly retreated back into the gateway, taking the wriggling wizard with it, as it did one thousand years ago.

A second idea struck Bale, right between the eyes, leaving a dull ache where it had hit him. With the stiffness of zombies, all of the remaining demons also retreated through the doorways whence they came.

Then what had never happened before took shape. Bale had a third idea within the confines of one day. He now possessed a headache that would stick with him for a week, but he accepted the suffering to make the proper choice. He rested the fist of the staff in his hand and made his way down the mountain path to the base, near an open doorway.

Once there, he squeezed, pulverizing the wood into splinters, releasing all five stones. All the doorways shrank, healing what they were etched upon. As the aperture nearest Bale closed, he threw the stones inside. The doorways shut, never to be reopened.

Having nothing to fight for and no leader to be found, Praeker's diminished army of monsters and men disbanded, simply heading in all directions looking for a better possible fate than what they had witnessed. Praeker himself was nowhere to be found.

And neither was Daedalus.

Silver and Diminutia ran to Bale, never so happy to see the grotesque ogre in their lives. "Bale," Silver said. "That was brilliant. Well done!"

"It's true, Bale," Diminutia added. "How did you think of that?"

"Simple," Bale replied with a smile. "I just thought of what I could do that would one-up you two so good that you'd never be able to one-up me again ..."

CHIRTY-FOUR

DIMINUTIA FED the pigs. Fruits and vegetables that he and his recent bride deemed unsatisfactory for their meals ended up in the pig trough. A few over-ripened apples, a couple of plums in the same state, tomatoes with evidence of sun withering, weak and wilted carrots. The quantity was far from overwhelming, but there were only four pigs and two piglets to feed, so there was enough to satisfy their hunger.

Diminutia set down the basket that had held the discarded food and leaned against the fence to rest. Chuckling to himself, he still found it difficult to recognize these lands as his even after living here for two full harvests. *My farm*, he thought. *My farm.*

Swatting a mosquito searching for an early evening meal, he looked to the small orchard of apples, plums, and apricots, then to the large garden of tomatoes and carrots. These seemed like such foreign ideals on foreign lands. The stables offered him some comfort, as did the humble farmhouse he called home. But even they felt like a hermitage isolated from the rebuilt capitol, Phenomere, by a full valley.

The farm life satisfied him, as did marriage and looming fatherhood. In two seasons, he would find out if he could do a better job at parenting than his father did. He already seemed to be a better husband. But how could he fail at that? He was married to the most beautiful woman he had

ever seen. And now that she no longer had to train and fight while within the army's ranks, her body relinquished some of its muscle. Some, but not all since there was always some work to do around the farm. But enough to lose the bulging veins and deep striations. The bit of baby belly also helped add femininity.

As if on cue, Dearborn walked from the house with a decanter of water to share with her loving husband by the pig fence. She smiled, finding it hard not to any time she looked into his crystal-blue eyes. Even though she was a good half-a-head taller than him, he made her feel like a woman, and for that she pledged her very soul to him.

Diminutia took a gulp from the decanter. As he wiped his chin with the back of his hand, his eyes drilled hers as he offered a smirk. "I heard rumors."

Dearborn blushed at his words. She knew what rumors he had heard. She pledged to him to leave her life of military servitude behind, never to fight again, except to protect her family, if need be. Never again for king or country. Perciless had returned right after Phenomere had fallen to The Horde with a blended army of troops from both Albathia and Tsinel. With ease, they removed what did not belong, and with the same stroke signed a treaty with Tsinel ushering in a new era of peace. *King* Perciless had the undying support of his followers, two full nations worth, which allowed for quick rebuilding of the country, capital, and castle. However, the army became quite skilled in a short time, leading some suspicious minds to wonder. Traveling down the winding roads of scuttlebutt, Diminutia uncovered tales of a great warrior offering fleeting moments to consult, guidance, and training. Dearborn returned the smirk and his sardonic words. "I heard rumors, too."

Diminutia raised his eyebrows and then laughed. Sliding his hands around her waist, he pulled her in for a kiss; a sign to show that he conceded before the argument even began. For her, he forsook his larcenous ways. However, a shiny pendant or a jewel-encrusted tiara would disappear from a daughter of wealth at nighttime while the city slumbered. Corresponding with such disappearances, Diminutia would surprise Dearborn with expensive

330 | CHRIS PISANO and BRIAN KOSCIENSKI

bouquets, or a dress woven with rich fabrics, or even a striking piece of jewelry.

The newlyweds knew each other's secrets, but knew the other would never let it go so far as to destroy their family. And they loved each other for it.

The coughing and clearing of two throats interrupted their embrace. The lovers looked up to see Belhurst and Silver, both men looking out of place in long wizards' robes —Belhurst because they were so new and clean, no one envisioned him wearing anything other than tattered rags, and Silver simply because they were robes and not dyed silks ornamented with scintillating jewelry.

"Wow," Diminutia said, seeing his friend looking so alien.

Silver smiled. "What? You don't approve? Wait until I trade in the apprentice robes for those of a master."

"We certainly do approve," Dearborn said with a smile. To prove her point, she placed a small peck on his cheek.

"Well, I can't believe two people who saved the world have decided to become farmers," Silver said.

Looking at Dearborn, Diminutia said, "I wouldn't have it any other way." He turned back to his friend and continued, "Speaking of, any word from Bale or Phyl?"

Both Belhurst and Silver laughed. "They are still traversing from town to town with Lapin in search of a new tavern."

Diminutia laughed. "Truly?"

"Truly. 'Tis a shame, too. Nary a soul knows about the demon stones, but hardly an ear hasn't heard of what happened at Munty's."

"Well, at least their quest is noble."

"Verily!"

"Word is that when they finish *that* noble quest, they'll answer King Perciless's call to locate his missing brothers. Not even a sideways rumor about the whereabouts of either Oremethus or Daedalus."

"Couldn't imagine a more intrepid group."

The friends shared one last laugh. Then it was time for Silver to move on.

"So your training in Phenomere is nearly finished?" Diminutia asked.

"Yes. The training so far has been little more than classroom conjecture. The only way I can learn about the world's workings is to see the world," Silver replied.

Tears accompanied hugs and farewells. The wizened wizard and his apprentice went on their way. Diminutia watched as their shapes turned to silhouettes turned to specks, then vanished, and thought of the grand adventures his friend would certainly encounter. He then turned to Dearborn and placed his hands on her belly and realized that he would certainly have adventures of his own.

Made in the USA
Middletown, DE
15 October 2015